accidentally
in love

Also by Cathy Woodman

Follow Me Home

accidentally
in love

cathy woodman

PEGASUS BOOKS
NEW YORK LONDON

ACCIDENTALLY IN LOVE

Pegasus Books Ltd
148 West 37th Street, 13th Floor
New York, NY 10018

Copyright © 2016 by Cathy Woodman

First Pegasus Books hardcover edition November 2016

ISBN: 978-1-68177-238-7

10 9 8 7 6 5 4 3 2 1

Printed in the United States of America
Distributed by W. W. Norton & Company, Inc.

For Tamsin and Will

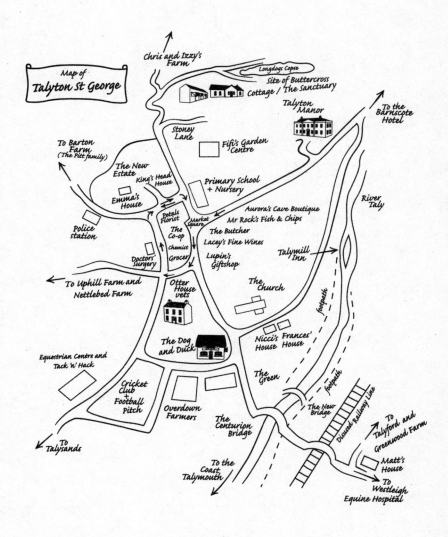

Chapter One

Rabbit, Rabbit, Rabbit

I'm on the early shift so there's nobody about when I turn up for work at Otter House, which isn't unusual.. What is out of the ordinary is the large cardboard box on the step in front of the glass doors at the side of the practice, which wasn't there when I locked up the night before. I take a closer look. The top is taped shut and pierced with holes, and someone has scrawled the words 'sorry, can't cope any more' along the side in pink felt-tip pen.

`I let myself into reception and return for the box, struggling to carry it into the consulting room. It isn't particularly heavy, but it only just fits through the door. I lower it onto the table, when whatever it is inside starts to scrabble about. I tear off the tape and open the lid very carefully.

One, two . . . no, six pairs of eyes look up at me. I stare back at six of the cutest baby rabbits I've ever seen: two cinnamon, three orange and one white, with pricked ears and manes of fluff.

'Oh, you are gorgeous,' I say, picking the white one

1

out and cuddling it against my cheek. 'It must be my birthday.'

'Hello, Shannon. Did I hear someone say it's their birthday?' Frances joins me, placing her handbag on the table and lifting out one of the orange babies, which matches the colour of the nest of false hair on top of her head, and clashes with her purple and lime-green tunic. She's in her late sixties, too old to update her look and redefine her style, I suspect. She's been on the verge of retiring from her position as practice receptionist for a while now. In fact, she reduced her hours and even left for a couple of months, but she's always come back. I can't imagine her not being here. She's like part of the furniture.

'How sweet,' she sighs, as she strokes her baby rabbit between the ears with the tip of her finger. 'This must be a vet nurse's dream.'

'It is, but I don't understand how anyone could bring themselves to abandon them. They can't be more than four or five weeks old.'

'Where did they come from?'

'I was hoping you might have some idea.'

'I'll keep an ear to the ground,' Frances says. 'On the subject of news, is it true that your mum is putting Petals up for sale?'

'I'm sorry?' My forehead tightens into a frown as she continues, 'Only several people have spotted one of the estate agents from Talymouth – Smith and Ryder-Cole – parked outside the shop.'

'When was this?'

'Yesterday afternoon.'

'There's no way she'd ever put it on the market. Floristry is her life. And, given it's also our family home, I think I'd know if my mother was planning

2

to sell the shop. I guess even estate agents – with their reputation for outrageous descriptions and dodgy dealings – have occasion to buy flowers, just like everyone else.' Smiling, I return to the rabbits. 'I'd better take these little guys through to isolation – they'll be better off in there than in Kennels with the dogs and cats. Please can you call Jack from Animal Welfare when you have five minutes? He should look into this.'

'I don't understand why the person responsible didn't contact the Sanctuary direct. That's what Talyton Animal Rescue is for – to take in and rehome unwanted animals without judging the owners.'

'It's easier to say than do,' I point out. 'Everyone knows that rabbits breed like rabbits, and I'd be pretty embarrassed at having to admit that I hadn't thought about contraception. They don't appear to have been badly treated; they have food and it wasn't cold last night. Do you think you'd be able to take a couple of them on?'

'I couldn't.' Frances puts her rabbit back in the box with the rest. 'I have three very messy hedgehogs at home already. How about you?'

'I couldn't have them, not with the dog. I wouldn't trust Seven with a small furry . . .' The lining of my nose starts to prick and I pop my baby back before I sneeze. I make a mental note to take some antihistamines as soon as I can for the rabbit allergy I acquired a couple of years ago.

The phone rings in reception and Frances goes to answer it, taking up her post behind the desk, while I carry the box of baby bunnies out the back to isolation, where I make sure they have plenty of hay, food and fresh water. I put them all inside the stainless-steel cage and close the door. The sound makes them skitter about, scattering hay across the floor.

I sweep up the mess, catching sight of the reflection of a skinny young woman of twenty-six, with a naturally pale complexion, blue-green eyes ringed with black lashes and a couple of sets of studs in each ear. I have long straight hair, dyed a reddish-brown shade of Irish setter and pulled back from my face with a French plait. I strike a pose with the broom. Some people say I remind them of Kristen Stewart, but I'm not as pretty as her, I think, as Frances calls me away to admit two cats for neutering. I dispense a repeat prescription before I set up theatre ready for the morning's ops.

Later, I get to help one of the partners with a collie who's under sedation for X-rays of his elbow. Keeping an eye on the dog, who's snoring lightly on the prep bench, I watch my favourite vet dithering over the X-rays. Maz is in her late-thirties, tall and slim with light blonde hair tied back with an elastic band. She's wearing black combat trousers with a top printed with cartoon dogs and cats. She holds the film up against the light of the viewer on the wall and is wondering aloud if the dog would really benefit from what the owner is pushing for – joint replacement surgery at a specialist hospital – when Frances appears, looking flustered.

'I'm afraid there's been a mix-up. Jennie's brought Lucky in for his investigations today instead of tomorrow. I've told her you're busy, but she won't budge.'

'That's just what I need when we're a man down.' Maz turns to me. 'I can manage here while you go and have a word with her. Looking on the bright side, though, if we do it today, we'll have a spare slot tomorrow.'

I join Frances in reception. A middle-aged woman dressed in a spotted summery dress, woollen cardigan and wellies is standing there with a scruffy dark grey terrier on a lead. Jennie is married to one of the local farmers and has a flourishing business baking cakes. Lucky has become what Izzy – our head nurse – calls a 'frequent flier' over recent months, attending the practice with various niggling problems from arthritis to a runny nose.

'Hello,' I say, before bending down to stroke the dog, who turns his back on me and faces the exit.

'Thank goodness you're here, Shannon,' Jennie says. 'I'm hoping you can make sense of the situation. According to Frances, Lucky isn't booked in, but she definitely told me to bring him today.'

'I've looked and he isn't on my list.' Frances scans her monitor with her glitter-framed glasses perched on the end of her nose.

'I don't like to make a fuss but, in my business, the customer is always right.'

I smile to myself. My mum follows the same principle – the customer is always right, except when they're wrong.

'I've just remembered.' Jennie pulls one of our appointment cards out of her bag. 'Look, Frances printed it out and told me to bring him in starved.' She hands it to me. 'I feel so mean – he's had no breakfast and he's been hanging around Reuben's highchair, waiting for a cornflake or some scrambled egg to fall from the sky.'

I check the date and time on the card as she continues, 'Please, don't tell me you have to rebook. I can't stand the stress. I just want this over with. I need to know what's wrong with him.' I notice how her dark brown hair is streaked with grey and there are shadows beneath her eyes. 'I'm so worried, I can't sleep.'

'Jennie is right.' I look to Frances. She does make mistakes – we all do – but it's becoming a habit.

'I must have had a moment,' she says, apologising.

'It's all right anyway because Maz says she can fit him in this morning.'

'That's brilliant, thank you.' Jennie's voice softens. 'I'm sorry for being so sharp, but this is a stressful time. Adam, my oldest, is very upset. He loves this little dog.'

I show her into the consulting room.

'Maz will go through the consent form with you as soon as she's free, and give him an injection of sedative.'

'I think it's me who needs the sedative,' Jennie says dryly, picking Lucky up while I collect the consent form that Frances has printed off at reception.

'I can't believe I did that,' she says sadly.

'Never mind. These things happen.'

'I know, but why do they have to keep happening to me?'

'Have you contacted Jack about the rabbits?' I ask to divert her.

'I have indeed. He's collecting them later. There's space for them at the Sanctuary until they find new homes.'

I'm pleased because with a bit of luck their new owners will register them with us for veterinary treatment and I'll get to see them again.

When Maz is ready, I fetch Lucky from his cage in Kennels.

'You wouldn't think there was anything wrong to look at him,' I observe as he tries to wriggle out of my arms.

'He's a typical terrier. They fight to the end.' Maz frowns as I utter three sneezes in a row, making the dog jump.

'I'm sorry. It's the rabbits.' I lift Lucky onto the prep bench and stroke his neck to calm him down, finding several lumps and bumps that shouldn't be there. I glance up.

'He has generalised lymphadenopathy,' Maz explains, drawing up some sedative. 'All his glands are up.'

I hug the dog tight to keep him still for her to administer the injection into the vein in his front leg, at which he grows limp in my arms and drops off to sleep. I lay him down on his side, check his heartbeat and the colour of his gums, and make sure his tongue is pulled forwards so he can breathe freely.

'Is everything all right?' Maz asks over the sound of the clippers that I've left clean and oiled on the bench.

'He's gone very deep.' I pinch his paw, but there's no reaction. The sedation has hit him unusually hard. I grab a mask from the drawer, attach it to a breathing circuit and slip it over his muzzle to give him some oxygen. 'He's breathing and his pulse is okay, but he's a bit blue.' After a couple of breaths, I check his gums again and they've turned pink, like litmus paper dipped in acid. 'That's better.'

Maz clips the hair from one of the lumps in Lucky's neck. I vacuum up the loose fur and scrub his skin while she prepares to take a biopsy. She also takes blood, X-rays his chest and tummy, and goes on to take some bone marrow to send off to the lab. Eventually, she injects the drug to reverse the sedation, but Lucky remains out for the count. We stand together, watching and waiting for him to wake up.

'I'm afraid he's sicker than I thought,' Maz says.

'Is it cancer?' I stroke the sleeping dog's ears.

'I'm hoping against hope that it's some kind of infection. I was going to set up the microscope to see if I could give Jennie an answer today, but it's packed away ready for the builders to start, so we'll have to wait for the path lab to come back to us. I'll ask Frances to organise a courier. If this is what I think it is, the sooner we start treatment the better. Wakey, wakey, poppet.' Maz sounds like she's talking to one of her children – she has three under seven: George, Henry and baby Olivia. 'It's coffee time.'

'You go. I'll stay with him,' I offer.

'Thanks, Shannon. You're a star.' She washes her hands and disappears through the swing doors into the corridor. I clear up, rinsing the used surgical instruments and soaking them in hot bubbles of detergent, keeping an eye on the patient at the same time. When I approach him again, he manages to lift his head.

'Another ten minutes and I could have missed this week's practice meeting altogether,' I grumble lightly. I lift him up and put him back in his cage under a blanket to keep him warm. He responds with a wag of his tail. Smiling, I leave him to join the rest of the team in the staff room.

Tripod, the black and white practice cat who helps me and Izzy run this show, is perched on the back of the sofa. He's called Tripod on account of him having three legs. Maz amputated the fourth one when Alex Fox-Gifford ran him over in the middle of the night and brought him to Otter House. According to Frances, he could easily have done the op himself at his practice at Talyton Manor, but at the time he was looking for any excuse to see Maz. It doesn't seem like a terribly romantic idea to me, but that's vets for you. They're a breed apart.

Tripod reaches across and taps my shoulder with his paw as I sit down. Eventually I relent, and he hops down and settles on my lap, purring and gently kneading my leg with his prickly claws while I take a jam doughnut from the plate that Izzy holds out to me. Our head nurse has been forty-two for a few years now; she looks younger, with her freckled skin and short hair that has turned to silver. She's like Marmite – you either love or hate her.

'Have I missed anything?' I ask.

'We're discussing the plans for when the new vet arrives.' Emma, who set the practice up in the first place and persuaded Maz to join her as a partner later on, brushes some sugar from her cheek and grins. 'So much for the diet.' She's short and curvaceous, with dark brown hair cut into a geometric bob, and dressed in a blue and red patterned dress with a tie waist and navy Mary Jane's. 'It isn't so much that I wanted a second doughnut – it's more that I can't bear to see food go to waste.'

'It's still going to waste,' Izzy says lightly. '*Your* waist.'

'Very witty,' Emma says with a touch of sarcasm.

'I hope the new boy is going to fit in,' Frances says. 'He seemed very . . .' It takes her a while to find an

appropriate description, which is a little worrying.
'. . . pleasant when he came for his interview.'

'Is that the best you can do? He's all right. Emma asked him all the right questions . . .' Maz pauses and Emma finishes the sentence for her: 'Does he like doughnuts, for example?'

'It's an icebreaker, the first thing I ask at every interview.' Emma chuckles.

'I'm not bothered about his dietary preferences,' Izzy goes on. 'His suit was too small and his ego far too big. He seemed a bit raffish to me.'

'What do you mean by that?' I ask. 'I wasn't here when you interviewed him.'

'Well, if you must swan off to Ibiza with your boyfriend,' Izzy says.

'Ex-boyfriend,' I point out quickly, wanting there to be no confusion about my status as a single woman.

'I'm sorry, I forgot you broke up with him when you came back. What I mean is that I thought that Mr Curdridge seemed a little unconventional compared with Will. In fact, I wanted to book him in for a dematt . . .'

'Maz and I have taken a lot of trouble to find the right vet for the job.' Emma sounds slightly hurt at the criticism, even though she really should be used to it by now, due to Izzy's tendency to suffer from bouts of foot-in-mouth syndrome.

'The length of his hair has no bearing on his ability,' Maz says. 'He'll be fine. Don't you remember how long it took for you nurses to break Will in?'

'He wanted to refer everything – even the simplest, most straightforward stitch – up for an MRI scan,' Izzy says, 'and he was an expert in what we called "foreverectomies", because it took him so long to do any surgery as he was scared of cutting too much out.'

'Better that way than the other,' Maz says wryly. 'It's a pity he decided to leave, although I can imagine him teaching vet students.'

'He'll be very good at it,' Emma says.

'Except he'll train another load of new vets his way, and we'll have to start all over again with them,' Izzy sighs.

'Will was amazing,' I say in defence of our assistant vet, who left to take up a post at one of the vet schools last week.

'In the end,' Izzy agrees. 'Is there any other business?'

'Yes, but it won't take long. Two minutes at most,' Maz says. 'The builders are starting on Monday next week and we're hoping—'

'Against hope, I think,' Izzy cuts in. 'I don't know why you've given DJ and his cowboys the contract to convert the flat.'

'Better the devil you know,' Emma murmurs.

'I'm hoping,' Maz begins again, 'that they'll finish the work within two weeks as planned. I know we've had issues with DJ and his merry band before, but they've given us a reasonable estimate and were available to do the work as soon as Will moved his exotic pets out of the flat. DJ knows that if he messes up, I'll be on his tail like a shot.

'Anyway,' she continues, 'although moving the lab and office onto another floor frees up space elsewhere, our client list continues to grow. People are travelling from further afield, which means we have to make plans for further expansion. As far as I can see we have three options: to move out of Otter House and

11

set up in one of the barns up at Talyton Manor, to take on one of the industrial units at the end of town, or to keep Otter House and buy or rent a building as a branch surgery.'

'Move out of Otter House? No way,' Izzy says, and I can see from Emma's expression that this option isn't acceptable to her either.

'We *are* Otter House,' Frances chips in.

'I know that, but with more space, we could have a fourth vet and more support staff. We could increase the range of services we offer, like adding a hydrotherapy pool for our orthopaedic cases. We could attract veterinary specialists for patients like Merrie with her chronic skin.'

'I'd love to train for a qualification in hydrotherapy,' I say, warming to the idea, 'and we could expand the nursing clinics.'

'There's no way we're moving out of Otter House.' Emma puts her foot down. 'That was never in my vision for the practice. Not only that, we've invested a small fortune here.'

'So there's still the concept of a branch surgery, or two, maybe,' Maz goes on.

'That would split the team,' Izzy says. 'Our clients wouldn't like that.'

'I understand why you're all being so negative – that's what happens when you instigate change,' Maz goes on bravely. 'We should embrace it, not be scared.' She turns to Frances for support. 'You're on the front line. You know how hard it is to turn people away when we're busy.'

'I do my best to squeeze everyone in somehow,' she says rather stiffly. 'We do manage.'

'I think you're completely bonkers,' Emma cuts in

12

when Maz opens her mouth to pick up on what Frances has said. 'I've told you, it's too much to think about right now. I want to spend more time with the children, not less.'

'I'm thinking of the future. When the children have grown up and left home, we'll be free to work full-time again and, when we retire, there'll be a nice little extra for the pension fund.'

'*If* you retire,' Emma points out with a wry smile.

I keep silent, not wanting to be seen to take sides. I love Maz. She saw my potential and gave me a chance when I was a rather awkward teenager, but I don't know why she's thinking about money and pensions when she's married to Alex Fox-Gifford, who's loaded. His family owns half the land around here, and I'm not sure she even needs to work. I like Emma too, and I can see how upset she is at her partner's suggestion that they abandon Otter House altogether – it was her family home and she set up the practice as a tribute to her mother who passed away from cancer.

'So, when's the new vet arriving?' I ask.

'Tomorrow for eight, I hope,' Maz says.

'You hope? He'd better be here,' Emma says. 'I've arranged for Ben to have a daddy day with the girls tomorrow so I can show him the ropes.'

'It's okay. He's texted me to say he'll be with us by this evening. He's staying at the manor with Sophia for now and I must admit I'm nervous – I'm not sure how my mother-in-law will cope with a house guest. On the other hand, it'll be nice for her to have company for a while, now she's alone in that big old house.'

Izzy frowns. 'I hope it doesn't put him off.'

'I've told her that she's to look after him like he's one of the horses.' Maz grins. 'That way, he'll want for nothing, which will be fine as long as she doesn't feed him pony nuts for breakfast.' She grows serious. 'I'm sure I don't really need to do this, but I just want to remind everyone to make him welcome. Your job, Frances, is to persuade people to see Ross when they book appointments. Don't let them insist on seeing me or Emma, apart from the really special ones, that is.'

'I'm pretty sure that's all of them,' I observe brightly. All our clients are special, in more ways than one. 'Ouch!' Tripod turns and gives me a gentle bite to remind me to stroke him now that I've finished my doughnut. I run my fingers down his back, shocked to feel the knobbles of his spine.

'If we can transfer as many of Will's clients as possible straight across to Ross, that would be perfect. There's bound to be some teething trouble as there always is when a new vet starts.' Emma looks towards Maz. 'Are we done?'

'Not quite,' I say quickly before the meeting comes to a close. 'Has anyone noticed that Tripod has lost weight recently?'

'I thought he was at the water bowl more often,' Izzy says, as Maz and Emma shrug rather sheepishly.

'It's so typical of the vets not to notice anything.'

'That's why we have nurses.' Maz laughs. 'I'll have a look at him later, Shannon.'

'You won't forget?'

'You might have to remind me.' She glances at the clock on the wall. 'Let's get going. Emma, you're meeting with DJ about the plans for the flat, Frances,

14

you're at reception, and Shannon, you're helping Jack with the baby bunnies. I said you'd be happy to sex them for him before he boxes them up to take them up to the rescue centre.'

'You don't think they're too young?' It can be hard to tell the boys from the girls before they're six weeks old, and I don't want to make a mistake.

'You'll be fine. I'm supremely confident in your ability to distinguish male from female.' Maz turns to Izzy. 'You're with me for the visits.'

I head to the consulting room to unpack the drugs order, tidying the shelves and restocking the fridge with vaccines while Tripod 'helps', pouncing on imaginary mice among the boxes and packaging. When I've finished, I whisk him into reception to weigh him on the scales – he doesn't need a basket as he's an old hand, standing there waiting for the reading to come up. He has lost weight, which isn't good, but I'm quietly confident that he'll be okay. I help Jack with the rabbits, assigning three to the girls' carrier and three to the boys', and sending each of them on their way with one last cuddle. That doesn't help my allergy because, in spite of a dose of antihistamine, I'm still sneezing when Jennie arrives to collect Lucky much later in the day.

'Am I glad to see you?' Jennie scoops him up into her arms from the consulting room table, and plants a kiss on the top of his head. 'We've all been so worried.' The dog looks adoringly into her eyes. 'You look completely spaced out.'

'It's the sedation. It'll continue to wear off overnight,' I explain, before I show her out and lock up behind her.

'That's another day over.' Maz looks up from where

she's filling in a form to go with Lucky's biopsy samples in the prep room.

'Haven't those gone yet? The courier should have been by now.'

Maz stares at me. 'I asked Frances twice to arrange collection.'

'Shall I call her to check? She's gone home.'

'No, I'll organise it. You've done more than enough today, thank you. I'll have to have a little chat with her. This can't carry on. I can't keep sorting out her muddles.' Maz grins ruefully. 'I have enough of my own.'

'Are you going to be around for a while? Tripod needs to see a vet,' I remind her. 'I don't see why he shouldn't get priority treatment, seeing as he's staff.'

'Let me do this first – I'll be with you ASAP.'

I feed Tripod and clean the theatre from floor to ceiling – I learned a long time ago that Izzy doesn't miss a trick. The tiniest fleck of dirt or a single hair and she's onto it. As I empty the bucket and rinse out the mop, Maz pops her head around the door into Kennels.

'I'm sorry, I'll have to look at Tripod another time. I've got to dash – Sophia's got the children and George has fallen over and bumped his head. He might need a couple of stitches.' Maz's face is etched with maternal anxiety, but she forces a smile. 'Perhaps I'll bring him back here and do it myself to save waiting in A&E. I am joking,' she adds quickly. 'You were about to ask me if I wanted you to get a kit ready, weren't you?'

'The thought did cross my mind,' I admit. 'You'd better go. I hope he's okay.'

'He'll be fine. The Fox-Giffords are hard nuts to crack.'

I decide that there's only one way to get Tripod seen by a vet – I book him an appointment for the following day before I walk the short distance home through Talyton St George.

As I glance back along Fore Street, I notice how the evening sun casts its rays across Otter House, lending extra warmth to its clotted-cream coloured render. There's a poster in the window of the pharmacy, advertising the maypole dancing on the Green which happened over a month ago on the first day in May, as it has every year since anyone can remember.

On my way, I'm accosted by our biggest patient, a blue Great Dane who reminds me of Scooby Doo. He leaps up and plants his paws on my shoulders, almost sending me flying as he licks my face with a tongue like a dripping towel. I step back against the wall beside the greengrocer's as his owner shrieks at him and tries to haul him off.

'Nero, get down!' Mrs Dyer, the butcher's wife, struggles to drag him away. She's in her fifties at least, and has arms like a bodybuilder on steroids. 'I'm so sorry – he doesn't know his own strength,' she gasps, catching his lead around the adjacent lamppost to act as a brake. 'Are you all right?' she goes on as the bunting flutters in the breeze above us.

'I'm fine, thanks. It isn't every day you get a greeting like that.' I avoid Nero's gaze because I know that if I acknowledge him, he'll be back to give me another slobbery kiss.

'I must come in and make an appointment for him – he's been scratching at his ears something chronic.'

'You'll be able to meet our new vet.'

'I prefer to see someone I know and trust. You do understand?'

Unfortunately, I understand all too well. When you've had a bad experience, as both of us have with losing much-loved dogs before, you're much more wary the next time: once bitten, twice shy.

Mrs Dyer wishes me goodnight and releases the lead. I watch her go, being towed along the street, recalling the times I used to scurry away in the opposite direction or pretend to be on my mobile to avoid her. As an idealistic and rebellious teenager, I was involved in an act of vandalism, spraying the message, 'Meat Is Murder' across her shop window with red paint. I meant well. I was fighting for a cause close to my heart. The police knew who'd done it because a couple of friends and I had already been in trouble for chaining ourselves to the gates of the fields in protest where the new estate was being built; we were taken to the station, where we had a meeting with Mr and Mrs Dyer and our parents. We apologised and paid for the clean-up – I was lucky not to end up with a criminal record.

I stroll on across the cobbles in Market Square, stopping outside one of the shops, the place I call home.

I look up above the window where 'Petals the florist' is painted in gold lettering on a green background. There's a smear of mould in the top corner of the glass that Mum must have missed – not an unusual occurrence, as she is both vertically and visually challenged. The sign in the door is turned to 'Closed', but the lights are on and I can see a figure beyond the shelves and buckets of flowers which form a riot of scarlet, pink, yellow and orange among the different shades of green foliage. My mum, dressed in a tatty sweatshirt and jeans that are too tight for her, is sitting at a table, where the light from a desk-lamp creates a golden halo around her frizzy curls as she concentrates on wiring the stem of a bird of paradise.

I slip the key into the lock, give it a jiggle and a twist and push the door open, at which the bell jangles, bringing a big black dog flying out from the shadows, claws clattering across the lino.

'Seven!' I exclaim as he jumps up, squeaking and wagging his tail.

'Hello, Shannon,' Mum calls.

'Hi,' I call back as I squat down to stroke his ears. He's a labradoodle, the product of an illicit liaison on the Green between a Labrador and a standard poodle. Maz delivered the puppies by Caesarean, and the seventh puppy to be born had a hare-lip, which meant he couldn't suckle. The owner of the bitch couldn't cope with the commitment of hand-rearing him, so he became ours.

'There's egg, beans, tomatoes and mash for tea,' Mum says, cutting up blocks of oasis and placing them in baskets. 'Would you mind putting the potatoes on? I'm all behind, like the proverbial cow's tail.'

'Do I have to? I've been on my feet all day – I could do with a shower and a long sleep.' My nose fills with the scent of lilies.

'I've got this anniversary do at the Barnscote tomorrow and it's got to be perfect.'

'I'm sorry.' I walk over and hug her. 'I'll do cheese on toast, if that's okay.'

'Thank you, I don't know what I'd do without you, darling. Or you, Seven,' she adds, reaching down to pat him as he walks right in close to her and presses his nose against her thigh.

'He thinks you're having a hypo,' I point out.

'I do feel a little shaky.' She hunts along the counter among the bridal magazines and sample brochures for her tubes of glucose gel. She takes one and then uses her machine to prick her finger and check her blood.

'How is it?' I ask, peering over her shoulder.

'My sugar's been all over the place for the last few days.'

'Why didn't you say something?' I say, annoyed. 'Have you seen the doctor?' I look at her and she gazes back, her eyes small and her cheeks puffy. 'Clearly, you haven't.'

'There's no need to give me one of your lectures. I know all about diabetes. I have to live with it.'

'So you know how serious it is if it's out of control.'

'Yes, it could kill me, but I'm not going to let it. I'll see Dr Nicci tomorrow.' She relaxes a little and I can tell she's feeling better. 'Come on, lighten up. I don't want my daughter returning to the dark side.'

'Oh, Mum,' I groan. 'As if.'

She's referring to my Goth years when I dyed my hair black and hid behind dark, shapeless clothes. I change the subject. 'Frances says you had an estate agent round the other day. You would tell me if you were planning to put Petals up for sale?'

'The agency dropped a leaflet through the door a while back. I thought there'd be no harm in having an up-to-date valuation.'

'What on earth for?'

'I don't know,' she shrugs. 'One of the partners turned up – he says it's a remarkably attractive property and he'd be delighted to market it personally, if that was what I wanted.'

'So you aren't selling?'

'No,' she confirms, looking aside as if she can't quite meet my eye, which makes me wonder what she isn't telling me.

Chapter Two

Itchy Feet

I'm first at the practice the next morning to find that a new inpatient has arrived overnight. Emma, who was on call with Izzy, must have admitted the dog, a black standard poodle. I know who she is before I check the record card that's clipped to the front of the kennel.

'Saba, what's happened to you?' She looks up with mournful brown eyes and promptly throws up at my feet. 'Oh dear.' I clear up quickly and give her a clean bed. 'Never mind.' She's Seven's mum and one of our favourites, having lost some of the aloofness of her youth. Her coat is rough and going grey around her muzzle, although she's still immaculately turned out. 'No breakfast for you, I'm afraid.' Emma has scribbled 'poss op' on the card.

I feed Tripod and hang out the wet towels and pet bedding on the line in the garden, keeping half an eye on the robin that's hopping about at the foot of the lilac. I can hear the starlings chattering in the roof where they've made their nest and hatched their first brood of chicks. It's very peaceful, apart from the sound of a car now and again on the road outside. I love this time of day, although it's often the calm before the storm. It won't be long before Kennels fills with yapping dogs.

Gradually, the sound of a motorbike cuts through the calm, starting as a faint buzz like an annoying wasp, and growing louder, until it's so noisy that it could be a whole flight of Hell's Angels roaring through Talyton St George and heading this way. I hear it pull up somewhere outside Otter House, its engine throbbing like a pulse. It's the kind of sound that goes right through you, vibrating through your skull and all the way to your feet. Tripod flattens his ears and slinks back through the cat-flap. The robin flies up onto the garden wall and stays there, even when the engine eventually cuts out.

I carry on pegging out the last of the washing until the sound of the buzzer from reception calls me back inside.

'I'm on my way!' I hurry on through the practice, wondering which of Talyton's pets has come to grief and hoping that one of the vets will turn up soon, but when I get there, there's a man in a helmet and leathers leaning nonchalantly against the desk, one finger pressed down hard on the button for the buzzer.

'Ah, there is some sign of life, after all.' He lifts his gloved hand and raises his tinted visor to reveal a pair of lively dark brown eyes.

'I came as quickly as I could,' I say, bemused at his impatience. Where's the urgency? He doesn't have an animal with him. He isn't carrying any parcels, so I assume this isn't a special delivery either, and then

23

I remember that the courier's due to take Lucky's samples to the path lab today.

'I believe you're expecting me.' His voice is rich and laced with dark honey. He's very well spoken. In fact, he's what I'd call well posh, much like Alex Fox-Gifford.

'Oh, yes, of course,' I say, a little affronted by his rather superior attitude. He removes first his gloves and then his helmet, revealing a mass of dark, almost black curls that fall to his shoulders, which I can't help noticing are broad and decidedly masculine. His complexion is tanned and his cheeks are adorned with dark stubble. He is heart-stoppingly gorgeous, maybe because he reminds me of Kit Harington, my actor crush of the moment – to look at, at least. I want to make the most of this occasion – it isn't often, if ever, that a handsome guy, roughly my age, walks off the street into the practice, but I'm a little surprised when he places his helmet on the desk and unzips and strips out of his leather jacket. Underneath he's wearing a grey T-shirt with a wolf on the front, which is stretched taut across his chest.

This is getting interesting, I think, frozen to the spot, watching him, but if he's expecting coffee and a chat, he's going to be disappointed. I know what these couriers are like. They charge by the minute.

'Wait there,' I say, and I hurry out the back to grab the package I wrapped and labelled last night. I bring it back to reception. 'This is for you.' I hold it out to him and he stares at me, as if he's a bit dense. My forehead tightens as he places the package on the desk, depositing it between the display of dog tags and collars, and a cardboard cut-out of a big brown flea.

'Thanks for the welcome present, but there's no need.' He grins, showing off a set of perfect teeth, and holds out his hand. 'I'm Ross, the new vet.'

'Oh-mi-god, how embarrassing. I'm so sorry.' I shake his hand briefly. A great start, I tell myself. You've just mistaken the hot new vet for the courier. 'I wasn't expecting you to turn up on a motorbike.'

'It's all right. It isn't your fault. I take it that you're Shannon.' He smiles as if to put me at ease, but I can't help wondering if he's laughing at me being wrong-footed by his arrival. 'Maz and Emma talked about you when I came here for my interview.'

I'm not sure how to respond. I look away, focusing on the noticeboard and the posters on the walls advertising our puppy parties and our competition for Pet of the Month.

'Um, Maz isn't here yet. She's probably dropping the children off at school and nursery.'

'She's on her way. I saw her bundling them into the car up at the manor. I'm lodging – no, slumming it – with her mother-in-law, the one who sounds like a horse.'

'Sophia? She's all right,' I say in her defence. She's been kind to me in the past. A widow in her late seventies with a consuming passion for all things equine and district commissioner for the Pony Club, she rides even now. 'I used to waitress for her at the Fox-Giffords' New Year parties.'

'There was a pony in the drawing room – as she calls it – last night, a hairy thing with terrible wind. She was feeding it mints from a tin. And that house.' He shudders. 'It should be condemned.'

I find that I'm rather glad at his discomfort. He

might be good-looking, but his scent of leather and oil is getting right up my nose.

He fetches a small bag from his bike and I show him to the staff room, where he can change into the new scrubs that were ordered for him and wait for Maz and Emma to arrive. Meanwhile I escape, running into Izzy in the corridor on the way.

'I see the new vet's arrived,' she says.

'I thought he was the courier and tried to give him Lucky's samples for the lab.'

She smiles. 'I thought you'd know by now not to make assumptions about people from their appearance.'

'Yes, but he was wearing helmet and leathers – he doesn't look like a vet.' I follow her into Kennels where I hang on to Saba for her to check her temperature and put her on a drip since she's been sick for a second time. 'Emma took some blood last night – if the real courier doesn't turn up soon, we can send Ross on his bike.' She chuckles as we return the dog to her cage. 'I think that's it for now.'

'I'll catch up with you later,' I say, walking away.

'Hey, where are you off to?'

'I need to set up for the ops. There's a cat spay, dog castrate, and whatever they decide to do with Saba.'

'Oh no, you don't. You're looking after Ross.'

'Do I have to?' My heart sinks.

'Emma's been held up and I thought you'd enjoy hand-holding our new vet.'

'Why do I always have to be babysitter?'

'I think you'll find me quite a mature individual.' I turn abruptly to find Ross standing behind us, dressed in a dark purple scrub top, chinos and black lace-up shoes, and with a new stethoscope around his neck. His tone is serious yet his eyes flash with humour, which only adds to my embarrassment. My cheeks burn as he continues, 'I haven't needed a babysitter since I was about twelve.'

'You know what Shannon meant. It was a turn of phrase,' Izzy says sharply.

'Okay, I get it. Keep your hair on, Izz,' he joshes.

'The name is Izzy.' She looks down her nose at him, as if she considers him anything but grown up, and checks the fob watch pinned to her apron. 'Go on then, both of you. It's nine o'clock.'

It's going to be a long day, I think, but I'm on an early finish. I'll be out of here by four.

In the consulting room, I turn the computer on and glance down the list of appointments on the monitor. There's Mrs Wall and Merrie, and Cheryl with one of her Persian cats. I smile to myself. This is going to be a baptism of fire.

'Is there anything I should know about this first one?' Ross asks as I do a quick check on the number of vaccines in the fridge and make sure the spray for wiping down the table between patients is topped up.

'I don't think so.' If I hadn't embarrassed myself in front of him, I might have been inclined to be more helpful. 'Will has left all the info in the notes.'

'What does this mean?' Ross runs one finger along the screen. 'CTTKB and CCFI. Are they some kind of coded warning? Can you decipher it, or should I ask Izzy, though she seems to be a bit of a dominatrix? How do you cope?'

'She's a fantastic head nurse and a good friend,' I say, offended on her behalf.

'I don't doubt that – I'm just saying she's rather bossy.'

And you're rather judgemental and outspoken, I want to say, but I bite my tongue for now. No comment, I think, and I return to the subject of the abbreviations.

'CTTKB is "Client Thinks They Know Better" and CCFI is "Client Can't Follow Instructions".' I relent and reveal what I know about Mrs Wall. 'She's renowned for failing to give Merrie her tablets and she's also the local fortune-teller.'

'Really?' He whistles through his teeth. 'You're winding me up.'

'It's true. My friends and I used to call her the witch because she wishes warts away over the phone. I'm not sure she has a first name. I've never heard anyone refer to her as anything but Mrs Wall, and there isn't a Mr Wall, as far as I know. She lives alone in one of the terraced houses opposite the church, a few doors up from Frances. She's pretty harmless. You just have to humour her.'

'Why? So she doesn't cast a spell on me?' He grins and I begin to warm to him just a little. 'What planet is this?'

'I'm guessing that you didn't have fortune-tellers at your last practice then,' I say, amused.

'I was working in London for my parents until recently. Their practice is in Kensington and their clients are mainly lawyers and bankers, and a few celebrities, actors and musicians.'

'That sounds exciting. Why on earth did you leave?'

'I won't tell you now. It's a long story,' he says. 'Shall we make a start? Hand me the cloak of scepticism and syringe of reason then send her on in.'

28

I call Mrs Wall. 'The vet will see you now.'

'Come along, Merrie.' She smiles, revealing a set of poorly fitting dentures, as she stands up with the aid of a stick, an ebony cane with a silver top. She's an elderly woman with tinted specs, grey slacks and red shoes. Her small dog, Merrie by name and merry by nature, is supposed to be a West Highland white terrier, but looks decidedly rusty where she's licked and chewed at her skin. She sniffs at the doorframe on the way, as if she has all the time in the world, while Ross stands drumming his fingers against the table.

'Good afternoon,' he says.

'Actually, it's morning time,' Mrs Wall replies, apparently giving him the benefit of the doubt. She isn't stupid. She can recognise irony when she hears it. 'You must be Ross.' She pulls the dog along behind her.

'That's right. And how is Merrie?' He bundles her up and stands her on the table where she snuffles about, searching for a treat. He ruffles her fur as she wags her stump of a tail. 'You haven't stopped her tablets again, have you?'

'I learned my lesson the last time. She's had every pill as instructed, but they don't seem to be working any more. She keeps biting at her feet and crying.'

I take hold of Merrie, who's a wriggly customer, scrabbling about as Ross tries to grab a paw. In the end, I manage to grab one for him. He has a good look and prescribes a bath in a medicated shampoo after he's taken some skin scrapings and hair pluckings.

'We won't have a result today,' I say aside to him. 'The lab kit is packed away.'

29

'All I need is a microscope and a couple of slides. If you find it, I'll set it up. It won't take two minutes and I'd rather have an answer today than tomorrow. It's better for Merrie.'

I can't argue with that, although I suspect Maz might have something to say about it.

'Her allergy's getting worse, isn't it?' Mrs Wall says.

'We don't know that for sure. It could be something else. It could be mites.'

'Mice?' Mrs Wall leans closer. 'Are you trying to tell me Merrie has mice?'

'Mites.' Ross spells it out. 'M-I-T-E-S.'

'You should speak more clearly, my lover, or no one around here will know what you'm saying,' Mrs Wall goes on, dropping into a broad Devon dialect.

'Maybe you should have your hearing tested,' Ross says with a smile that could melt the iciest heart. I hold my breath, but all that Mrs Wall can do is glare at him.

'You, young man, are very rude.'

'It's a serious suggestion. I'm trying to be helpful.'

'Let me take Merrie,' I say, in case Mrs Wall should change her mind about leaving her with us. I carry her through to Kennels where I find her a comfortable bed next door to Saba before returning to help Ross with the rest of the morning's appointments.

'Who's next?' he asks. I notice that he's cleaned the table. That's my job.

'This is Cheryl, who runs the teashop and breeds long-haired cats. She calls them her babies.'

Ross rolls his eyes. 'I can't understand these people.'

'She does care about them. She has them tested for genetic diseases.'

'But they still look like they've run into a wall.'

I can't argue with that.

'Send her in.'

To my relief, he's polite to Cheryl, and gives the cat her booster vaccination without incident.

'Shall we see if we can find out why the lovely Merrie has such itchy feet? It's a pretty safe bet that it isn't mice,' Ross jokes at the end of morning surgery, and in spite of myself, I find myself smiling. I start to wonder if he's always this cheerful.

I fetch the microscope and a couple of slides from the cupboard in the corridor, leaving them on the prep bench for him. He examines the skin samples and prescribes a suitable shampoo. On the way to fetch Merrie from her cage, I notice that Saba has been given a reprieve from surgery. Good news, I hope, as I carry the Westie to the doggy bath, grabbing a couple of towels on the way. She is instantly suspicious, standing stiff as a statue in the bottom of the ceramic tray. I run the water from the shower head, checking that it's warm before letting it run onto the back of her neck. She shakes herself, splashing me in the eyes.

'Do you mind?' I exclaim, but clearly she doesn't, because she scrambles towards me and jumps up, placing her soggy paws on my chest. 'Get down,' I say firmly. 'I can see this isn't going to be a walk in the park.' I shampoo her, leave the foam on her coat for a few minutes, during which time she gives herself several more good shakes, before I give her a thorough rinse, after which she shakes herself again. By the end of her bath, I'm as wet as she is.

'Ah well, at least you know that you don't have mange,' Ross laughs when he sees me disappearing off to change my scrub top and trousers. So much for

31

making a good impression, I think with a rueful smile.

When Merrie's dry, I discharge her, making an appointment for a checkup the following day.

'I don't think much of the new vet,' Mrs Wall says. 'Merrie hasn't taken to him at all.' I'm not quite sure how she makes that judgement. Maybe she can read her dog's mind as well as seeing into the future. 'Can't we see one of the other vets instead?'

'I'm afraid not. Ross wants to see if she improves on the treatment.'

'I suppose that makes sense.' She squints at me through her tinted specs. 'I'm sure you won't mind me telling you this, my lover, but this year will be your year. I read the leaves this morning and now I've seen you, I understand what they were saying to me. Change is afoot – it won't all be plain sailing, but good fortune is coming your way in life and love.'

'Well, thank you,' I say politely.

'Don't turn away the stranger who comes a-courting,' she adds.

'Chance would be a fine thing.' I haven't exactly been lucky in love. 'We'll see you tomorrow.'

'Goodbye, dear,' she says.

After my lunch break, I catch up with Maz.

'You could have reminded me to have a look at him later rather than book him during afternoon surgery,' she observes when I place Tripod on the consulting room table. 'I've just had it in the neck from Frances because she's short of appointments. You know what she's like.'

'I tried that yesterday. It's no good because you're always rushing off to do something else. How is George anyway?'

'We waited for three hours in A&E and all they did was give him some Calpol, stick a couple of butterfly strips across the wound and tell me to keep him under observation for twenty-four hours. I was right. I could have dealt with it myself. I almost brought him in with me this morning, but Alex stepped in and took him out on his rounds. George didn't want to go at first, but I told him it would be far more exciting looking at cows with his daddy than sitting in a kennel all day here. Luckily, he's still at the age where he believes everything his parents say.'

'He is all right now?'

'He's fine – until the next time. We'll soon be on the at-risk register with social services, if we aren't already.' She changes the subject. 'How are you getting on with the courier?' She giggles. 'I heard.'

'He isn't like Will. I miss him.'

'Will was one in a million. Emma and I felt like we could trust him to handle any case, any situation. It's bound to take a while for us to get used to Ross and vice versa. I was impressed that he used his initiative and used the microscope, even if Izzy did have to put it away after him. He seems very efficient.'

'Either that or he's in a hurry to get through his appointments as quickly as possible. I think the clients might feel he's in too much of a rush, compared with Will, I mean.'

'We can't compare him with Will. That isn't fair.'

'I know.' I'm wondering how tactfully I can put it. I don't like to disappoint her, but this is her practice and her reputation at stake. If anything goes wrong, the buck stops with the partners. 'Ross and Mrs Wall didn't exactly hit it off. He was pretty sharp with her.'

'You mean, he was rude?' Maz hesitates. 'Frances

said she wasn't terribly happy when she paid her bill. She said she could foresee trouble ahead, not that I believe in that crystal ball of hers. Oh, never mind. We'll see how things go.' She strokes Tripod, tickling him under the chin. 'So, what's the problem?'

'I was hoping you'd be able to tell me,' I say cheekily.

Maz looks up with a weary smile. I feel sorry for her – she must have been up all night with the children. She starts examining Tripod from the tip of his nose to his tail. He's loving the attention, purring and rolling over to show his belly. Eventually, she looks up and glances towards the empty hook on the wall.

'Have you seen my—?'

'It's around your neck,' I cut in. 'And it isn't yours,' I add when she reaches the stethoscope. 'It's the one from the spares drawer.'

'All right,' she sighs. 'I'll put it back later.'

'I've heard that one before.'

'I promise.' Maz sticks the stethoscope in her ears to block me out as much as to listen to Tripod's chest. She grins when he continues to purr. 'I can't hear anything. Come on, pussycat.' She blows on his nose to make him pause for just long enough to hear his heartbeat.

'He's losing weight and drinking more. Izzy and I checked his blood pressure this morning and it's a little high. I thought maybe it would be worth taking some blood.' We could easily have taken some ourselves but decided it would be wise not to overstep the mark. 'It could be his kidneys, or thyroid, couldn't it?'

'There doesn't seem to be much wrong with him,

but we'll take some blood to check – anything to give you and Izzy peace of mind.'

'I know you think we're fussing, but there's definitely something wrong.'

'He's getting old, like Frances.'

'Are you taking my name in vain?' Frances's head appears around the door.

Maz looks up, her face pink. 'I wish you'd knock first. What is it you want?'

'Alexander is on the phone wanting to speak to you.' She means Alex. She used to call him Young Mr Fox-Gifford to distinguish him from his father, for whom she used to work.

'Tell him I'll call him back.'

'How long will that be? Only this is the third time he's called. It's about George—'

'There's nothing wrong?' Maz interrupts.

'Not with George. It's Alexander. He says he's had enough – he wants to know if there's a kennel free.'

'For him or for our son? Tell him I'll be five or ten minutes then I'll go and pick him up.' Frances disappears again, and Maz takes the blood, leaving me to give Tripod a cuddle for being so good-tempered about it before I pack the sample for transport to the lab.

Later, after I've said a quick goodbye to Ross, and George is ensconced in reception with Frances, some juice and a packet of chocolate biscuits, I overhear Maz telling Emma that she decided to run some blood tests on Tripod. I smile to myself. Sometimes, you can't tell a vet. You have to let them think it's their idea. It turns out that it's much the same with parents.

When I get home, I shower and serve up pasta and a mixed salad for tea, and we chat about the new vet and the latest gossip – being the local florist, Mum is a fount of knowledge when it comes to hatches, matches and dispatches. After we've eaten, I clear the plates from the table in the kitchen while she gazes out of the window, past a souvenir of Greece, a fishing boat with striped sails and a bronzed sailor at the helm, that she bought when we went on holiday a couple of years ago. He reminds me of a waiter who liked to flirt with her – we went to the same beach tavern every day for a week.

'What are you doing tonight?' I ask her.

'I need to order some more supplies and update the accounts.'

'What's that saying? All work and no play . . .'

'. . . makes Jack a dull boy.' Mum frowns. 'Do you think I'm boring?'

'Single-minded.'

'Sometimes I wonder if I should get out more.'

'That's a great idea. We can take the dog for a walk.'

At the word 'walk',' Seven turns up with his lead in his mouth, his trunk curving as he wags his tail.

'Oh, I don't know if I've got the energy,' Mum says, backtracking.

'It's too late. You can't possibly let him down now. He'll be disappointed.' I pause. This is where she usually says she isn't coming with us, but she surprises me.

'Why not? Let me get my shoes on and we can go down to the river for a nice chat, like we used to.'

We walk through town, along the Centurion Bridge and across the Green. Having passed through the kissing gate next to the stile, I check the field for sheep before letting Seven off the lead. He barks at Mrs Wall and Merrie, who are strolling along the far bank of the river, as I take a deep breath and survey the scene. The river Taly, its rippling surface glinting in the sun, meanders through the valley, and as we walk on, the air grows pungent with elderflower, sheep and a hint of river water.

There's the sound of splashing and a duck flies across the surface, landing among a flurry of ducklings that have been caught up in an eddy and spun into the shallows beneath the bank.

'I can hardly bear to watch,' Mum says, as the smallest is washed out into the middle of the river and carried downstream. It starts to make panicky, pipping noises as it struggles to turn back.

I make to run down and wade in, but Mum catches my arm and I wait, watching with my heart in my mouth, as the mother duck rounds up the rest of her brood before letting the current take the family to catch up with her lost baby. When we round the first bend, the ducklings are safely ensconced on a bed of silt at the edge of the water and the mother is expressing her feelings through a series of noisy quacks.

'We'll go back along the old railway line.' I whistle to Seven who's investigating the rabbit holes in the hedge before turning back to Mum. 'You're very quiet for someone who wanted to chat. If this is about selling the shop . . .'

'I'm not selling up. I would have told you if I was.'

'What is it then?' I walk through the gap in the hedge onto the clinker track that marks the old railway line, watching the creases at the corners of her eyes deepen. 'You're beginning to worry me.'

'I've met someone, a man,' she blurts out.

'Really? Who is he? How did you meet?' Mum doesn't go out that much, and it's a fact of life that the men who come in to buy flowers at Petals are either attached, suffering from unrequited love, or making up to their existing partners for a guilty conscience. I run through the eligible males in Talyton St George who are of a similar age. 'Is it Peter?' He's the greengrocer and recently divorced.

She shakes her head. 'We've been friends for years, but I couldn't be romantically involved with him. There's no spark.'

I'm uncomfortable with my mum talking of romance and sparks. She seems too old for that.

'Come on. You have to tell me. Don't keep me in suspense.'

'His name's Godfrey. He's sweet, funny and very good-looking.'

'Who does he look like exactly? I'm not getting the picture here.'

'A bit like George Clooney, I suppose. He's a little older than me, but what difference does twelve years make at my age? At least he has his own hair and is in possession of a full set of teeth.' Mum hugs her arms across her chest. 'He's the Ryder-Cole part of Smith and Ryder-Cole, the estate agents.' She pauses, gazing at me anxiously. 'I hope you don't mind.'

'Mind?' I give her a hug. 'I think it's amazeballs. Awesome! Why now, though, after all this time?'

'That's a question I've asked myself. When your dad passed away . . .' She bites her lip before continuing. '. . . it took me a long time to accept he was never coming home. It was all so sudden that I didn't have time to prepare myself. We were still young. We'd planned a long and happy life together and there, in the blink of an eye, it was over and I was planning his funeral and wondering how I was going to keep a roof over our heads. It was hard, raising an eight year old and running a business full time, but we survived. People were kind to us. As the years went by, I had offers, but I turned them all down. I suppose I was still grieving and afraid you would feel I was being disloyal to your dad's memory.'

My throat tightens as she continues, 'I know how much you loved . . . love him. You were always his special girl.' She gazes up at the canopy of leaves formed by the arching branches of the trees on either side of the track. The dappling sunlight catches her face. 'I hardly got a look-in when you were around.'

I glance away. Seven is trotting out of the ditch alongside us, emerging from the stinging nettles, his paws thick with red Devon clay. A memory of myself as a child, falling into a clump of nettles, and my dad whisking me into his arms and running me across the Green to find dock leaves to counter the rash. I remember the smell of crushed leaves, the green stain rubbed into my skin, and my father's arms around me. I miss him, always will.

'If he could see you now, he'd be very proud of you. You're a beautiful young woman, kind and caring, and I live in hope that you'll meet and move in with the man of your dreams one day. What will I do then? I'll be like a duck with an empty nest.'

'You know you shouldn't go looking for someone just because you're afraid of ending up alone,' I observe, wondering if she's trying to pre-empt this scenario.

'This has nothing to do with you, Shannon. I'm doing this for me.'

We walk on back towards the Green.

'Does he have family?' I ask.

'He's divorced and has a son and grandchildren.'

'Are you sure he's no longer married? You can't be too careful.'

'Please don't worry.'

'I don't want to see you get hurt.'

'Oh dear. I thought you'd got over your trust issues.'

'What makes you think I haven't?' I say, exasperated at myself, not Mum, because the episode she's referring to was years ago, when I was eighteen. Yet I still have my moments, times when I blame myself for being a complete idiot, for not realising until I'd become a pathetic, obsessed and lovesick shadow of myself that I was being played by the man in question.

'It's such a shame that you decided to finish with Mitch while you were on holiday. It came quite out of the blue.'

'It wasn't a lack of trust that broke us up. The relationship had run its course. It didn't feel right any more.'

'What I don't understand is why you're still seeing each other. I don't think I could remain friends with an ex.'

Mitch and I were mates long before we got together, and we've hooked up a couple of times since our return from Ibiza in the way that exes sometimes do when neither of them has moved on. I'm still fond of him.

'I like Mitch,' Mum goes on with a sigh. 'Sometimes I wonder if you'll ever settle down.'

'I don't need a man to make me happy.' I change the subject. 'How long have you known this Godfrey?'

'It's been three or four weeks now. We've been to

the café on the promenade at Talysands, he's popped in to the shop, as you know, and we're going out for dinner later in the week. I'm not rushing into anything – it's friendship first.' She hesitates. 'I'd really like you to meet him sometime. You can give me your opinion.'

'I'm hardly the best person to ask,' I say wryly. There was Drew, the lying locum, Diego, the beautiful Spaniard I spent a summer with when he came to work in Talymouth, and Mitch. None of them worked out, and I can't help beginning to wonder if there's something wrong with me. Why do I always choose the wrong kind of man? Because I tend to focus on the positive aspects of their character, ignoring the flaws until it's too late and I've fallen for them hook, line and sinker.

I think about Ross as an example of the male species. There's the charming version with the melting smile, and the rather less endearing one who is impatient and somewhat rude. Is it any wonder that I find men confusing?

'Well, will you join me and Godfrey for coffee or a meal?' Mum repeats.

'I'd love to meet him,' I say, and we head for home, Mum with a smile playing on her lips and me deep in thought.

Chapter Three

Paws for Thought

The prospect of meeting my mother's new man turns out to be the least of my concerns because, when I return to work the next day, the new vet has another run-in with Mrs Wall. It's our last appointment of the afternoon when she brings Merrie into the consulting room for her checkup.

'Is she feeling better?' Ross asks without any preamble.

'She's hardly scratched at all since I put the crystals in her bed last night.' Ross raises his eyebrows as she continues, 'I swear by quartz and jade.'

'You don't think the improvement in her skin has more to do with the shampoo and injection she had here yesterday?'

'You shouldn't be so sceptical,' Mrs Wall says coldly.

'Why? Because you have special powers?'

'At this moment, I can see into your past,' she says, holding his gaze.

'You don't have to tell me about it – I was there.'

'You should take time to reflect on what's happened, because the past informs the decisions you make in the future.'

'I'm sorry, I haven't got time for this. I'm fully booked so, if you don't mind, I'll just get on and look at the dog,' he says politely but firmly.

As Mrs Wall opens and closes her mouth like a fish, I pick Merrie up and pop her onto the table. Ross examines her and dispenses some tablets with a warning.

'I don't need special powers to predict that without the full course of medication, Merrie will not get better. I will be able to tell if you haven't followed my instructions.' He relaxes a little, a smile crossing his lips. 'There are no known adverse reactions with any crystals, be they jade or quartz, so if you insist on using them you can continue, reassured that they will do no harm – and absolutely no good either.'

I notice how Mrs Wall grinds the end of her stick against the floor. She is not happy, and neither is Merrie, who is looking in vain for her treat.

'Will always gave her a biscuit when he'd finished,' I say. 'They're in the drawer by the computer.'

The concept of treats seems alien to Ross, so to keep Mrs Wall and Merrie on side, I give the dog a biscuit myself.

'Are you drumming up takers for your nurse-led slimming courses?' he says when they've left the room.

'Of course not. It's good PR and I love it when the animals come in all keen and pleased to see us.' I pause. 'You could at least try to humour Mrs Wall like Will used to. He had such a lovely pet-side manner.'

43

'Whereas I don't?' Ross says harshly. 'I don't pander to people and their ridiculous ideas. Jade and quartz as a cure for allergic dermatitis? I've never heard such utter garbage.'

'I'm sorry. I was trying to be helpful. I didn't mean to criticise.'

'I do what I think is right. The patients are my priority.'

But you have to treat the clients too, I want to say. That's one of the first things Maz taught me when I started work at Otter House. They are the ones who are paying your wages. If you lecture them or make them feel guilty, you drive them away.

'I'd prefer it if you didn't feed the animals,' he continues. 'I'm sorry if that makes me sound like a killjoy, but I can't teach clients about diets and obesity when the nurse is giving their porky pets extra calories. We're going to have to agree to disagree on certain things when we're working on the same shifts. I believe we're spending the night together –' his mouth smiles, but his eyes do not – 'and I have to say, I can't wait.'

'Great,' I say, matching his insincerity. I'm really not sure about him. I don't know where I stand when he's always in a rush and determined to make his mark by making sure everything is done his way. Perhaps he's feeling the pressure of being in a new job. I decide to give him the benefit of the doubt.

We manage to survive the rest of the day without further incident, and I'm cleaning the waiting area when Ross is preparing to leave the practice. He's wearing his leathers, and has his helmet under one arm as he fishes about in his pocket.

'Cheer up, Shannon.' I bang my bucket with the

mop, sloshing some suds across the floor. I *am* cheerful. 'If you're lucky, it'll be a quiet night,' he goes on. 'I can't imagine you get that busy. Everything around here closes at five. The place is dead.'

'People move here for the peace and quiet. If you don't like it, you know what you can do.'

'I was making an observation,' he says, looking hurt, but I don't believe him. 'It's just that I'm used to being called out three or four times a night – it was hardly worth going to bed.' He rolls an earplug into a squishy ball and slips it into one ear.

'Don't speak too soon,' I warn him. 'That's like tempting fate.'

'You sound like Mrs Wall. You'll be telling me that a black cat crossing your path is bad luck next.' He's grinning as he slips an earplug into the other ear.

'It is, if it makes you swerve off the road. Unlucky for you, lucky for the rest of us.'

'I'm sorry, I can't hear you,' he mouths, pointing at his ears.

'Take the stupid things out then,' I say, a little irritated that he's cut the conversation without waiting for me to finish. 'I don't know why you wear them anyway.'

'Because the bike's noisy and I want to preserve my hearing for as long as possible. I can lip-read, you know.'

'Yeah, it's funny how you can only hear what you want to hear,' I say as he slips his helmet on. 'I assume you're taking the phone for now. That's the accepted routine. The vets take the calls while the nurses are on standby.'

He frowns, looking at my mouth as I repeat what I've just said.

'Phone?' I say. 'You are taking the phone.' Finally, as I'm about to explode, he gets it.

'Actually, I was planning to go for a spin, if you don't mind, that is.' His expression is soft now, entreating. 'I could do with a break.'

What about me? I want to ask. I wouldn't mind going for a swim.

'I can't hear the phone above the sound of the engine . . .'

'Can't you put it on vibrate or something?'

'I wouldn't feel that either. She's a monster of a bike.' He gazes fondly towards the car park, then turns back to me. 'It doesn't have to be a special favour – I know I'm not your favourite vet – but I won't forget that I owe you one. I'll be half an hour, tops.' And he's off before I can either agree or argue, striding out of reception and up to his bike where he swings his leg over with one light movement and sets it going with a kick-start. I cross my arms as I watch him ride away, slightly irritated with myself because I can't help thinking that there's something very sexy about the combination of man, leather and machine, even if the man alone is a pain in the—

The sound of the phone interrupts my train of thought and I run back to the desk to grab the duty mobile.

'Otter House vets . . .' I don't need to ask what's wrong because I can hear the sound of a dog yelping in distress, and my heart sinks because I have no vet and no way of contacting him. I don't even know where he's gone.

'It's Declan here from the Old Forge,' a voice says. 'I think Trevor has gone and broken his leg. He's in a lot of pain.'

'Okay, we'll be there with you shortly,' I say to reassure him.

'Thanks. Is Maz about?' he asks hopefully.

'Ross is the vet on call tonight. He's very . . .' If it had been Will in the early days, I'd have described him as 'nice', but I can't say the same for Ross. '. . . professional,' is the best I can come up with. Okay, he's downright hot as well, I think as I cut the call and phone him.

I grab the visit case with the phone tucked under my chin, leaving a message with the address at Talyford and an outline of the problem, because he isn't answering, but as I get into the ambulance, he calls me back.

'Where are you?' I can hear the throb of his motor-bike in the background.

'I'm on the escarpment, looking down at the sea. Don't worry. I can be back at the surgery in ten minutes.'

'Didn't you listen to my message?' I say, slightly miffed. 'It has to be a visit.'

'Really? The dog will need to come in for X-rays anyway.'

'Trevor is one of Maz's specials. She'd authorise a house call, without question, and bring him back in the ambulance if necessary.' I give him no option except to meet me there, and set out, yearning for the good old days with Will.

I drive out of Talyton St George along the one-way system of narrow streets originally designed with single-file horse-drawn traffic in mind, and north along the road signposted to Talyford. I cross the ford where the water is clear and only a couple of centi-metres deep, and carry on down the hill where the stream passes in front of a row of pink cottages that seem to glow in the evening sunshine, a shop with a post office, a small church or chapel and a courtyard of converted barns. I park outside one of the cottages, the Old Forge, carrying the stretcher and visit case across the narrow wrought-iron bridge over the brook to the house. The door is open.

'Come on in, Shannon,' Declan says, showing me through to the back garden. He's about my age, maybe a couple of years older – in his late twenties, anyway. He's tall and skinny and dressed in jeans and a T-shirt with 'Kaiser Chiefs' emblazoned across the chest.

'The vet's on his way,' I say, secretly crossing my fingers. Where the hell is he, I wonder? He should be here by now. I walk across to where Penny, Declan's partner, is leaning down from her wheelchair to cuddle a young chocolate Labrador who's whimpering and holding up a front leg.

'What happened?' I ask.

'I let him out in the garden as usual. He heard something, a fox or a cat, and went haring off across the lawn, where he tripped over the well cover, bowling himself head over heels.' Penny looks up. She's wearing a mock fur gilet, and wisps of hair of many different colours emerge from beneath the scarf that's tied around her head. The age gap between her and Declan never fails to amaze me – she's at least forty, probably more. 'He's really hurt himself,' she goes on, almost in tears.

Never before have I wanted to hear the roar of a motorbike. Come on, I mutter under my breath as I check Trevor over.

'Has he broken it?' Declan hovers anxiously at my

side, making me nervous. There isn't a lot I can do apart from provide reassurance, because I can't make a diagnosis or give painkillers without a vet's say-so.

'He has hurt his leg,' I say, stating the obvious, but I can't help feeling that Trevor's being a bit of baby. However, he seems genuinely scared by the sight of a man in black when Ross finally turns up. He tries to hide under the wheelchair and howls.

'I'm sorry, I took the wrong turning – all these lanes look the same and I couldn't see a single road sign.'

'Probably because you were going too fast,' I say.

'The one on the way into the village has been stolen.' Declan shakes Ross's hand and introduces himself. 'This is Penny, and that's her dog, Trevor.'

Penny smiles. 'Why is he always my dog when he's in trouble?'

'It's a shame about the circumstances, but it's good to meet you all.' Ross removes his jacket and puts it to one side. 'Ah, he's only a puppy.'

'He's six months old,' Penny says, as I hold on to Trevor, who winces when Ross finds a painful spot.

'We'll take him back to the surgery after I've given him a shot of something to calm him down and reduce the pain. I don't think he's broken the leg, but we'll X-ray him in the morning to check. Is that all right?'

'I suppose it will have to be,' Declan says.

'I don't like the idea of him being alone in the kennels all night,' Penny says.

'He'll be fine,' Ross says, but I'm not sure he's won them over yet.

'I'll stay in the practice with him,' I offer. 'He won't be on his own.'

'I'm going to miss him so much,' Penny goes on.

'He's such a sweet dog.' Clever Trevor as I called him, was the nice but dim one at my puppy parties, scampering about on his enormous paws and bumping into the other puppies.

Penny chuckles. 'You always have such high hopes for your babies, but he's never going to be a genius.'

'As long as he's smart enough to work,' says Declan.

'He'll learn. It isn't rocket science. He's booked in for his residential training later this year and I know I'm going to feel like a terrible mother, sending him off to boarding school.'

I undo the stretcher, but Trevor gets back on his feet and hops three-legged through the house. Declan thanks us as he shows us out.

'I'll call you tomorrow to let you know how he is.' Ross turns to me as Declan closes the door behind us. 'I'll meet you back at Otter House, if I can find it.'

'You'd better follow me,' I say, and he does, riding his bike close up behind the ambulance and sometimes alongside, breaking all the rules of the road.

When we arrive at the practice, Trevor has forgotten that he's hurt himself and leaps out, landing on the tarmac with a yelp.

'Penny and Declan are an odd couple,' Ross says, catching up with me as I take him through to Kennels.

'Some people consider her to be a cougar, snagging a toy-boy like that, but she didn't go out to hunt him down. He was her carer and their relationship grew from there.'

'They're like overprotective parents.'

'Trevor's their baby, and he's caused them plenty of sleepless nights already. He's had treatment for

50

running onto a stick and throwing himself off the sea wall so far. I know him from my puppy parties.'

'Did he fail the course, by any chance?'

'We don't use that word any more.'

'It's no wonder there are so many dogs out there who don't know how to behave – so much for progress.' He stares at me, slowly shaking his head.

'It was a joke,' I point out. 'Are we X-raying him now or in the morning?'

'Well, let me think. I was going to leave it, but I've no doubt that Maz, Emma and my predecessor would do it straight way.'

'You're mocking me now.'

'Are you really staying to puppy-sit?' he goes on, without answering my question.

'I promised Penny that I'd be here to keep an eye on him.'

'If that's the case, we might as well get on with it.' He throws on a surgical gown, sedates the dog and I set up for the X-rays. I switch on the machine and choose a suitable cassette loaded with film, making sure it's labelled before placing it on the table. I collimate the beam of light, look up the exposure and slip into a lead apron that is so heavy it makes me waddle – it isn't a good look.

Ross positions the dog so the X-ray beam is centred over the sore spot before we go outside the radiography room, and peer through the viewing pane in the door that's only a few inches square. We're so close that I can hear his breathing. I can't help feeling a bit flustered. I glance towards him. His eyes dart away, and I wonder if he's noticed.

'Ready?' I'm holding the controller on the lead that runs from the X-ray machine under the door, so I press the button, then leave him with the dog. I pass the film through the automatic processor and wait for it to come out the other side. Ross has a look at it, holding it up to the light.

'It's nothing to worry about, just a greenstick fracture that should heal pretty quickly with him being a young dog, as long as he doesn't charge about and run into any more walls.' He splints the leg with a quick-setting cast that I cover with a layer of self-adhesive bandage – I choose purple – and we return Trevor to the kennel where he continues to snooze.

'Thanks for the help.' Ross removes his gown and dangles it over the door of an empty cage. 'I'll be off now.'

I bite my tongue. Will used to stay on for a while and make the tea while I tidied up after him.

'I'll see you tomorrow, if not before. I assume you'll field any calls, seeing you're staying up.' With that, he's gone again, his feet marching away along the corridor.

How inconsiderate is that, I think, unimpressed. If only he'd asked, rather than 'assumed' . . .

Trevor's first reaction when he wakes up is to sniff at the cast; just as I'm beginning to think he's going to be fine with it, he starts to nibble at the top, tearing at the bandage.

'Oh no, you can't do that. You're going to have to wear the cone of shame.' I spray some bitter tasting chemical onto the cast, and put a collar on him, a soft fabric cone, not one of the older-style plastic ones. He stands up, bumps into the sides of the kennel and tries to rub it off.

His impulsive nature reminds me of my new colleague. How many more night duties are we going to be forced to do together? I toy with the idea of talking to Maz again. What if Trevor had been more seriously injured and Ross hadn't turned up? Why should I take the phone when it's the vet's responsibility?

I wonder if I'm being unfair. His lack of patience, uptight approach and sarcasm could be a front, I suppose. Like any relationship, it takes time to get to know someone. I'm willing to give him a chance to redeem himself.

In the morning, Tripod comes out to the garden with me when I'm taking Trevor out to stretch his legs. He doesn't like to use the cat-flap now, partly because he has a strong sense of his position in the practice hierarchy, secure in the knowledge that if he sits peering out of the flap, someone will come along and open the door for him. The dog lunges at him, but Tripod saunters casually past, keeping just out of reach of the end of his lead. Trevor turns his attention to one of the bees that's homing in on the remains of the apple blossom, but he misses that too. I smile to myself as I hear Ross's motorbike arriving in the car park on the other side of the wall. Like Trevor, I need to keep a grip on my sense of humour and carry on.

It's Thursday and, once I've got through the ops this morning, I have a long weekend off: three whole days to sleep, swim, walk Seven and catch up with Mitch and Taylor.

Ross joins me in Kennels, placing his helmet and a paper bag on the prep bench. 'I reckon we could use breakfast before we start. Coffee and bacon rolls from the baker's.'

'Oh,' I say, surprised and touched at his thoughtful gesture. 'Just coffee for me though, thank you.'

He frowns. 'It's a peace offering – I'm not trying to poison you.'

'It's kind of you, but I don't eat meat.'

'I see,' he says slowly. 'I should have asked. Idiot! I'll get you an egg sandwich next time.' He unwraps a roll and stuffs half of it into his mouth. 'I'm starving.' He grins. 'Still, one woman's vegetarianism is another man's gain.'

'You can't eat and drink in here,' I say. 'It's practice rules.'

'What are rules for but to be broken?' he says dismissively.

I stand my ground. 'Take it to the staff room, please.'

He gazes at me and, just as I'm expecting him to refuse, he backs down with a shrug.

'As long as you come with me. We can run through the ops list at the same time – I'll pick up a print-out on the way.'

It doesn't take long. Frances buzzes from reception to say that the first patients have arrived, and Ross goes to admit them while I make sure I have the right surgical kits lined up ready. I feel slightly apprehensive. It's all rush, rush, rush, and he works so quickly that I've barely recovered the first cat spay before he's anaesthetising the second one.

'You aren't used to working at speed, are you?' he says cheerfully as I join him at the prep bench. He's clipping the cat's flank there, leaving a ragged patch of skin. He scrubs up while I finish preparing the patient. He starts the operation but, part-way through, he pauses and stares at his hand.

'I've torn my glove. Can you fetch me another? Today would be good,' he mutters as I move around the table. In my hurry, my arm catches against the instrument tray, sending forceps and swabs flying across the floor.

'I'll get a fresh set,' I say, my face burning. I haven't dropped a kit since I was a trainee. I fetch a pack of gloves and another set of instruments.

'I don't know about you, but I'd like to finish by midnight.'

Smarting, I turn my attention back to the cat. I don't know where I stand with Ross. One minute he seems quite human, the next he's having a meltdown. I take my break outside with Tripod; when I return to Kennels, I hesitate at the door. I can see Ross sitting on the prep bench and talking on his mobile.

'No, I'm talking about the younger nurse, Shannon – she's just knocked my spay kit on the floor, can you believe it? Yes, I know, it was a pretty dopy thing to do.'

I push the door open. He looks up and continues, 'About the dog, there's no way I can have him here this weekend. We'll discuss it again later. I have to go.' He slides down onto his feet. 'I don't know how much you heard,' he says quietly. 'I was sounding off, that's all, and I'm sorry.'

'I don't care,' I say, although I care deeply about his criticism when it was just a clumsy mistake. I didn't do it deliberately. I fetch the next patient and we finish the ops in virtual silence. Ross appears contrite, but it's too late. As I leave to go home in the afternoon, I'm still too upset to speak to him.

I say goodbye to Maz, Izzy and Frances, glad to get away. I collect my car and drive to the leisure centre in Talymouth, where I swap my clothes for my costume in the changing rooms that smell of chlorine and sweaty trainers. I grab the locker key, fasten the bracelet around my ankle and walk out to the pool, where the lifeguard is putting the floats away now that lessons have finished for the day. I watch him reorganising the tapes that divide up the pool, leaving two lanes in place, the fast one for speedy swimmers like me and the slow lane for the oldies who swim breaststroke with their heads above water, not wanting to splash their specs or mess up their hair. He's good-looking, blond, clean-shaven and lightly tanned, with blue eyes, a square jaw and the perfect six-pack, and I know for a fact that he waxes his chest.

I twist my hair up and stretch my swimming hat across my head, and glance across at my reflection in the glass that divides the pool area from the spectators. I don't look bad, but if I could alter anything about my appearance it would be to add a few curves to my slim, rather straight, boyish figure.

'For goodness' sake, stop admiring yourself and get in that water,' Mitch calls. 'Fifty lengths.'

I turn and give him a cheeky grin. 'I'll race you.'

'Not now. I've been lifeguarding and teaching all day. I'm going to get some food and chill for a bit.'

'You're making excuses because you know I'll beat you.' He's stronger than me in the water, but not as fast – built more for stamina than speed. 'Dream on, Shannon.' Something – or someone – catches his eye and his attention drifts. I follow his gaze to the young woman who's walking up the steps out of the pool. It's Gemma, one of the leisure centre receptionists. She has a chain of flowers tattooed around one ankle, but Mitch isn't looking at her feet.

'Put your tongue away,' I tell him lightly.

'Are you jealous? You are, aren't you?' Mitch grins.

'Don't be ridiculous,' I say, wondering how I really feel about him. We aren't in a relationship any more, but I still feel drawn to him.

He moves up closer, touches the small of my back and gives me a kiss on the cheek before whispering in my ear, 'We should catch up again for old times' sake, just the two of us.' His hand slides down to my buttock.

'Hey.' I point to the pool rules on the sign on the wall. 'No petting.'

He chuckles and steps away. 'You do love me?' he says lightly.

'You know I do.' I've known him a long time. We were at school together, although we didn't become friends until I took up swimming three or four years ago. We started going out with each other about eighteen months ago and then, as I've said, we finished it while we were on holiday, having realised that we didn't want to spend the rest of our lives together.

'How's the new vet?' he asks. 'Is he behaving himself?'

'He's being a bit of a pain, but I haven't come here to talk about work. I'll catch you later – for a coffee,' I add, to make my intentions for the rest of the evening perfectly clear.

'Are you sure you wouldn't like to come back to my place tonight? I have a bottle of tequila, some pizza in the fridge, and a couple of new DVDs.' Mitch tips his head to one side.

'It's tempting, but no, not tonight. I had very little sleep last night – I'm shattered.'

He studies my face for a moment. 'You do look tired,' he agrees. 'Another time then.' He looks past me. 'Here's Taylor. Hi, we're over here.' He waves. 'She's forgotten her contact lenses again.'

'There you are.' She squeals with laughter. She is shorter than me and wears a shocking pink swimsuit that matches her nails. She has her long blond hair extensions tied back.

'I didn't think you'd make it with your other commitments,' Mitch teases.

'The next module of the management training course starts on Monday, and as I'm at a loose end, I thought I'd do a few lengths and catch up with you at the same time.' Taylor has recently been promoted to assistant manager at the garden centre on Stoney Lane. 'Of course, we could always skip the swim and go straight to the pub.'

'Shannon's planning on a quick coffee followed by an early night,' Mitch says.

'You can't,' Taylor says.

'Oh, I can. You'll have to forgive me for being such a lightweight – I was on call last night.'

'With the new vet?' She links her arm through mine. 'I want to know all about him. Come on, you can join us for one drink.'

'No, really. We're going out for your birthday tomorrow and I'd like to be awake enough to enjoy it.'

'In that case, you tell me all about him while we swim.' She turns to Mitch. 'I'll catch up with you later.'

There's hardly anyone in the pool – just me, Taylor, an elderly couple and a pair of teenage girls who are practising under the watchful eye of their coach for the next local gala. When I swim alone, I'm focused on getting as many lengths in as possible, but when

I'm with Taylor, I find myself setting out with good intentions, but usually end up drifting alongside her as she swims breaststroke with her head out of the water, so we can catch up. We discuss the course she's started and the trainer who sounds quite promising as a potential date, and we talk about Ross, but I want to enjoy my time off, so I don't say much. The less said about him the better.

Chapter Four

That Monday Morning Feeling

For the first time I can remember, apart from around exams at college when I was panicking about the practical day, I have that Monday morning feeling.

'Don't go in if you aren't feeling well,' Mum says as I rinse out my cereal bowl in the kitchen sink. 'No one is indispensable.'

'If I'm not there, Izzy will have to look after two vets on her own.' Emma doesn't work on a Monday, so it's just Maz and Ross. 'They'll have to cancel some of the ops.'

'What's going on? You've been very quiet.' Mum picks up a tea towel and wipes the dishes. 'Is it what we talked about the other day? I'm sorry if bringing up the subject of your dad brought back memories.'

'It isn't that.' I think of my father often and visit his grave at least once every couple of weeks. I just don't talk about it.

'Are you missing Will and Jess? You used to see quite a lot of them.' She smiles as I shake my head.

'We're still in touch. I'd like to go and see them, but

they're busy settling into their new house and planning their wedding.' Jess and I met when we were doing the vet nursing course at the local college. I introduced her to Will and the rest is history, as they say.

'Are you worried about Tripod? I wish you didn't get so attached to your patients.'

'His blood-test results should be back today.' I let the water out of the sink, watching it whirl down the plughole. 'It isn't about Tripod either, although I'll be devastated if anything happens to him. It's about having to spend all day with Ross. I just can't work with him, and Izzy won't rearrange the rota because she says we have to learn to get along.'

'It's easier said than done, but you shouldn't let people get to you.'

'I know. There's Mrs Wall, Trevor, the way he puts me under pressure and patients at risk when he rushes the ops, and on top of that he made me feel really bad about knocking the kit off the stand in theatre the other day when it was an accident. I'm going to have to have it out with him today, whether he likes it or not,' I tell her.

A loud ping from Mum's tabard pocket diverts her. She takes her mobile out and checks her texts. 'It's Godfrey.' Blushing, she turns away and starts typing a text back. 'He's planning to drop by for lunch. I don't suppose you could spare an hour to mind the shop?'

'You know I can't. I can't even guarantee I'll have a lunch break.'

Mum sighs. 'Never mind. Another time.' Her mobile pings again, once, twice and three times, and I have to smile. It comes as a bit of a shock to find that your mother receives more texts in a day than you do.

I leave her to it and head out for work, arriving at about eight to find a grubby white truck parked across the entrance to reception. A long-haired black dog leans out of the window, sniffing at the air. Maz's car is here too, and the practice is open. I step past a stack of timber, boxes of tiles and tubs of adhesive into the waiting area, where Maz and a squat man in dirty overalls and a cap are staring at a pot of paint that has disgorged its contents across the floor.

'I hope you're going to clear up after yourselves,' Maz says, acknowledging me with a glance. 'Stay there, Shannon. I don't want anyone walking paint through the practice.'

'I'm sorry.' The man I recognise as DJ, the boss, removes his cap and screws it up in his hand. 'I'll be onto it straight away, as soon as humanly possible.' He turns to me. 'Good morning, my lover.'

'Hi,' I respond, as the sound of banging comes from above our heads. I hope it isn't going to be like this all day – the cats will go ballistic.

'You need to get on with it,' Maz says. 'We have clients turning up in the next hour.'

'Don't fret. We'll be out of your hair by then,' DJ says confidently, giving Maz a wink as he reaches out and leaves a dusty handprint on her sleeve. With a sigh she rubs it off. 'You know us.' He winks again. 'Satisfaction guaranteed.'

I go around the side of the practice to the back door to avoid the paint and find Tripod waiting for me in the corridor outside Kennels. He mews and I mew back. He turns his nose up at his usual food, so I cook him some chicken, recalling with a rueful smile how

I cremated a whole carcase, wrecking the microwave soon after I started work at Otter House.

'There you are.' I place his bowl on the floor. 'Chicken for breakfast.'

Tripod laps at the juice, leaving the pieces of meat in the bottom of the dish. I shake my head, hoping it's just a tummy bug, as he ambles away. I throw a load of laundry into the machine and return to reception to answer the phone until Frances arrives. The paint has been cleared to an extent – there's a cream stain across the floor and some spatters across the bags of pet food on the shelves.

'I think the next couple of weeks are going to be interesting,' Maz says, joining me. 'I asked DJ and his boys to take their gear around the back, but did they listen?' There's another series of crashes, as if someone is throwing an elephant down the stairs. Maz rolls her eyes and turns to her emails to look for Tripod's lab results in her inbox.

'So his kidneys are packing up,' she says matter-of-factly.

'Oh no, I told you he was ill,' I say sadly as we compare the figures with those for a healthy cat. 'How long do you think?'

'Who knows? Weeks, maybe. Months, I hope.' She instructs me to put some medication ready for him and order some prescription diet to support his failing organs.

'I don't think he'll eat it,' I point out. 'He wouldn't eat fresh chicken this morning. Shouldn't he go on a drip for a day to flush the toxins out of his system?'

'I suppose so, but I don't like to put him through too much stress.'

'It's what we'd do for some of our other patients.' I can't understand why she isn't desperate to give him a chance, and I wonder if she's in denial about how sick Tripod is, even though the blood results are there in black and white in front of her.

'Okay, Shannon, if you get everything together, I'll come and set it up, but I'm only going to do this once to give him time for the medication to work.'

Result, I think. I'm surprised how cool she's being about it, but I reckon she's putting on a front to hide the fact that, like me, she's gutted.

'Lucky's coming in at ten thirty to start on some chemo,' she continues. 'Izzy's going to phone Jennie to confirm that the drug order's turned up before then.'

'So it is cancer?' This isn't a good start to the day.

'The prognosis isn't great, although there's a small chance of remission with treatment.' She changes the subject. 'How are things with Ross now?'

She looks frazzled – she hasn't brushed her hair and there's a stray Rice Krispie stuck to her top – and I can't bring myself to start whinging about how we don't get on and everything else.

'Your silence speaks volumes,' she says with a wry smile. 'I'll catch you shortly.'

However, it's Izzy who sets up Tripod's drip with her because I'm needed in the consulting room where I call the first client in from reception.

'Mrs Dyer, you can bring Nero through now.'

'Or he'll bring me,' she chuckles as she gets up from her seat, tucking the ends of her polka-dot scarf inside her mac.

I smile to myself as the Great Dane tows her out through the double doors into the glazed porch. She grabs the doorframe and hangs on in desperation.

'Can I help?' I say, walking up to her.

'Oh no, he'll have you over. You're such a slip of a thing.' She yells at the dog. 'Nero, you are a very naughty boy!' She lets go of the doorframe and hauls him back with two hands on the lead, like she's in a tug-o'-war, bringing him into the consulting room where I shut the door before he can shoot back out.

She removes her mac and scarf and puts them on the table. She slips out of her cardigan and places it on top of the mac. I catch Ross's eye. He raises one eyebrow. Is she trying to impress him with her physique or preparing to do battle?

'Hello,' she says eventually, when she's caught her breath. 'I'd like you to check his ears.'

Great, I think. I open the drawer and discreetly pull out a consent form, assuming that Ross will want to admit Nero for the morning. He starts chatting to Mrs Dyer, focusing on the dog's general health first.

'He looks well,' he begins.

'He's a butcher's dog,' she beams. 'What do you expect when he lives on tripe and marrow-bones?'

'He's been having too many pies. Have we weighed him recently?'

'Maz said not to bother any more – she had difficulty fitting him on the scales the last time she tried.'

'We'll have another go. He hasn't got a waist . . .'

'I can feel his ribs under the muscle,' she says defensively.

'Show me,' Ross says.

'Here, and here.' She waves vaguely in the direction of the dog's chest. Ross prods and pokes.

'I can't feel any ribs or muscle,' he proclaims as he straightens up. 'It's all fat.'

I cringe. Why can't he be more tactful? It's embarrassing.

'I like to see a bit of weight on a dog,' Mrs Dyer says. 'Anyway, he's very fit. He has regular walks – on the lead because he will knock people over, not in a nasty way, but when he's pleased to see them. I don't think it's anything to worry about. Look at me, I'm perfectly healthy and you'd have a hard job finding my ribs.' She prods her fingers into her side. 'Here, have a feel.'

'Er, that's some offer, but . . .' Ross takes a step back behind the table.

'Oh, I'm sorry.' She smiles and her cheeks turn a darker shade of scarlet. 'I didn't mean . . . I wasn't giving you the eye or anything. I'll have you know I'm a married woman.'

I notice how Ross's eyebrows shoot up behind his fringe of curls. He pushes his hair back from his face.

'Let's get him on the scales,' he says.

'Can I make a suggestion?' I say, not waiting for his response because I'm going to make it anyway. 'It would be better to look at him first and weigh him on the way out to avoid another fight to get him back in here.'

'He'll be fine.' Ross gives me one of his 'don't inter-fere' looks. 'I've handled racehorses before.'

'Are you sure? He's a real handful.' I wouldn't nor-mally say anything in front of a client, but . . . 'What's the point of me being here for my experience when you don't take any notice? I know Nero.'

'He's a lovely boy, a friendly giant. He doesn't know his own strength, but you're a strong-looking lad.' Mrs Dyer hands Ross the lead. I open the door, and as I predicted, Nero takes advantage and bounds out into reception with Ross hanging on for dear life behind him.

'You see, he's quite an athlete,' Mrs Dyer says with pride.

'He's hardly Usain Bolt,' Ross observes, determined to squeeze the enormous dog onto the scales, which are more suitable for a Labrador than a Great Dane. He has the front end and I have the back, while Mrs Dyer stands in the middle giving orders.

'Back a bit. That's right. Oh no, his paw's come off. He can't do it. He's too long in the body.'

Two more clients look on, one with a puppy on their lap and one with a cat hiding beneath a towel in its carrier. Ross looks at me, his face flushed and hot, and I find that I have absolutely no sympathy. When we do get the dog onto the scales, I have to reset them by which time, dopy Nero has reversed a step so that his hind paws are back on the floor and we have to start all over again.

Eventually, to the sound of cheers, we obtain a figure for Nero's weight. Mrs Dyer covers his ears, making him yelp.

'That hurts,' Ross observes. 'Let's get him back and have a look.'

It takes the three of us to persuade a reluctant Nero into the consulting room for a second time. I find the extra-large attachment for the otoscope, the instrument with a light at one end that's designed for looking down ears.

'Thank you.' Ross takes it from me. 'Now, if we reverse him into the corner, you can hold onto his head for me.' I look at the dog. I look at Ross.

'You are kidding me? Tell me you're going to admit him so he can be sedated for this.'

'Are you questioning my judgement?' he says, staring at me. I keep my eyes fixed on his and his expression starts to soften, as if he's decided to back down. 'I was brought up by two vets, I had a real stethoscope for my sixth birthday and I trained for five years to do this job.'

'It's just that he's a big dog and Maz—'

'I am not Maz,' he says sternly. 'I'm sure Mrs Dyer would prefer to take her dog straight home rather than leave him with us all day.'

'Yes, I'd much rather that. Everyone knows how protective I am when it comes to my Danes.'

Giving in, I take Nero's neck and head in a canine cuddle to restrain him while Ross shines the light right down into the depths of his ear. Nero tenses and I tighten my grip. If he goes, I won't be able to hold him. It's like asking me to wrestle with a fully grown man. I don't know why, but the thought of wrestling with Ross crosses my mind. I suppress it quickly.

'Hold on,' Ross warns as Nero wriggles.

'I am holding on,' I say curtly, but the more he faffs around, the more Nero feels like a coiled spring.

'He has a lot of wax down the left ear and a little down the right one,' Ross explains.

'It's no wonder he takes no notice of me,' Mrs Dyer says, amused.

'I'm going to pop some ear cleaner into each ear and show you how to clean them. We'll give it a week or so and check to see if it's cleared up or whether he needs further treatment.'

'I used to use olive oil with my other dogs,' Mrs Dyer says doubtfully. 'Old Fox-Gifford – he was my vet before Emma set up the practice here – used to swear by it.'

'I've heard he used to swear by many lotions and potions, but this is the twenty-first century.'

'I could try olive oil, couldn't I? It's natural,' she says, with a Devon accent, pronouncing it 'n'art'ral'.

'I'd keep the olive oil for salad. I would choose this product myself because it's hypoallergenic and quick-acting.'

I clear my throat. I wish Ross was quick-acting. I can't hold on to Nero for much longer.

'Well, if you'd use it on your own dog . . .'

'I have done.'

'You have a dog? What kind?' Mrs Dyer says, suddenly impressed.

'He's a bitser – bits of this and bits of that.' His tone brightens as he talks about his pet. 'He's a big dog – not as big as your fella here, though.'

Mrs Dyer gives him the go-ahead and he squirts the bottle into Nero's ear. The contact with the cold solution sends the dog into a spasm. He starts to scratch my arm with his back leg.

'Hold on,' Ross says.

'What do you think I'm doing?' My arms are killing me. 'Good boy. Stay still. It won't be for much longer.'

Ross massages Nero's ear, then starts hunting for something to wipe away the excess solution and loosened wax. Typical, I think, no forward planning. As he turns away, Nero can no longer restrain his urge to shake his head and scratch. He wrenches himself from my grasp, pushing me back so I end up on my bottom on the floor.

'No!' I get back onto my knees and tackle him, throwing my arms around his neck. Almost . . . Nero strains and breaks free . . . No, not that . . . He shakes his massive head, spattering brown gunk everywhere, up the walls, over me, Ross and Mrs Dyer.

'For goodness sake, Shannon!' Ross exclaims, exasperated.

'I'm so sorry.' I throw my hands in the air. 'I couldn't hold onto him any longer.'

I can feel drops of ear wax mixed with cleaning solution on my cheek and in my hair. How can such a small volume of liquid spread so far? Nero gives himself another shake while Ross offers Mrs Dyer some paper towel. She rubs it against a brown blob on her blouse.

'It's no good. That won't come out, not in a month of Sundays. Oh dear, oh dear, we are in a pickle.' She starts to laugh while Nero stands at the door, pushing at it with his nose. 'It always happens to me. My last dog had a problem with his eye, and I ended up with a yellow stain that ruined my top.'

Ross runs his fingers through his fringe and holds up a nugget of black ear wax. He looks at it and looks at me and, just as I'm expecting him to have a complete sense-of-humour failure, his lips curve into a smile.

'I've never seen so much ear wax in my life. I think this consultation had better be on the house – Otter House. I'm sorry.' He's choking with laughter now and, in spite of everything, I can't help smiling too. 'You'll have to excuse me,' he adds, ducking out into the corridor as he lets loose an unrestrained guffaw.

'Do you think that's it?' Mrs Dyer says as we stand there, listening to his hearty belly laughs on the other side of the door. 'Has he finished?'

I don't think so, I muse as the laughter continues.

'He's done with Nero for now,' I say, showing her

70

out to reception. 'If you'd like to make an appointment for next week . . .'

I clean up the consulting room as best I can, but the scent of dog's ear remains. When I put the spray back beside the sink, a red-faced Ross intercepts me.

'You've got some . . .' His hand hovers at his cheek '. . . just there.'

'Ugh.' I grab a tissue and wipe my skin. 'Has it gone?'

'Here. Allow me.' He reaches towards me and touches my face. I freeze at the contact. 'Got it,' he says, turning and flicking a piece of gunk into the bin.

I don't thank him.

'Are you mad at me?' he asks quietly.

'I'm not happy about this,' I say, standing my ground.

'You did find it funny though.'

'In the end,' I admit.

'I owe you an apology if I've made life difficult for you.'

'There are no "ifs" about it. I can't say I've enjoyed working with you so far. I hope you can see it from my point of view when I say that we need to find some kind of compromise. You can't expect me to carry out my nursing duties properly when you're rushing the clients and patients through like you do. It isn't a conveyor belt. You can't treat everyone as if they're the same.'

'I don't think you can accuse me of not caring. That's what you're saying, isn't it?'

'I'm sure you do care. It's just that the way you race through the consults and ops makes it seem as if you don't.'

'You're probably right.'

'I am right.'

'Look, I've said I'm sorry for what I said about you knocking the instruments onto the floor the other day, and I know it's difficult to unsay something when you've already said it, but I was hoping you'd be able to accept my apology in the spirit it was intended.'

'You described me as "dopy".'

'I don't think you're dopy, far from it. I said it was a dopy thing to do. And you wouldn't have done it if I hadn't been stressy with you about the gloves.' He pauses, gazing at me, his expression gentle.

'Okay, apology accepted,' I say grudgingly.

'That's good. I'm glad,' he says. 'I'm sorry too because I realise it's no excuse, but I've felt under pressure. The local bobby stopped me for speeding on the road from the manor on the way to work this morning.'

'I've no sympathy,' I say coolly.

'I wasn't concentrating. Maz gave me a lecture on client and nurse relations last night; I had a phone call before breakfast – my ex turning the emotional screw – and then there's the stress of starting a new job, wanting to make the right impression and getting it totally wrong. When Maz offered me accommodation, I thought it would be ideal, but my room is damp, the water's always cold, and there are dog hairs everywhere, and I can hardly sleep for the barking. But none of that is reason to be rude to you, and I'm very sorry. I know you're just doing your job.' He pauses. 'I've been a dick, haven't I?'

'You said it. You know, it would have been easier to admit Nero rather than trying to hold him down.'

'I don't think Mrs Dyer would have left him here for the day without a fight, do you? I've read the notes.' He gazes into my eyes, his expression filled with compassion. 'Were you here when she lost her last dog?'

I nod. 'I was there.' It was a black day for the dog, for the Dyers and for Otter House, and I remember it as if it was yesterday. 'It was the locum,' I say, my throat running dry. 'Drew . . .' There, I can say his name. 'The dog had cancer and the only chance of saving him was surgery to amputate his leg. Drew carried out the op and I was in theatre with him.'

'That must have been a dreadful experience.'

'He was in a rush – that's why I'm nervous about vets who are in a hurry – and I hadn't been nursing for long. It wasn't until he'd finished that he realised he'd taken off the wrong leg, and then, instead of admitting it, he asked me to help dress the wound and put the dog back in his kennel. He was too scared to admit what he'd done and it wasn't until the next day that Maz found out. Brutus had to be put down. Maz was devastated. We all were.'

'I know they shouldn't, but these things do happen.'

'I should have been more careful – I never let a vet operate on anything without double checking that they're working on the right leg, or lump, or whatever part of the patient. And Drew was careless, slap-dash . . . and a coward,' I add, unable to disguise the bitterness in my voice. 'He ran out on us, left the country.'

'That sounds a bit drastic.'

'That's what he was like.'

Ross picks a piece of sticky ear wax from his scrub top.

73

'You've got some more in your hair,' I point out, half smiling at his discomfort. 'I think you came off worse.'

He tips his head forwards and ruffles his curls. 'That's disgusting.' He peers up through his fringe and grins, and he looks so cute that I can't help grinning back. 'We're not getting anywhere standing here. Who's next?'

'Don't you want to change your top first? I'll fetch you a clean one.'

'I can get it.'

'You'll never find it.' I leave him and return with a freshly laundered tunic. As I open the door, I find him waiting, stripped down and bare-chested – I say 'bare', but you can't miss the V of dark curly hair running across his chest and narrowing down towards his taut, muscled belly, and the tattoo across his left side, an eagle with its wings spread, reaching around to his loin, its tail feathers disappearing beneath the waist of his trousers. It looks so real, I want to reach out and touch it . . .

'What took you so long?' he says.

'Frances ambushed me with a query about a sick rat.' I try not to catch his eye, but it's difficult to know where else to look. He's even more attractive without his clothes on.

He clears his throat and holds out his hand, and I give him the clean top.

He slips it on and fastens the poppers at the neck. 'Does that meet with your approval?'

'Well, yes.' For a moment I wonder what he means, then I realise he's asking me if he looks better without the ear wax. At least I think he is. 'Yes, it does,' I confirm.

'Good. Let's crack on then.'

We see the two clients who have been waiting for a while, after which I call in the next one, but they haven't turned up yet.

'Where are they?' Ross asks.

'I don't know. Frances is the oracle. Ask her.'

He pops his head through the consulting room door. 'Has the next one called in to say they'll be late, or are they a no-show?'

'It's Ally bringing one of her boys' pet rats in,' Frances replies. 'She's always late. She has to shut up shop, you see. The boys usually help her out behind the counter, but they'll be at school. Don't worry, she'll be here in her own time.'

'What about my time?' Ross scowls. 'That's so annoying. I hate falling behind. It wrecks the whole day—'

'Hey, chill, remember,' I interrupt. 'You'll have a heart attack before you're thirty.'

'I didn't think you cared.' His eyes flash with humour. 'Don't say anything,' he adds quickly. 'I'd prefer to labour on under the illusion that you merely hate my guts, rather than want to kill me.'

'I thought we were getting somewhere with the ear-wax breakthrough,' I say.

'Shannon doesn't hate anyone,' Frances cuts in. 'She's a pacifier.'

'You mean a pacifist,' Ross corrects her.

'There's no need to be picky with me,' Frances says. 'You know, Shannon, I reckon our new vet could do with signing up for your puppy parties to learn some manners.'

'I've been wondering if he's been properly socialised,' I say lightly, and I'm relieved to see that he takes my joke in good spirit. 'Where is DJ?' I ask, noticing that his truck is no longer in the car park.

'Oh, he's gone,' Frances says. 'They took their supplies up to the flat and left. I'm surprised that he isn't trying harder to impress Maz – you know how he flirts with her, winking at her all the time. Mind you, she doesn't believe me. She puts it down to a nervous tic.'

He has no chance with my boss, I think, smiling as Ally Jackson arrives with a rat peeping out from the collar of her pale blue lace jacket, which she wears over cropped trousers. She's in her late thirties, early forties, I think, and one of those women who has appeared to grow younger over the years. She's gone from wearing tight suits to clothes that my friend Taylor might choose; she wears subtle make-up and has her hair coloured.

'Good morning.' Frances keeps well back behind the desk as she clicks the mouse to change the status of the appointment to 'waiting'. 'We missed you at WI the other night. You are still available to judge the creative writing competition next week?'

'I'm not sure I'm up to that.' Ally bends her neck and kisses the rat on the nose.

'You were very creative when you used to write those articles for the *Chronicle*.'

'Was I?' Ally feigns seriousness, then breaks into a smile. 'I did have an awful lot of pages to fill.'

'Ally's in newspapers. She took over the newsagent's a while ago,' Frances says in an aside to Ross before turning back to her. 'So you will do it?'

'If there's cake involved, then yes, all right.' Ally's a single mum with teenage children, and has lived in Talyton St George for as long as I can remember.

Ross shows her into the consulting room and I follow, shutting the door behind us.

'This is Electra, my middle son's pet.' She extracts the rat from where it's dived into her cleavage and under her blouse. 'She hasn't eaten for two days and I'm wondering if it's her teeth. Oops, I'm sorry, I'm flashing.' She places the rat – a hooded creature with brown eyes and a long scaly tail on the table – before refastening her buttons.

I stay back to let Ross pick the rat up.

'Is she friendly?' he asks, diving straight in.

'Oh, she's beautiful,' Ally says, but Electra twists her head around and nips him on the finger.

'There doesn't seem to be much wrong with her teeth.'

'How embarrassing.' Ally takes over. 'Let me hold her for you. You scared her, rushing in like that without making friends first.'

Ross makes the sensible decision to admit Electra for sedation and a thorough examination. Ally is distraught, which is quite normal for her. I remember her crying her eyes out almost every time she brought her hamster to see us.

At the end of morning surgery, I help Ross with the rat. Her teeth are growing overlong at the back so he trims them down, making sure there are no rough edges. Looking at a rat's molars isn't the easiest task in the world.

'That should do the trick,' he says eventually. 'What's next?'

'That's it until this afternoon,' I say, assuming he's going to rush off somewhere. 'I'll wait for her to come round.' I nod towards Electra, who's asleep on a heated pad.

He takes off his gown and drops it on the bench before tapping his notes into the computer and chatting.

'Here's a photo of Bart.' He shows me on his mobile.

'He's a handsome dog.' I study the picture of a muscular, sandy-coloured dog with heavy jowls like a bull mastiff. 'Don't you miss him? I mean, he isn't with you . . .'

'I do, but I saw him this weekend and I'll be seeing him again soon. He lives with my ex during the week and spends some weekends and holidays with me.'

'Oh, that's a little unusual.'

'It works for us. We rescued him from the local dogs' home – he was on death row because he'd been there for months. He's a lovely dog, friendly and fun to be with, but people couldn't see past the fact that he kennel-guards. Whenever anyone went to look at him, he'd growl and throw himself at the bars to try and get out, which is understandable when his previous owners kept him in a cage all the time when he was a puppy. Oh, and he isn't great with cats, apparently. He did pass the child test with flying colours.'

'I can't imagine how anyone would allow their baby to be used to check a dog's temperament.'

'It's done under controlled conditions.'

'I know that, but I still can't understand it.'

'Anyway, we bonded straight away so we took him on. He's my running buddy and Heidi's baby, and when it came to the split, neither of us was willing to give him up.'

'I see.' Now there are some people who would say that it's only a dog and you can go and get another one, but I know that dogs are individuals and you can't just replace one with another in your heart.

'I'm surprised that you're so soft on him,' I say quietly.

'I finished the relationship and she found it difficult to accept that it was over at first. I was afraid I was going to lose all contact with Bart, but then she suggested the dog share and I jumped at it.'

'Joint custody? How does that work exactly?'

'I have Bart one weekend in four, and for holidays, or if she's away.'

'So you see your ex quite a lot?'

'Which is different from seeing quite a lot of her. Yes, we still have contact.' He bites his lip. 'A clean break would have been easier all round, but luckily we didn't get married or have a baby which would have made it even more complicated.' He gazes at me. 'We'd been together for seven years. I loved her, but I wasn't in love with her.'

'That sounds like a cop-out to me.'

'Maybe you're right.' He smiles ruefully. 'I didn't feel the same about her any more and it wasn't fair to lead her on. I should have questioned my relationship with her before, but I was too busy having fun and living in the fast lane to think too deeply about anything much, until something happened to make me stop and reflect on where my life was going. I'm sorry, I'm not sure why I'm telling you all this. I just don't want you to think I'm a complete bastard. Although I wouldn't blame you after the way I've behaved recently.'

'It's all right. I can forgive you.' I've been there. I've had my heart broken. I've been led on and let down before.

'It would have been so much worse to have carried on and let her down later, and although Bart is confused, coming from a broken home, it's much better for him with us not being at each other's throats all the time.' Ross hesitates. 'Maybe I've said too much. I'm sorry to have gone on. That's enough about me. How about you? How was your weekend?'

'It was great, thanks. We had a few drinks for my friend Taylor's birthday. I've been swimming and walking the dog, and listening to my mum going on about her new man.'

'You get along well with your mother?'

'Most of the time – I live with her.'

'At the flower shop?'

'That's right.'

'She doesn't expect you to carry on the family business then?'

'She's never tried to push me into floristry – she knows it isn't my thing. How about you?' I've asked him this question before. 'Why aren't you working for your father?'

'He doesn't approve of the way I've chosen to live my life. He was furious when I broke up with Heidi – I rather think he fancied her himself. He's very controlling. When I went to India to volunteer with a rabies charity there, catching and vaccinating stray dogs, I had to beg him for a few weeks of unpaid leave. The practice comes first. In fact, that's all there is, in his opinion. As for me, I've always been a rebel.'

I like the idea of him being a rebel. I smile to myself. Maybe we do have something in common, after all.

During afternoon and evening surgery, he can't stop himself rushing, speaking so quickly at times that I have to interpret and repeat what he's said to clients when I show them back out to reception, which then delays me from helping him with the next one. When I return to the consulting room after our last patient, he logs off from the computer.

'Was that better for you?' he says with a cheeky smile.

'Yes, thank you.' If he was grumpy and short-tempered about it, he managed to hide it well. I find myself warming to him a little and wondering if I'd feel quite differently about him if we didn't have to work together.

Chapter Five

It Shouldn't Happen to an Estate Agent

Since when has my mother been buying underwear that is smaller, skimpier and prettier than mine? I tuck the bra – made of the lightest tulle with magenta pink embroidery and bows – back into the basket of clean laundry and run to get changed into my uniform. I grab my bag and say goodbye as I pass through the shop where Mum is typing a text on her phone.

'I'm off,' I say as she puts her mobile down.

'Oh, just a moment. Are you free to meet Godfrey this evening, only he's offered to take us out for dinner?'

My fingers tighten on the strap over my shoulder. 'I'm not sure. I'd feel really awkward.'

'You mustn't worry about being a gooseberry,' she says, snipping lengths of floristry wire from a reel.

I smile. 'It's called a third wheel nowadays.'

'I'd love you to meet him.'

'Okay, I'll join you. Thank you.'

'You seem more cheerful. Has everything settled down at work?'

'It's better than it was. I think it's safe to say that Ross and I have come to an understanding. We actually got to talk yesterday and have a proper conversation.'

'I'm glad.' She swaps her wire cutters for her mobile again, her face lighting up as a message comes in from Godfrey, I assume. 'I'll see you later.'

'Have a good day,' I say, but she's reading her texts, like a distracted seventeen year old, and I can't help thinking that she's fallen for this man far too quickly. I only hope he's worth it.

On the way to the practice I receive a text message from Mitch who's at the pool.

How about drinks tonight? ☺*xx*

Four words and Mitch's customary sign-off that mean so much more than meeting for drinks. What he means is, how about we catch up for a kiss and cuddle, and more? I text back.

Not tonight. Meeting Mum's new man-friend x
Tomorrow? ☺*xx*
I'm on call. Sorreeeee! Another time. X

Another time? As soon as I've pressed 'send', I regret it. It's a cop-out because I'm beginning to realise that, for me, there won't be 'another time'. I thought I could deal with our current arrangement, but it's beginning to make me feel cheap.

☹*xx* comes back, and then nothing, no friendly banter or gossip about what's going on at the pool. I make to send him another text, but change my mind. We need to talk face to face.

I reach Otter House, unlock the door and switch on the computer at reception before going through to the back where Tripod greets me with a loud meow. He stands up and strolls towards me. I pick him up

and carry him through to Kennels where I warm
some of his special kidney diet in the microwave and
feed him by hand.

DJ and his team turn up and stay for several hours,
spending much of the time sitting in the truck, eating
sandwiches and drinking coffee, and the rest of the
day runs pretty smoothly.

'Well, that's the last one. Thank you, Shannon,' Ross
says, closing the door behind Mrs King, who brought
in Cleo, her cat, wanting advice about fleas. He starts
to remove his vet's tunic, unfastening the poppers at
the neck.

'It was almost a pleasure,' I say, teasing him.

'Aren't you ever satisfied?' he jokes back and, even
though I know he's pulling my leg, I blush. 'I've been
doing my best to give every client my full attention
so they don't feel rushed, and to the detriment of my
health. I've heard more than I ever wanted to know
about Lynsey Pitt's children and how she gave birth
to one of them here at Otter House, and which TV
programmes the greengrocer guy played to his
cockatiel to cure its compulsive feather-plucking.'

'That's good,' I point out lightly. 'It means you're
becoming part of the community. Are you off home
now?'

'I have a report to write up first. I'd better be getting
on with it.'

I leave him to it, going to make a start on the weekly
cleaning routine, starting with isolation and working
back through to reception.

'Are you going swimming tonight?' Ross asks
when he's on his way out of the practice half an hour
later, dressed in his leathers with his helmet under
his arm.

'I wish.' I squeeze the water out of the mop as I finish cleaning off muddy paw-prints from the floor in reception – it's been raining all day. 'I'm going out with my mum to meet her new man. He's treating us to a meal at the Barnscote, the posh place to eat around here.'

'Oh, that's nice, I suppose.' He grins and my heart melts.

'Hardly.' I can't explain how I'm feeling because it would sound unreasonable and petty. It's been eighteen years since I lost my dad – a lifetime; yet I feel as if I'm letting him down by agreeing to meet my mum's new man. Equally, I'll be letting Mum down if I don't go.

'Aren't you curious to know what he's like? I would be.'

'They haven't been together for more than five minutes. I only hope they aren't going to make a spectacle of themselves—'

'Like you have done on occasion,' Maz interrupts. I turn at the sound of her voice. I thought she'd gone home.

'Me?' Inside I'm saying, don't go there, please, not in front of Ross, but she appears oblivious, continuing, 'I've seen you dancing on the table up at the manor with a bottle of champagne in your hand. You were a wild child.'

'Thanks a lot.' My face burns as I recall one particular New Year's party when my waitressing shift had ended and we finished the open bottles. There were a lot of open bottles. 'You're never going to let me forget that, are you?'

'I thought you were such a mouse until then,' she teases. 'You hardly spoke for the first few months after you started working here. Have a good evening, both of you,' she adds.

'And you,' I say. 'I hope it isn't too busy.'

'I don't mind.' She's on duty tonight. 'The more the merrier.'

'Mad Maz,' says Ross once she's gone. 'She loves this place, doesn't she?'

'She does, and she's pretty hands-on, even with having the children, whereas Emma's happy to take more of a back seat. They get on well together, presumably because they accept their differences, but I wouldn't like it, having a partner who doesn't work as hard as I do.'

'Emma does a lot behind the scenes – the accounts, for example.'

'Yes, but she could employ someone else to do that so she could concentrate more on being a vet.'

'Hey, are you trying to push me out of a job? If Emma put more hours in, they wouldn't need me.' Ross picks up the bucket.

'You don't have to do that.'

'I want to . . . I'd hate you to think I do less around here than you.' He grins.

'Thank you,' I say gracefully, checking my watch. 'I'd better get going. I don't want to keep the gorgeous Godfrey waiting. You can tip the water down the sink, by the way,' I add.

'Anything for you.'

'You're so kind,' I say with a touch of sarcasm.

'I haven't been out on a date for a while.'

'Am I supposed to commiserate with you?'

'Are you, you know, seeing anyone?'

'No, I broke up with my ex a couple of months ago. Going out on someone else's date is the nearest I've had to a date for ages.' I can't help chuckling. 'I'm so sad!'

'We could go out together, if you like. Maybe we could go out and dance on some tables together some time,' he suggests, walking alongside me with water splashing out of the bucket all over my clean floor.

'You are joking.' I stare at him. 'I meant, you are joking about dancing on the tables. I didn't mean about going out with you sometime.' I find the words are sticking to my tongue. 'As friends,' I mutter, to clear up any misunderstanding, because somehow his presence manages to throw me into confusion. To hide my blushes, I throw some shapes with the mop, cleaning up after him.

'That's a date then,' he says.

'Not a date.' I gaze at him. His pupils are dark and dilated, reminding me of a cat drunk on a pre-med. I think he means it. 'Definitely not a date.'

'If that's what you think's best,' he says, his tone one of regret.

'I don't go out with people I work with,' I say firmly, although looking at him it's tempting.

'That's probably a good idea,' he says, and I can hear the smile in his voice, which suggests that I haven't offended him by rejecting his offer. 'Have a lovely evening and I'll see you tomorrow.'

I wish him goodnight before heading home to meet this man with the looks of George Clooney, the sex appeal of Brad Pitt and the charisma of Barack Obama rolled into one. I walk through the shop, filled with flowers and perfumed drifts of chrysanthemums and roses, to be greeted by Seven, who comes running up to me with a wedge of oasis in his mouth.

'Drop it,' I say, but he trots in circles around me,

just out of reach. 'Come here.' I pat my thigh, and he makes a half-hearted approach before backing off again. 'I thought you were a good boy.' He looks up at me as if to say, 'I am.'

'Please don't eat that,' I go on, as he drops the oasis on the floor and starts to rip it up. 'I don't want to have to call Maz. Why don't you eat a biscuit like any other dog?'

At the word 'biscuit', Seven stops and looks up, tipping his head to one side and lifting one paw.

Smiling, I walk on through to the kitchen, aware of him following closely on my heels. If the way to both a man's and a cat's heart is through their stomachs, it's the same with a dog, and I'm giving Seven a biscuit from the tin when Mum appears in a red dress I've never seen before.

'Hello, love. What do you think?' She looks down at her outfit. 'I couldn't decide what to wear. I went through my wardrobe the other day, realised I had nothing suitable and ordered this online.'

I gaze at her. The colour in her cheeks and the way she's straightened her hair makes her look ten years younger.

'You look fantastic.'

'I like to make an effort. Godfrey always looks smart.' She gives me a twirl and I notice how the material clings to her curves.

'It's very different for you – quite a showstopper,' I say tactfully.

She bites her lip. 'I'll go and get changed if you think it's tarty.'

'There's no need to do that. It's more fitted than the clothes you usually wear, but it's fine, really.'

'Are you sure? Only I'm not wearing any pants.'

She giggles. 'I tried but they gave me a VPL.'

'Too much information,' I groan. 'I don't understand you – I'd never risk going out commando.'

'I can't believe that you're such a prude,' Mum
exclaims.

'I'd like to credit you for the way you've brought
me up, but now I somehow doubt it. Are you sure
you want me tagging along?' I'm hoping she'll say
don't bother, but she insists.

'We need to get going – we're meeting him at Mr
Rock's at six thirty.'

'What happened to the Barnscote?'

'There's been a bit of a mix-up with the booking –
but never mind, it's one of those things.'

I glance down at Seven who is at my feet, holding
his lead in his mouth.

'No, I'm sorry.' The look in his eyes fills me with
guilt. 'Hasn't he had a walk today?'

'He's having you on,' Mum chuckles. 'I took him
out at lunchtime.'

I promise him that I'll take him out early the next
day, and we let him have the run of the shop and
downstairs while we're out – although, if anyone
broke in, they'd be more at risk from being licked to
death than being savaged. Mum and I walk along to
Mr Rock's, the fish and chip shop, where a Mercedes
in metallic brown is parked with its wheels up on the
pavement. An old man – I don't know why this is a
surprise to me – with grey hair that's smoothed down
with gel, gold-rimmed glasses, and wearing a crum-
pled pale beige linen suit, steps out from beneath the
awning. He holds out a bouquet of flowers wrapped
in pale green tissue paper.

Now, I would have thought that flowers were the

most unsuitable gift you could buy for a florist. Mum spends all day surrounded by them, she dreams of them, sometimes waking in the early hours to sketch an idea she has for an arrangement or colour scheme, but when Godfrey hands her the bouquet, she doesn't stare at it as if registering the quality of the blooms, the number and arrangement, and the artistic merits. Instead, her face crumples.

'Oh Godfrey.' She holds the flowers in one arm and throws the other around his neck, kissing him on the cheek. 'No one has ever thought to buy me flowers before. They're so beautiful.'

His face flushes, and he goes up one tiny notch in my estimation, even though he doesn't bear the slightest resemblance to either George Clooney or Brad Pitt.

'This is my daughter, Shannon,' Mum says. 'Shannon, this is Godfrey.'

'I'd never have guessed – you look like sisters,' he says, which makes me wonder if he should have gone to Specsavers, considering that we look so different that in the past people have actually wondered if I was adopted. 'It's lovely to meet you at last – your mother's told me a lot about you.'

'All good, I hope,' I say lightly.

'It must be wonderful being a vet nurse, looking after those cute, fluffy animals.'

'Some of them are cuter than others. The job's more about looking after the vets, making sure they have a stethoscope to hand when they need one, organising their diaries and even babysitting their kids.'

'She's been showing the new vet the ropes,' Mum says. 'Apparently, he needed taking in hand and given further training.'

'I didn't say that exactly,' I say, but I'm not sure either of my companions is listening.

'How marvellous,' Godfrey responds. 'Shall we . . . ?' He opens the door with a flourish and the three of us head inside and sit at a table in the restaurant area. Godfrey moves the chair for my mother and sits down beside her, holding her hand and locking lips with her for a full five minutes. Unsure where to look, I clear my throat and slide a menu towards them. 'Shall we order?'

'Oh yes, we must.' Mum pulls away from her beau, who slides his arm around her shoulders. 'What would you like, darling?'

Darling? I think. How long have they known each other?

'Finding your perfect woman is like finding your dream house. One has to be open-minded. It's all very well going in with a list of fixed criteria, like "must have great kerb appeal and original features".' Godfrey gazes at my mother – he can't keep his eyes or his hands off her. She giggles and whispers into his ear, and just as I'm wishing I'd stayed at home, I hear the sound of a motorbike pulling up outside, its engine making a deep-throated growl before it cuts out. A familiar figure in black leathers dismounts, removing his gloves and helmet as he enters the restaurant. Ross catches my eye and waves.

'What are you doing here?' I say as he approaches our table.

'Looking for something half edible. Same as you, I expect,' he says. 'I thought you said you were going to the Barnscote.'

'There's a private party there tonight,' Godfrey says. 'Elsa, who owns the place, was most apologetic.'

'I've come to pick up a takeaway – Mrs P, the woman who does and doesn't do it very well, left a beef stew on the hob, and most of it has stuck to the bottom of the pan. I couldn't salvage any of it.' Ross wrinkles his nose. 'I can see I'm going to have to eat my chips with only the Fox-Giffords' drooling gun dogs for company.' He picks up a menu from the adjacent table. 'What do you recommend?'

'Oh no, you must join us,' Mum cuts in. 'It's all right with you, isn't it, Godfrey?'

He looks relieved, as if it's taken the pressure to perform off him.

'Well, yes, of course. A double date it is.'

'It isn't a date,' I say hastily, but Godfrey isn't listening, and I wonder if he's deaf as well as short-sighted.

'Thank you,' Ross says. 'It's very kind of you to let me join you. I feel a little embarrassed about gate-crashing your evening.'

'Not at all,' Godfrey says. 'You're Shannon's young man, I presume?'

'He's one of the vets – I work with him.'

'This is the one you said you've been training,' Godfrey blunders on.

'No.' I touch my face – my skin feels like it's been deep fried. 'I didn't say that.'

Ross raises one eyebrow.

'So you aren't an item?'

'Sadly not. I don't think she'd have me,' Ross teases. 'I don't know why –' he looks in the direction of the wall tiles that are decorated with fish – 'I'm a great catch.' He takes the chair beside me and pulls it up to the table, and we place our order of fish, chips, mushy peas and cola. I have a bean-burger.

'This is wonderful,' Godfrey says, as we wait for Mr Rock's daughter to mix a fresh batch of batter and fry the chips, 'a real treat, and it's on me.' He turns to Ross. 'I hope you don't mind me asking, but my son has just bought a Dalmatian puppy for my grandson – it has bald ears and a spotty belly.'

'It's supposed to have spots,' Ross says, deliberately misunderstanding. I cringe at Godfrey's lack of tact.

He chuckles. 'You are a bit of a wag, Ross. What I mean is—'

'I know what you mean,' Ross cuts in. 'Your son should get the puppy checked out.'

'So it isn't worth waiting to see if it goes away?'

'I wouldn't recommend that.'

'And there's nothing you could let me have . . .' He's persistent, I'll give him that.

'No,' Ross says firmly, as a mobile rings at our table.

'Excuse me.' Godfrey pulls his BlackBerry from his pocket and checks his messages. 'If you don't mind, I'm going to call my client back. The vendor's had a change of heart.' He heads off outside and stands on the pavement deep in conversation.

'I'd be pretty miffed if my man took me on a date and spent his time on his phone,' I observe.

'He can't help it. It's business.' Mum turns to Ross. 'Shannon tells me that both of your parents are vets.'

'There isn't room for three of us in the family practice, which is why I'm here,' he says smoothly.

'It must be in the genes. Unfortunately, Shannon hasn't inherited my enthusiasm for floristry.'

'My sisters have gone into other careers. One is an optician and the other is a nurse who's married a

consultant otorhinologist – who gets right up everyone's nose.' He laughs. 'We aren't close.'

My mother looks past him as the food arrives and
her man-friend returns. He leans down and kisses
her on the cheek.

'I'm sorry.' He removes his jacket and sits down.
'I'm selling four houses and the vendor at the top of
the chain is having cold feet. It happens all the time.
You wouldn't believe what I've done to keep sales
from falling through. I was selling a farm at Bottom
End one time and at ten a.m. on exchange day, the
vendor's solicitor said that the three rickety old goats
that they kept in the yard were no longer included in
the sale. The buyers were so fed up – negotiations
had been long and hard because the vendor was an
eccentric old boy – that they threatened to pull out
completely, and I had to source three goats and pay
for them from my own pocket to pacify them. It was
worth it, though. It was a big sale.'

He smiles and turns to Ross. 'I think vets are higher
in the popularity stakes than us agents. When I go to
someone's house to value it, they want you to advertise it at a higher price than it's worth and then it
either sells quickly and the vendor gets annoyed
because it appears that I've done no work for the
money, or it takes months to sell and I'm accused of
overvaluing it, or not trying hard enough. Having
said that, I don't like to blow my own trumpet,' he
says in a pompous tone that suggests the opposite,
'but I'm pretty good at my job.' He looks towards my
mother. 'I've made a small fortune out of property
during my lifetime.'

'I've always wanted to be a vet,' Ross says, as Mr
Rock's daughter brings salt, vinegar and ketchup to

the table. 'My first memory is of being in my mother's arms in a darkened room while she showed me some X-rays. I can still see her face and the reflections in her glasses, and smell her perfume and the chemicals from the developer. It's strange – it felt quite magical.' He shrugs. 'I can't imagine doing anything else.'

'I bet you have some wonderful stories to tell,' Godfrey says.

'Most of them are rather gory.' Ross looks at me with a twinkle of mischief in his eye.

'I don't think I want to hear those,' Godfrey responds. 'I'm not good with blood – just the thought of it makes me feel queasy.'

'Ketchup?' Ross offers him the bottle. I bite my lip to suppress a giggle.

'No, I prefer mayonnaise, thank you.' Godfrey mops his brow with a cotton handkerchief from his pocket.

'Do you live locally?' Ross says, changing the subject – a relief, I think, because I was afraid he was going to go on and talk about rabbit abscesses to put Godfrey off mayonnaise.

'I have a house in Talymouth, a des res on the north side of town with sea views. I'm planning on renting it out.' There's a clunking sound from beneath the table. Godfrey winces and his fork drops off the edge of his plate. 'I'm talking about one day,' he adds, looking at Mum and leaning down to rub his ankle at the same time, 'not in the immediate future.' He dips a cheesy chip into mushy peas, and takes a bite. A green gobbet of food rests on his chin until my mother reaches across and wipes it with the corner of a napkin. He gives her a long and hungry look, as if he might eat her.

'How are you finding Talyton St George?' Mum asks, looking at Ross as Godfrey slides his arm around her back.

'It's great for motorbikes. The roads are so quiet compared with London, and the people are interesting too.' He flashes me a smile. 'I mean that in a good way,' he adds, 'although it's driving me mad having to stop and talk in every shop. Every time I go into the baker's or the Co-op, there's a queue at the till and I feel as if I'm obliged to have a conversation before I can leave.'

'I love a good gossip,' Mum says.

'I don't mind talking when there's a point to it, but when you yack on regarding the weather or the price of apples, it's a complete waste of time, don't you think, Godfrey?'

'I've made a good few sales over the years through chance discussions. It's always useful to keep one's ear to the ground.'

'I guess it's different for you,' Ross says, glancing towards me, his expression one of mock seriousness. 'When people raise the subject of their pet's ailments, it's usually because they're trying to obtain free advice and avoid a trip to the surgery.'

I have to stifle my laughter at this comment, clearly aimed at Godfrey, who loads his fork with mushy peas and stuffs them into his mouth. When he's swallowed them, he starts to speak again.

'I do love plain and simple food now and again. It makes a change from the rich dishes you get at business lunches and dinners.' He belches. 'Excuse me.' He holds a paper napkin to his mouth.

My mother isn't fazed by his behaviour. I think she would forgive him anything.

At the end of the meal, Godfrey's credit card is turned down. He checks through his wallet and looks bashfully at his date.

'You must think me a fool – I'm out of credit and I haven't any cash on me.'

I start to wonder about the fortune he's supposed to have made from property.

'I'll pay,' Ross says.

'No, I'll settle up,' I say, embarrassed, but he ignores my offer.

'That's incredibly generous of you,' Godfrey says. 'I owe you.'

We stand up and make our way outside to the pavement. Ross asks if anyone would like to join him for a drink.

'Shannon?' he says gently.

'Yes. Yes, why not?' I say, slightly shocked that he's keen to spend more time in my company.

'No, thank you,' Godfrey says. 'I shall escort my lovely lady back to her establishment.'

'I'll see you later,' I tell Mum, assuming they would appreciate some privacy and, once we've said good-night to her new man, Ross and I walk the short distance to the Dog and Duck at the bottom of town. I prefer the Talymill Inn, but it's further away.

'I'll come back for the bike,' Ross says, locking it up before we make a move. 'Your mum seems nice and Godfrey isn't so bad – a little too full of his own self-importance maybe. They seem very close for a couple who've only just met. How long have they been together?'

'I'm not sure exactly. I suspect it's longer than Mum claims. I reckon she's kept it quiet because she thought I'd disapprove.'

'And do you?'

'As long as he makes her happy, I'm happy.' I glance up at him. His eyes are in shadow and I can't tell what he's thinking. Sometimes, he seems preoccupied and hard to reach, as if something is bothering him, but I don't feel I know him well enough to ask what. We walk along in silence until we reach the pub. Ross holds the door open for me.

'What would you like to drink?' I ask as we enter the bar, which smells of stale beer and old carpet. It's pretty quiet – Nobby Warwick, the church organist, is snoring at a table in the corner, and a couple of other old men are playing cards.

'I'll get them,' Ross says.

'No, let me. You paid for dinner.'

'It wouldn't feel right. I'm not bragging – I'll point that out because I know you think I'm an arrogant so-and-so – but it's a fact that I earn more than you. Which often seems a little unfair to me, considering some of the things you have to do.' He grins. 'I get to do the good bits while you clear up. Go on, put your purse away and I'll get the drinks in. What would you like? No, let me guess.' He looks me up and down, his eyes seeming to linger appreciatively on my figure. 'White wine?'

'White or rosé.'

'A large glass of each?'

'Are you trying to get me drunk or something?' I say lightly.

'It's an attempt to make up for us getting off on the wrong foot. I don't think I've thanked you for the way you've helped me out since I arrived at Otter House. I'm very grateful.'

'I'll have a rosé then,' I say, pleased that he's

recognised my contribution at last.

He orders wine and half a pint of bitter, one of the locally brewed ales from the Taly brewery, and we sit down opposite each other at one of the empty tables. At first, we struggle to find anything to talk about, but soon we're sharing our views on music, pets and hobbies. I like indie music while he prefers rock. I can't see the attraction of racing around the country-side on two wheels, while he detests swimming pools because of the chlorine. He's a carnivore with an appetite for exotic meats like ostrich and kangaroo, while I'm a vegetarian. It doesn't matter that we don't have a lot in common. It makes him interesting, intriguing even, and the conversation flows far better than I expected.

It crosses my mind that our differences wouldn't make a good basis for a relationship, but I can't help wondering what it would be like to kiss him. I know, I'm letting my imagination run away with me, which is what happened with Drew. I fell for him – but he was a fantasy man, a chimera, as it turned out; poles apart from the person he portrayed himself as or the adoring lover I wanted him to be. I'm attracted to Ross. I'll go as far as to admit that, but after Drew there's no way I could let things progress to a rela-tionship when we're working together – if that's what he wanted, of course. What if it should all go wrong? It would be intolerable.

His phone rings and he checks the caller ID.

'I'm sorry, I'll have to take this – it's the dog.' And I have a vision of Bart, the big dog in the photo, dial-ling up his master. 'Heidi, what's up? Yeah, yeah. Not bad. I'm in the pub.' He pauses and I notice that he doesn't say he's with me. 'It's rather soon after the last visit and it really isn't the best weekend to choose – I'm on call and at the Country Show on the Saturday. I know. I can have him with me at the practice, but it isn't ideal, is it? You know how stressed he gets when he's left home alone.' He flips a beermat into the air and catches it between two fingers. There's a slight edge to his voice when he continues, 'Of course I'd rather see him than not. I'm not being difficult. It's the way it is. Okay, have it your way. I'll see you then. Goodnight.' He takes a deep breath, cuts the call and drains his glass.

'So I get to meet Bart this weekend,' I say.

'I suppose I should be thankful that Heidi's willing to bring him down here at all,' Ross smiles ruefully.

'You can hardly fetch him on the bike.'

'I let her hold onto the car because she has the dog. It seemed fair at the time.'

I wonder if it's more the case that letting her have the car assuaged some of the guilt he felt at finishing with her. Whatever it is, his mood has changed since the phone call.

'Shall we go? I could do with an early night,' he says. He stands up and throws on his jacket, leaving it open at the front. He opens the door for me as we head outside where he makes a show of holding out his arm for me in such a way that I feel I can't refuse. I slip my arm through his and we walk the short distance to Petals where I let go, wishing I didn't have to.

'Thank you for the wine,' I say.

'Thanks for the company. I feel I've got to know you a whole lot better this evening,' he says and as he leans slightly closer, raising the hairs on the back of my neck, I realise how much I'd like him to kiss me.

'Goodnight, Shannon.' He smiles and takes a small step back. 'I'll see you tomorrow.'

'Tomorrow,' I echo. I watch him return to his bike, wondering if I'm reading too much into it. He's been a gentleman tonight – it doesn't mean he fancies me.

Two minutes later, as I let Seven out into the garden, I hear the engine power up and the rev and roar of the bike as he rides away through the narrow streets before I follow the sound of the television to find Mum sitting on the sofa.

'I thought Godfrey might still be here.' I settle on one of the armchairs as she mutes the volume with the remote.

'Oh no, he's gone home.' She pauses, toying with the fringe on one of the cushions. 'What do you think?'

'He isn't quite what I expected . . .' I'm being tactful. I don't want to hurt her feelings.

'I agree. I've always been under the impression that estate agents are dull and boring, but Godfrey's quite the opposite.'

What's that saying? Love is blind. Mum strokes Seven absentmindedly.

'You will be careful,' I say.

She looks up abruptly, a blush spreading across her cheeks. 'What do you mean?'

OMG, I groan inwardly. She thinks I want to speak to her about safe sex. 'I'm talking in general terms. Godfrey could turn out to be too good to be true.'

'Don't you think I know that? I don't know what he sees in me, but I'm going to make the most of it, even if it doesn't last.'

'I can see why he likes you when you have so much to offer,' I point out. 'You have a thriving business, and your own place, which is worth quite a bit of money.'

'So, he has his eye on my assets. Equally, I have my eye on his.' She giggles again.

'Mum, I wish you'd be serious about this.'

'And I wish you had someone to have fun with. Ross is not what I expected at all from the way you've described him – much better looking than you said, very friendly and a bit of a tease. Luckily, Godfrey didn't mind.'

I'm not sure he noticed, I think, before I go on to say, 'I'd rather you hadn't let him pay for the meal.'

'He wanted to. He insisted.' She pauses. 'Shannon, there's something I need to run past you.'

'What is it?'

'How would you feel if Godfrey moved in with us?'

'Moved in? Have you gone totally mad?

'I'm not saying that it's been decided. It's just an idea at the moment.'

'Is that why he mentioned renting out his house in Talymouth?'

Mum rests her hand on my shoulder. 'We want to spend more time together so we can get to know each other properly. Let's face it, if we find we aren't suited, then the sooner we find that out the better, and what better way is there than sharing the same living space?'

'Why can't you live in his house?'

'Because I have to run the shop. You know the hours I keep. I'd hardly see him.'

'I know . . . Why the rush though?'

'Neither of us is getting any younger . . . He looks and acts like a forty year old, but Godfrey's actually quite a few years older than me.'

I bite my tongue. It shouldn't be surprising after her experience with my dad that she's already afraid that her beau is going to die while in his prime.

'There's plenty of room for the three of us – and Seven,' she goes on. 'Naturally, Godfrey and I would share a bedroom.'

'Ugh, that's too much information.'

'So what do you think – of the idea, I mean. Could you live with it?'

'With Godfrey, you mean?' The bean-burger and chips sit like a cold weight in my stomach. 'I really don't know. It's all a bit of a shock. When did he get divorced?'

'Is that relevant?'

'Well, yes, I don't like to think of him rushing from one woman to another.'

'You're very prim and proper all of a sudden,' Mum smiles, 'but no, he isn't like that. He and his wife divorced a year ago. There was no one else involved – Godfrey says they grew apart. Anyway, it doesn't matter. It's in the past and I'm concentrating on the future.'

'Well, it's nice to hear you being so positive.'

'All I'm asking is that you think about it.'

'I will,' I promise her, but I can't help thinking there is nothing I can say to stop this plan coming to fruition, and nor can I imagine sharing our home with anyone else, least of all Godfrey. I'd be living with a stranger and I wouldn't feel comfortable chilling out in my pyjamas on my days off. I wish Mum goodnight and head for bed, with Seven padding along behind me. I feel a sense of unease as I start to wonder what the future holds.

Chapter Six

One's a Kiss, Two's a Letter,
Three's a Wish for Something Better

The next morning I find a silk tie and a file of property details under the coffee table which Godfrey must have left the evening before, and I realise that – whether I like it or not – he is moving in gradually anyway, almost by default. I join Mum in the shop where she's unpacking a fresh delivery of flowers, dividing them up and bunching them for display. I fetch a couple of buckets from inside the door for her.

'About what we talked about last night – I'm cool with it.'

'Are you really?' Mum gives me a long hard stare before breaking into a smile. 'Thank you, darling. You don't know what this means to me,' she adds, but I can tell – I haven't seen her this happy for ages. 'I'll speak to Godfrey. Have a lovely day.'

'I hope so,' I say, knowing I don't have to worry any more about my position with Ross. In spite of myself, I can't wait to see him.

On arriving at Otter House, I find Izzy is already

looking after the inpatients, so I spend the few minutes before morning surgery making up the repeat prescriptions – 'spot-ons', tablets, shampoos and eye ointments – ready for clients to collect.

'Is everything under control?' I ask Frances as I deliver them to reception.

'At the moment – touch wood,' she looks around and reaches for the shelf behind the desk, 'but, Shannon, I've been a little dizzy. Look, I managed to double-book the operations today. Maz isn't happy with me at all.'

'How did you manage that?'

'I got confused with the dates.'

'So what's happening?' I feel sorry for her because she prides herself in doing a good job.

'She sent two of them home – I don't know, she found some excuse to rebook them. Anyway, it's sorted now and everything else is running like clockwork. DJ is here – he says they're putting the new units for the lab in today. And there's more good news.' She clasps her hands together and tucks them under her chin. 'Fifi's booked a celebrity guest to give out the prizes at the Country Show.'

'Who is she? He?'

'I'll give you three guesses.' I can hear joy bubbling up in her voice.

'Well, from your reaction, I'd say Robert Downey Junior.'

'Robert who?' Frances's pencilled eyebrows shoot up behind the strands of hair that have escaped her bun.

'The actor. Or Kit Harington?' I giggle. 'If it isn't him, I'm not interested.'

'It isn't him,' Frances confirms. 'One more try.

Come on, I'll give you a clue. He's on television every week day, has been for years.'

I'm thinking along the lines of the presenter of a show like *Countdown*, but I don't know his name so I plump for Jeremy Kyle. Frances shakes her head.

'It's Bray from the local news – you know, Bray Molland.'

'I'm sorry, I haven't got the foggiest idea who he is. I can't picture him at all.'

'Tall, has a twinkle in his eye and the most wonderful voice, smooth and deep like rich chocolate sauce. I can't believe you've never heard of him. All the ladies at the WI have a crush on him.'

'That explains a lot. How old is he? Ninety?'

'You may mock, but you'll be ninety one day. No, he's in his early sixties, I'd guess; not far off retirement, I suppose, like me.' She pauses, appearing upset again. 'I'm sure Maz and Emma are going to ask me to leave.' She looks past me. 'Oh, here's Ross's first appointment. Good morning, Ally.'

Two minutes later, Ross and I are together in the consulting room with Ally and a purple pet carrier.

'Would you like to take the first one out while I draw up the vaccines, Shannon?'

'What are they?' I ask, wondering what I'm letting myself in for. Will used to delight in surprising me with all kinds of creepy-crawlies.

'Have a look,' he says, smiling.

'Oh, they're rabbits.'

'Well spotted,' Ross says dryly.

I open the front of the carrier, finding two youngsters with manes of fur, one cinnamon and one white.

'They're called Mojo and Flyte,' Ally says. 'The boys chose the names.'

'Are they from the litter I found on the doorstep?'
Ally nods. 'We go up to the Sanctuary to help out
when we can – I used to write about the rehoming
campaigns for the local paper. Anyway, we saw these
guys and fell in love with them.'

I pick the braver one out of the box. His brother sits
towards the back of the carrier, twitching his nose.

'That's Mojo,' Ally says as I cuddle him, waiting
for further instructions from Ross.

'So they're here for their first vaccinations and a
chat about neutering,' he says. 'Close your ears, boys.'

'We want to make sure we do the right thing.
They're wonderful characters. Mojo is the quiet one,
very affectionate, while Flyte is the bossy one.'

'I'll just check,' Ross says, giving Mojo a myxi jab.

'They're both boys,' I say, feeling slightly offended.
'I sexed them before they left the practice,' but he
looks at them anyway.

'I like to be sure,' he says. 'Mojo is a boy, but
Flyte . . .' he takes a second look ' . . . is a girl.'

'Are you sure?' I exclaim.

'What do you think?' He turns to me with a big grin
on his face.

'I'm sorry,' I stammer. 'I must have got it wrong.' I
recall that I wasn't sure about one of them and
assumed that someone else would eventually check.
I glance from Ally to Ross and back, feeling embarrassed and rather stupid.

'It's one of those things,' Ross says. 'They were very
young, and it's hard to sex rabbits at that age.'

'It wouldn't be any good asking me.' To my relief,
because I thought she'd be annoyed, Ally giggles.
'Something similar happened to me before. We had
a hamster, Harriet, who turned out to be a Harry. My

fault. I thought she had cancer but the lumps turned out to be . . . well, you know what I'm talking about, man parts. I'll book them in for neutering as soon as you recommend.'

I swap Mojo for Flyte. Ross gives him his vaccination too and, once he's back in the carrier, Ally wishes us a good day before seeing Frances on the way back through reception. I clean the table as Ross types up the notes.

'Is everything all right?' he asks, looking up.

'I have a few things on my mind, that's all. I'm fine.'

'If you want to talk . . .'

'Oh, it's my mother. When I got home last night, she asked me how I felt about the idea of Godfrey moving in with us. I've told her it's fine with me, but I'm worried about the prospect of having to live with that rather pompous old man.'

'He means well, I think,' Ross says.

'I'm afraid he'll drive me mad. He's bound to be set in his ways.'

'Cheer up. It might never happen.'

'I am pretty sure it's a foregone conclusion.'

'You should have put your foot down.'

'How could I? Mum seemed so happy. I didn't want to upset her. It's her house, after all.' I throw the paper towel in the bin. 'Hey, don't worry about me. You're falling behind.'

Smiling softly, he calls in the next client. It's Jennie with Lucky, for a blood test to check the effect of the chemotherapy. Ross gives him a thorough checkup while I prepare the syringe and needle, and the blood tubes.

'He's doing well,' Jennie offers. 'He was sick the first day after he had the drugs, but he's been better since, more lively. In fact, Guy had to tell him off this morning for chasing the cows.'

I hold onto the dog while Ross takes the blood. Lucky wriggles and fights, but we manage to get enough.

'He's growing to hate needles,' Jennie says. 'I'm only putting him through this while there are signs of improvement. If he goes downhill, we'll stop.'

'That's what I'd do if he was mine,' Ross reassures her.

'When I first heard the word "chemo", I thought the worst. I pictured all his hair falling out, but when Maz explained that she wouldn't be giving him enough of the drugs to make him bald, I thought, let's give it a go.'

'We'll be in touch with the results, then we can confirm the go-ahead for the next round of treatment.' Ross rolls the blood tubes gently between his palms to mix the blood with the anticoagulant inside them, before I label the tubes and take them through to reception to pack them up for the courier.

Morning surgery continues right through coffee time. I am manning the desk at reception while Frances takes her break, and Ross is hanging around waiting for me so we can have our breaks together, when DJ comes bursting into the waiting area, closely followed by his mate, their faces white with shock.

'You tell Maz I'm not staying here another minute,' DJ bellows, thumping his fist on the desk. 'It's almost given my mate here a heart attack.'

'Excuse me. What are you talking about?' I say, wondering if I should call her from the staff room.

'There's a bloody great snake in the flat.'

'Wrapped around the hot water pipe,' says DJ's mate. 'Massive thing, it is.'

'One bite and it could kill a man,' DJ goes on.

'I don't think so,' I say. It must be one of Will's exotics that somehow got left behind, so it's either a harmless cornsnake, or a small python, which might squeeze a small creature to death, but not a slightly overweight builder. I'm not keen on snakes. The idea of handling one makes my hair stand on end, but I already look like an idiot, making a mistake with the rabbits, and I'm not going to show myself up in front of Ross for a second time by failing to tackle it. 'You wait here,' I tell them, 'I'll sort it out.'

'I'll come with you,' says Ross.

'I'm waiting in the truck,' DJ says, scuttling outside, his mate following on behind him.

I collect a snake hook and bag from the cupboard in isolation and lead the way to the flat. I open the door and survey the chaos. The new units are partially fitted, but the water and heating pipes along the back wall are still exposed, and wrapped around one of them is a small python about three feet long.

I laugh as I approach it. 'That's more like an earthworm than a snake.'

'I'll get it.' Ross tries to step in front of me, but I won't let him.

'I'll do it.' I unravel it from the pipe, holding it by the neck and body. 'It seems quite weak.' I hold it out for Ross to examine. 'What do you think?'

'I reckon it's hungry. Let's take it downstairs and put it in isolation. It needs food and warmth.'

'If it's one of Will's, he can have it back.'

We put the snake in the plastic incubator before I go outside to give DJ the good news.

'Are you sure there aren't any more surprises in there?' he says. 'I felt like I was in *I'm a Celebrity*. It's like a jungle. I can't believe it.'

Inside, Frances is catching up on the latest developments. She offers to contact Will while Ross and I go to the staff room for our break but, as we reach the door, we catch the sound of raised voices inside. I hesitate, unsure whether or not we should interrupt. Ross holds me back, his hand on my waist, sending an unexpected thrill of longing down my spine.

'Will kind of blended in whereas Ross is a much bigger, stronger character,' Maz says. Ross's fingers tense and relax again. 'It would help if we weren't all tripping over each other,' she goes on. 'We have more clients coming through the door than we did last summer, and you're in more now the twins are older. We need more space.'

'Oh no, not that again. Please, don't go there. We agreed. No expansion. No empire building.' Emma's voice softens. 'Isn't this – Otter House – enough for you? It's all I ever wanted.'

'Where's your ambition?'

'I'm a wife and mum first – as you are, or have you forgotten that?'

'What do you mean?' Maz sounds hurt – as well she might, I think, because she's a great mum, full of fun, and not as serious as Emma.

'If we go down the route you're suggesting, when will you ever have time to be with Alex and your kids? It's hard enough, juggling all the balls now.'

'He understands.'

'He understands, yes, but are you sure he doesn't mind hardly seeing you?'

'You know how it is. We're rushed off our feet now,

111

but in a few years' time, the children won't need us in the same way—'

'And our neglected husbands will have run off with someone else,' Emma counters.

'Alex wouldn't.' Maz laughs. 'He knows I'd find him and book him in for castration if he did.'

There's a long pause when I wonder if we should just burst in, but Ross continues to restrain me. I can hear his breathing and smell his scent of antiseptic and shower gel, and I can't help wondering if he's making the most of the situation to be close to me. I turn my head. His face is near mine, his eyes dark with desire. My heart leaps because his expression tells it all – that the attraction isn't one-sided. I smile and he smiles back. He does fancy me. I'm sure of it.

'Of course it is,' Emma responds eventually. 'Do you remember when I first invited you here? Or rather, when you first found the time to accept my invitation?'

'It was for a few days' break in sunny Devon, I seem to recall.' I can tell from the tone of her voice that Maz is smiling.

'I was at breaking point. I hadn't had a holiday since I set up the practice. I was exhausted and, even though Ben was a darling, being totally supportive and helping out with the decorating and night duty, it wasn't fair on him either.'

'Times were hard. The bailiffs were coming in at any minute.'

'I have no appetite to return to a situation like that, which is why I'm so anti-expansion. I'm afraid we'd overstretch ourselves, time-wise and financially.'

'What if . . . ?' Maz begins.

'Oh, Maz,' Emma sighs.

'What if we at least look into the possibility? I'll call the accountant and ask him to do some costings and get in touch with the estate agents to see what's around in the way of suitable property. There wouldn't be any harm in that.'

'I find it almost impossible to argue with you when you put it like that,' Emma says.

'Thank you, partner,' Maz says lightly.

'I haven't said I'd do it.'

'I know,' Maz responds, but I can tell from the tone of her voice that she thinks she's well on the way to expanding Otter House vets. 'One other thing,' she goes on. 'We need to talk about Frances.'

My ears prick up, just like a baby rabbit's, when Emma agrees.

'It's time she retired. We can't keep taking risks with her. She does her best, but something will go badly wrong and then we'll kick ourselves for not facing up to the problem and dealing with it.'

'I'll talk to her. I'll put a positive spin on it, that she'll have time to relax and enjoy life and spend more time with Lenny. She can hardly argue with that.'

'Oh, she will though,' Emma counters. 'She comes here for the social aspect. She doesn't need the money – she'll have a decent pension.'

The lining of my nostrils prickles. I want to sneeze. I should have taken the antihistamines after handling the rabbits. I pinch my nose, trying to distract myself from the imminent explosion.

'What about a replacement? We'll need a new receptionist.'

'We'll ask around. Keep it quiet for now,' Emma says. 'Speak to Frances first.'

I can't contain the sneeze any longer. I sneeze once, twice, three times in a row. Ross snorts with barely suppressed laughter. The door flies open and I'm face to face with my bosses, with Ross right behind me.

'Oh, I'm sorry,' I say, stepping to one side. 'I didn't realise there was anyone in there. I'm on my break.'

'That's okay,' Emma says. 'We've saved you each a doughnut.'

'Did we miss anything – the practice meeting?' I stammer.

'I reckon you've probably caught up on all you need to know,' Maz says, glancing at her partner, who grins and adds, 'And probably more besides. What was DJ yelling about?'

'They found a snake in the flat.' I explain that it's been secured in the incubator.

'There's never a dull moment around here,' Emma observes.

Suitably embarrassed, I retire to the staff room with Ross. Tripod joins me, curling up on my lap. He purrs as I sip my coffee, thinking about what I've discovered about my feelings for my new colleague and his about me, as well as what I've just overheard relating to Frances and the practice.

'I don't know how Frances will take it. I'm afraid she'll be completely gutted. I wonder if I should warn her, or leave it to the partners.'

'I don't think it's our place to say anything.' Ross changes the subject. 'I wouldn't mind being involved in this branch surgery idea. What do you think?'

'It could be good for me – I'll never be head nurse while Izzy is here. If she moved, I might get a promotion.' I'm not incredibly ambitious, but it's frustrating to think that the only way of progressing is to change practice and move out of the area. 'I wouldn't raise your hopes, though. It sounds like there's a long way to go.'

Ross checks his watch. 'We'd better make a move. Frances has lined up a visit for us, a cat for vaccination and a pedicure – that's your department.'

As it turns out, the cat has done a runner before we get there. The owner is suitably apologetic, providing us with tea and cake before we go back to the practice. Ross insists on carrying the visit case for me and I can't help hoping that this is further proof of his feelings for me. During the afternoon, I find myself daydreaming that he is putting himself in my way, brushing against me as I restock the shelves in the consulting room or happening upon me in the big cupboard, entering and closing the door behind him so he can get me alone.

'I'll see you tomorrow, unless you'd like to go out for another drink, or something to eat?' he says at the end of the day.

'I'm sorry. I'm going swimming tonight. Another time,' I say quickly, not wanting him to feel that I'm fobbing him off when I'd be more than happy to spend more time in his company.

'You bet,' he says. 'By the way I've checked on the snake. It's fine and it's going to one of Will's reptile clients until he's able to pick it up. DJ and Co are still traumatised – according to Frances they went to the pub to recover. Goodnight, Shannon.'

I say goodbye and, having tidied up, I pick up my car and go for a quick swim. I run into Taylor who is getting out of the pool as I'm getting in.

'How are you?' she asks, hesitating with one hand on the rail by the steps.

'I'm well, thanks. I've been pretty busy so far this week.'

'So have I.'

'I bet you didn't have to catch a stray snake.' I slip into the water and duck my shoulders under the surface.

'No way?' She stares at me. 'You hate snakes.'

'I wanted to impress the new vet,' I say lightly.

'Oh yes? I thought you didn't like him.'

'Things have changed. He's mellowed.'

'Tell me more.'

'There isn't much to tell except . . . not only is he extremely fit, he's funny, friendly—'

'And you fancy him,' Taylor adds for me.

'A little, maybe,' I admit.

'You do.' She laughs. 'You're blushing.' She grows serious again. 'Does Mitch know?'

'He doesn't need to, but I am going to talk to him. We've hooked up twice since we broke up – I know, I'm not proud of it, and I'm afraid that Mitch is beginning to take it for granted. It isn't right.'

'I agree – how are you going to move on if you still have some kind of attachment to your ex? You definitely need to speak to him.'

'You won't say anything?'

'Of course not.' She shivers. 'I must go – I've got some work to do for this course. I'll catch you another time.' She smiles. 'Don't forget to keep me updated.'

Once she's gone, I swim fifty lengths before returning home to find Godfrey's car outside. I walk through to the kitchen where he and Mum are admiring a commercial coffee machine.

'It will have to be plumbed in, and then you'll

wonder how you ever survived without one. It can make one hundred espressos an hour.'

I wonder if his enthusiasm for caffeine might explain his hyperactive behaviour.

'Godfrey's brought a few bits and pieces with him,' Mum says when she finally notices me.

'Hello,' he says bashfully, making me realise that he isn't finding this situation easy either.

'I've made a space for his shoes in the under-stairs cupboard,' Mum says as I spot a packet of muesli on the table. That must be Godfrey's too – we don't eat muesli.

Seven takes two seconds to decide that he approves of our new housemate.

'You are a disloyal creature,' I grumble lightly when I'm giving him his food. He looks up with his tongue hanging out and a grin on his face. 'I'm glad you're happy about it.' I know that Mum is too and I'm pleased for her, but I'm not sure how long I'll be able to live with Godfrey. At least though it looks as if I'll be able to go out with Ross now and again to escape.

In fact, I'm going to spend the coming weekend of the Country Show on call with him and, with just two days to go, I can hardly wait for the opportunity to show him around one of my favourite events and get to know him better.

Chapter Seven

Piggy in the Middle

As I walk along the Green with Seven early in the morning, I picture how I'll spend the day with Ross, meeting his dog, and introducing them to my friends and acquaintances at the show.

'Hello, Shannon.' I look up to see Wendy, the dog fosterer, walking five dogs of various sizes and shapes on leads, the group as a whole looking like a drunken spider with its legs moving in all directions. I wave and move on. The sun is up and a pair of swans are floating down the river. It's going to be a good day.

I put Seven on the lead for the stroll back into town across the Centurion Bridge – or the new bridge, as it's sometimes called, to differentiate it from the old one that was washed away in the floods a few years ago. On the way, I call Ross to offer him a lift. I'm taking the ambulance to the show so we have first-aid equipment to hand in case of accidents. Last year, I helped Emma treat a pair of terriers who had become embroiled in a scrap over a cheeseburger. Both dogs had bite wounds to the head and neck, and the cheeseburger came off pretty badly too.

'There's room for Bart in the back,' I say when he hesitates. He sounds as if he's just woken up.

'Um, no, it's all right. Thanks for asking, but I'll make my own way there. I'll see you later.'

'Bye,' I say, and the phone cuts out. Maybe Maz has offered him a lift from the manor. I dismiss a pang of disappointment. It doesn't matter how we get to the showground because I'll be spending the rest of the day on call with him anyway.

Back outside Petals, Mum is loading the van with boxes of bouquets, corsages and buttonholes.

'Thanks for walking the dog,' she says, smiling when she sees us. 'There's tea in the pot, but I can't stop. I really must get a wriggle on. These are for the judges – Fifi twisted my arm for a contribution to the show in return for free advertising.'

'Isn't the man going with you?'

'Please don't call him the man. It's Godfrey.'

'I know. GOD-frey. Four letters away from the superior being he believes himself to be,' I say with sarcasm. I know I'm being childish, but I don't like having to share our home. He's stayed three nights now, hung some linen and tweed suits in Mum's wardrobe, cleaned his shoes and done some ironing. There is no sign that he will ever leave.

'I like having you and Godfrey here.' Mum moves in for a hug. 'I love both of you.'

'I love you too,' I say, relenting. I feel like the squab of a wood pigeon Izzy picked up from the ground the other day on the way to work, and I start to wonder if it's time to fly before I'm pushed out of the nest.

'We're meeting up later. Smith and Ryder-Cole have

a trade stand for the day. He has badges for the members' area and I'm looking forward to my strawberries and clotted cream.'

'You won't forget to take your insulin,' I say quickly, then wish I hadn't because her eyes narrow to dark slits and I know that I'm about to get a lecture.

'For goodness' sake, I'm the parent here. You really have to stop feeling responsible for me.' She's snappy and I wonder if she's having a hypo. I glance down at Seven, but he's unconcerned, licking at his paw to remove some sticky buds that have caught in his fur. 'There have been times when I didn't look after myself and I'm sorry, because I wasn't a good mother back then, but I'm all right now.' She bites her lip as I move towards her and rest my hand on her arm, giving it a squeeze.

'You couldn't help it,' I say softly. 'You were ill. I know we fall out now and again, but you're the best mum in the world.'

'Thank you.' She gazes into the back of the van at the profusion of red and white blooms before she slams the door shut. 'I'll see you later.'

Indoors I grab a mug of tea and head for the bathroom. As I round the corner on the landing, I walk straight into Godfrey. He's completely naked. I utter a scream of horror as he tries to retrieve his modesty with one of mum's flower-arranging magazines from the shelf outside their bedroom.

'Gosh, apologies,' he blusters. 'I thought you'd gone out.'

'I'm going to have a shower,' I say as he sidles, crablike, across the carpet and reverses into the bathroom.

'I won't be long,' he says, the door closing behind

him, but he takes a good half an hour, and when I finally fight my way through the steamy scent of *my* shower gel and his aftershave, there's no hot water, and all I can do is fantasise about how to get rid of him while I wait for it to warm up.

Having collected the ambulance and parking pass from Otter House, I drive out of town along the lanes, taking a back route towards the showground in the hope of avoiding the long queue of traffic that normally builds up on the way in. There are no cars, no lost grockles and no slow tractors, and I'm tempted to put my foot down so I can spend as much of the day as possible with Ross. I have to tell myself to calm down because I'm looking forward to seeing him far too much.

The road is narrow and winding with a bank of red sandstone, bushes and tree roots to one side and a hedge of blackthorn and brambles to the other. I take the next bend a little too fast and find myself around the corner, face to face with an obstruction in the middle of the lane. I jam the brakes on, slewing the ambulance across the potholed tarmac until it comes to a stop. There's a jolt and a giant marshmallow of an airbag punches me in the nose. The scrunch of crumpling metal and plastic is followed by silence, and I sit shaking, with the metallic taste of blood on my lips and shooting stars arcing across my vision. Gingerly, I check for my nose. It's still there. That's all I need to know, I think, as an enormous spotted pig gazes at me through pale, pink-rimmed eyes, as if to say, 'mind how you drive'.

I'm not sure I can take any more surprises. Keeping my eye on the unexpected pedestrian, I slide out of the driver's door to inspect the damage.

'Hello,' I say. 'You're lucky you didn't end up as bacon just then.' The ambulance is a different matter; it's wedged on the base of the bank with part of a tree embedded in the bonnet. That's going to take some major surgery. 'You might still be sausages when Maz and Emma see this,' I add wryly.

The pig grunts as she (for it is a girl, I can tell this time) ambles up to me. She seems to enjoy me scratching her hairy back and I take advantage of her friendly nature, directing her towards the adjacent gateway, but she plants her trotters in the grass on the verge and refuses to budge. At a loss, because she's at least as heavy as I am, so I can't pick her up or give her a push as I would with a dog, I call the emergency services to report the accident, and Ross, because he's the first person who springs to mind.

I wait for him to answer, my heart pounding. Delayed shock, I think, trying to calm myself down so I can actually speak.

'Hi, Shannon. What's up?'

'I've broken the ambulance.' I clutch at my throat as I relive the experience. 'I came around the corner and found a pig in the middle of the road. I swerved and ran into a tree.'

'Are you okay? Have you called an ambulance?' he says urgently.

'I'm fine. The pig's fine, but I need help to get her to a safe place.'

'Tell me where you are and I'll be straight over.'

'Thank you. I'm sorry to be a pain . . .'

'Don't be silly. It's no trouble.'

I explain how he can find me and, within minutes, he's tearing up on his motorbike and parking a little way back so as not to scare the pig. He leaves his helmet perched on the seat and comes running over.

'Thank goodness you're okay,' he says, taking me gently by the arms and looking me up and down. The relief and softness in his eyes sends hot tears rolling down my cheeks. I have never been so pleased to see someone, and secretly I'm flattered that he cares enough about me to race to my rescue. It seems to confirm that he has feelings for me as I suspected. 'Let me get you some tissue or a swab for your nose. You look as if you've taken quite a knock.' He releases me and reaches into the ambulance, takes the key and fetches some paper towel from the back. 'Have this.'

'Thanks,' I say, snivelling.

'There's an ice pack in the first-aid kit – I'll see if I can find that too. It might help keep the bruising down.' Ross grabs it, breaks the sachet inside the pack to activate it and hands it to me. With shaking fingers, I hold it to my nose.

'Ouch,' I exclaim. 'That's freezing.'

In spite of everything, Ross laughs. 'It's supposed to. Stop complaining. Let's get Miss Piggy off the road before she holds up the traffic,' he adds as local policeman, Kev, arrives in a patrol car. He opens the window.

'Is that one of Elsa's happy pigs?' he asks.

'I've no idea,' I say. 'It's a friendly pig.'

'I was only eating one last night – I took Heidi out for dinner at the Barnscote,' Ross says. 'She's staying for the show.'

'Oh?' My heart sinks into the soles of my Doc Martens. I thought I was going to have him to myself. It reinforces a suspicion that's been taking root in my head, that there's more to his ex than he's led me to believe. I don't know why it should concern me, but it does. I suppose he's become more than a colleague – like Will, I see him as a friend. In spite of the way my mind has been running away with me, imagining that Ross fancies me, and picturing me and him in a lustful embrace, it's all fantasy. I know it can't go any further and Heidi's appearance has confirmed that. I try to put a positive spin on it. At least I won't have to worry about whether or not I should enter into a relationship with someone I work with.

'What do you know about pigs?' I ask him.

'Silly question. He's a vet,' Kev points out, 'and I could have booked him for speeding back there.'

'I was in a hurry to rescue a damsel in distress.'

I take offence at being described as such, but he continues, 'Pigs are smarter than many people I know, and they make a great pork pie.'

'Please don't talk about meat in front of her,' I say, as she snuffles around at my feet.

'I'll get the stretcher. We can use that to direct her into the field.' Ross turns back to Kev with a wicked grin on his face. 'Aren't you going to help?'

'I'm staying put, thanks.' Kev gazes back. 'This is the kind of situation best left to the experts. I'll get on with logging a record of the accident and tracing the owner.'

Ross fetches the stretcher. He takes one end and I take the other and we guide the pig to the gate. Twice she doubles back, but the third time we cajole her far enough into the field to be able to close the gate behind her, by which time Kev has decided it's safe to emerge from the patrol car and inspect the ambulance.

'Do you think it's drivable?' I ask.

'More importantly, are you fit to drive?' Ross asks. 'I could take you to the show and come back and get the bike later.'

'There's no need to do that. I'll manage. It isn't far.'

After some debate, we decide that I can drive it the short distance to the showground and then, if necessary, call out a recovery vehicle, or borrow someone with a tractor to tow it back to the practice. It's up to Maz, I suppose. I'm not sure what happens about the insurance – you can hardly sue a stray pig for damages.

Kev returns to his traffic-directing duties, and Ross rides his bike behind the ambulance, weaving along the lane, revving the engine, and taking his hands off the handlebars and his feet off the footrests.

'You show-off,' I say, getting out when he pulls up alongside me in the exhibitors' parking area at the showground.

'What did you say? Can't hear you.' He grins as he removes his helmet.

'I said . . . oh, never mind. You can't park here – you haven't got a pass.'

'Who cares?'

'Fifi does.' I give him a nudge as I spot an older woman marching towards us, all dolled up in a coordinating outfit in baby blues and pinks, and a splendid hat of matching feathers. 'She's the local busybody.'

'I've met her up at the manor. Sophia introduced us.' Ross locks his bike as fast as he can, but it's too late. Fifi is on to him like a heat-seeking missile.

'It's only a bike,' I start, before she has a chance to open her mouth.

'What do you mean, it's only a bike?' Ross cuts in,

with an expression of mock hurt in his eyes. 'She's the apple of my eye.'

'What I'm saying is that I don't see why Ross needs some official pass to park here.'

'Oh, I'm not here to talk about that – although you really shouldn't be in the exhibitors' car park without one. No, this is about another matter entirely.' Fifi turns to Ross, and gives him the sweetest of smiles. 'My celebrity guest has spent the past hour driving around the lanes and is threatening to go straight back home. I've managed to persuade him to wait down at Bottom End for an escort. Our lovely police officer refuses to leave his post for a second time, but with your motorcycle, you can be there in an instant.'

'I'm not sure. I don't want to lose my parking spot.'

'You have my special dispensation to park here when you get back,' Fifi says.

'Well, that would be handy, but I'm still not sure . . .' Ross casts me a cheeky glance and I realise that he's stringing her along. 'I'm on call for the practice and I don't want to be too far away.'

'It isn't for me – it's for the people of Talyton St George. I'll pay for your fuel and make a donation to a charity of your choice. There is no one else . . .' Just as her padded shoulders begin to sink, he puts her out of her misery.

'All right. I'll go.'

'You are a hero,' she says delightedly, and for a moment I think she's going to kiss him. She watches him ride away, her hand shading her eyes from the sun. 'It just goes to show that you shouldn't make snap judgements based on appearances. I wasn't sure about him when I first met him up at the manor, but there's a lovely person somewhere under all that hair.' She smiles. 'Are you all right? You seem to have had an accident.'

'I ran into a tree, thanks to a stray pig.'

'Come along to the members' enclosure – I'm sure we can find you a restorative brandy.'

'No thank you, I can't, I'm on call.'

'Come and have tea and a cake then. You can wait for Ross in comfort. I'll introduce you to Bray Molland as well. You can take a selfie, or whatever it is people do nowadays.' She checks her watch. 'I hope they're going to hurry up. The show hunter championship will be over shortly.'

A few minutes later, I'm looking out of the members' tent towards the main arena, where an elderly gentleman in tweeds and a rotund middle-aged woman in a floral dress, jacket and wellies are judging some horses that stand in a row, their bits gleaming in the sunshine. One steps out of line; the rider gives it a dig in the ribs and a slap on the shoulder with a cane and it moves back.

'Maybe there is something to be said for a motorbike, after all,' Fifi observes when Ross returns, walking into the tent with a brown-haired man who towers over him. 'Our vet on two wheels has saved the day.' She rushes over to greet the celebrity – he looks vaguely familiar, but then I don't often watch the television news. I rely on the Internet. 'Thank you so much for agreeing to award the prizes at our humble Country Show,' she gushes. 'And thank you, Ross, you've made a lot of women very happy.'

'I believe you're flavour of the moment,' I say, grinning at him. 'What next?'

He looks past me and I turn to find Maz – dressed in a pink jacket, navy trousers and long brown boots

– walking towards us. George is with her, skipping along in a yellow T-shirt and bright blue shorts. My heart sinks because now I'm going to have to confess, but it's too late.

'We saw the ambulance on our way here,' she says. 'What happened?'

'It will have to go to hospital, won't it, Mummy?' George says.

'I think it might be beyond recovery, darling.'

'It's drivable,' Ross says optimistically.

'I'll get onto the insurance company. Was it one of those "a tree jumped out into the road" episodes?'

I shake my head, smiling in spite of my worries about Maz's reaction. 'It was a pig.'

'You ran into a pig?'

'No, I was avoiding the pig. She survived.'

Maz's mouth curves into a smile and she starts laughing. 'OMG, only in Devon. Are you all right, Shannon? You haven't hurt yourself?'

'She took a punch in the nose from the airbag,' Ross says.

'I'm fine though,' I insist.

'Are you sure?'

'I've been checked by a vet.'

'Oh, I'm not sure about him,' Maz chuckles. 'Wouldn't you like a second opinion?'

'Hey,' he says, pretending to be offended.

'Heidi's on her way,' she goes on. 'The last time I saw her was about half an hour ago, queueing up for the car park. I have my judge's badge so we were fast-tracked, weren't we, George. George? Where are you?' She looks around the tent and a giggle emerges from under the trestle table that's covered with a white cloth, bowls of peanuts and vegetable crisps, and trays of champagne flutes. 'Come out of there, will you? Now!' she goes on. 'Your grandmother has Henry and Olivia, and Daddy wants me to help get the ponies ready for Seb and Lucie before the best pet competition starts.' Seb and Lucie are George's half-siblings, who visit during the school holidays and turn up for special occasions such as the Country Show.

'I don't think he's taking any notice of you,' Ross observes.

Maz grimaces. She's too nice to everyone: her clients, their pets and her children. Feeling a little sorry for her, I walk to the table and squat down.

'Out you come or you'll miss the show.' I grab onto the cloth as it starts to move and the glasses begin to rattle on the trays. I lift the corner to find George sitting on his haunches, eating a handful of crisps from a bowl at his feet. 'Did anyone say you could help yourself?'

'No,' he says, his teeth gleaming from the near-darkness.

'Doesn't your mummy feed you?'

'No,' he confirms with another giggle.

I look back at Maz. 'Would you like me to have him for a while?'

'Would you? It's a bit of an imposition, but he really isn't into horses.' A flicker of amusement crosses her face. 'Sometimes Alex jokes that he'd like a DNA test to check that George really is his son.'

'He takes after you,' I say.

'I know. I'm a complete disappointment to Sophia. I'll catch up with you later.' She fumbles about in her bag, an oversized tote with a pink and navy design, and pulls out a twenty-pound note.

'Oh no, you don't have to pay me.'

'Take it. You can buy an ice cream or drinks.'

As soon as she utters the words 'ice cream', George is out and standing in front of us, his eyes wide with expectation.

We arrange to meet at lunchtime, when Maz is free again, and I persuade George to take a walk around the showground. Ross tags along with us.

'You don't have to,' I say, assuming that he would prefer to catch up with Heidi and his dog. 'I have my mobile if you need me.'

'I want to,' he says as he follows us out of the members' enclosure. 'If you don't mind . . .'

What about Heidi? I want to ask. Won't she be looking out for him? More questions chase through my brain. Where did she sleep last night? Did they have separate rooms at the manor, or did she and Ross share a bed for old times' sake?

Chapter Eight

Cuddly Crocodiles and Silver Balloons

We pass the Talyton Animal Rescue stall, where Tessa and some of the volunteers are running a tombola. Ross stops to buy a strip of tickets and George turns the handle on the revolving drum before picking a winning number. The prize is a bottle of bubble bath, but Tessa swaps it for a Rubik's cube and gives him a quick demonstration.

'We've rehomed all the baby rabbits from Otter House,' she says. 'It wasn't difficult – they definitely had the cute factor.'

We move on.

'Isn't that Merrie over there?' Ross touches my shoulder, the contact like an electric shock shooting down my spine. I try to shake off the feeling of longing, following his gaze to where Mrs Wall is sitting at a small table outside a small, wigwam-style tent with candy-striped canvas. Merrie is perched on a cushion on a chair beside her. 'Let's go and see what planet our local soothsayer is on today.'

'Oh, don't be mean. Promise you'll be kind to her.'

'I'll try,' he grins. 'George, have you met Mrs Wall, the fortune-teller?'

'No, but I'm really hungry now,' he pleads.

'You've just had a bowl of crisps,' I point out.

'I'm hungry for ice cream.'

'So am I,' Ross says. 'We'll go and get one as soon as we've spoken to Mrs Wall. I can check on Merrie's skin at the same time.'

When we approach, she looks up from her crystal ball, which looks very much like an empty snow-dome. She's wearing a black coat with a lining of purple shot silk over her everyday clothes, and a scarf wrapped around her head like a turban.

'Cross my palm with silver, my lovers, and I'll read your fortune.'

'Silver?' Ross says.

'Actually, it's a fiver for the full works, three questions for the crystal ball and a palm reading.'

'Oh, go on then,' he says, but she declines the money that he takes from his wallet.

'I can't read the hand of a sceptic.'

'Shannon, how about you?' Ross pays for me before I have a chance to argue that she's read my fortune using astrology at a previous year's show, so I know that I'm going to be lucky in love and lead a long and happy life. However, I decide that I have nothing to lose by going along with it.

'How would you like me to interrogate the crystal ball?' she says, moving both hands over the glass.

'I'd like you to ask if there's a message from my father.' I swallow past a lump that forms in my throat.

'You don't believe in this stuff, do you?' Ross whispers from my side.

I turn to him sharply. 'I believe in the afterlife.'

132

'I'm sorry,' he says, backing down. 'You go ahead.'
'Don't you?'
'No.' His voice is thick with sorrow and his eyes are fixed on Mrs Wall's hands. 'When you're gone, you're gone,' he adds, his scathing attitude replaced with regret, and I wonder who's on his mind.
'Hush,' she says. 'I have something.'
'How do you know you're in touch with the right person?' Ross asks.
'Don't question what you can never understand.'
'I'm trying to figure it out.'
'So you can mock and undermine me when I'm merely a channel along which the unexplained energies of the universe transmit. Hush,' she repeats, holding one long finger to her lips. 'There is indeed a message.'
My heart leaps. 'You've found him?'
'What a bit of luck,' Ross says with sarcasm.
'Ross, shut up.'
'He has found you,' Mrs Wall says, ignoring him. 'He says to look out for the rainbows, darling, just as we used to.'
How does she know that? I think, feeling hopeful although not entirely convinced. My dad used to take me out hunting for rainbows.
'Is he happy?' I want to know. 'He doesn't feel . . . pushed out or forgotten, because you must tell him that he isn't; that he's always in my thoughts.'
Mrs Wall's hands do an elaborate sashay above the crystal ball.
'He knows he is loved and he loves you. And the appearance of a man with a name beginning with G has made no difference to him.'
'Godfrey,' I sigh.

'What a surprise,' Ross cuts in.

'It's all right. Everyone knows he and Mum are an item. I'm glad Dad's cool with him.' I wrap my arms around my chest. 'Is there anything else?'

'Nothing,' Mrs Wall says quietly. 'I'm so glad he came through for you. Now, give me your hand.' She puts her tinted specs on top of her turban and examines my palm. Her eyes are remarkably green, calm and cat-like when she looks up at me.

'You recall that I said you would be lucky in love – well, it's clear that you will be married, very possibly within a year from now.'

'Really?'

'That all sounds rather vague to me,' Ross comments.

'Palmistry isn't an exact science.'

'It isn't a science at all. It's smoke and mirrors.'

'We'll see, shall we? I'm not normally a gambling woman, but I'll make an exception. If Shannon isn't making plans to marry by this time next year, I'll give you a ten-pound note – and vice versa.'

Ross hesitates, as though taken by surprise, before shaking her hand. 'Done,' he says. 'Can you tell her how many kids she's going to have?'

'Why? Do you think she's going to marry you?' she asks with a sly smile.

He chuckles. 'I doubt it somehow.'

Mrs Wall takes a second look at my palm, counting the tiny lines on the edge of my hand opposite the base of my thumb. 'There will be five children, all boys.'

'That's too many,' I say quickly. 'I mean, I'd like a baby in the future, one or two – not five.'

'Just imagine taking five mini-bikes to motocross

every weekend,' Ross teases, and a picture of him on his bike with five boys on bikes in a row behind him, like a duck with ducklings, springs to mind.

'It would be so cute, but these are my babies, not yours.'

'The lines indicate the potential for you to have five children. It doesn't necessarily mean that you'll end up with that many.'

'All these rules made to be broken,' Ross starts again. 'Really, you can say what you like.'

'I hate to say this, but you're right,' Mrs Wall says. 'People take their own truth from my words.'

'They pick and choose to suit their circumstances, you mean.'

'Listen, young man, we are never going to agree on anything.'

'I know. Would you mind me having a quick look at Merrie, seeing as she's here?'

'You're welcome, but don't ask me to cross *your* palm with silver afterwards. I'm not made of money.'

Ross grins as he strokes the dog, running his fingers through her coat and looking closely at her skin, checking her ears and paws in particular.

'She's looking better,' he says.

Mrs Wall thanks him and George, who's been watching intently, asks if he can have a go at the crystal ball.

'We must ask Mummy first.' I don't want him having any hang-ups because of what Mrs Wall tells him. I don't think his parents would appreciate him having nightmares about the ghosts she can conjure up. We wish her a good day and Ross and I take George to join the queue outside the ice-cream van, and the three of us are eating vanilla cones with flakes and strawberry sauce when a woman appears with a dog that's almost as big as Nero.

'Hi,' she calls, and the dog bounds in on the end of his lead to greet Ross.

'Meet Bart,' he says, looking at me as he hugs the dog, who is standing on his hind legs with his paws on his master's shoulders.

'That is a giant dog,' George marvels, wiping his face with the back of his hand.

The woman smiles. 'That's so typical, introducing the dog before me.'

'I'm George,' George says.

'Heidi, this is Shannon. Shannon, Heidi.' Ross pushes Bart down so he has all four feet on the ground. The dog hangs back with his ears and tail down as he sniffs the air and holds my gaze with a cool stare. I avert my eyes, uncertain about his reaction when I'd expected him to make friends.

'Let's hope Maz is right and it won't be too busy on call today,' Ross goes on.

'I hope so. You promised to take me out to see the sights tonight.' I notice how Heidi rests one hand on his shoulder. She has shiny French-polished nails with immaculate white tips. Her hair is sleek, blonde, and feathered down past her high cheekbones, and her clothes – a rugby shirt with a bold stripe, crops and canvas shoes – are Joules and Musto. 'Hello, Shannon. It's lovely to meet you.'

I'm not sure what to say. My first impression of Heidi is that she's okay, vibrant and beautiful – in fact, I'm not sure why Ross would give her the push.

He walks ahead with George, trawling all the stalls for freebies – pens, fluffy creatures for the dashboard of the car, badges, a sample of disinfectant for cleaning your cowshed and three silver balloons on sticks – while Heidi and I wander along behind with Bart between us.

'I know Ross doesn't like it much, but I felt like the lady of the manor this morning, waking up in that lovely old house.'

'What about Bart? Does he get on with the Fox-Giffords' dogs?'

'We decided not to risk finding out – he slept in the bedroom with me and his dad.'

It takes me a moment to register that by 'his dad' she means Ross. So that's it then, I muse. He really is unavailable. He and Heidi are still sleeping with each other. His status is what I'd describe as 'complicated'.

'This is so much fun,' Heidi goes on. 'I feel as if I've stepped back in time. There's a Punch and Judy show and a stall selling old-fashioned sweets and candy sticks,' she says brightly. 'I'd love to live somewhere around here. It's beautiful.'

'So you're thinking of moving to Devon?'

'Not seriously. It's a long way to bring the dog, but I need to stay where I am for work.'

'What do you do? You aren't a vet . . . ?'

'I couldn't do what Ross does. I'm a biologist – I work in a research lab in Surrey. I specialise in tissue cultures.'

It's funny, but I imagined she'd do something more glamorous. I'm finding it hard to picture her in a white coat when, with her figure, she could be a model.

'Who looks after Bart while you're at work?'

'I'm very lucky – my mother has him for doggy day-care.' She flicks her hair back. 'Ross seems happy here. I thought he might hate it. It sounds as if he's making friends. He was at the pub the other night when I called him.'

'We had a drink at the Dog and Duck.'

'I see,' she says slowly. 'Oh well, I expect you spend a lot of time with him.'

'Mostly at work.' I don't think she likes the idea of me fraternising with her ex after hours, but that isn't my problem, I think, as Bart pulls her across the avenue between the stands. He introduces himself to a spaniel, which lifts its lip to reveal a full set of teeth as the hairs on Bart's hackles rise.

'Bart, come here.' She tugs at the lead. 'No,' she adds, as he ignores her, and she has to resort to dragging him away by his collar. 'I'm supposed to have taken him to dog training, but I haven't had the time.' She looks at me, her face flushed. 'It's no use asking Ross to do it – there'd be no consistency or routine. He's always been like that: getting up in the morning and taking off on his bike whenever he feels like it. I suppose that's one of the things I love about him, his spontaneity, even when it does lead him into making some pretty dim decisions.'

I'm not sure what to say. I don't like talking about Ross behind his back, so I settle on a safer topic of conversation.

'Bart seems like a lovely dog,' I begin, even though I'm not sure about him yet. 'How long have you had him?'

'A couple of years now. Ross and I had been together for five years – we met at university – and we gave Bart a home on the assumption we'd stay together. We talked about marriage, I bought the dress, and then things began to unravel. I've seen it before. Man gets serious. Woman accepts proposal of marriage. Woman buys wedding dress. Man gets cold feet.'

'I didn't realise . . .' That isn't the impression he gave me when he talked to me about ending his relationship with her, and I wonder whose version is closest to the reality of what did happen between them.

She tips her head slightly to one side. 'I'm hoping it won't take him too long to see what he's missing and then, who knows? Maybe . . .'

'You mean, you want to get back with him?'

'You seem surprised,' she says, her brows arched in question.

'No, not really,' I stammer.

'I wouldn't expect Ross to talk about personal matters with one of his vet nurses,' she says. 'Besides, you know what men are like. They're never good at expressing their true feelings.' She seems to accept my silence as mutual agreement, when it's far from it. I haven't noticed her ex having any trouble letting people know exactly how he feels. 'Well, it would be great to be a family again,' she goes on, giving Bart's ear a rub. He grunts with pleasure. 'And, maybe, in the future . . . well, look how good he is with George . . .'

Why didn't Ross mention this possibility?, I wonder, as George comes running back with a green soft toy crocodile that's almost as big as he is, having given up the Rubik's cube.

'I've got a ginormous crocodile,' he shrieks, proceeding to wrestle it to the ground until it's lying on its back and he has his foot on its yellow belly. 'Gotcha!' he bellows.

'I think it's time we took you back to find your mummy.' I turn to Ross. 'What was in those ice creams?'

'I dread to think.' He grins at George. 'Now you've subdued that giant croc, you can pick it up and carry it.'

'It might still bite me,' he says, flexing his skinny arms.

'How about tying the string from one of the balloons around his nose?' Ross suggests. George nods in agreement, and Ross unfastens the knot on one of the strings, lets the balloon go floating off into the sky, and wraps the string around the crocodile's mouth, finishing it with a bow. 'How's that?'

George waves his hand in front of the crocodile's face and pronounces the move a success.

I wish Ross and Heidi goodbye before I take George and the crocodile along to the ring, where Maz is judging the 'best pet in show' class. Her top three are Sherbet, a sausage dog belonging to one of our clients; the pair of baby rabbits – Mojo and Flyte – who are safely ensconced in a white wire basket, and a very grumpy long-haired cat that's also in a cage.

'Which one would you choose?' I ask George.

'The rabbits, because then my crocodile could eat them. Snap, snap.'

I ruffle his hair. 'You'd better not let your mum's clients hear that.'

After some deliberation, Maz picks Sherbet as the winner, honouring his handler, a little girl in a red dress, with a matching rosette. The rabbits are second, and the cat third, and as the competitors parade around the ring to the sound of applause from the assembled audience, Maz spots us and comes over to the ringside that's marked out with rope and straw bales.

'Look what I won.' George holds up the crocodile.

'That's wonderful, darling. Thanks for that, Shannon. Where am I going to put it?'

'It was Ross,' I say.

'I'll be having a word with him later. You don't fancy having George a little longer? Sophia wants me to help supervise the Pony Club Mounted Games.'

'I want to go with you, Mummy,' George says.

'Of course you do.' Maz takes his hand. 'I expect you want to catch up with some of your friends too,' she adds, looking at me.

'That's the plan.' George is lovely, but sometimes you can have too much of a good thing. Taylor isn't able to make it to the show because she's working at the garden centre all day, but Mitch has texted me to let me know he'll be about this afternoon. I check my watch. It's almost midday. I decide to have a wander and see how Frances has done with her entries in the WI competitions.

I check I have my mobile to hand in case Ross calls me to help out with any emergencies, and step inside the marquee. It's buzzing with both people and some bees that are confined, I hope, behind some netting, and two beekeepers dressed in protective clothing. The scent of honey and sweat mingles with the fragrance of English roses that reminds me of the shop.

It takes me a moment to identify Frances amongst the crowd – she's wearing a tunic printed with big black and white squares, white cropped trousers and cork sandals, and wearing a rosette. I thought that wasn't the done thing in the WI, where winning is everything as long as you don't make a spectacle of it. I make my way across the trampled grass to congratulate her.

'What was it? The chutney?'

'Of course,' she smiles. 'It's my secret recipe that does it every time. Have you seen Bray Molland? He gave me this rosette.' She touches the red ribbons. 'Can you believe it? He shook my hand.'

'I hope Lenny doesn't mind,' I say, teasing her.

'He knows I'd never be unfaithful. He has a crush or two himself.' She reaches for my arm. 'Is that Lucky over there, under the table?'

I follow her gaze. He's lying on his side, gasping for air. I rush over to him, pick him up and look for somewhere to put him amongst the plates of scones that haven't been judged yet.

'You can't put that there. It's unhygienic,' someone says.

I glance aside, catching sight of Fifi coming towards me, handbag at the ready, as if she's about to take a swipe at me. Frances intercepts her and starts to move the scones onto the next table, fitting them between the flower arrangements and a sign reading, Theme: the movie, *Frozen*.

'Is Jennie here somewhere?' I ask as I check Lucky over. The effect of moving him appears to have had a beneficial effect – his breathing is steadier.

'She's judging the Victoria sponges,' Frances says, but Jennie's already on her way across to us.

'What's wrong?' she asks.

'I don't know. I'm calling the vet.'

'Is it Maz, only she's been treating him—?'

'It's Ross.' I turn away to speak to him on my

mobile. 'I need you at the WI marquee right now, this minute.'

'That's what they all say,' he says lightly. 'I'll be right over. What's wrong?' His voice catches as he starts walking.

'It's Lucky. He's collapsed.'

Ross arrives within seconds. He diagnoses heat exhaustion and takes control of the situation, ordering some water and cloths. I pour a couple of bottles of spring water onto a tea towel and dampen Lucky down. He isn't impressed, giving me a look as if to say, 'What do you think you're doing?'

'Do you think it's the cancer?' Jennie asks.

'It could be that, or a side-effect of the chemo, or he could be stressed out because he's here rather than resting at home.'

'I knew I shouldn't have brought him, but he looked so sad when I said he couldn't come with us.' Her eyes fill with tears. 'My poor Lucky.'

She leans down to kiss the dog, just as Ross reaches out to stroke his head, and kisses Ross's hand instead. She steps back abruptly, bumping into Frances.

'I'm so sorry. I kissed you.' Suddenly, she laughs out loud. 'Oh dear, this is bizarre and very embarrassing.'

'Don't worry. I have this way with women,' Ross says, lapping up the attention. 'Let's make a plan. I would suggest that you take Lucky home and call me in an hour to let me know how he is. If he's comfortable, we'll book him in to see Maz on Monday for a check-up and a chat. Shannon and I are on duty all weekend, so you can ring at any time.'

'Thank you,' Jennie says. 'Frances, please can you pass me my bag? I left it on the cake table—'

'Where do you think you're going?' Fifi interrupts.

'Home.'

'What about the Victoria sponges? You hadn't come to a decision.'

'Oh, sausages to them. I have to go.' Jennie takes her bag and lifts Lucky into her arms. 'Someone else will have to do it.'

'But who? You're the expert. You're our Mary Berry.'

Jennie looks in Ross's direction. 'Why not ask our answer to Paul Hollywood here? I'm sure he eats cake.' She whisks Lucky away and leaves the marquee.

'Would you?' Fifi asks. 'Bray Molland has returned to the member's enclosure – he is "in his cups", to put it mildly. I do believe I'm going to have to put him up for the night because there's no way he's fit to drive.'

'It will be a pleasure,' Ross smiles, as I'm trying without words to impress on him the fact that it isn't a good idea.

'Whichever you choose as a winner, you'll be accused of favouritism,' I whisper as we make our way to the row of sponges.

'I can handle it. Watch me and learn.'

I notice his eyes glazing over as Fifi explains the criteria for the judging, talking at length about texture and presentation.

'What really matters is that it has to taste bloody good,' Ross says, summarising as he cuts himself a big chunk of the first cake and bites into it. 'That's a ten.' He tries the second one and frowns.

'Is there something wrong?' Fifi says hopefully. 'It's the one Frances baked.'

'Yup, there's a big problem.' He has cheeky twinkle in his eye. 'That one's a ten as well. There are a lot of tens around here.'

He goes through several more slices of cake, finishing every one and proclaiming that they're all worthy of his top mark.

'You have to make a decision,' Fifi says.

'I'm going to give an award for flavour and consistency, and another for artistic merit.'

'There are some who might consider the Victoria sponge an art form, but I'd argue that you can't possibly create a new award for spreading jam and sprinkling icing sugar.'

'You'd argue about anything, Fifi,' Ross says, and I would swear it is at that instant, as he's teasing and flirting with her, that she falls in love with him.

'Oh,' she gives him a gentle nudge, 'you are a cad. I'll go and find an extra rosette and certificate.'

Ross turns to me. 'You see: that's how it's done.'

'I'm impressed.'

'Would you like to join me and Heidi, and Bart of course, for lunch in the members' enclosure? Fifi said to just turn up as a thank-you for going to find that Bray chap.'

'No, thanks. I'm going to have a look around the rest of the show.'

'I'll catch you later then.' He acts out doffing a cap. 'I'm one of the country set now, you know.'

'Enjoy,' I say with some irony. I don't want to mix with a load of old farmers and horsey people, and I have no desire to schmooze with the businessmen and women like Mum and Godfrey, but these are convenient excuses when I'm really trying to avoid seeing Ross with his ex because the idea that they're still seeing each other makes me feel a tad jealous. I know it's irrational when it's clear that I have no claim on him, but I can't help it.

'I will,' he says with a cheerful grin.

Outside the marquee, Ross goes one way and I go the other. I watch some Morris dancing and sheep shearing before catching up with Mitch in the middle of the afternoon. We sit on the grass outside the beer tent, watching Dexy's Dancing Diggers in the main arena. I hold onto my bottle of elderflower cordial as a breeze catches my arms, raising goose bumps across my skin, which is turning pink in the sun. Mitch is wearing a cap, a vest with 'In at the Deep End' printed across the front, and knee-length denim shorts.

'So what did you want to talk to me about?' He touches the mouth of a bottle of lager to his lips. I become aware of his hand slipping under my top, touching the small of my back. I shuffle a little to one side and he shifts closer. 'You said in your text you wanted to talk. What's wrong, Shannon? Are you playing hard to get, only I thought we'd make the most of a free day together? My brother's band's playing a gig in a pub near Exeter tonight. I thought we'd go, just the two of us. It feels like we haven't caught up for ages.'

'I'm sorry. I can't.' I can't quite bring myself to let him down, so I add, 'I'm on call this weekend.'

'You mean, you don't want to come with me?' He leans back and rests on his elbow, putting some space between us.

'I'm serious. I'm on duty.'

'You're always working,' he complains.

'It's the nature of the job.' I tuck my cardigan

around my shoulders. 'Aren't you supposed to be at the pool?'

'I am allowed out now and then. There's something else, isn't there? You've been different recently.' I pick at the grass and let it drift as he goes on, 'Apart from swimming, Taylor says she's hardly seen you.'

'I've been busy,' I say with a twinge of guilt.

'You don't text or talk to me any more.'

'I'm talking now. Oh, I'm sorry,' I repeat. 'You're one of my best friends.' I gaze at him with a sick sensation in the pit of my stomach. I have to tell him because I can't go on living a lie, pretending that I'm cool about it.

- 'Look, I want to stay friends, but without the other thing. It isn't working for me.'

'The sex, you mean.' His eyes are dark. 'I've never heard you complaining before.'

'I'm not complaining. It's been—'

'Fun,' he finishes for me. 'So why can't we carry on? No ties, no attachment.'

'I thought I could do it, but I can't. After we broke up, it felt comforting to be back in your arms.'

'Comforting?' he interrupts. 'Am I really that bad in bed?'

'I didn't say that, and anyway, we agreed after the first time: no recriminations.'

What we didn't talk about in advance was how we would deal with it when our arrangement came to an end, because it has as far as I'm concerned. I don't want to be close to Mitch any more. In fact, the thought of a drunken fumble right now makes me feel slightly sick.

'There has to be somebody else.'

'There isn't, but I want to be free to move on.' I

147

pause as two of Dexy's Dancing Diggers clash buckets. 'This isn't right for me. When I go home the next morning, I feel kind of used.'

'You've been using me too,' he says, raising one eyebrow.

'I want more from my life, Mitch. Don't you?'

'Not really. I'm happy as things are. I suppose I've been half expecting you to dump me for a second time,' he continues morosely.

'I'm not dumping you. We aren't a couple.'

'Oh, you're right. It's hurt male pride. I'll be all right.' His expression softens. 'How about one for the road?'

'No, I'm afraid not. Just to make it perfectly clear – no more drinks and no more falling into bed with each other,' I say firmly.

'Okay, but you can't blame me for trying.' He looks at me with a rueful grin. 'Cheers!' He raises his bottle and touches it to mine. 'Good luck.'

'You too.' I sip at my drink, the fragrant bubbles popping sharp and sweet at the same time on my tongue. It's a relief to know that we have a clean break this time. Mitch will find someone else. And me? I look down the avenue where I catch sight of Ross strolling along with the dog. Heidi is on his arm, carrying a silver balloon on a string, a carved duck and several carrier bags. Somehow the prospect of a night on call with him no longer appeals in quite the same way as it did, but I'll have to get over it. It's probably for the best because it would be a shame to complicate mine and Ross's growing friendship with romance.

'I'll be off then,' Mitch says, getting up and brushing the grass from his shorts. I stand up with him, putting my arms around his shoulders to give him one last hug. He squeezes me tight and gives me a forceful kiss straight on the lips. 'Keep in touch.'

'I'll see you at the pool,' I say, taking a step back.

He turns and strides away. I pick up our empty bottles and drop them in the recycling bin nearby, not noticing Ross and Heidi until they are almost on top of me.

'Hello again,' Heidi says, as if she's my best friend. Bart hesitates, raising one paw off the ground and growling when he sees me.

'Hey, shut up,' Ross says jovially. 'I'm sorry – he's rather opinionated.'

'Is that your other half?' Heidi asks. 'It's a shame he had to run away – we could have made it a foursome.'

'That's Mitch, my ex.' I'm blushing for no good reason, except I'm acutely aware that Ross is studying my face rather intently. 'He's a lifeguard and swimming teacher at the leisure centre.'

'I thought he looked rather fit.' Heidi turns to Ross with a coquettish flick of her hair. 'Not as gorgeous as you, though.'

I have to admire her confidence. She's determined she will win him back.

'I'm glad we ran into you,' Ross says. 'We've been called back to the surgery. Heidi can give you a lift.'

'It's all right,' I say quickly. 'I'll drive the ambulance.'

'If you're sure.' He frowns. 'It isn't desperately urgent, but it's a puppy with an upset tummy that needs to be seen today. Promise me you'll take it slowly.'

'I'll be careful.'

'Great. I'll ride the bike, and Heidi can bring Bart. Meet you there.' He places his hand on the small of Heidi's back as we walk towards the car parks.

Back at Otter House, Heidi waits in reception with Bart while Ross and I attend to the puppy, a ten-week-old tricolour terrier with a black patch over one eye. Ross decides to admit him and we put him in isolation on antibiotics and a drip. As soon as I close the door of his cage, the puppy – called Pirate – is sick. I clean up after him, give him a new bed and, as soon as my back is turned, he vomits again.

Oh, joy, I think.

'How is he?' Ross asks, returning from reception, where he's been completing a consent form with Pirate's owner.

'He's thrown up twice in ten minutes.'

'I'll give him something to stop that.' Ross hesitates. 'Would you mind hanging around for a couple of hours? I would offer to stay myself, but Heidi wants to take Bart up to the escarpment for a run. We can let him off the lead up there because there aren't many dogs about.'

'He's a bit funny with other dogs, isn't he?' I say, remembering how he behaved with the spaniel.

'I don't think it's him,' Ross says protectively. 'It's more a case of the other dogs picking on him.'

I let it go, amused to find that Ross is a typical dog owner who can't accept that his pet can do any wrong.

'I don't mind staying.' I haven't got anything better to do at the moment. In fact, I feel a little flat, because the day I've been looking forward to hasn't gone as I'd hoped.

'Thanks.' He leans across and brushes his lips

against my cheek in a gesture that takes me by surprise. 'I owe you.'

I stay at the practice all night, sleeping on the sofa in the staff room and checking on the puppy every couple of hours. In the morning, I'm up when Ross arrives in jeans and a T-shirt with his hair still damp from the shower.

'Did you have a good evening?' I ask him.

'It was okay, I suppose. It was nice to catch up with Heidi and what's going on with our friends.' He sighs. 'I'm afraid I've lost touch with some of them, mainly the women who have – not surprisingly, I suppose – chosen to take Heidi's side. How is the puppy?'

'He hasn't been sick again. Can I feed him?'

'You can try him with a little chicken before we see the two patients I've booked in,' he says.

I take fresh chicken breast from the fridge and cook it; the puppy devours the few pieces that I let him have. Tripod turns up and he has some too, even though he probably shouldn't.

We see a cat with an abscess on its head and a dog that can't walk in a straight line without falling over. Ross lances the abscess and dispenses antibiotics for the cat, and diagnoses the dog with an inner ear problem for which he prescribes the appropriate drugs and rest. When they've left the surgery, he checks on Pirate and decides to send him home.

'He'll be happier in his own surroundings, a bit like Bart really. I enjoyed the show. I didn't think I would. Do you think I'd get a job presenting *Bake Off*?'

'I don't think so. Do you watch it?' I ask, grinning.

'Oh, avidly.'

I gaze at his face, which is a mask. Is he winding me up? I don't think so . . .

'Do you really?'

He grins. 'Of course not. I've seen it a couple of times in passing. It isn't my cup of tea – and, talking of which, would you like a drink? You look weary – I don't suppose you slept much.'

I yawn in response.

'Why don't we run up to the Copper Kettle? I fancy some cake now. My treat.'

'Cake? At this time of day?'

'Why not? I'll call Pirate's owner. Once they've picked him up, we'll go.' He smiles wryly. 'Unless anyone else calls us in the meantime.'

Later, we share a plate of different types of cake in the teashop, which is open for business on Sundays throughout the summer to take advantage of the tourist trade.

'So what marks would you give the lemon drizzle?' I ask him.

'That's a ten, and so is the chocolate sponge, and the walnut and coffee.' He changes the subject. 'I found out what happened to the pig. Heidi and I ran into the policeman – not literally,' he chuckles. 'When we went to grab a bite to eat at the Talymill Inn last night, he told us that they'd traced the owner, who came with a trailer to take her home. Apparently she broke out of their garden and took herself off for a walk. She's a pet, which explains why she was so tame.' There's a buzzing sound from his pocket. He takes out his phone and checks the screen.

'Ah, good. Heidi's back safely. She wasn't going to stay at all, but when I told her about the show, she wanted to see what it was like. I'm glad – I don't think I'd have coped with Bart as well as being on call.'

'When will you have him again?' I chase the last crumbs of cake and icing from the plate with a fork.

'It depends on Heidi.'

In that case, I think, it will be very soon.

'Shall we go?' he says. 'I'll hold the fort while you go home and take a break.'

'Thanks, Ross.'

'There's no need to thank me. It's you who's done me a favour.' He settles up with Cheryl and we part outside the Copper Kettle. 'See you later maybe,' he says, and I start to walk towards Petals. I stop and turn partway along the road. Ross is watching. I wave and he waves back. I can hardly believe how much my opinion of him has altered since he arrived at Otter House. He's a good friend and great vet, and I'm growing fonder of him every time I see him. I smile to myself because, if we should get called out again, I won't mind in the slightest.

Chapter Nine

Snow White

There are no further emergencies or urgent cases to deal with on Sunday or during the night, and I don't see Ross again until Wednesday, because he has two days off due to some tweaks to the vets' duty rota while I have only one. I find that I miss him when he isn't at the practice. It's rather dull without him.

Wednesday and Thursday pass without incident, and the next day I have that Friday feeling. Just evening surgery and some babysitting to get through, and then I have another long weekend off: three whole days to catch up with friends, take Seven out for walks, swim, maybe hit the shops with Taylor; anything to avoid lolling around the house with Mum and Godfrey, I think ruefully. It occurs to me, not for the first time, that I should buy a motorbike and disappear for days out like Ross does, touring the countryside and stopping off wherever he likes.

At eight thirty in the morning, Fifi Green is standing at reception with her hair set in immaculate waves of copper and gold highlights, and a handbag which coordinates with her teal jacket and skirt. She leans across the desk and I can't help staring at her neck, where her skin is stretched remarkably smooth for a woman of her age.

'It's rather good, isn't it?' she says quietly. 'Just don't breathe a word to a soul. Our secret.'

'Oh? Yes, of course.'

'I can give you his card.'

'I'm sorry?'

'For my surgeon. It wouldn't hurt you to invest in a little help for those frown lines.'

'There's no way I'd consider it – Botox is a poison.'

'I'd rather die with it than without. You'll change your mind one day, you'll see. Now, where is Ross?'

'I'm afraid he isn't in yet. Can I take a message?'

'I'd prefer to speak to him in person.'

'You can wait if you like – he should be here soon – unless you're in a hurry.'

'I'm in no rush.' She sits down to wait until he turns up, parking his motorbike before striding in with his helmet under his arm.

'Hello,' she says, intercepting him.

He hesitates, looking at me as if he's expecting me to take over.

'Fifi wants a word with you,' I say as Frances joins us in reception. I move aside to let her take up her place behind the counter.

'I'm afraid you'll have to be quick,' he says lightly. 'I'm a busy man.'

'Aren't we all?' Fifi hands him a business card. 'I wanted to thank you again for saving the day last weekend – and, while I'm here, I've brought you the number for the barber. I couldn't help noticing that you're a little overdue for a haircut.'

Ross appears completely bemused.

'You mean, you want me to conform?' I can hear laughter bubbling up in his voice. 'Don't you like my style?' He places one hand on his hip, coils a lock of hair around his fingers and casts her a sideways glance, fluttering his eyelashes.

'You're a very handsome young man.' She mirrors his body language – I'm not sure if it's deliberate or not – resting one hand on her hip and playing with her hair, tucking a wave behind her ear. 'If I were twenty years younger—'

'Oh come on, Fifi,' Frances interrupts, 'thirty years at least.'

Fifi glares at her. They haven't always seen eye to eye in the past.

'Twenty-five then,' she accedes.

'And not married,' Frances adds sharply, a reference to Fifi's fondness for the male species. There have always been rumours that she hasn't been entirely faithful to her husband throughout their marriage.

'Well, thanks for thinking of me,' Ross says, tucking the card into his pocket.

'The pleasure is all mine,' Fifi says.

'I really must be getting on,' Ross says. 'Shannon, you're with me.'

Smiling, I follow him into the consulting room and close the door behind us.

'I think you've got yourself a stalker,' I say in a low voice.

'I'll go and change,' he says, and he returns a few minutes later in his tunic. 'Has she gone?' he asks.

'Yes, I checked. Penny's waiting for you with Trevor.' I open the door to let them in, and Penny reverses the wheelchair into the corner so that Ross has space to lift the dog onto the table. Trevor's cast is looking a little the worse for wear. He jumps up and head-butts Ross on the mouth and wees at the same time. I clear up and wash my hands, but when I turn back, Ross has his fingers pressed to his lower lip.

'You're bleeding.' I hand him a swab from the tray on the worktop.

'I'm so sorry,' Penny says.

'It's all right,' he mutters. 'I'm fine.'

'Let me see,' I say, moving up to have a closer look.

'Am I going to live?' he says with mock concern.

'I'm not sure,' I tease. 'I'm only a nurse, remember. I haven't got the benefit of your superior knowledge.'

'You look like you've been in a bit of a scrap,' Penny says worriedly. 'I don't know what to do. I really need to talk to you about Trevor.'

'He's all right,' he says. 'It's just youthful enthusiasm. Some dogs never grow up.'

Like some vets, I think to myself.

'That's hardly reassuring,' Penny says, but although I suspect she wants to say more on the subject of Trevor's behaviour, Ross seems keen to keep to the schedule so we don't fall behind with the appointments. He checks the nibbled top of the cast and covers it with a new bandage, the camouflage version in green this time.

'He wears the cone of shame when he's alone, like at night, but I keep finding Declan has taken it off because he says Trevor doesn't like it.'

'He won't have to wear it for much longer. Book him in for a day in three or four weeks' time and we'll

157

sedate him to repeat the X-ray. If, as I'd expect, the break's completely healed, we'll remove the cast.'

'Will he be back to normal after that? Will we be able to take him for walks?'

'As long as you build up the exercise slowly and don't let him do too much at first.'

'Thank goodness. He's driving us mad.' There's an edge of desperation in her voice, reminding me of when Seven was about Trevor's age, constantly pestering me to play with him and take him out. 'He has far too much energy.'

'He'll be able to run it off soon enough.' Ross steps aside to type some notes onto the computer.

I'm not sure any time will be soon enough for Penny. Call it a nurse's instinct, but I don't think Ross is getting the message. He doesn't mean to be insensitive. He's too focused on the veterinary aspects of the case, not looking at the broader situation, the relationship between owner and pet. Pets are very much like people: you can love them with all your heart, but not like them very much at times.

'I'll see you in a couple of weeks,' he adds.

'Yes, thank you.' Penny struggles to get out of the door as Trevor leaps up and down and runs around the chair, his lead tangling with the wheels. I accompany her, taking hold of the Labrador's collar, and telling him to sit while I retrieve the lead. I have to ask him three times before he plonks himself on my feet, looking up with his tongue hanging out and an 'I'm such a good boy, aren't I?' expression on his face, the kind of expression that makes you smile even though you know you shouldn't.

'How do you do that? You're like a proper dog whisperer. I have to shout to get him to listen to me.'

To my horror, Penny's lips start to tremble and her eyes brim with tears. 'Oh, this is so silly. I feel like a complete failure.'

'Let's have a chat.' I grab the box of tissues from reception, looking towards Frances, who nods as if reading my mind.

'Ross has one more to see and then the consulting room will be free,' she says. 'I'll put the kettle on.'

'Thank you, but I don't want to hold you up.'

'You said you needed to talk about Trevor,' I say firmly, 'so that's what we're going to do. The floors can wait.'

Ten minutes later, Trevor is pottering around the consulting room. He cocks his leg against the bin, but I don't think Penny notices. Her hands shake as she sips at the tea. I can't drink mine – it's as if Frances has used the sugar content of the brew to represent the seriousness of the situation.

I let Penny speak.

'You remember Sally?' she begins.

'Of course I do.' She was her first assistance dog, a golden retriever who loved her work so much that she got herself a reputation as a serial shoplifter, although the items she picked off the shelves were always returned undamaged and unopened.

'She had her foibles, but she was sweet and well meaning, and a good worker. She saved my life, too, when she kept worrying at that mole on my leg that turned out to be a melanoma.' She bites her lip. 'I miss her very much and I know you shouldn't compare, but when I look at Trevor . . .'

'He's still a baby,' I say softly. I'm quite fond of him.

'It isn't that. I'm not a pushy parent, as such. I haven't got high expectations. He doesn't have to be

159

a genius, or even particularly clever, but I really don't think he's going to be able to carry out the simplest of tasks. The other day, I found him pulling the washing out of the basket and ripping it up. I'm not saying he's stupid. He's just very impulsive.'

I gaze at him – he's calmer now, looking at us with his soft eyes, all innocence, a young dog barely out of puppyhood who's just having fun. I wonder if it's a case of him being the wrong dog for Penny. Like humans, dogs have personalities and sometimes they clash, although I've always found her to be pretty laid back.

'When's he due to go off to the centre for training?'

'In four months' time, but Declan's worried that he'll have hurt me by then – not deliberately, but by accident. I have bruises all over my legs where he's knocked into me.' She lifts one trouser leg to show me her mottled shins. They are black and blue.

'Oh, that looks painful.'

'He wants me to give him up, but that would break my heart.' She shakes her head. 'I'm at the end of my tether, I don't know what to do.'

'I'm no expert. You can speak to one of the vets and have him referred to a behaviourist, or if you're prepared to wait until after his cast comes off, I could do some work with him.'

'Would you?' She brightens. 'I'd pay you for your time.'

'I'm not a qualified trainer,' I point out.

'He likes you and I know you wouldn't be mean to him. I'd be very grateful.'

'What about Declan?'

'I think as long as he knows that I'm giving Trevor

this one last chance, he'll go along with it.̄ I'll just have to wear lots of padding for a while.' She smiles. 'Thank you.'

'I'm flattered that she asked me, and worried that she's expecting too much,' I say to Ross later when I find him in Kennels, having a moment with Tripod. I have my trusty mop and bucket filled with hot suds. 'Why are you still here anyway? I thought you'd gone.'

'I'm in no rush.' Tripod purrs in his arms as he reverts to the subject of Trevor. 'When you lose an old dog, it can be a bit of a shock to the system taking on a puppy. I've seen it before.' He pauses and clears his throat. 'I was wondering if you fancied going out somewhere tonight, if you're at a loose end, that is.'

He seems uncharacteristically awkward, hesitant, but it's no big deal – my fantasies of falling into his arms remain just that, especially with his ex apparently still in the picture, and we've already agreed, albeit tentatively, that there'll be no dating, no relationship . . . yet my pulse beats a little faster and my bucket seems lighter in my hand.

'I'm sorry, I'm busy,' I say, disappointed.

'Never mind. It doesn't matter.' He shrugs. 'I forget that you have a social life.'

'It isn't that. I've promised Maz and Emma that I'd babysit.'

'Of course. They're going to a party. That's why they swapped the rota about. I'm on call with Izzy, but we could still have gone to the local, the Dog and Duck.'

'The Talymill Inn's a better class of hostelry,' I say brightly.

'I like a traditional pub where you can almost smell

161

the sawdust on the floor. Anyway, you can't go, so that's that. Another time.'

I gaze at him. He looks downcast and I wonder if he's lonely. I almost suggest he joins the WI as a joke, but decide against it. He doesn't seem to be in the mood for jokes.

'How about popping over for a drink as you're only next door? You can help me out. In fact, you can entertain George while I read to the twins, or vice versa. Or you can look after Henry and baby Olivia if they wake up.'

'I'd love to,' he says, looking more cheerful.

'Drop round any time after eight.'

'I will do, unless I'm called out. Thanks.'

'You might not be thanking me later. They're quite a handful.' I notice the way Tripod nuzzles up against his shoulder and smile to myself at my reaction, giving myself a stern telling-off for being jealous of a cat. Ross lets him down onto the floor and straightens up.

'I'll see you later,' he says with a smile.

Having checked with Maz that it's all right for him to help out with the babysitting, I return home to shower and change before I drive to Talyton Manor, leaving Mum preparing for a wedding the next day. Godfrey is supervising, wearing the apron he uses when making coffee, because he says it makes him feel like a barista. As I close the shop door, the bell jangling discordantly behind me, I feel as Ross must sometimes do: excluded. Godfrey has taken my place, helping my mum when she's under pressure from a deadline. I expect she'll be up all night – as I could be, I muse, depending on how the children behave and what time Maz and Emma get back.

When I reach the manor, I park in front of the stables, at which a pack of gun dogs, Labradors and spaniels, ambush my car, barking and jumping up. One runs across the bonnet as a nearly new four-by-four pulls up beside me and a man jumps out. He yells at them and shoos them away, at which they come running in to welcome him. It makes me chuckle. Why is it that vets have no control over their dogs?

Alex, dressed in mucky overalls and wellies, opens my door.

'Hi, how are you?' he asks as I get out. He's tall, and his hair is short and wavy, dark, yet turning to silver. He's handsome and pretty fit for his age, and I can see why Maz fell for him.

'Good, thank you.' I know he's a nice guy, but I still feel unnerved by him – a throwback, I think, from the way almost everyone used to treat the Fox-Gifford family with awe. They own half of the land around Talyton St George, have their own burial crypt in the church, and it would be an understatement to say that Alex's father was a difficult man.

'I hope you'll still be in one piece after an evening with our little monsters.'

'I'm sure we'll be fine,' I say as he growls at the dog that's taking a second run across the bonnet of my car.

'Off, Flossie.' She jumps down and promptly jumps back up again, but he doesn't apologise. 'You can see why they're called springers,' he grins. 'Come on in.'

I follow him across the yard, past a row of stables and a horsebox to the converted barn where he lives with his family. Inside, Maz looks up across the open-plan living area, from where she's loading the

163

dishwasher in her party dress, and George comes running over and throws himself into his father's arms, oblivious to the odour of cow that emanates from Alex's clothing.

'Daddy, Daddy!' he cries.

'I wish you'd leave your boots at the door,' Maz says. 'Emma will be here any minute and you know what she's like about the twins and germs.'

'A few friendly bacteria won't hurt them,' Alex laughs, but I notice that he returns to the front door and removes his overalls and wellies, before giving George a piggyback.

'Where have you been anyway?' Maz continues. 'We're going to be late as usual.'

'I was up at Barton Farm, helping Leo out with a calving.'

'Does he really need your assistance?'

'Lynsey offered us afternoon tea. It would have been rude to refuse.'

'Oh really, Alex. Here I am rushing around trying to get the children ready, tidy up and change, while you've been gossiping and eating cake.'

'And cottage pie.' He grins again as he lowers George to the floor, walks across to his wife and wraps his arms around her.

'Ugh, you stink,' she complains, but I notice she doesn't push him away, and I can tell he's forgiven. According to Frances, every woman over thirty has been in love with Alex at one time or another. Having divorced his first wife when she left him for a footballer, he fell for Maz when she moved here from London. They've been together ever since through various ups and downs, and I think it's very romantic that they're still so obviously in love.

'Let me have a quick shower,' Alex says, kissing her.

'Do hurry.' She glances past his shoulder out of the window. 'Emma's here and we're supposed to be at Matt and Nicci's for eight.'

'They're both medical. They understand.' Alex steps away and disappears off upstairs.

Maz looks at me with a rueful smile. 'He'll be asleep by nine, no doubt. Never marry a vet. They're too much trouble. I should have gone for an accountant, or a builder.'

'A builder!' I exclaim, thinking of DJ and his motley crew.

'Imagine having a husband who starts work at eight and finishes by four, or more often than not by midday. Anyway, thank you for agreeing to babysit. I don't like to leave them all with Sophia. She'd love to have them, but they're too much for her. Here are the instructions and the number for Nicci's landline in case there's no mobile signal.'

Emma brings the twins indoors, leaving her husband in the car. Lydia and Elena are wearing matching floral dresses, frilly socks and sandals. Lydia is clutching a book.

'I wonder if I can guess what we're going to be doing,' I say, greeting them.

'I'm sorry, I tried to persuade her to leave it at home.' Emma looks up as Alex comes down the stairs in a check shirt and dark trousers, his hair wet from the shower. 'You made it then,' she smiles. 'Ben and I are really looking forward to an evening out.'

'I'm not sure about bringing kids up on a diet of fairytales,' Alex observes. 'It's like feeding them false hope of the happy-ever-after.'

'You're such an old cynic,' Emma says.

'Less of the old, thank you.'

'Once upon a time, a handsome prince swept me off my feet,' Maz joins in.

'My mum read them to me and I turned out all right,' Emma says. 'I wish she'd been here to read to my little girls. She'd have been such a wonderful grandma.'

'She would,' Maz confirms softly. 'She was a lovely lady.'

It's another half an hour before the adults are off to their party, but I'm grateful because Maz manages to get the babies off to sleep in their cots upstairs, with the monitor set up so I can hear them snuffling about, and I'm left to entertain George and the twins who are very excited about having a sleepover. They're sharing a room – the barn is pretty crowded and I'm surprised that the Fox-Giffords don't move their growing brood into the manor house next door.

I make chocolate milkshakes for George, Lydia and Elena, and let them share the packet of biscuits Maz has left for them. It's a mistake, I suspect, because the sugar appears to go to their heads and they're off, running up and down. George is screaming like a cat with its tail caught in a door.

'Please calm down,' I beg them. 'You're frightening the mice.'

'What mice?' George stops in his tracks.

'I not like mice.' Lydia bursts into tears and her twin rushes up to comfort her.

'There aren't any,' I say quickly. 'It's just a saying.'

'So we can carry on playing.' George picks up a trolley of wooden bricks and tips them all over the floor.

My heart sinks. It's going to be one of those nights.

A loud rap at the door sends George running over to open it.

'Hello, Ross,' he says, letting him in. 'What are you doing here?'

'I've come to see you and Shannon.' Ross flashes me a smile. 'I can hear you from the manor.'

'Please, will you play crocodiles with me? The twins don't like that game.'

'I'd love to – let's have a go at sleeping crocodiles. You have to lie down very quietly and pretend to be a crocodile waiting to attack.'

'Okay,' George says. 'You have to lie down too.'

'I can do that,' Ross says, looking around for somewhere comfortable. 'Why don't you take the fluffy rug over there while I have the sofa?'

'Can I get you a drink?' I ask.

'I'm all right, thanks. I'm on call so I don't know how long I'll be able to stay.'

I notice how the twins join George on the mat, not wanting to miss out, and Ross stretches out on the sofa with his hands behind his head and his feet over the arm.

'What are you doing tomorrow?' I ask him as I clear up the dirty glasses. 'We could go to the beach for a swim, unless you have other plans.'

'Are you sure? The last time I swam in the sea was in Thailand.'

'I can't promise you crystal-clear waters, but I can give you a lift.'

'I was going out on the bike to meet a mate of mine, but he's in hospital with suspected appendicitis, so he won't be going very far. That would be great, if you don't mind me tagging along – I don't really want to be on my own tomorrow.'

'I'll pick you up from the manor in the morning. I'll text you a time.'

'Thanks, I really appreciate it.'

'Stop talking,' George moans. 'You're spoiling the game. Crocodiles can't talk.'

Ross falls silent for a few minutes, but he can't do quiet for long.

'Sometimes I play this game with my nephew,' he begins.

'I'm not playing this game any more,' George pipes up. 'It's boring.'

'I've got a couple of games on my phone,' Ross says, sitting up, and soon he's surrounded, showing them his fancy mobile, which occupies them for a good twenty minutes.

'I'm thinking of subcontracting the babysitting to you,' I say. 'You're a natural.' However, it doesn't last because he's called out to the surgery to see a farm dog suspected to have eaten rat poison.

He wishes us all a goodnight and I watch him from the window, walking across the yard under the moonlight, back to the manor to pick up his helmet and leathers.

'Please don't wake the babies,' I breathe as his motorbike roars out of the yard. I listen for a moment after he's gone. There is a god after all, I think, as the monitor continues to transmit the sound of contented snuffles and snores. I persuade George and the twins to change into their pyjamas in return for a story.

'Just the one,' I remind them as the twins and I settle on the double airbed on the floor, Elena on one side and Lydia on the other, while George bounces on his bed.

'Again,' Lydia says, and somewhere during the third or fourth reading, when Snow White eats the poisoned apple and succumbs to a deep sleep, the twins do too, and George and I stay up chatting and playing robots versus crocodiles until his parents return home. I enjoyed the evening, but I can't help feeling that I would have had much more fun if Ross could have stayed for longer.

Chapter Ten

Life's a Beach

I have yet to find my handsome prince, but my mum has found hers; the next morning, he is knocking on the bathroom door.

'Are you going to be in there much longer?'

'Five minutes,' I say.

'As long as that? I'm in a bit of a rush. I have things to see, people to do,' he adds jovially. 'And I could do with availing myself of the facilities with some urgency before I leave the building.'

'Oh, all right.' Sometimes I wonder if Godfrey's bathroom demands are part of a campaign to persuade me to move out. I grab my toothbrush and paste and go to the kitchen to clean my teeth before picking up my bag and leaving for the manor. Ross is waiting for me there at the bottom of the drive. I suppose I was expecting to see him in his scrubs or leather jacket, but he looks different, dressed in a grey, zip-up sweat top, cargo shorts and leather sandals – cool ones, like a surfer-dude would wear.

'Hi,' I say, lowering the window. 'I almost didn't recognise you.'

'Thanks for the lift.' He smiles as he gets into the car and throws a small rucksack onto the back seat. 'Sophia has linseed and barley simmering on the range again, there's some filthy horse rug in the washing machine, and I found a dead mouse in my shoe – *after* I put my foot in it. I couldn't wait to get away.'

'I know the feeling. I know he can't help it, but I really don't think I can accommodate Godfrey and his prostate for much longer. He's driving me mad.' I glance towards Ross as he settles beside me. He seems to be in a hurry, as usual, just like he is at work. I think we're going to have an interesting day.

'How was the babysitting after I left?' he asks.

'It was fun – I've learned Snow White off by heart.' I smile. 'Did you have a busy night?'

'I readmitted the rabbit that Maz operated on a couple of days ago, the one with the abscess. It's a bit of a worry really. Izzy's hand-feeding him and I've given him some drugs to try to get his gut moving, but you know what rabbits are like. They're always sicker than they look.'

'I hope he'll be okay.' I grind the gears by mistake. I'm not sure why, but the situation is making me nervous. What if we haven't got anything left to talk about?

'I'll feel bad if he pops his clogs, but it's Maz's problem – she's working today and I'm going to enjoy my time off.' He gazes out of the window. 'Let's get going while the sun's still shining.'

Although it's the last weekend in June and another three weeks until the schools break up for summer, the road to Talysands is jammed up with holiday traffic and we have no choice but to sit behind a caravan travelling at about ten miles an hour for most of the journey. Ross fiddles with the radio to find some music and then sits, drumming his fingers on the dashboard.

'By the time we get there it'll be time to come back.'

'It's early yet and the beach doesn't close.' I glance at him. The muscle in the side of his cheek is twitching. I start to feel a little irritated.

'Why do people think it's necessary to drag caravans around with them when they go away?' he blurts out. 'I don't understand. They don't need all that gear with them.'

'There's nothing wrong with a caravan holiday. You can go wherever you want.'

'What, in this traffic?' he exclaims. 'If I had my bike, I could drive straight past all this lot.'

'Tell you what,' I say. 'Why don't I just drop you back at the manor and you can do just that?'

'Are you telling me to get on my bike?' I can hear the hint of a smile in his voice.

'Yes, I suppose I am.' The caravan in front stops altogether. I put the handbrake on and turn to my passenger. 'We're stuck in a traffic jam. So what? We have the whole day ahead of us. Just chill, will you? It's exhausting.'

A shadow crosses his eyes. 'I'm sorry. I didn't realise I was being an—'

'Well, you are,' I cut in. 'Anybody would think you were still at work.'

'Okay, point taken.'

'You really need to learn to relax.'

'Are you offering to teach me?' The sound of

hooting breaks into my consciousness and a grinning Ross gives me a nudge. 'Move on, Shannon. You're holding up the traffic now.'

Flushing, I let the handbrake off and put the car in gear but, as I make to drive away, the engine stalls. I restart it, inwardly thanking him for not making some cheeky comment about my driving, and continue in the slow-moving queue down the hill to the resort. At the bottom I turn off and drive under the railway bridge, past the amusement arcade and shops selling brightly coloured buckets and spades, windbreaks and body-boards. Ross opens a window and rests his hand on the roof of the car, letting in the scent of the sea mingled with fresh doughnuts and chips, while we look for a parking space.

'There's one,' he says.

'I won't fit in there.' I drive on past the rows of cars with sunlight glinting from their bonnets, looking for what I consider to be a wide enough gap – I haven't the best sense of spatial awareness when it comes to parking. Eventually, I find a space near the dunes where the heat is shimmering from the tarmac. Ross grabs his rucksack; I pick up my bag and lock up. When I look up, my companion is striding across the slatted wood pathway through the sand and spiky clumps of marram grass. He turns and shades his eyes.

'Are you coming or not?' he calls.

'I thought we might have a coffee . . .'

'Let's swim first. We can have coffee any time. Let's not waste a minute.' His voice fades as he looks out to sea, and I wonder if something is bothering him. It's as if he's trying too hard to have fun. 'I thought you loved swimming.'

'I do,' I say, and I join him to walk through the

173

dunes, across the promenade and down the steep stone steps to the beach. I take off my canvas shoes while he sets up his territory among the encampments of sun-tents, windbreaks and deckchairs, with his rucksack and towel, fitting us in between what appears to be a focus group of three adults debating how best to build a sandcastle, and a couple lying side by side on sunbeds, reading ebooks.

'Come on. What are you waiting for? Get your kit off.' I avert my gaze as Ross strips down to his shorts. 'What's wrong?' he adds.

'Nothing,' I respond. Feeling shy I turn away to slip out of my T-shirt and skirt, revealing my black Lycra go-faster costume beneath. When I turn back, I'm grateful to find that Ross is already down at the water's edge, where the waves are gently caressing the sand. The sun is shining and the sea is calm and blue, giving the illusion of a tropical beach – but this is the Devon coast.

'That's going to be cold,' I observe as I reach his side, a flock of goose bumps leaping to attention across my skin.

'Imagine it's a hot bath. That works for me.'

'You must have a very good imagination.' I sense the lightest touch on my wrist and the brush of his fingers as he gently takes me by the hand. With a tiny shiver of surprise and uncertainty, I turn to face him.

'Hey, you're as jumpy as a rabbit.'

'I'll be all right once I'm in. It's the thought of it.' I take the first step with him, wincing as the water swirls around my ankles. 'I told you,' I exclaim, trying to resist as he steps behind me, places his hands on my hips and drives me towards the breakers where the next wave breaks across my knees.

'It's freezing,' I gasp, but I'm laughing at the same time, enjoying the pressure of his fingers against my flesh. Another wave breaks over my hips, pushing me back against his body as his arms wrap around my waist and carry me kicking and screaming into the deeper water. He lets me go, laughing with me.

'You see, it isn't so bad when you don't faff around,' he says.

I drop my shoulders under the surface and dip my head, breathing out bubbles of joy as I re-emerge with water up my nose and salt on my lips.

'Last one to the rocks buys the ice creams.' I dive and resurface a couple of lengths ahead, listening to him coughing and spluttering. I roll onto my back and call back, 'You aren't supposed to drink it.'

'I'm going to get you . . .'

'Catch me if you can!' I swim crawl, pacing myself so that I reach the rocks, a sandy red outcrop adorned with a wig of seaweed near the cliffs at the west side of the bay, with scarcely any change to my breathing. I skirt the edge, finding a suitable place to scramble out, scraping my feet on the barnacles and limpets on the way to the top, where I sit on a patch of sun-warmed stone, looking down at Ross who's clambering up the slope to join me. 'The ice creams are on you!'

I watch the rapid rise and fall of his chest and the water glistening as it trickles down his broad chest and the slabs of his six-pack. He bends his neck and shakes his head, scattering silver droplets from his hair like a dog.

'How do you do that?' He sits down beside me. 'You're like a fish.'

'It's taken hours of practice. If you work out the

number of miles I've done in the pool, I've probably been to the moon and back.'

Our thighs are almost touching, driven together by the contours of the rock, so close that I can feel the heat radiating from his skin as we dry off in the sun.

'This is such a beautiful place. It reminds you how lucky you are to be alive.' All I can hear is his breathing, my pulse and the waves lapping at the rocks as I wait for him to continue speaking.

'What's wrong?' I ask him eventually. 'You don't seem your usual self.'

'I'm okay . . .'

'If you don't mind me saying, you don't sound convinced.'

'I'm sorry. I shouldn't have inflicted myself on you today. I should have gone out on the bike, taken myself off somewhere.'

'Oh, Ross, what is it?'

'I lost my best friend two years ago today.'

'I'm so sorry.' I pause, wondering if he wants to talk about it.

'My friend, Zac . . .' He struggles to utter his name. 'We were out riding our bikes – the weather was like this, and we were out exploring with plans to meet Heidi and his fiancée, Luisa, for a pub lunch.'

I feel sick for him. I can kind of guess where this is going.

'We might – or might not – have been going too fast, I'm not sure,' he goes on. 'I remember this long winding road without much traffic. We overtook a couple of cars, slowed down through a village – I can still see the sign someone had set up by the pond, saying "Drive Careful, Ducks".' His voice grows harsh as he continues, 'As we left, we sped up – it's all part of the fun, and Zac had the better bike at the time, and he was just ahead of me, that's when I think we touched the speed limit. I pulled back, but he kept accelerating up the hill and around the next bend . . .

'I was just close enough to see the lorry pull out in front of him. The bike went underneath, he came off and was flung across the road onto the verge. He survived the impact and, who knows, he might still be here today – he would have been – if a driver who drew up to help hadn't made a terrible mistake, completely misjudging the situation. There was no reason for anyone to interfere. He was complaining of pins and needles in his leg, and some aches and pains, and the ambulance was on its way, but this idiot – he said he was a first-aider at work, but it turned out he hadn't kept his qualification up to date and, of course, he'd had no preparation for dealing with the aftermath of an RTA.'

He means a road traffic accident.

'I told him to sit with him and not let him move while I checked on the lorry driver – I thought he was having a heart attack from the shock. He was in a right state, even though it wasn't his fault. He'd been delivering grain to a local farm, checked both ways as he pulled out of the drive, but hadn't seen the bike until it was too late. I called for a second ambulance and, when I looked round, the car driver was removing Zac's helmet.' Ross swears under his breath. 'I could have punched him. When I tackled him, he said Zac had been panicking, that he couldn't breathe.'

'I can understand why he did it.' Resuscitation starts with the ABC, airway, breathing and circulation. 'If he wasn't getting enough oxygen . . .'

'Zac had broken his neck, and the act of taking off

his helmet displaced the bones and damaged his spinal cord. He was paralysed.'

'That's terrible.' I don't know what to say. I'm still pretty sure that I'd have done the same thing as the driver, given the situation.

'He died from pneumonia three months later. I saw him every day, but I felt so impotent and useless not being able to do anything. He had no movement from the neck down, and little feeling. He would never walk again, never make love or ride a bike . . . He wanted me . . . he asked me about euthanasia.' Ross gazes at me, his eyes glazed with tears. Quickly, he brushes them away. 'It's the salt,' he mutters.

I reach out and rest my hand on his shoulder as he continues, 'I couldn't do it, of course, which makes me a coward. I do it every day for my patients, but I couldn't do the one thing Zac wanted, to put him out of his misery.

'I bet you wish you hadn't asked me along today. I'm spoiling it for you.'

'Not at all. It's fine.' I'm touched that he feels he can talk to me about it and reveal the man behind the mask of relentless action, impatience and humour, one who is capable of expressing regret and heartache – and love.

'Thank you,' he says, recovering himself. 'He was my best friend, we'd been to school together, moto-cross; even went to the same university, although he was doing a different course. I wish I could have helped him at the end.'

'How can you bring yourself to ride a motorbike after that?' I ask. 'No, you don't have to answer that. Don't talk about it if you don't want to.'

'It's all right. I'm beginning to feel that I could talk

to you about anything.' He catches my wrist and gives it a quick squeeze. 'It wasn't the bike's fault. I know it's a cliché, but the accident reinforced my belief in living each day as if it's your last. I promised Zac I wouldn't give up motorbikes. If I woke up paralysed from the neck down, would I look back on a life lived the way I wanted, that I was proud of, or would I wish I'd done things differently?

'I began to question everything I was doing: working for my parents; planning to marry Heidi; buying a house.'

'Is that why you left the family practice? I've been wondering.'

'It's part of it. My dad went ballistic when I was back on the bike for Zac's send-off, but it got worse. Earlier this year, I found him in a clinch with the head nurse. I'd suspected him of having an affair for a while . . .' He swears. 'He was living and working with my mum, taking her on holiday and holding dinner parties for their friends, yet behind the scenes he was having it away with a woman twenty years younger than him.'

'What did you do?'

'I was completely torn. I didn't know whether to keep my mouth shut so Mum didn't get hurt, or whether to risk getting the blame for telling her and breaking up their marriage. I hate cheats and liars so I gave my father an ultimatum. He couldn't bring himself to say anything, so I did.' He grimaces. 'As you can imagine, I wasn't very popular. Mum was devastated and my father was furious with me. He dumped the nurse and made a show of getting the marriage back on track, but it was too late. The damage was done. At the moment, my parents are in the process of divorcing. Dad's back with his fancy woman and I'm here, getting away from it all.'

'It wasn't your fault. You can't blame yourself.'

'I think they would have stayed together if I hadn't said anything. I reckon my mother knew all along and chose to ignore it out of convenience, or misplaced loyalty, or for the sake of the practice, I'm not sure. Anyway, I'm *persona non grata* and I don't want to be involved in the fall-out.'

'Do you think you'll ever go back?'

He shakes his head. 'My father is hoping to buy my mother out so she can take her share in the value of the practice and go and work part-time for a friend. I've lost all respect for him. I used to think the sun shone out of his behind. I was going to work with him and take over the business when my parents retired, cruising off into the sunset, or buying a house in the country or whatever they chose to do.'

'What's he like?' I ask, thinking about my dad. I can remember his smile, his smell and the way he used to sweep me off my feet and spin me around until I was giddy with laughter.

'He's a clever man and a good vet; conventional, predictable . . . some might describe him as boring. He's quite controlling too – I guess that's why I rebelled.' Ross gazes at me, his expression gentle. 'How about your dad? You've never talked about him.' He clears his throat. 'Frances told me what happened: I'm very sorry. It must have been incredibly traumatic.'

'It was a terrible shock. I was eight years old. I was at school – I remember it as if it was yesterday – it was lunchtime, and my gran came to take me to the hospital, but it was too late. He'd already passed away.' A lump catches in my throat. 'Mum told me he'd fallen asleep, which left me hoping he'd come back one day. It wasn't until a couple of weeks later that she and Gran found the strength to explain that he'd died from bleeding into the brain. He had an aneurysm which could have blown at any time – it waited until he was forty.'

'What did he do?'

'He worked hard. He was a spark, an electrician, and when he wasn't rewiring houses, he helped Mum out in the shop and walked me to school. We'd stop at the newsagent and buy sweets – he'd joke around and say we'd have to eat them so Mum didn't find out because she didn't want him spoiling me. He used to bring me to the beach and we'd take shells home so we could listen to the sea.' I smile. 'That's what he used to say, anyway.' I stare down at the water and Ross takes my hand to comfort me.

'Shall we go back?' he suggests after a few minutes' silence, and we swim back to the shore. I beat him to our patch of beach and throw myself onto my towel to watch him walk out from the sea with his wet cotton shorts clinging to his masculine contours. His hair and skin glisten. His muscles are defined and his belly is taut, with a line of dark hair and the tail of the eagle tattoo diving down beneath the waist of his trunks. He has an air of confidence, but not arrogance, and he doesn't realise how hot he is, I muse – an attractive and rare trait in the male of the species, in my experience.

'You mentioned Godfrey and his prostate earlier,' he begins as we settle down to dry in the sun.

'Don't.' I pause. 'I shouldn't mock him, should I? One day that could be me.'

'Um, Shannon, you did do anatomy at college?

Only, unless I'm very much mistaken, you don't and never will have a prostate.' He looks at me appreciatively. 'You're very definitely feminine.'

I can't help giggling at his comment. 'You know what I mean though, that I will eventually get old and be struck down by some inconvenient affliction. I wouldn't like to be talked about like that behind my back. It isn't his fault, but it isn't just that. It's his scintillating conversation at breakfast – I'm being ironic, in case you hadn't noticed – and the way he and Mum are forever checking out each other's tonsils. It's so awkward. I mean, neither of them are spring chickens.'

'There's life in the old dog yet,' Ross grins. 'It's reassuring to know that desire and lust don't wear off with age.'

'It shows no sign of fading anytime soon. In fact, I'm seriously thinking of finding my own place. It's about time,' I add wryly. 'I've never lived anywhere else.'

'Never?' He whistles through his teeth.

'There's never been any reason to. And I suppose with losing my dad and Mum getting ill with bouts of depression, and then being diagnosed with diabetes, I've felt responsible for keeping an eye on her. It's only recently that she's started muttering about me moving out. I feel a bit hurt that she doesn't really want me there any more.

'It's been just the two of us for as long as I can remember. I didn't go away to university or anything, and I did my training on day-release, so there was no need to move.' I pause to pick up a handful of sand and let it trickle through my fingers. 'I was this –' I hold my forefinger and thumb a couple of centimetres apart to demonstrate – 'close to leaving once, and I'm ashamed to say I would have walked out, leaving a note, because I couldn't bring myself to tell Mum to her face.'

'Was that when you almost ran off with the locum? Frances told me all about that as well,' he goes on when I don't respond.

'It was a long time ago. Drew was a lying bastard – it was a good thing I found out before it was too late. I had a lucky escape.' I smile. I can talk about it now. 'After that, there were occasions when I could have moved out, like when my friend, Taylor, bought a house. I could have shared with her, but it didn't happen. Mum has diabetes – she has these hypo attacks and they come on so quickly that she doesn't realise until too late that she needs sugar. I've found her collapsed and semi-comatose more than once.' I shudder at the memory. 'It's really scary.'

'Does she still have these attacks?'

'She's been much better recently. She controls the diabetes much more tightly, and Seven's been a life-saver, literally. If her blood sugar falls, he's right there.'

'Wow, that's amazing. Did you have him specially trained?'

'He did it all himself. Of course, I still worry that he might miss something, but he's been one hundred per cent reliable so far.'

'So you can move out now? And you'd leave Seven with your mother and Godfrey?'

I nod.

'Perhaps we should look for somewhere together.'

'You are joking?' I say slowly.

'Why not? It was a light-hearted suggestion,' he

continues, 'but the more I think about it, the more it makes sense. I want to move out of the manor before I grow hooves and start neighing, and you need to get away from Godfrey and the prostate. We can find somewhere with two bedrooms and share the bills. I'm being serious. I don't want to buy my own place – I'm not ready to put down roots. I'd rather rent for a while, find a place with a garden so I can still have Bart to stay at weekends . . .'

'Oh? You mean you're thinking of leaving us?' I feel a stab of disappointment at the idea that he might move away just as I've got used to him being around.

'I'm not going anywhere. I like it here. Devon holds a lot of attractions.' I feel his eyes on me and my skin tingles in the heat of his gaze. 'Any more questions?'

'What would people think? Your ex, for example?' I clear my throat. 'I don't believe it would help your case if you have some inkling that you might get back together in the future.'

'I have no intention of doing that.' His eyes narrow. 'What gave you that idea?'

'Heidi gave me the impression that you might try again. Actually, it was more than an impression. She told me.'

'I can't imagine why. She must have been having a moment,' he says dismissively.

'With reason, I suspect. She hinted that you still hooked up now and again.'

'In her dreams. We shared a room when she came to stay, but that was only because it's about the only one that's still habitable.'

I'm not sure I believe him.

'Who cares what anyone thinks?' he goes on. 'It's

nobody's business except ours; if it doesn't work out, neither of us has lost anything.'

'It could be fun. I'd love to see the look on my mum's face if I told her we were moving in together.' I think for a moment. 'We have more in common than I imagined when I first met you.'

'Not difficult, considering you thought I was a courier in the beginning.'

'We'd have to decide on some house rules,' I go on.

'No way. As you know, I don't like rules – as far as I'm concerned they're only there to be broken so I don't think we should bother.' He pauses. 'So, shall we do it?'

'I'm not sure . . .'

'You seem shocked.'

'It's a bit of a surprise, that's all. I've only known you for three weeks.'

'Some people get married in less.' Ross looks at me through a fringe of damp curls. 'Your face! Don't worry, this is a purely platonic arrangement. We get along well – at least I think we do. We'll make good housemates.' He gives me a wicked grin. 'At least I know the floors would always be spotless.'

'Ross!' I flick the end of the towel at him.

'I thought it might help you out, knowing your situation.' Chuckling, he holds out his hand. 'Shake on it?' I take his hand and shake it. He holds on to my fingers for a fraction longer than necessary, his skin grazing mine as he withdraws. I gaze at him, losing myself in the depths of his brown eyes, and suddenly what seemed like the perfect plan feels like it could be One Big Mistake. Working and living together in the same house? I stir up the sand between my toes.

'If you feel homesick,' he says, perhaps misinter-preting my silence, 'I'll remind you of Godfrey and his prostate. Let's not waste time. We'll ask him to find us a nice place to rent. '

'Straight away?'

'Why not? I'm a man of action.' Ross leans back and closes his eyes and, just as I'm about to remind him about the ice cream he owes me, his mouth opens slightly and his breathing deepens; within seconds, he's fast asleep.

I sit back and stare towards the horizon, listening to the cries of the sea birds overhead. What on earth have I done?

Later, we pack up and stroll along to the beachfront café for chips and ice cream. We sit side by side at a table inside to avoid the dive-bombing gulls and chat about our plans for our new home.

'So what kind of house would you choose to live in?' Ross asks.

'A castle at the very least.' I smile as I dip the end of a chip into tomato ketchup. I notice how Ross has picked mayonnaise.

'Is that one with a moat or without?' He chuckles. 'It sounds too draughty for me.'

'How about a thatched cottage with roses around the door?'

'That old cliché,' he sighs.

'I wouldn't like to live in a modern house, unless we absolutely had to. Mind you, I'm not sure I can afford to be fussy. We'll have to agree on a budget.'

'Oh, that's too boring. Let's not worry about money.'

'It's important to me,' I say firmly.

'I'm sorry.' He reaches out and touches my hand.

'I shouldn't be flippant. It's just that I'm really excited about this. I can't wait to leave the manor – I never thought I'd say that – and move in with someone who isn't completely bats. I'm looking forward to being able to have friends to stay – if you don't mind, that is.'

'Of course I don't mind. I'd like to meet them.'

'And then there's Bart. We'll need somewhere suitable for a big dog so he can spend weekends with us. It's pretty well impossible for me to have him at the manor with the Fox-Giffords' dogs. I've tried, but he hates them.'

'They are rather overwhelming,' I agree.

Ross picks up the salt cellar from the table and tips it up. Nothing comes out, so he taps it and gives it a shake. Still nothing. He unscrews the lid and tilts the container; a few grains fall and the rest come tumbling out onto the remains of his chips. He swears lightly.

'Have some of mine,' I offer. 'We're going to have to get used to sharing,' I add when he hesitates. 'Go on. There are too many here for me.'

We move on to ice cream afterwards. I have mint choc chip and Ross has raspberry ripple before we walk along the seafront and back before making a move.

'So, do you want to speak to Godfrey, or shall I?' Ross asks as I'm driving back to Talyton Manor. 'I don't want to hang about. The sooner we get the ball rolling, the better.'

'I'll talk to him tonight. I'll explain what we're looking for: somewhere close to the practice with two or more bedrooms and a large garden for the dog.'

'Haven't you forgotten something?'

'I don't think so.'

'Off-street parking for the bike, preferably under cover.'

I didn't remember the bike, I think, recalling how he talked of the tragic loss of his friend. He seems more cheerful now, as if the day out has done him good.

As the sun begins to set, I pull in to the drive leading to the manor.

'You can leave me here,' Ross says. 'I'll walk the rest of the way.'

'If you're sure.'

'You don't have to hang around. You've done enough today. I really appreciate it, Shannon. Thank you.' He leans across and kisses me on the cheek. 'That was platonic, by the way,' he adds with a grin on his face.

'Goodnight,' I say, wondering why it didn't exactly feel that way. 'See you soon, housemate.'

When I return home, I find Mum with her feet up and Seven lying on the sofa beside her with all four paws in the air, and Godfrey in the kitchen, washing the dishes.

Mum looks up from a bridal magazine and smiles. 'Have you had a good day?'

'Great, thanks. Ross and I have been talking and we've decided we're going to be housemates.'

She frowns. 'Isn't he still living up at Talyton Manor?'

'It was supposed to be a temporary measure, a stopgap while he got to know the area, but he's had enough of it now and this is the perfect solution. This place is too small for the four of us – or should I say five, including the prostate? This means you and Godfrey can have your own space.'

'I have to confess this is a bit of a shock,' she says eventually. 'You said there was nothing going on between the two of you and now you're moving in with him.' She can hardly criticise, seeing how quickly she and Godfrey moved in together. 'Have I missed something?

'We're friends, that's all,' I insist.

'Sure,' Mum snorts sarcastically. 'There must be more to it than that. Did he ask you or did you ask him?'

'It doesn't matter. We're going to have separate bedrooms and all that.'

'I think you're completely barking if you really believe that you can work with him, live with him and be "just friends".'

'We've agreed that it's a platonic arrangement.'

'Wonderful. What could go wrong? Sometimes, you can be very naïve. Ross is charming, charismatic . . . and very attractive, and if I were twenty years younger—'

'I'm not sure I like the idea that you have a secret crush on my new housemate.'

'Perhaps it's best not to mention that to Godfrey.' She giggles before growing serious again. 'Why does Ross want to share? You have to ask yourself that question, when it's patently obvious that he can afford to buy or rent his own house on a vet's salary. Do you think he's gay?'

'I don't see how that has any relevance, but he definitely isn't gay.'

'In that case, does he want you there to wash his socks and iron his pants? Or both.'

'Is this a reference to the fact that Godfrey will insist on leaving the ironing board out so you can iron his boxers?'

'I don't do any laundry for him. He does it himself.' She sighs. 'All I'm saying is, be careful. I know you – you're very good at hiding your true feelings. If you're harbouring hopes that you and Ross might get together, this won't help if he doesn't feel the same way, and vice versa.'

'But I'm not. He is good-looking, kind, funny—'

'There you go then,' Mum cuts in as I list his attributes. 'He's perfect boyfriend material.'

'He's also impatient, a little sharp at times, can be inconsiderate, and I suspect he still has feelings for his ex. I think those are more than enough reasons to prove that he isn't.'

'When you put it like that,' Mum agrees.

Later, Godfrey comes to find me. 'I hope you aren't moving out on my account,' he says.

'It isn't you,' I say, amused that I find myself unable to hurt his feelings. 'I've been thinking of moving out for a while now, and it feels like the right time.'

'If you're sure.' I nod and his face lights up. 'In that case, I can help you find a suitable property. Give me a list of your requirements and I'll be onto it straight away.'

I thank him.

'Move in in haste, repent at leisure,' Mum reminds me, and I wonder if she's regretting her situation, but when I see her and Godfrey sidling off upstairs to the bedroom, I doubt it very much. I also begin to doubt myself. Can friends of the opposite sex really live together and remain just good friends?

Chapter Eleven

The Home Front

During the week, we have several more conversations about what kind of home we are looking for. We go out for another drink one evening – at the Talymill Inn this time – and have a couple of quiet nights on call. I swim just once. Mitch isn't at the pool, and when Gemma tells me he's changed his shift to mornings, I can't help wondering if he's done it to avoid me. I try phoning him, but the call goes to voicemail. I don't leave a message. I'm sorry that our friendship – or whatever it was – has ended this way, but I did the right thing. I no longer feel as if I'm living in limbo. Life is exciting, sometimes challenging, but I'm loving it.

The prospect of choosing a place to live with Ross occupies my thoughts. Neither of us wishes to delay the move any longer than necessary, so on the following Saturday morning, we're all set to go house-hunting. I've been out for a walk with Seven and I'm finishing my toast in the kitchen, while Godfrey, dressed in one of his linen suits, prepares himself an espresso from the machine, which hisses and blows steam into his face.

'Today, I'm showing you three properties. They're very different, but I'm sure you'll love them all.' He removes his glasses, breathes on the lenses, and wipes them with the end of his bright red tie. At the sound of a motorbike, he cocks his head. 'Shall we go?'

He drains his coffee cup and we head through the shop to meet Ross at the front.

Tucking his helmet under his arm and unzipping his leather jacket, he shakes Godfrey's hand, but his eyes are on me.

'Hi, Ross. I couldn't sleep,' I say. 'You probably think I'm mad, but I'm so excited. This is a new experience for me.'

He chuckles. 'I'd reserve some of your enthusiasm for moving in with me until after the first couple of weeks when you're complaining about the bike magazines and gear all over the place.'

'Oh no, it's going to be fun. I can't wait.'

'We'll see. Can I leave my bike out there?'

I gaze out of the window, past the twisted hazel Mum has used to dress the display. It's market day and Jennie is already setting up her cake stall in the square, unfurling the stripy pink and white canvas surround and fixing it to the frame. One of her daughters is with her, unloading boxes of freshly baked muffins and fairy-cakes from the boot of a four-by-four. I wonder briefly how Lucky is.

'It would be best to bring it around the back,' I suggest. 'If you go left and left again, there's a drive-way where you can park behind the shop.'

He thanks me and disappears, returning a few minutes later, and we head out in Godfrey's car with Ross in the front and me in the back.

'I can't persuade you to reconsider buying rather than renting?' Godfrey negotiates his way through the preparations for the market, narrowly avoiding a crate of eggs and a small queue at the hot drinks stand. I press myself back against the seat, checking I've fastened the seatbelt as he waves one arm and swerves away from the pavement to avoid Mrs Dyer and Nero, who appears to have his eye on the pet-food stall. 'Don't forget about the potential investment opportunity. You can buy, save through a mortgage and sell later for a profit. Simples.'

I wish he wouldn't say that – his attempt to be down with the youngsters sounds lamer than a three-legged donkey.

'As I've said before, I'm not ready to put down roots,' Ross says.

'You can easily let the place out if you decided to move on, and buy another property. I've never met a poor vet.'

'I could buy a place, but I don't want any complications. Keep it simple: that's my motto. I don't want to be tied down to anything longer than a twelve-month lease to begin with, then Shannon and I will decide whether or not we want to make it a more permanent arrangement.' He turns round and winks at me. He has to be kidding. 'Thanks for doing this when Saturday must be your busiest day.'

'I try my best to be accommodating as only an estate agent can.' Godfrey laughs at his own joke.

'Where are we going?' I ask.

'We've arrived,' he says, and he pulls into the road that leads into the new estate, not far from Emma's old house and almost opposite Taylor's.

'I thought we'd said no to this one.' I look out at a terrace of modern houses, but Godfrey's already out of the car and holding the door open for me.

'It's the one on the end. I know this doesn't quite fit the brief, but I'd like you to be open-minded because this is about location and price. There are two bedrooms and two bathrooms, one en-suite on the first floor, and a large kitchen/diner and snug living room downstairs. It's well presented and has a garden suitable for a dog.'

Ross whistles through his teeth as he looks out onto the patch of lawn at the side. 'I don't think there's room for Bart's body and tail at the same time.'

'It is a little – what shall we call it? – bijou, but it's small and perfectly formed.'

Spare me the clichés, I think, smiling to myself.

'Bijou,' says Ross. 'That's the name of a Siamese cat I treated for lily poisoning. There's one big drawback to this house – there's no room for the bike. I can't possibly live here.'

'There's plenty of space on the drive.' Godfrey waves his arm expansively, as though gesturing across acres of parkland, not a couple of square metres of tarmac.

'I did tell you we needed off-street parking.'

'I wish you could be a little more open-minded. Think of the alternatives. You can leave the bike at your place of work and walk here.'

'No, no, she'll get nicked or vandalised.'

'There's very little crime in Talyton St George. I think you're being very pessimistic.'

'Godfrey, this one isn't for us,' I say firmly. 'Let's move on.'

'Don't dismiss it out of hand.' He puts the key into the lock on the front door. 'At least, have a look around. The interior boasts a good number of electrical sockets.'

'I don't need to see inside, especially if that's all you can say about it.' Ross turns to me. 'Do you, Shannon?'

'Not if you don't like it,' I concede, wondering how I can have become so hypocritical in my old age. When I was a teenager, I objected to the new estate – I actually protested with my friends at the desecration of an open field – but now I'm considering living here.

'You like it?'

'It isn't bad. I could live here.' I could live anywhere if it meant not living with Godfrey. 'It's close to town and Taylor is just around the corner. I know we discussed what we wanted, but it isn't going to be that easy to find.'

'That is music to an estate agent's ears. It's a real benefit being able to be flexible in your requirements and expectations. It isn't everyone who can see the potential in a property.' Godfrey stares at Ross, who looks in through the downstairs window.

'It's still a no. You couldn't swing a hamster in there.'

'I hope you don't change your mind – a property like this will always be in high demand, and they don't come along very often.'

'A bit like the buses in Talyton St George. Mrs Wall was telling me how the bus company's cutting the number from three to one a day. Soon, you'll be able to leave town, but never come back. I offered her a ride on the back of the bike, but she declined.' Ross grins. 'It's probably a good thing – I wouldn't like to be responsible for scaring her to death . . . I really don't like this house. It's just a box. It's boring.'

'So it's absolutely, definitively and decidedly a no. Never you mind,' Godfrey pats Ross on the back, 'there's more to see. Let's move on to the next property, a spacious end-of-terrace in a prestigious address, ultra-convenient for all the local amenities.'

We get back in the car and Godfrey drives us back through town, pulling up outside the church, a massive gothic-looking building built from grey stone, covered with gargoyles like rabid dogs, with bulging eyes and lips drawn back to reveal their teeth. The graveyard surrounding it is bordered with an iron railing and dark green yew trees, underneath which nothing grows. I know the names of the ancient families of Talyton St George etched into the gravestones by heart.

'It's that one, number one.'

'Oh no,' I say quickly. 'I couldn't.'

'That's almost next door to Frances,' Ross says. 'She lives at number three.'

'So you know you have friendly and responsible neighbours, willing to help you out if you need them,' Godfrey says, putting a positive spin on the situation.

'And when you don't,' Ross adds.

'The house is of a good size and spread over three floors.' Godfrey gets out of the car.

'Are you coming, Shannon?' Ross asks when I hesitate. The biggest bell in the tower tolls the hour: ten booming strikes.

'I'm not sure.'

'What's wrong?' He grins. 'Are you worried about the other neighbours, the ones across the road?'

I don't know why, but a wave of sadness suddenly hits me, and I'm my eight-year-old self again, sitting beside my mum in the black car behind my father's hearse, and she's crying because I've just asked her for the hundredth time when he's coming back from heaven. My throat tightens and tears prick my eyelids.

'Oh god, your dad. You told me.' He reaches his arm around my shoulders. 'I'm sorry. You must think I'm really insensitive.'

'It isn't your fault. I thought I'd be fine about it. I mean, I come and visit him often. I sit or stand at his grave and, when no one is listening, I tell him what's going on in my life, and how I wish he was still here.'

Okay, I don't know if he can hear me. I don't even know for sure, even with the evidence from Mrs Wall's crystal ball, if there's an afterlife, but if there's any chance he's about in some form or another, I'd hate him to think I'd forgotten him. It's comforting in a way. I'll come here if I've had a really bad day at work. I didn't talk to him about Mitch, and I haven't told him everything about Ross. It's hard to talk to your dad about the other men in your life, dead or alive.

I take a deep breath and wipe away a tear with the tissue Ross hands me. It's got some grease on it from the bike, but I thank him anyway.

'Shall I tell him we want to go on to the next place?'

I shake my head. 'I'll come and have a look. We don't have a lot of choice – when people move to Talyton St George, they never leave.'

He takes my hand to help me out of the car and we

cross the road, following after Godfrey, who ducks his head to enter the house through the front door straight from the pavement.

'This lovely house has oodles of character,' he says as we catch up with him in the first room on the ground floor. 'Look at those beams and that fireplace – all original features that have been sensitively restored. It's absolutely charming.'

'What do you think?' Ross asks me.

'I'm not sure. In some ways I like the idea of being close to my dad, but I don't think I can deal with seeing the grave every time I look out of the window.' I can just make it out among the stones on the north side of the churchyard.

'Your dad? Your father.' Godfrey's voice wavers as he raises his fist to his forehead.

'He's buried here,' I say quietly. 'Didn't Mum tell you?'

'I knew she was a widow, of course, but we've never talked about it . . .' He frowns. 'Never mind.'

I mind, I think. It's as if she's betrayed my father's memory. She used to walk Seven and our old dog, Daisy, in there all the time. I wonder if she ever does that now.

'What do you think of the house?' Ross says.

'We should look at the third option before we make a decision. I do like it. It feels homely and it's handy for the practice – maybe too handy. If people find out we're living here, they'll be on our doorstep at all times of day and night with their animals. I think we'd be better off out of town.'

'Let's move on then,' he agrees.

The final property on Godfrey's books is in Talyford, just along the road from the Old Forge where Penny and Declan live. It's a barn conversion with a stable door, shared courtyard for parking at the front, and long windows onto the garden at the rear that backs onto fields. There's even a shed where Ross can park his bike.

We go inside the house and have a look around.

'This is more like it,' he says.

'It's perfect.' I look out across the fields and the Taly valley. There's a large kitchen/diner and small sitting room with a wood-burning stove; two bedrooms, one en-suite which, as Ross quietly reminds me, means I won't have to worry about sharing a bathroom if his prostate should give him trouble prematurely.

'Can we have pets here?' I ask.

'I've already spoken to the landlord – I've checked the tenancy agreement which is for twelve months, and they're happy with one small dog or a cat.'

Twelve months is a long time if we don't get on, I muse as he continues: 'Size is relative, and Bart wouldn't be here full-time anyway.'

'I can picture you two sitting here on a winter's evening in front of a flaming log fire,' Godfrey says, 'or sitting out on the patio with wine and salad in the sun.'

Ross smiles at these pictures of cosy domesticity.

'How much?' he asks.

Godfrey responds with a monthly figure and my heart sinks.

'That's too much,' I say.

'There may be a little wriggle room for negotiation,' Godfrey says, but I think he's being overly optimistic.

'Oh, who cares?' Ross says. 'It isn't much over.'

'We said we'd stick to the budget.'

'I'll leave you two to explore while you discuss it,' Godfrey says tactfully. 'I'll be in the motor.'

Ross and I move to the kitchen to talk.

'It's pretty much perfect,' he begins. 'It's fully furnished so we don't need to buy much. It's tucked away so we won't run the risk of having clients knocking at the door at all times of day.'

'Except perhaps for Penny and Declan – they live almost opposite and Trevor's prone to accidents.'

'If you're worried about the money, I can pay the difference.'

'You can't do that. I won't let you.' I couldn't. I'd hate to feel under any obligation to anyone, especially him. 'We have to be equals in this arrangement.'

'I know, but I earn more than you and I want to live here, so it seems fair.'

'But we set a limit—'

'Godfrey's right. If we don't take this one, someone else will snap it up and we'll have to look further afield, and I'm not sure Maz and Emma would be happy with that. We can't be too far away when we're on call.'

I stare at him. Why does he have to be so insufferably right?

'If you don't want to go in with me, if you're having cold feet, don't worry. I'm going to move in here anyway. I've made my mind up.' He grins. 'So, are you in? Please say you're in.'

I take a moment to think. It's a beautiful place and I can see us living here. If I make a few adjustments, I can pay my share. That is non-negotiable. If I turn this down, I'll either have to pay more for a home of my own or spend more time with Godfrey. I make my decision.

'I'm in.'

'That's great!' Ross grabs me by the hands and spins me around the kitchen until I'm giddy, breathless and laughing. 'We are going to have so much fun. We'll stock up the fridge with beer, have a bit of a party.'

'Beer? No way. It has to be wine.'

'Both then.' He tips his head to one side. 'You see, I'm prepared to compromise. I am going to be your perfect housemate.'

Godfrey is delighted.

'Good decision,' he says when we return to the car, although I'm sure he'd have preferred us to take one of the other rental properties off his hands. 'We can go down to the office and sign the agreement if you're sure. There's no time like the present.'

'When can we move in?' I ask, looking back at the house as he drives us away.

'Within the week,' he replies, and I wish he didn't look quite so smug at the prospect of him and Mum having Petals to themselves. 'We'll deal with the paperwork and then go out and celebrate.'

We have a quick coffee at the Dog and Duck before Ross returns to the manor to go out for a ride on his bike.

Later the same day, Taylor tries to persuade me to change my mind. I meet her at the Talymill Inn, taking up her offer of staying over at her place for the night. I'd thought the prospect of a house party would be uppermost in her mind, but she isn't happy about my plans.

'Are you sure about this?' Taylor says over a large glass of Prosecco. 'You tried to stay friends with Mitch after you broke up and look what's happened.'

'Where is he? I did text him.'

'I'm afraid he's feeling neglected since you let him down at the show. Don't worry about it. He'll come round.'

'I don't understand.' I stare into my wine glass, where a single bubble rises slowly to the top. 'He's always been cool about it, about us.'

'Not that cool, as it turns out, not since the new vet rode into your life on that sexy motorbike. The trouble is that it's true that you always want what you can't have and, now he knows for sure that he's lost you, he wishes he'd gone about things differently.'

'It has nothing to do with Ross.'

'Are you sure about that? Come on, Shannon. It seems a bit of a coincidence that you spoke to Mitch not long after Ross appeared on the scene.' She smiles. 'You can squirm as much as you like, but I'm right, aren't I?'

'Some people can deal with continuing to sleep with their exes, but I realised I wasn't one of them, that's all.' I run my fingers up and down the stem of my wineglass. 'It's hard to explain. It didn't feel right any more.'

Taylor arches one eyebrow as she plays with a beer mat, flicking it over and over on the table.

I fetch two more glasses of Prosecco.

'You might think you're capable of being just friends with Ross, but romance and lust could be bubbling up under the surface, ready to burst out at any opportunity – and there will be an awful lot of opportunities when you're living together. Are you sure he doesn't want more out of this? If anything does happen, it could make life very awkward. How will you feel if you do fancy him, and he brings a girl back? Have you talked about that?' She interprets my silence correctly as a 'no'. 'What about you? Will you feel comfortable taking a guy back for coffee?'

'Keep going,' I say mutinously. 'Give me the complete reality check.'

'Oh, I'm going to,' she says with a smile. 'You've said he's untidy at work. What will it be like living with him?'

'We'll share the cleaning and cooking.'

'Dating while sharing a house could get very messy. It should be a slow reveal. I mean, you don't want your date to know how much time it's taken you to make yourself look amazing, do you? When you live with someone, they know from day one how long you spend on your hair and make-up, and ugh, gross, they see you without it. You know how you like to look good.' Taylor warms to her theme. 'What if you date, break up and have to continue living together? Can you imagine the stress?'

'His ex, Heidi, is still in love with him – she lives in hope that they'll get back together and, although he says he wouldn't get back with her, I'm pretty sure he has feelings for her. They shared a bedroom at the manor when she stayed over for the show, so any relationship is off-limits.'

'How can you be sure he will stick to that? Would you want to move in with a boyfriend before you even went on a first date? No, I thought not. Yet that's what could be about to happen – and who will be left to pick up the pieces? Me.' Her tone softens. 'All I'm asking is that you reconsider.'

'It's too late. We've put down a deposit and we're moving in next Saturday.'

'I think you're mad, but there's always the faint

possibility he wants you as a housemate so you can introduce him to lots of hot girls.'

It hadn't occurred to me.'

'I'm not interested. I'm not looking any more.' Taylor giggles.

'Have I missed something? I say, frowning.

'His name is Dave.' She leans towards me with a conspiratorial gleam in her eye. 'He's the new chef at the garden centre. Invite me to your housewarming and I'll introduce you.'

'Has he asked you out?'

'Of course not.' She grins. 'I asked him. For once, Fifi listened to one of my suggestions for the garden centre, which was bringing in a fresh eye when it came to the food. The restaurant is stuck in a rut, serving the same old English breakfast, tea and cakes, and roast dinners as it's always done. People want more nowadays. Their tastes have changed. They want bruschetta and ciabatta, lamb tagine and couscous.'

'Are you sure? I've always been under the impression that customers go there because it's boring and predictable, and therefore they know exactly what they're getting.'

'I think it's time to shake things up. Innovation, planning and execution.'

'You've been doing too many courses.'

'Maybe, but I'm determined to make a go of it. One day, I'll run my own business, although it won't be a garden centre.'

'What's this Dave like, then?' I'm pleased for her – Taylor ended a long-term relationship earlier this year. The guy was one of the engineers who worked on the farm machinery for her father. He was pleasant enough and reasonably good-looking, but I can only describe him as oily – and that's in more ways than one, with his dirty nails and greasy attitude to women. He thought nothing of chatting me up at parties if Taylor wasn't about, and on one particular occasion, when we were at Talymouth's answer to Blissfields last summer, he tried to kiss me. Mitch saw him off and I told Taylor, but she forgave him, saying it was the drink. It wasn't until the New Year when she found texts from another woman on his mobile that she saw him for what he was and dumped him. 'How old is he? What does he look like?'

'He's lovely, and looks delicious in his chef's whites. He's divorced and has a three-year-old daughter who's living with his ex-wife – he has her two nights a week. He's funny, kind . . . and he's Irish.' She pauses. 'It's all right, I'm not letting my imagination run away with me this time.'

'That sounds like a good plan,' I agree. I wish I could do the same.

Chapter Twelve

Moving On Up

Maz offers us the use of the Fox-Giffords' horsebox as a removal van. Ross takes up her offer, while I take my possessions, consisting of a few bags and boxes, a suitcase and duvet, in my car.

I'm at home – that sounds strange because in another hour or so it won't be home any more – packing the last few bits and pieces in my room, when Mum walks in and sits on the bed. Seven jumps up beside her.

'You don't have to rush off, you know. It's all been rather a whirlwind,' she begins. 'I'm going to miss you.'

'I won't be far away. I thought you wanted this place to yourselves.'

'Shannon, darling, you have to admit it's felt a little crowded at times, but now . . .' She plays with a loose thread on the mattress. 'It's silly but it feels like the end of an era. My little girl is finally leaving home.'

My heart aches for her. I move around the bed and

give her a hug. 'I might be back, like one of those boomerang kids. Who knows?'

'You're always welcome, remember that. Drop in for tea anytime.'

'Of course I will. Seven will still want his walks.' I shove a pair of socks into a bag and suppress the sadness that wells up inside me at the thought of leaving him behind. I'd love to take him with me, but Mum needs him and I couldn't leave him home alone all day. It wouldn't be fair. 'You don't walk him through the churchyard any more,' I say quietly. 'Godfrey didn't know about Dad being there. He said you hadn't really talked about him.' I look towards the mantelpiece above the fireplace. There's a photo of my father dressed in an Exeter City football shirt – he was a keen supporter who spent Saturday afternoons following his team.

Mum follows my gaze.

'You probably won't understand. I don't want to go on about how wonderful your dad was in front of Godfrey – behind the bluster, he's a sensitive soul and he might feel that he can never match him.'

'But it feels like you've erased him from your memory,' I argue, hurt on my father's behalf.

'I'm sorry for upsetting you, but we deal with things in different ways. I loved your dad and I love Godfrey too, and I can't stay stuck in the past.' She hesitates. 'Would you like a hand with those bags?'

'Please.' I hand her my sports bag with my swimming kit, then grab the photo of my dad and tuck it into the pocket of my suitcase, before picking the case up and taking it outside to the car. Seven waits on the doorstep, sniffing at the air and watching Mum and me stacking my luggage in the boot.

'That's it.' I try to shut the tailgate as my belongings start to spill out again.

'Not quite.' She dashes back indoors as I squash everything back in.

'You've done it.' Mum returns with a massive bouquet of flowers – roses, lilies, gypsophila and blue-green foliage. 'For you and Ross, as a moving-in present.' She presses them into my arms and I thank her, swallowing past the lump that forms in my throat.

When I'm driving to Talyford with the radio on, my regret at leaving is replaced by a sense of excitement and anticipation of what lies ahead. Ross is waiting when I pull in alongside his motorbike in the courtyard outside the house. He emerges from the front door with a bottle of beer in one hand.

'You're starting early,' I smile. 'It isn't even lunchtime yet.'

'Might as well.' He opens the boot of the car. 'You look like you could do with some help. I've left my things in the hall and returned the horsebox. The groceries and booze have arrived so we're ready to party.'

I grab the flowers from the passenger seat and hand them over to him.

'You shouldn't have,' he teases.

'They're from my mother.'

He holds my gaze and my cheeks flood with heat.

'That's very sweet of her. Have you brought a vase?'

'I didn't think,' I begin, 'and me a florist's daughter.'

'We might find one indoors.'

The owner of the house is working on a long-term

contract abroad and has left it fully furnished. I head inside, Ross following on behind me with his beer and the bouquet. In the kitchen, I look in several of the cupboards until I find a suitable receptacle in the form of a red bucket.

'This will do for now,' I say, filling it with water and a sachet of flower food before placing the flowers into it. 'Where shall we put them?'

'You choose – you're the lady of the house.'

I leave them on the breakfast bar and survey the worktops where Ross has left the bags of groceries.

'What are you doing?' he says as I turn my attention to them.

'What do you think?' I open the fridge to put the butter, bacon and sausages away, but it's full of wine and beer. 'You can't leave all that in there. What about the food?'

'You have to get your priorities right.'

'Very funny,' I say dryly.

'It won't go off – we'll have eaten it by the morning. It's going to be a great party.' Ross grins. 'Relax, Shannon. Have a drink.'

'Not yet,' I say, feeling a little awkward because we are no longer at work or out and about, and I realise that I don't know him as well as I imagined – and he doesn't really know me either.

'There are some veggie sausages somewhere in those bags. I remembered. This is going to work,' he says quietly. 'I'm going to be the best housemate you've never had.'

I can't help grinning. 'You can start by helping me put everything away first.'

'Of course. You want to show the place off.'

'Well, yes.' I walk across to the patio doors, push

them open and look out at the view. The sun is blazing high in the sky and a buzzard circles above the black and white cows in the field beyond. I can't resist the urge to run across the lawn to the hedge, screaming. I reach the end of the garden and turn to find Ross staring in my direction.

'You're mad,' he yells.

'Delirious,' I shout back as I look at the house. This is our home for at least a year, and suddenly life seems like a great adventure.

'What will the neighbours think?'

'I didn't think you'd care!'

He laughs as I jog back across the grass.

'Let's get the place exactly how we want it.'

'All right then. I guess the sooner it's done, the sooner we can chill. Heidi was the same when we moved in together – although it was under different circumstances,' he adds quickly.

Heidi again, making a small hiccup in my happiness. Why, I don't know. She's bringing Bart with her tonight and staying for the party, but ultimately it has nothing to do with me who Ross decides to invite.

We return inside; he sets up his speakers to play music while I sort out the kitchen and carry my bags to my room. I unpack, hang my clothes in the wardrobe, and shower and change into a long skirt and green vest top, which has a school of dolphins embroidered in silver thread on the front. I do my make-up and dry my hair, leaving it loose, and return downstairs.

The party starts at seven – we keep countryside hours in Talyton St George – and our guests start to arrive. Our immediate neighbours turn up and stay for an hour for a drink and pizza. Maz and Izzy, who are on call, make an appearance. A couple of Ross's friends and their girlfriends arrive on motorbikes. They are what Fifi would describe as 'respectable' people, with degrees, good jobs and haircuts.

Taylor brings Dave, the chef, with her. Ross offers them beer or wine.

'Or both,' he laughs, 'depending on your preference. Let me guess. You are Taylor.' He grasps her by the shoulders and kisses her on both cheeks, making her blush. 'And this is?'

'Dave,' she says, stepping aside to allow them to shake hands and give me time to assess her new boyfriend. He's taller than Ross, dark-haired, confident and smiling. He wears jeans and an orange T-shirt that seems to emphasise rather than disguise the fact that he has man-boobs and a paunch. Considering how particular Taylor is about appearances, I'm surprised at her choice.

'Hello.' He holds up two bottles and thrusts them into Ross's hands. 'It's great to meet you,' he goes on in a strong Irish accent. 'It's a lovely place that you have.'

Everyone has drifted out onto the patio to enjoy the evening sunshine, and we show Taylor and Dave through to the kitchen where they linger for a while as Ross fills the last empty glass and a mug with red wine.

'What's that burning?' Dave asks.

I turn to the oven. 'Oh no, who left the pizzas in?' I move to open the door, but he beats me to it.

'I'll get it.'

'No, you mustn't,' I say. 'You aren't at work now.'

'It's all right,' he grins, as he opens the door, releasing a cloud of smoke, grabs a tea towel and pulls out two blackened objects that look like frisbees. He drops them in the bin.

I open a couple of fresh ones, but Dave takes over. Taylor touches my arm.

'Leave him. He's a workaholic.'

He smiles at her. 'You'll always find me in the kitchen at parties. Have you any cheese? Chili? These could do with spicing up.'

'Yes, chef,' I giggle.

Ross finds some extra toppings and grates cheese while Taylor and I look on.

'Have you got any salad?' Dave asks, as Bart comes running into the kitchen and jumps up at Ross, licking at his hands and face.

'Get down,' he says, but Bart takes no notice until Heidi strolls in behind him. She looks amazing in a low-cut floral top, jeans and heels. Taylor gives me a look as Heidi puts her bag on the worktop, kisses Ross on the cheek and picks up a bottle of wine.

'Where are the glasses, darling?'

'You'll have to have it in a mug, I'm afraid,' Ross says.

'Oh god, you're really slumming it. Never mind. It'll taste the same.' She checks the label. 'Pretty awful, I imagine.' She changes the subject. 'I'd like you to have a look at Bart's tail. I took him to see your dad, who gave me some cream to put on the scab, but it's no better.'

'What did you go and do that for?' Ross says, annoyed.

'What am I supposed to do when you've abandoned your only child and moved so far away?'

I glance at Taylor who rolls her eyes. Dave turns his attention to Bart.

'What a fantastic dog,' he says, bending down to let the dog sniff his hand, at which he snarls and lunges at him, grabbing Dave's hand with his massive teeth. 'Ouch!' Dave yelps as Ross dives in to pull the dog off by the collar.

'What the . . . ?' I exclaim.

'Bart, that's enough,' Ross scolds. He turns to Dave. 'I'm sorry about that. Are you okay?'

As Taylor takes her boyfriend's hand to inspect the damage, he sways. I grab a chair.

'Sit down,' I say, placing it behind him. 'You've had a shock.'

He takes a seat, his face pale and shiny with sweat.

'It's all right. I'm fine. No harm done,' he says, repeating himself several times.

'You've been lucky,' Taylor says, giving him a beer. 'There are teeth marks, but he hasn't broken the skin.'

'Ross, aren't you going to put the dog away? He can stay in my room for the duration,' I say.

'There's no need for that,' he says gruffly. 'Dave must have reminded him of someone in his past. He wouldn't actually hurt anyone.'

I'm not happy with his verdict.

'That behaviour was really threatening.'

'He sounded aggressive, but it was all talk,' Ross insists. 'If he'd really meant it, he'd have drawn blood.'

'I disagree.' I turn to Heidi for moral support. 'You know Bart best. What do you think?'

'I think we should listen to the vet,' she says sweetly, looking down her nose at me. I get the impression she doesn't like me sharing a house with her ex.

'If he bites somebody, you'll always regret it.' I

refuse to give up. I don't want any of my friends to get hurt. 'How would you feel if Bart ended up on death row?' I look back at Ross. 'This is our home and these are our guests. This has to be a joint decision.'

'Except you win so it's down to you,' he says dryly. 'Okay, I'll take Bart upstairs.'

'He'll wreck the place,' Heidi says. 'You know what he's like.'

'I'll take the risk,' I say firmly. 'Thank you, Ross. I appreciate it.'

'I'll leave him in my room and check up on him now and again.' Ross drags Bart away while Heidi wanders out to speak to his biker friends and Dave continues preparing the food.

'I can't understand what he saw in Heidi,' Taylor says.

'Sees,' I correct her. 'She's staying over tonight.'

'Oh? But you aren't jealous, remember?' Taylor's earrings glint in the spotlights as she goes on with a mischievous smile, 'You're just housemates.'

'That's right.' I relax and sip at my wine. Now that Bart is safely locked away, I can enjoy the party, except perhaps for Heidi's presence. We move aside as Dave lays out the freshly cooked pizzas on the worktop and goes into the garden to announce that the food is ready.

'I'm glad you've met someone new. He seems like a lovely guy.'

'I'm very lucky,' Taylor says. 'I haven't known him long, but it feels like we've been together forever. The only hitch is the ex-wife and mother of his child. She's quite demanding, expecting him to change his plans at the drop of a hat.

'He's a great dad, though, and Chloe's quite cute

– she's his daughter.' She smiles. 'I never thought I'd
say this, but I love taking her out and about. We went
to the beach the other weekend and her favourite part
of the seaside was the pebbles. She cried when we
had to go home.' She pauses. 'Shall we eat? I'm
ravenous.'

A few glasses of wine later, I turn the music up,
clear the patio and start dancing. Dave leads the way
with the conga and some Irish dance moves mixed
in. Taylor grabs him by the waist, Ross grabs Taylor
and I grab Ross, my hands on the hard muscle of his
loins, and we snake our way across the lawn and back
when Heidi pushes in, shoving me aside and inserting
herself between me and her ex. Dave rushes forwards,
there's laughter and screaming, and the line falls
apart. I notice how Ross catches Heidi as she stumbles
into him, deliberately, I think.

I felt sorry for her when she told me about how
Ross let her down, but now I'm not so sure. She's
pushy and thinks she's superior to me, a lowly vet
nurse, but she's wrong. I'm worth more than she is.
I wonder how Ross feels about her as he holds her
up, pulls her close and dances a slow dance with her.
She has her eyes half closed as she rests her head
against his shoulder and locks her manicured fingers
around his neck in a gesture of possession. He, meanwhile, glances towards me, gives a hardly perceptible
shrug of his shoulders and smiles, before turning back
to whisper something in her ear.

'Come and dance with us.' Taylor grabs my hand
and I end up in a clumsy group hug with her, Dave
and one of the bikers, who introduces himself as
Charlie, and the four of us end up in the living room
chatting until way past midnight, when the party

breaks up, the sober guests heading for home, Taylor and Dave deciding to walk and the rest crashing around the house.

The last time I see Ross, he's helping a very tipsy Heidi up the stairs. Does it matter to me if he's sleeping with her this time? It shouldn't, I think, trying to ignore the dull ache in my chest, but it does.

The following morning, I wake up slightly the worse for wear and head downstairs to find Ross feeding Bart in the kitchen.

'We don't have any dog food,' he says, breaking up some pizza and cold sausage into a bowl.

'You lecture Mrs Dyer on how to feed Nero, and here you are giving your dog fast food.'

'I know. I'm having to improvise.' He chuckles. 'Is that it then? One night and we've already settled into a pattern of mundane domesticity, with you nagging me?'

'Hey, don't knock it. It's been brilliant so far – no Godfrey, no prostate, and a great party.'

'I thought you were going to mention my amazing company.' He raises one eyebrow.

'And that as well.' I pause. 'Is Heidi about?'

'She's upstairs.'

'You seemed very . . . close last night.'

'Would you like some of this pizza warmed up?' he asks.

'No, thanks, not now.'

'Why?' He grins. 'Are you hungover?'

'A little,' I confess.

'I've left Heidi to sleep it off.'

So he slept with her again, just as he did when she came down for the Country Show, I think, my heart sinking.

'What are you doing today?' he goes on.

'I'm going swimming and I'll probably drop in to Mum's to see Seven on the way back.' I pause. 'What are you doing for tea?'

He frowns. 'You mean dinner?'

I nod. 'Will she still be here?'

'No, we're going to walk Bart before she takes him home. I'll cook tonight.' He gives me the sweetest smile that makes my pulse quicken, even though I know it shouldn't because, whether he fancies me or not, nothing can happen between us while Heidi's on the scene, and she's going to be around for some time because of their commitment to the dog. 'You can do the meal tomorrow.'

When I return to the house in the afternoon, I find Ross in the kitchen again. This time he's clearing up the last of the cans and bottles.

'I'm sorry.' I unpack my swimming stuff straight into the washing machine. 'I should have given you a hand.'

'It's fine. Heidi stayed for a couple of hours to help out.' He ties the top of a bin bag full of rubbish and puts it outside. 'I'll make a start on dinner. There's a film I'd like to see later.'

'A rom-com?' I say hopefully.

'A spy thriller.' He laughs. 'Does that make us incompatible?'

'It means we'll be fighting for the remote.'

We settle down for our first evening as just the two of us in our new home, making plans to buy one or two bits and pieces, such as a new kettle because the current one is broken, a rug for the hall and a couple of spare towels for visitors. I feel comfortable sharing with Ross, but it's a few days until I'm happy kicking around in my trackies in front of him. He has no such reservations, wandering into the kitchen with just a towel – and a small one at that – wrapped around his waist for breakfast in the morning, or pacing up and down the living room in a pair of stretchy boxers, talking on his mobile. I'm not sure what to think. Should I ask him to cover up his blatant masculinity or should I let him carry on? I text Taylor to request her opinion. She says, 'If I were you, I'd keep quiet and enjoy the view', so I do.

One morning just over a week after our move, I'm on an early – Ross is on a late because he did a swap with Maz. I swing through reception at Otter House, pausing at the desk to say good morning to Frances.

'I can't say that it's good,' she says quietly. Her eyes are red and her hairpiece has slipped to one side. 'I've been given the sack. Maz and Emma have told me that I have to go.'

'They haven't said that,' Izzy interrupts as she emerges from the consulting room.

'What are you doing here?' I ask.

'I'm doing a couple of hours of overtime.' I offered to collect Trevor on my way to work – he's due to have his cast off today. She turns to Frances. 'They've asked you to retire.'

'Same difference.' She shrugs.

'I'm sorry.' I look around for the tissues and hand her the box.

'It's hard to take. Look at me. I'm capable and active. I have years of experience and now, because I've made one or two mistakes, I have to leave.' She dabs at the mascara tears that run down her cheeks. 'I'm not the retiring kind.'

'We know you aren't – in more ways than one,' Izzy

says with a gentle smile. 'You have Lenny, the hedge-hogs and the WI. Once you've had time to adjust, you'll wonder how you ever had time to go to work.'

'Life won't be the same,' she says, and I have to agree. With Frances leaving, it's the end of an era.

'You'll always be welcome to drop in for tea and a chat, as long as you bring one of your legendary cakes.' Maz walks in from the corridor, fastening the poppers on her tunic, which is covered with cartoon cats. 'Seriously, we're going to hold a barbecue in your honour. Everyone is invited, including partners. It will be at Emma's – she's roped Ben into doing the cooking.'

Frances forces a small smile.

'We'll never be able to replace you,' Maz continues, 'but I have spoken to someone who's keen to train to be a veterinary receptionist. She's called Celine – you might know of her. I met her a while ago, dropping the children off at nursery, and we got talking. She gave up work to have her kids and now she's ready for a break from full-time motherhood.'

'Celine?' Frances taps her nails against the desk. 'I know who you mean, the blonde lady who wears too much fake tan. Her house has the fountain and statues of naked women outside.'

'They're supposed to be nymphs,' Maz smiles.

'What does she know about working at a vet's?'

'I'm not sure,' Maz says cheerfully, 'but we're going to find out. She's starting on Monday on a month's probation, so you can teach her everything she needs to know.' She looks past me. 'Here's my first one.'

I open the door for Jennie. Lucky is in her arms, clinging to her with his paws around her neck.

'He's so much better than he was at the show,' she

says as I lead her into the consulting room. 'He still goes mad whenever anyone turns up at the house, but he sleeps a lot. I think he's been better off the chemo and I'm wondering if we can just forget it, and let nature take its course. What would you do if he was your dog? Be honest with me.'

'You know him best, but I agree, I don't like to see him feeling sick for those few days after each round of treatment.'

Jennie turns to me. 'What about you, Shannon?'

I hesitate. 'It's your decision.'

'You've nursed him,' Maz says. 'You can have your say.'

I gaze at Lucky, who glances towards me and wags his tail.

'No one likes needles, but Lucky's beginning to hate them. Every time he comes in for a blood test or treatment, it's a battle.'

'I'd like his last weeks, or months, to be happy ones, so we should stop,' Jennie decides. 'I'd rather not prolong his life at any cost. It seems selfish.'

'You can say you did your best for him,' Maz reassures her. 'No more needles then?'

'No more,' Jennie says.

'We won't make any more appointments – call me once a week to let me know how he is and we'll go from there.'

'Thank you. We're going to spoil him from now on.'

Jennie seems to be holding it together, but Maz and I are struggling as I open the door to let her out. I duck out and grab the box of tissues back from Frances.

'We should have shares in Kleenex,' Maz sniffles.

I take a break after morning surgery, sitting in the

garden with a mug of coffee. Tripod lies in my arms, purring. He fixes his gaze on a blue tit, which is pecking at the feeder that hangs from one of the branches on the apple tree. Deciding that he can't be bothered to chase the bird, he butts his face against my chin, asking to be stroked, but at the sound of a motorbike, he wriggles out of my arms, jumps down with a light thud and stalks away towards the back door. Faithless creature, I think: so like a man.

'You have poor taste,' I call after him, but I'm generalising. Ross is untidy around the house, but he's a great cook, and I'm telling the truth when I say that my inability to prepare anything but basic meals was not a deliberate strategy to force him into the role of house chef.

On the way home at the end of my day – I finish at four – I pop into Petals to see Seven. I have a quick chat with Mum, who's worried that I'm not eating properly, which is ridiculous because I'm eating better than I ever did at home. I buy a couple of reed diffusers and fragranced candles at cost price, and take them back to the house, where I start preparing dinner.

'Are you intending to burn the place down?' Ross says when he walks in much later. 'It smells like a whore's bedroom.'

'I wouldn't know . . .'

'Me neither.'

'I've incinerated a pair of your socks – you left them on the kitchen floor.' I glance towards the living-room window, where the garden brazier is aglow with some burning weeds that I pulled up from between the slabs of the patio earlier. 'I wish I'd brought a set of forceps home to pick them up with.'

'Shannon, you haven't?'

'Not really. I put them in the washing machine – I even put detergent in and switched it on.' I'm being sarcastic. 'Would you like me to give you a lesson?'

'I'm sorry. We're definitely incompatible when it comes to housework.' He pauses and gives me a weary smile. 'Would you like me to move out?'

'No, of course not. I want it to be . . . homely, that's all. I don't mean to nag. How did the rest of your day go?'

'Frances couldn't cope and went home early, so Izzy had to take over at reception. I see that Tripod's looking better.'

'You've noticed?'

'Of course. It's my job.' He smiles. 'I know how fond of him you lot are.'

By 'lot' I assume he means me, Maz and Izzy in particular. He changes the subject. 'Have you had dinner?'

'There's vegetarian lasagne in the oven.' I hesitate. 'Having said that, I can't smell it.' I dash out to the kitchen where my worst fears are confirmed – I haven't turned the oven on. I swear out loud as Ross walks up behind me and rests his hands lightly on the curve of my waist.

'Never mind,' he says. 'It's the thought that counts. How long do you think it will take?'

'An hour by the time it's come up to temperature.'

'Let's have a glass of wine while we wait.'

'Are you sure you want to wait?' I find myself leaning back into him. His breath is warm against the side of my neck. I can hear my heartbeat, pounding, persistent, and I feel slightly sick in the best possible way. Ross reaches past me and turns the oven on.

'White or rosé?' he says, apparently oblivious to the way he makes me feel.

'Have you heard from Heidi recently?' I have to ask.

'She's texted a couple of times – she sent me a selfie of her and Bart in Richmond Park.' He hesitates. 'I was wondering about buying some kind of fold-up bed in case she wants to stay over again. That sofa is –' he swears – 'uncomfortable.'

'Oh?' I turn. 'I thought . . .'

'What did you think?' he says, amused. 'That I'm sleeping with her? No way.' He frowns. 'I'm not into one-night stands, especially with an ex.

'But you danced with her and helped her up the stairs,' I point out, wanting to prove once and for all whether or not there is anything going on between them.

'I suppose the dance was for old times' sake and she was was so drunk I felt I had to make sure she made it to bed.' He looks at me, his expression serious. 'It didn't mean anything. I've told you before – without the dog, I wouldn't see her again, especially after the other night at the party. She was pretty rude, looking down her nose at you and pushing you out of the way. I'm not blind.'

We look at beds on the Internet, using Ross's tablet, but we don't end up buying one. All I can focus on is the revelation that there is nothing going on between him and Heidi. My housemate is both irresistibly gorgeous and quite possibly available. My imagination runs riot.

Chapter Thirteen

Receptionist Wars

Tripod continues to improve and I'm hopeful that he'll be with us at least for the rest of the summer. Maz announces at one of our practice meetings that the finances are falling into place for the purchase of a branch surgery, which is everyone's preferred option for expanding the practice, and the builders move out. Ross and I settle down to some kind of routine. We make a good team – when we're on duty, we take it in turns to go out. Either he will ride off on his motorbike, or I'll go swimming.

Last night, he cooked an amazing dinner of bean casserole with garlic bread and green salad, and we spent most of the evening chilling on the sofa with him at one end in jeans and a T-shirt and me at the other in my summer pyjamas, shorts and a vest top, watching comedies and a detective drama. I'm not sure I got the gist of the story because my mind – and my eyes – kept drifting towards my gorgeous house-mate and the gap between us, wondering how to close it.

This morning, I'm up drinking tea in the kitchen, but Ross hasn't made an appearance yet. I text him. There's no response so I head upstairs, knock on his door and push it open.

'It's time to get up. You'll be late for work.'

He sits up abruptly and swings his legs so he's sitting on the edge of the bed, naked with the duvet strategically placed across his belly and thighs. He runs one hand through his hair, shaking out his curls before looking up.

'I couldn't sleep last night,' he mutters.

Neither could I, I think. What is that saying? Familiarity breeds contempt. It doesn't apply in this case, because the more time we spend together, the more I get to know him and the more I want him. I yearn for the pressure of his lips on mine and the taste of his kisses. I dream that he'll sweep me off my feet and carry me into his room – I glance down at the heap of laundry on the floor, the open laptop and glasses of water and food wrappers – okay, it would have to be my room, where he would lay me down on the bed and . . . well, let's close the bedroom door on what I'd like him to do to me.

He gets up, dragging the duvet with him, and takes a shirt from his wardrobe.

'I'm off,' I say, quietly turning away.

'I'll catch you up. Cover for me if I'm a few minutes late. Say I had trouble starting the bike or something.'

'Is that ethical?'

'Hardly, but I'd do the same for you.'

I get to Otter House in time, but if Emma notices that Ross is a few minutes late, she doesn't comment. She's in reception, introducing Celine to Izzy and

Frances, who stands behind the desk, her handbag and glasses on top of it, as if she's guarding her territory.

I'm not sure what to make of our new receptionist. With her blonde hair extensions, false nails and eyelashes, less than subtle fake tan and hint of an Essex accent, she could have walked straight out of *TOWIE*.

'Frances is going to show Celine how we do things at Otter House,' Emma says.

Frances opens and closes the till with a loud crash.

'I'll let you all get on with it then,' Emma continues brightly. 'Izzy, you're with me. Shannon, you're with Ross. Where is he, by the way?'

'His bike wouldn't start,' I say, amazed at how glib I sound.

He catches up with me about ten minutes later, and we see the morning appointments and go out on a couple of visits, after which I spend some time in the office with Celine, explaining the system for obtaining a repeat prescription. She writes notes on her iPad.

'I want to get this right,' she says.

'How are you getting on so far?' I ask. She must be a few years older than me, in her early thirties, and she has what I suspect she'd describe as some post-baby weight to lose.

'I'm struggling with Frances – she won't let me do anything, yet I'm perfectly capable of inputting data into the computer and taking payments. All she's allowed me to do is make the tea, but when I did that, she poured it down the sink and started again. She keeps running through her list of criteria for a successful receptionist: being able to cope with unpleasant discharges and secretions. I can do that – I have two

226

kids and a baby –' she grins – 'and a husband. He's a sales team leader in Exeter – we moved here because of his job.'

'Do you have any pets?'

'Not yet.'

'You will do. It's an occupational hazard.' I smile. 'Frances is all right when you get used to her. She doesn't want to retire, but it's come to the point where she has to for her health . . .' And our patients' safety, I want to add, but don't because it would feel disloyal. 'Don't hesitate to ask me if you're unsure about anything.'

'Thank you. I'd better get back to my post.'

'Good luck,' I say, wondering how long she'll stay.

Ross's favourite – I'm being ironic – arrives with Merrie towards the end of afternoon surgery. Both Frances and Celine show her through, as if they're in competition to provide the best welcome.

'You must be charging too much if you can afford two receptionists,' Mrs Wall mutters, unimpressed. 'I should ask for a discount.'

'How is Merrie?' Ross asks, as I pick her up and lift her onto the table.

'She's the best she's ever been.' Mrs Wall leans on her stick.

'What do you put that down to?' he asks in a slightly challenging tone.

'Mr Curdridge, I have opened my mind to the possibility of synergy between the ancient healing arts and modern science. You would do well to do the same. What if the addition of a crystal to the drinking water allowed you to reduce the dose of tablets you prescribe?'

'That would be a fine thing indeed, but it's pure

fantasy. I base my treatments on evidence-based medicine.'

'I thought that now her skin is under control, I should wean her off your drugs and onto some homeopathy.'

'The itch is under control because of the drugs.' Ross runs one hand through his hair in exasperation. 'Take Merrie off them and she'll start scratching again.'

Mrs Wall squints at him. I can understand why he finds some of our clients infuriating.

'If you don't trust me to do what's best for your dog, then you should see one of the other vets,' he goes on quietly.

'Oh no, I wouldn't like that. I do trust you. Really, I do. It's conventional medicine that I have a problem with. You are a marvel. I like a man who calls a spade a spade.'

'That's settled then.' Ross smiles and she smiles back. 'I would suggest that you leave Merrie here for an hour so Shannon can give her another bath.'

'She does love coming here for a shampoo and set.'

Little does she know the trauma that we go through each time, I think, amused.

'Take her through, please,' Ross says. 'You can collect her any time after four, if that suits you.'

'I shall have a wander around town.' Mrs Wall pats Merrie, fumbles for her stick and walks out of the consulting room, tripping over her own feet on the way. She regains her balance and continues out of the practice while I take Merrie for her bath. As usual, I end up soaked through and smelling of dog shampoo, while she turns out clean, white and fluffy. I give her a pedicure, trimming the fur between her toes and clipping her nails, but before I can put her in a kennel to await her owner, Ross comes to tell me that she won't be going home for a while.

'Mrs Wall's been carted off to hospital. She was in the church – she had a fall.'

'Is she going to be all right?'

He shrugs. 'I'll find out later.'

I glance across to where Merrie is sitting in a nest of towels, her ears pricked and her expression hopeful, and my heart goes out to her because she's going to be disappointed at not going home yet. We walk back to the consulting room.

'Who's next?' Ross asks, closing the door behind us.

'Trevor,' I say, checking the monitor.

'It isn't very long ago that his cast came off. What's he done now?'

'It says he's suffered a wheelchair injury – Penny's run over his paw.'

Suddenly, the sound of yelping carries through from reception.

'He's here,' Ross says with a sigh. 'That's definitely Trevor.'

Luckily, his foot is merely bruised, so he goes home with a couple of days' worth of painkillers and orders to rest.

'You're done –' Celine pops her head around the door when we've seen the last client – 'and so am I. I'm not working with Frances again. She's doing my head in. She won't let me do anything or get a word in edgeways.' She looks at her iPad and reads from the screen. 'Mrs Wall has phoned from the hospital to ask if we can look after Merrie. I didn't run it past

Frances – I just assumed that we would as these are circumstances beyond anyone's control.'

'It's good to find someone who can use their initiative,' Ross says.

'I'm going to call Maz. I can't work under these conditions.' She touches the corner of her eye, as if dabbing at a tear, sending her gold bracelets jangling down her arm.

'You aren't going to leave?' I say anxiously. 'You've hardly started.'

'I'm not staying to be treated like a child. I've had a customer service role before so I have at least half an idea of what I'm doing.'

Ross rolls his eyes as she heads out in her heels with a massive designer handbag over her arm. 'Is Frances still here?'

'I think she's gone home,' I say, pulling the rubber cover off the table and putting it to one side so I can clean underneath it.

'What is this? Receptionist wars?' He turns away and closes down the computer. I reach out and place both hands on his waist to ask him to move aside, but he freezes – we both do – at the contact. My breath catches in my throat as I feel the heat and hardness of his flesh through my fingertips.

He turns his head to face me and gives me a long, smouldering look. Fighting a wave of desire, I force myself to take a step back, clasping my hands together and popping the joints of my fingers as a distraction. It's dangerous being in such close proximity. It would take very little to tempt me to move in closer and slide my arms right around his waist, but it cannot be. We're colleagues and housemates, and that's how it has to stay.

'I wish you'd stop cluttering up the room. You're in my way,' I say lightly, before returning to the subject of our new receptionist. 'It's wrong to expect Frances to train someone new. It's like rubbing a puppy's nose in it when they've had an accident in the house – and besides, she's too set in her ways. She'll only teach Celine how *not* to do it.'

'I'm glad to hear your opinion,' Emma interrupts as she arrives in the consulting room via the other door, with a bottle of injectable antibiotic which she puts back on the shelf.

'I didn't realise you were listening,' I say awkwardly.

'It's all right. I'm going to suggest that they do alternate half-days until Frances leaves the practice. The rest of us will have to help Celine out – we can't afford to lose her.' Her eyes narrow as her gaze settles on Ross, who is standing very close to me, reaching past me for the disinfectant spray. 'Is everything okay?'

'Yes, fine,' I say a little too quickly.

'It's all good,' he adds.

'You will remember to send us an invite?' Emma continues. 'For the wedding,' she adds with a giggle. 'Come on, it's so obvious.'

'There's nothing going on,' I stutter.

'Sure,' she says, retreating. 'See you later.'

Ross starts cleaning the table.

'You don't have to do that.'

'And you don't have to be quite so vehement in your denial.' He glances up with a spark in his eye and a flash of his teeth. 'There is some truth in the saying: methinks the lady doth protest too much.'

'That's ridiculous,' I argue, half laughing because

he's right and I don't want to admit it. 'Remind me
to feed Merrie, won't you?'

'I'll take her home,' he decides.

'That's a little unconventional,' I point out. 'She can
stay here overnight.'

'That seems a bit mean when she isn't an inpatient
as such.'

'I don't mind – in fact, I'd like to have a dog
around the place – but I didn't think you'd provide
your least-favourite client with such a personal
service.'

'She's a strange old bat, but I have to admire her. I
like people who stick to their guns. She's all right.'

Later in the evening, we settle on the sofa with
Merrie between us. Ross has a cushion across his lap
where the dog rests her head. She seems to like men,
or maybe she's enjoying the novelty, having been
living with Mrs Wall. I sit back with a glass of apple
juice – I'm trying to be healthy – and rest my feet on
the footstool, stretching out my long bare legs.

I sense Ross's eyes on me and the warmth of his
gaze sends flickers of heat through my body. When
he becomes aware that I'm watching him, he looks
away abruptly. I reach for another cushion and hug
it tight.

'I'm off to bed,' he says suddenly. 'I'll put the dog
out – she seems to think she needs to go out rather
often.' He gets up and moves past me, stopping to
lean down and brush his lips against my cheek, not
once, but twice. His breath lingers on my skin as he
kisses the side of my mouth then my lips. 'Goodnight,
Shannon,' he murmurs.

'See you in the morning,' I say, touching my face.
He kissed me. My heart is doing somersaults. I'm not

sure where we are, or where we're going? I can't stop thinking about him and I start to wonder if I'm going mad.

The next day at work, I manage to fix it with Izzy so that I can spend a couple of hours at the end of the day setting up the lab, now that the builders have gone. It's out of the way of the hustle and bustle of the practice, and I can clear my head as I set up the microscope and pack the spare sample tubes, slides and chemicals into the cupboards.

'So this is where you've been hiding?' Ross puts his head around the door.

'It's lovely, isn't it? DJ did a good job, even if he did miss the deadline.'

'I'm off home. I'm going to make a curry – vegetarian, of course – if you'd like it.'

'Ah, no thanks. I'm going straight to Talymouth for a meal with a couple of the girls I met on the vet nursing course. It'll be fun – I haven't caught up with them for a while.' It was a last-minute arrangement. I contacted them via Facebook this morning and they both happened to be free.

'Are you going without me?'

'It's a girls' night out,' I add to make it clear.

'You're bored with my company already,' he says lightly.

'Of course not.' Far from it, I think. He is always in my mind. That's why I have to go out to put some distance between me and the object of my affection. 'You have Merrie,' I point out.

'I'm going to walk her back to Mrs Wall's before I jump on the bike. It turns out that it was just a sprained ankle, so she's home. Have a good evening. I'll see you later.' He smiles. 'I'll be able to have the remote to myself. Oh, I forgot to say, Bart's coming to stay this weekend.'

'It's all right, you don't need to ask. That was part of the agreement when we moved in together.'

'I know you aren't keen on him.'

'I don't think he's keen on me either.' I force a smile as I try to dismiss my memory of his aggressive behaviour at the party. 'We'll get used to each other eventually.'

Ross disappears again and I return downstairs to change and drive to Talymouth. The girls and I have a good laugh, sharing our vet nursing stories, including mine about the builders and the snake, and gossiping about our love lives. I don't say much about that. I talk about how I'm sharing a house with one of our vets, but I don't let on how I feel about him.

Chapter Fourteen

Two Little Kittens

I don't see Ross in the morning, at least not until I get to work. I get up late and take coffee and toast to my room, and wait for him to leave before I pick up my bag and keys and drive to the practice. He calls up the stairs to let me know he's going out and check that I haven't gone back to sleep.

'I'll see you soon,' he says.

'Okay,' I call back, but even when I reach Otter House, I occupy myself with feeding Tripod and checking the drug order so I can have a few more minutes before starting work with him. Ross catches me in the corridor.

'Are you trying to avoid me or something?' He stands in the doorway with one hand on each side of the frame, his bulk creating a shadow across the floor. 'You would tell me if I'm stinking of *l'eau* de dog's bottom? I've just been squeezing some anal glands.'

'No?' I stammer. 'I mean "yes". Oh, I don't know. I'm sorry. I've got a bit of a headache.' I smile weakly.

I feel very awkward. It was a kiss, just a kiss, even if it was on the lips.

'Are you sure that's all it is?'

'You know how sometimes you just need a bit of space . . .'

'That's when I shoot off on the bike for a couple of hours.' He smiles. 'You need a motorbike so you can get away from it all.'

'No, thanks. It doesn't appeal to me. I'd rather go swimming.'

'If you can bear my presence for a couple of hours, I could do with a hand in Kennels.'

'Okay, anything for you,' I say, 'but you'll have to move,' I add, as I try to pass him in the doorway, catching his scent of fresh deodorant and shampoo. He's wearing a new shirt, short-sleeved and striped. It seems as if he's made a special effort and I can't help hoping that it's for me. Grinning, he steps aside, apparently unaware of how he makes me feel. 'What is it?'

'One of the cats Jack has trapped and brought in today, a feral with aspirations to be a tiger.'

'Oh, thanks. I think I've changed my mind.' I glance at the silvery, thread-like scars, evidence of previous cat attacks on my arms, as we make our way into Kennels and he holds the door open for me.

The cat is in a crush cage, which is hidden underneath a towel for privacy. Murmuring sweet nothings, I push the inner bars of the cage up close to her so she can't turn around. Ross lifts the corner of the towel and injects her through the bars, at which she hisses and pants, open-mouthed, scared and angry at the same time.

'She's a feisty little thing,' he observes.

'You could say that.' We step away for a few minutes, keeping an eye on her from a distance while she wobbles then sinks onto her tummy, looking completely dazed. I prod her gently through the bars. She doesn't respond with any more than a slight quickening of her breathing.

'It looks like she's good to go,' Ross says from over my shoulder. 'Are you wearing the gauntlets, or am I?'

'I think that's traditionally been the role of the vet nurse,' I say sarcastically.

'Of course, the vet's safety is paramount,' he teases.

I put on the leather gauntlets just in case, but the cat is out for the count and I'm able to take them off as soon as I've transferred her to the prep bench.

'I'll make this quick.' Ross checks her over. 'She's got milk. Jack didn't say anything about her having kittens when he dropped her off,' he adds, and my heart sinks.

'I'll call him when I have five minutes.'

Ross spays her – I have to remind him to use stitches that dissolve under the skin because there's no way she'll let us catch her again – and soon she's recovering in the trap, in preparation for release late the same evening or the next day. When I phone Jack, he says he isn't aware that she has any kittens.

'If she does, they'll be hungry by now,' I say to Ross. 'I'll go out at lunchtime to see if I can find them.'

'They'll be okay if she's back with them tonight.'

'Jack isn't sure how long she'd been in the trap.' She hangs around the barns at the equestrian centre. Apparently the owner, Delphi, acquired a couple of young cats from the Sanctuary some time ago, but in spite of prepaying for neutering when she

237

picked them up, she didn't get round to having it done. She took them on for pest control in return for bed and board. The strategy worked – the number of rats fell, but the number of cats went up. 'I really think I should go and have a look.' A trip out will give me the chance to put some space between us, but it turns out that Ross wants to come along too.

'Let's X-ray the dog that Emma admitted this morning, then go. We can take the ambulance now it's back from the garage. According to Maz, the insurance company made a pig's ear of the claim.'

'Very funny, but I'd rather you didn't remind me.' The repairs have taken ages.

The X-rays are not helpful. Ross makes a diagnosis of BATS, but when I'm marvelling at his superior knowledge and ability to diagnose obscure orthopaedic conditions, he turns round and explains that it means 'bugger all to see'.

'Do you want to drive, or shall I?' he asks when I've stopped laughing.

'I'll drive as long as you promise not to go on about the traffic or criticise my ability behind the wheel.'

'I can agree to the former. I'm not sure about the latter. When you gave me a lift in your car the other day, I thought we were going to end up in the ditch.'

'It wasn't my fault.' I was avoiding the fox that sauntered across the lane in front of us.

'Hey, you two are beginning to sound like an old married couple,' Izzy says, walking in to the prep area with a cat in a basket. 'Shannon, can you find room for Toby? Maz wants to monitor him for the next twenty-four hours.'

'Is there any chance you can do it? We're about to go and look for these kittens.'

'Yes, of course.' Izzy's forehead is lined with concern. 'I wish we'd had some idea before. I wonder why Delphi or someone else at the stables didn't mention it.'

'Perhaps they didn't know.' I give them the benefit of the doubt. 'We'll be off then. That way, we'll be back for afternoon surgery.'

'Good luck. I hope you find them.'

'We'll do our best,' Ross says.

I collect a few items of equipment, load them into the ambulance and drive to the stables, turning off the main road into a driveway and passing a sign reading 'Letherington Equestrian Centre'. There's a small warehouse-style building on one side and, on the other, a field divided into sections by electric fencing, where several horses are grazing, some of them reminding me of aliens in fly-masks that cover their eyes and ears. We travel on past a modern barn and into a car park, where Ross takes the carrier out of the back of the vehicle and hands me a towel and the gauntlets.

'I don't think we'll need those.' Smiling, I hand the gauntlets back, and we go and speak to the member of staff who's grooming a big, dark brown horse tied up outside one of the stables. The groom is a couple of years younger than me and her jodhpurs are so tight you can see the ripple of cellulite beneath. She introduces herself and gives Ross an appreciative once-over.

'Delphi says she's sorry she can't see you because she's teaching. There are kittens – someone should have told the guy who came to pick up the cat in the trap. They're in the old barn, which is through the passageway over there.' She points towards the end of the stable block. 'I can put Star away, and give you a hand to find them, if you like.'

'We'll manage, thanks,' Ross says quickly.

'Any time.'

'You disappointed her.' I follow him into the barn where the air is warm and heavily scented with dried grass and sweaty horse. 'She fancies you.'

'Did she? I didn't notice. I only have eyes for you.'

'I could have you for harassment.' I give him a gentle shove.

'But you won't because you love me,' he says, giving me a push in return. 'You aren't quite ready to admit it yet.'

'Ross! Stop messing about. You'll frighten the kittens.'

'Which, it turns out, they did know about, but forgot to mention.' I recognise the impatience in his voice when he continues, 'They could have saved us a trip.'

I flick a fat bluebottle from my arm as we emerge from the far end of the passageway back into the bright sun.

'Did you ever ride here?' he asks.

'I was never part of the horsey set. Mum said riding was too dangerous for her only child, and she couldn't afford it anyway. How about you?'

'I spent some time at a racing yard when I was a student. I had a go at riding, but give me a motorbike over a horse any time. Horses have minds of their own, and although the thoroughbreds are quick, they aren't fast enough for me.' He unfastens the rope which holds the gate into the barn closed. When he opens it, it drags across the ground. 'What is it with people? It's just like being at Talyton Manor. Everything's tied up with string.'

'They spend all their money on the horses. Maz told me how much it cost to keep one at livery here. I had to ask her to repeat herself because I couldn't believe it.'

We step into the darkness, which is cut through by swathes of light entering between the wooden slats, illuminating a stack of traditional hay-bales at one end and some bags of shavings and a couple of wheelbarrows without wheels at the other. 'We should have brought a torch,' I go on.

'Why are you whispering?'

'I don't know. Because it's . . .' A shiver runs down my spine. 'Spooky.'

'Really, Shannon.' Ross chuckles. 'You have an overactive imagination.'

If only he knew, I think. I'm here in near darkness, alone with the hottest man in the universe and a million dangerous, delicious and positively wicked thoughts running through my head. House rules, I remind myself. Even though he didn't want them, I created some for myself.

'Your eyes will soon adapt. Stop.' He touches my arm, making the hairs stand on end, in the nicest possible way. 'Listen.'

'I can't hear anything.' I hold my breath, but the sound of my heartbeat is deafening in my ears.

'Sh! There it is.'

I catch a faint mewling noise from the depths of the barn.

'Kittens,' I say, smiling.

'A great deduction, Holmes, but where are they?'

Ross says wryly as he moves towards the source of the sound, which is coming from somewhere above our heads. 'This could be like looking for a needle in the proverbial haystack.'

'I don't think there's anything proverbial about it. It's a monster.' I look up towards the top of the stack, which is piled at least ten bales high and twenty wide, with several random gaps where bales have been removed to feed the horses.

'I'm going up,' Ross decides.

'I'm coming with you.' I throw the towel around my neck.

'Do you need a leg up?'

In answer, I reach up, grab the edge of a bale and dig my foot into a space between two more, jumping up and reaching the first platform partway up the stack. He tries to follow, but slips back.

'Pass me that.' I reach for the carrier, and place it beside me. 'Now, give me your hand.'

'And you'll pull me up?' He raises one eyebrow.

'I'm stronger than you think. I swim at least three times a week, remember. Go on.'

He reaches up for my outstretched hand, our fingers touch and interlink. I take a firm grip.

'After three,' I say. 'One, two, three.'

He springs up and I pull, and he ends up on his stomach, wriggling onto the platform next to me.

'All we've got to do now is get to the top.' I take a breath and look up at the timbers and corrugated iron, adorned with dusty cobwebs, above our heads.

'I can't hear anything now.' He moves up and sits beside me, his thigh touching mine. I can smell his scent of musk and surgical scrub, and the coffee on his breath. I turn to look at him and his gaze locks onto mine, and for a single delicious moment, I think he's going to lean towards me and . . . the expression in his eyes is suddenly guarded. Biting my lip in frustration, I pull my knees up to my chest and wrap my hands around my shins.

There's another mew, a louder one.

'Someone's calling for their mother,' Ross says quietly, and we climb onto the top of the haystack. 'They're over there, in the corner down between the bales.' He starts to shift the hay, perspiration shining across his forehead and his cheeks growing pink with exertion.

'There. I can see them.' He moves one last bale aside to reveal two tiny spitting kittens. 'They're so not cute,' he says, grimacing.

'Like mother, like daughter . . . and son,' I say, relieved that we appear to have found them in time. I can't be sure of the sex, but there's a tortoiseshell and white, and a ginger one, so it's a reasonable assumption that they are girl and boy respectively.

'Are you certain about that?'

'It's an educated guess. I'll check them later. You aren't going to let me forget about the rabbits, are you?'

'Probably not. It's too much fun winding you up. Let's get the kittens into the carrier and take them back to Otter House.'

'How do we know they belong to the cat we have at the surgery?'

'We'll have to rely on circumstantial evidence.' I feel like I should offer to mop his brow like I do when he's operating. 'We'll take them anyway. If they are hers, they need feeding – they can't be more than ten days old. We'll see if we can reunite them with mum and, if it goes well, we can release the three and re-trap the kittens in a few months' time before they can produce more babies.' He reaches down to grab one, but the kittens have other ideas, wriggling back into the dark tunnel between the bales and the wall.

'I'll move this – you be ready to catch them.' As he lifts the closest bale, hauling it up by the strings, I scoop the kittens up in the towel and pop them straight into the carrier.

'Gotcha,' I say as I secure the front.

'Thank you.' Ross checks his watch. 'We'd better be getting back.' He climbs down and I hand him the carrier, which he places on the ground before helping me. I slide down, missing my footing as I land and falling into his arms. He jumps back as if he's been bitten. No touching. It's too close, too intimate. I grab the carrier, and walk back to the ambulance, flustered and hot.

When we arrive at Otter House, I let Celine have a brief glimpse before I take the kittens straight through to Kennels to see if I can reunite them with their mum, but she isn't having any of it. The kittens cry plaintively when she's spitting at them as if she's never seen them in her life. Part of me wants to put them in the cage and leave them to work things out in a forced re-adoption, but I fear for their safety because the mum's so ferocious I think she'll kill them. Even though I've handled them in a towel, they must smell different. Either that, or they've been apart for too long.

'How's it going?' Ross asks, checking up on them.

'Not great.'

He reaches out and touches my hair.

'Anyone would think you'd been rolling in the hay,'

he says, grinning as he drops a piece of dried grass into the bin. I wonder if I should reward him with some kind of treat to reinforce this good behaviour. 'That's such a shame, after all the hassle of going to catch them,' he goes on with a sigh. 'I guess I'd better do what's best—'

'What?' I turn to face him, my chest tight with apprehension. 'You don't mean?'

'I know it seems harsh, but it's the sensible option. We can't put them back. They're too young to fend for themselves, and it's obvious that mum isn't going to look after them.'

'You can't do that.' I gaze at the kittens, two tiny bundles of fluff with bright eyes that haven't been open for long, and my maternal instinct – such that it is – kicks in. 'I'll look after them. I'll rear them by hand.'

'You can't. It's a twenty-four/seven occupation, and you already have a full-time job.'

'I did it with Seven. It was hard work, but I managed, and it won't be long until they can be weaned onto solid food.'

'There are already hundreds of other cats looking for homes.'

'I know that, but these two could be neutered –' I gaze at him hopefully – 'by their lovely vet and be homed as farm cats. There are lots of farms around here.'

He reaches out and scruffs the ginger kitten to pick it up, at which it explodes into a mini-tornado of fury and scratches him.

'Ouch!' Swearing, he pops the kitten back into the box. 'He's drawn blood.' Ross holds out his finger.

'Good. It's no more than you deserve.' I pick up the

bottle of surgical spirit and squirt it over the tiny wound.

'What did you do that for? That's made it ten times worse.'

'It serves you right. I have no sympathy.' I cross my arms across my chest, a wall of hot tears building behind my eyelids. 'I'd never have let you come with me if I'd known you wanted to put them to sleep. You're a vet – you're supposed to love animals.'

'I always do what I think is best for them.' His brow is deeply furrowed. 'I wish you'd stop looking at me like that. I don't enjoy this side of the job.'

'Let me rear them then. I can give it a go at least, then if it doesn't work out . . .' I can't bear the thought of them not having a chance of life. Their eyes have only just opened. 'You don't have to have anything to do with it if it's against your principles.'

'Now you think I'm a mean bastard,' he sighs.

'There's no thinking about it. You are!' I hesitate. 'You gave Bart a chance. You gave him a home.'

'I heard raised voices.' Izzy's sudden appearance makes me jump. She raises one eyebrow. 'Your first appointment is here, and Celine says you have kittens. Oh, aren't they sweet?' she goes on, looking into the box.

'Ross doesn't think so. He wants to bump them.'

'Oh no, we can't do that.' She reaches into the box, but before she can pet them, the tortie and white kitten is spitting furiously.

'Have you reared wild kittens before?' I ask her.

'Yes, with some success. I'll give you a hand with them. There's some cat milk substitute somewhere, along with a feeding bottle. And you'd better make a sign, Do Not Touch.'

'Thanks, Izzy.'

'Mind they don't bite your hand off.' Ross shows off his war wound, but Izzy is scathing, claiming that she can't see it, and I'm grateful that she's on my side.

'You are up to date with your tetanus jabs? And you've cleaned them properly?' she says.

'Thank you for showing so much concern for my health, when Shannon here seems determined to make me suffer.'

'I'm not doing it for you,' Izzy says. 'I don't want Maz and Emma left in the lurch if you end up incapacitated in hospital.'

'I'm supposed to be in the consulting room with Ross now,' I say, hoping that she will offer to take my place so I can play with the kittens.

'It's all right. I can manage. I'm a big vet now,' he mutters, disappearing off to see the appointments.

Izzy digs out a bottle and mixes up some milk substitute while I have one last attempt at reuniting the kittens with their mum, but it's no good. I cover her cage again with a towel so she can have some peace before Jack turns up to take her back to the stables and freedom.

How do you pick up a feral kitten? The answer is carefully. I manage to get hold of the girl by the scruff and lift her out onto a blanket on the prep bench. She hisses, revealing a pink tongue.

'Temper,' I say softly. 'I'm afraid you're going to have to get used to this.' I offer her the teat on the bottle, letting a drop of milk trickle into her tiny mouth. At first she won't take any, and I'm beginning to despair when she gives in and starts sucking, barely stopping until her belly is full and the bottle is empty. She's a fighter, a good sign. As she lies in the blanket holding the teat in her mouth and giving it the occasional hopeful suck, I take a closer look, catching sight of some dark spots in the white patches of her fur. They're ticks. I pick off a couple between my thumb and fingernails, making sure I don't leave their mouthparts embedded in her skin, but she's soon fed up with that, so I have to stop. They'll have to come off one way or another. I make a mental note to ask Ross to recommend a suitable product to get rid of them.

I use a piece of damp cotton wool to wash the kitten and encourage her to go to the toilet – her mum would lick her, but I'm not up for that! I pop her back in the box and repeat the whole exercise with the ginger boy, who is slightly calmer. Eventually, I put them back together. They rub faces and settle down together.

'Ah, they're so sweet. What are you going to call them?' Izzy asks when she returns a little while later.

'I thought Tilly and Kit.' I don't know why, but the names stick.

I take them home and feed them every two to three hours to begin with. Ross makes me breakfast the next morning.

'How are they?' he asks over coffee and poached eggs on toast.

'They're fine.' I yawn. 'I'd forgotten what it was like – I'm shattered.'

'You must let other people help you.'

'Are you offering?' I ask brightly.

'If you're saying I could stay up with you all night, then yes . . .'

'Cheeky sod.' I grin.

248

'I can take them off your hands for a night at the weekend.'

'That's really kind of you, but—'

'You don't trust me?'

'They'll be used to me by then.'

'You know where I am if you need me. How about Izzy?'

'Izzy works on the farm after work – I can hardly ask her.'

'Wouldn't Frances like to have them for a day or two?'

'She means well, but no.'

Ross touches the top of Tilly's head. She growls and flattens her ears.

'There's some way to go. Please don't build your hopes up, and don't wear yourself out.'

'It's okay,' I joke. 'I'm not going to let these babies change my life.'

'That's what all new mums say,' he teases.

I gaze at them fondly. I promised myself not to get attached to them, but I'm afraid that it's already too late. I'll be devastated if they don't make it.

Chapter Fifteen

Patients Permitting

The kittens thrive. In spite of his reservations about hand-rearing, Ross takes turns with me to feed them day and night for the rest of the week. At first, I was put off him a little by his suggesting that they should be put to sleep, but when I saw him holding a tiny kitten in one hand and a bottle in the other, my heart melted and I began to forgive him.

By the time the weekend comes along, I'm starting to relax and look forward to Frances's retirement do, especially when Heidi drops Bart off without staying for more than a quick coffee, because she's going to a hen do at a Cornish spa. Bart is calmer than he was at the party, but I keep the kittens shut in my bedroom just in case.

Ross and I are on duty, but we go along between calls. I drive and he sits with the kittens in a cat carrier on his lap, while Bart is shut in the back.

'Are you sure we should have brought him with us?' I ask.

'I asked Emma and she said it was okay.'

'She didn't see him at the party,' I remind him.

'That was a one-off – he took a dislike to Dave,' Ross says. 'You're being paranoid. He's a lovely boy.'

'I'm worried about the children.'

'You don't give up, do you?'

I feel chastened, which is wrong when he's the one being unreasonable. I glance towards him. The muscle in his cheek tautens and relaxes.

'I'll keep him with me, on the lead,' he says eventually. 'Happy now?'

'Thank you,' I say as I pull into the drive outside Emma's house.

Who needs a designer handbag when a pair of kittens are a vet nurse's favourite accessory? Wherever I go with them, people talk to me, although this is somewhat nerve-wracking at the party where the children want to stroke them. I sit on a blanket on the lawn in Ben and Emma's garden with Celine, while Ross – with Bart on the lead – chats to Ben, who's playing with the barbecue. Maz is frantically wrapping a present on the garden table with Henry toddling about under her feet and the baby asleep in the buggy alongside her, while Emma is bustling around with plates of food.

She and Ben moved from the new estate to this lovely old white house just outside Talyton St George. It's my idea of a dream home, and I'm sure Godfrey would have waxed lyrical about it when he marketed it. It has views of the Devon hills and the moors beyond, a walled garden where we are now, with a small orchard behind it, and although the house has original features, such as beams and wooden floors, it's been updated with a new kitchen and bathrooms.

The garden contains a trampoline, various ride-on vehicles and a two-storey playhouse kitted out with everything you can think of in miniature for the twins, yet George, Lydia and Elena are intent on getting their hands on Kit and Tilly.

'I'm warning you,' I say sternly. 'They look cute, but they bite and scratch. They are more dangerous than any crocodile.'

George gazes at me, uncertain about whether to argue that point or not.

'Please don't touch, otherwise I'll have to take them straight home, and your mummy will have to take you to hospital again to have your fingers sewn back on.'

His eyes grow wide.

'I've left their bottles of milk warming up in a bowl in the kitchen. It would be a great help if you could fetch them for me,' I say.

'You're so devious,' Celine says, when the three of them disappear into the house. 'I'm not sure I'd have even thought of that with my little monsters. I should be taking notes.' She looks into the carrier. Kit hisses at her. 'You and Ross? I've been meaning to ask. Are you . . .?'

I shake my head, wishing the children would hurry up with the bottles, at which they appear with the twins carrying one each.

'I would if I wasn't married,' she giggles. 'Maz calls him the boy racer – she says she prefers a man in tight breeches.'

I take Tilly out of the carrier and feed her first. She drains the milk and hiccups.

'She burped.' George laughs, making the twins laugh too.

'It won't be long before I start weaning them onto

solid food and then we'll have to decide what to do
with them,' I say, thinking aloud. 'It will be hard
letting them go.'

'I'll give one of them a home,' Celine offers. 'I don't
mind which one. What do you think?'

'That would be great as long as they're tame enough
to fit into normal society.'

'I'm not sure I'd describe my family as normal.' She
changes the subject. 'I hope Frances is going to turn
up soon.'

'I expect she wants to make a grand entrance,' I say.

'It's her prerogative,' Ross says, joining us with a
glass of shandy in his hand. 'It's her party, after all.'

The kittens settle down to sleep and the children
run off to the playhouse. Bart grabs a stick from the
flowerbed alongside us and starts chewing it. I give
Ross a nudge to suggest he takes it away, but he lets
him carry on. Maz joins us, topping up my glass of
apple juice.

'I have some exciting news,' she says.

'You aren't pregnant again?' I say, squinting into
the sun.

'No way,' she chuckles. 'No, Emma and I looked at
a property in Talymouth this morning – that's why
we're running behind. We've made an offer and we're
waiting to see if it's been accepted.'

'That's brilliant,' I say, uncertain how I feel about
a branch surgery now that it is more likely to happen.

'There's a long way to go before we can make any
decisions about staffing, and it needs some work – if
we get it, of course.' Maz gazes at Bart, who's tossing
the stick in the air and catching it. 'I can think of
someone who'd make a great branch manager.'

'I wonder who that is,' I say as she walks away.

'I reckon she's talking about the dog,' Ross laughs. 'You see, you needn't have worried. He's being angelic.'

We continue to chat and, half an hour later, when Ben is beginning to stress over his organic beefburgers and vegetable kebabs, Frances arrives with her husband, Lenny.

Ross smiles. 'Good, I was worried we wouldn't get to eat before we're called away again.'

Once we've demolished the barbecued food and salads, Maz gives Frances her presents – a watercolour of Otter House that she commissioned Penny to paint, a pen and a gift voucher – and brings out one of Jennie's celebration cakes with a knife and plates.

'I hope you've enjoyed the party,' she says. 'I know you didn't want a fuss, but we couldn't let you go without one. I'd like to wish you all the best for the future. I've been looking up definitions and the one I like best is that retirement is when you get up in the morning with nothing to do and by bedtime you haven't done a tenth of it. Knowing you, Frances, you'll be so busy that you'll wonder how you ever had time to go to work.'

She pauses. 'On a serious note, I'd like to say that Frances has always kept us very well informed about what's going on with our clients, and she makes the best cup of tea in Talyton. She's provided us with a shoulder to cry on from time to time, and she's always been completely committed to the practice, for which Emma and I are eternally grateful. We couldn't have done it without you. You will be sorely missed.' Smiling through tears, she picks up a box of tissues from beneath the table and hands them over. 'Help yourself.'

Frances thanks her, and wipes her eyes.

Maz looks at Emma and they start to sing, 'For she's a jolly good fellow', and everyone else joins in. Maz cuts the cake, a rich sponge with 'Good luck' iced onto the top, into irregular pieces.

'Call yourself a surgeon,' Emma jokes.

'Don't you want any then?' Maz says with a smile.

'I didn't say that.' Emma holds out a plate for a slice of fluffy chocolate sponge oozing with buttercream. At the same time, Ross's mobile rings with a call from a client whose cat has been hit by a car.

'We'll have to leave the cake,' he says. 'Let's go.' He wraps Bart's lead around his wrist. 'Don't forget the kittens.'

'As if.' I give Frances a hug. 'We'll catch up soon, I hope.'

I miss her. When I'm admitting the patients for their operations one morning after the party, I find that each time I go into reception, I have to readjust to finding Celine there instead. She's efficient, and although she doesn't know much about the veterinary side of her job, she's learning quickly. I leave the kittens behind the desk with her in between feeds so she can look after them, taking them out when she has five minutes to accustom them to being handled by more people.

Today, it's like a game of 'How many people can you fit into a consulting room?'

Ross is in the corner, reaching across the table to shake hands with Stevie from Nettlebed Farm. She's in her thirties, a farmer's daughter who left Talyton St George and came back when her father and their cowman began to struggle with looking after their dairy herd. She set up an alternative business, a petting farm where people take their little kids to stroke rabbits and cuddle chickens. Occasionally, she'll bring one of their small furries to Otter House for treatment, but her husband Leo, who works for Alex at Talyton Manor Vets, looks after the sheep, goats and donkeys.

Stevie has her child – a girl – strapped into a buggy, and a big dog on a lead. He opens his mouth and yawns nervously, emitting a pungent scent of halitosis into the mix of disinfectant, wet canine and farmyard.

I've met Bear before. He's a cuddly patchwork of various breeds, with odd eyes and one ear up and the other down, the kind of character who brings a smile to your face without even trying.

I step inside the room, pull the door shut behind me and press myself against it, while both Maz and Izzy enter through the other door from reception, Izzy with the consent form, and Maz wanting to have a word with Ross.

'I'm delighted to point out that Stevie has her own vet, yet she's chosen us to look after Bear,' she says. The Otter House and Talyton Manor vets can get quite competitive.

'Leo says he doesn't want to get the blame if something goes wrong. Not that anything will, I'm sure. Bear has been here before for a dental,' Stevie explains.

'I remember,' Maz says. 'I think we clipped most of his hair off too.'

It was me. I clipped him and gave him a bath. He was filthy – not Stevie's fault, I hasten to add. Bear's neglect had been another sign that her father wasn't coping with running the farm.

'I'll leave you to it then,' Maz continues. 'I'll catch you later, Ross.'

Ross gives Bear a once-over before giving him a shot of sedative, a low dose appropriate for an old dog.

'I don't mind how many teeth you take out; anything to make him smell sweeter,' Stevie says. 'It's a shame because when he comes up to say hi, everyone backs off.'

'We'll see what they're like,' he says, but you can tell from a mile away.

Stevie, who was confident at first, suddenly has a wobble as she signs the consent form.

'I do hope he'll be all right.' She drops the pen and squats down to hug Bear and kiss the top of his head.

'There's no reason why he shouldn't be fine. Maz took some blood the other day to check his kidneys and everything looks hunky-dory.' Ross catches my eye and gives an almost imperceptible shrug in reply. Since when has 'hunky-dory' become a technical term?

'I'll take him through and find him a bed for the day,' I say, aware that he wants to get on.

'You be a good boy. Love you.' Sniffing, Stevie stands up and hands me the lead. 'I feel such an idiot.'

'You can't help it. They're part of the family,' Ross says, and I wonder if he's thinking of Bart.

I take the forms, glancing down at Bear's details. Under breed, it reads 'mostly collie'. He was an old dog when he first turned up at Otter House, but he's aged considerably since I last saw him. His nails click-clack along the floor when I take him through to Kennels – I can't wait to give them a good trim while he's under anaesthetic.

He is the last patient to be admitted, so I'm free to finish setting up in theatre. I remove a set of instruments, hot from the autoclave, while I'm waiting for Ross; he turns up a few minutes later, changed into his scrubs. I can hardly tear my eyes away from the V of his top where the dark hairs that adorn his lightly tanned skin curl across the base of his neck, and at the muscles in his arms that flex and bulge. It's no good. The more I try to suppress the feeling, the more I fancy him. Concentrate, I tell myself, as he puts on a theatre cap.

'What are you staring at?' he says, as he tucks his hair inside it.

'That cap. It isn't a good look.'

'I'd rather be wearing my helmet. Perhaps I should do that: design some cool theatre gear.'

We anaesthetise the first patient, a cat for spaying, and while I finish preparing her for surgery, Ross scrubs up at the sink before gowning and gloving.

'We're getting rather good at this,' he says, when we've finished all the sterile ops by coffee time, and there's only Bear's dental left to do.

'Not bad.' I survey the mess he's left behind him – he's been rushing me and I haven't had time to tidy up yet.

After the break, I fetch Bear. We lift him onto the prep bench where he sits drooling calmly as Ross injects a touch of anaesthetic so he's sleepy enough to be tubed and connected to the anaesthetic machine. I turn the oxygen on.

'That is what I call dog breath.' Ross grimaces as he hands me a mask and puts one on himself.

I check Bear's colour and reflexes. His breathing is regular and his pulse is steady.

'All's well. He's ready when you are.'

'He hasn't got many teeth left. He had ten removed the last time, according to his notes,' he says, looking inside the dog's mouth.

'I don't think Stevie took the advice I gave her the last time about regular brushing.'

'You can take a horse to water, but you can't make it drink. I don't expect you have time to clean Seven's teeth every day.'

'I do actually. Most days. As you do with Bart, no doubt.'

'Unfortunately not. He isn't the most obliging dog when it comes to dental hygiene.' He picks up a set of dental forceps, and plucks out a tooth.

'Look how easily that one fell out. You would have thought Leo would have noticed something was wrong before now.'

'I don't think he lives in the house with them. He's a yard dog,' I say, in Leo and Stevie's defence.

'There's one more to come out at the back, then you can scale and polish, if you like.'

'Can I?' I say, pleased that he's confident to let me do more. Maz has allowed me to scale and polish teeth a few times before, whereas Emma prefers to do it all herself.

'I'll be here, keeping an eye.'

'Do you want to do any X-rays?'

'I'm sure Maz will have talked to Stevie and Leo about that. Bear's an old dog, it adds to the cost, and this seems pretty routine, so no, I'll just whip this molar out at the back.'

Bear is fine under the anaesthetic, even when Ross takes the electric saw to the tooth and cuts it into pieces. I relax, but after fifteen minutes of watching

Speedivet struggling to remove it root by root, I start
to worry. This isn't like him at all.

'I'm having trouble with this one,' he admits
eventually. Red-faced, he starts to lever out the last
root with some force, leaning on the dog's chest so
hard that I have to warn him not to interfere with his
breathing.

'Shall I go and get Maz?' I don't think it's an
unreasonable suggestion, considering that two vets
can sometimes be better than one, but Ross gives me
a glare.

'What do you think she can do that I can't? I am
perfectly capable!'

'I'm sure you are, but—'

'Just shut up and let me concentrate.' He leans
back over the dog and, suddenly, there's a terrible
crack.

'What was that?' I exclaim.

'That's never happened before. I don't understand.'
He swears as he examines Bear's mouth. 'Set up for
an X-ray,' he adds sharply.

I hesitate, wondering if it's safe to leave the patient
when the vet appears to be in a state of shock.

'Go on. I'll watch the dog and check on the bloods
that Maz took to see if we missed something.'

I set up the X-ray machine to take a couple of views
of Bear's jaw. As soon as the pictures emerge from
the processor, even I can see there's something very
wrong. The bone is broken. I feel the same depth of
nausea and sense of inevitability that I did when
Drew made his fatal error with Mrs Dyer's dog. All
kinds of questions run through my head. Doesn't
Ross know his own strength? How will he tell Stevie
that Bear is going home with more of a problem than

he came in with? The thought occurs to me: *If* Bear goes home . . .

'I wasn't expecting that – it's no wonder that jaw snapped.' Ross looks at the X-rays on the viewer and points out an area where the bone has been destroyed by some kind of cancer. I have mixed feelings, because it proves that it wasn't his fault, but it makes the outcome look worse for the dog. He turns on his heels and walks away.

'What do you want me to do?' I call after him. 'Wake him up?'

'Keep him under,' he calls back, before returning with Maz for a second opinion; a little ironic, I think uncharitably, considering how he wanted to deal with it all himself. I overhear them discussing the options, but the general agreement is that it would be kinder to put the dog to sleep than put him through any prolonged, painful and potentially fruitless attempts at treatment.

I don't know if Bear can hear me, but I talk to him quietly too, treating him as I'd want someone to treat Seven if he should ever end up in this situation.

'I can speak to Stevie,' Maz offers. 'I don't mind.'

'I'll do it, thank you,' Ross says. 'It's my responsibility. He's my patient.'

'You don't have to take everything on your shoulders. I booked him in for you this morning. It could easily have been me or Emma in your . . .' She looks down and up again with a wry smile. 'Clogs.' She reaches out and touches his arm. 'Come on, let me do it. Stevie's a friend of mine.'

The vets disappear for a few minutes, leaving me with Bear. I stroke him, hoping that he's had a happy life.

When Ross comes back, he looks a little pale and weary.

'What's the decision?' I ask.

'I'm going to put him to sleep without waking him.'

'Stevie doesn't want to say goodbye?'

'She says it would be wrong to let him come round so she could have him home for a couple of days. She doesn't want him to suffer.'

I remember how upset she was when she left him. I think she had a feeling when she brought him in that she wouldn't be taking him back to the farm. I fetch the blue juice, Ross injects it into the catheter in the vein and Bear utters one last sigh as I whisper goodbye. I take a deep breath. Sometimes the final stillness catches me and I have to turn away for a moment before I can help slide him into a bag.

'Stevie's sending Leo down to pick up the body – they're going to bury him at home.'

I tag the bag, but when I write his name, 'Bear', I can't hold back any longer and I burst into tears. No one is to blame, but I still feel guilty. We're here to save lives, but there are times like this when it doesn't work out.

'Hey, come here.' I attempt to step away, but Ross slides his arms around my back and pulls me close. I can feel his fingers stroking the nape of my neck as he murmurs into my ear, his breath damp against my skin.

I press my hands against his chest, afraid to lean into his embrace and give away my feelings. He's a friend, we're having a hard time at work and he's trying to comfort me, nothing more.

Eventually, he releases me and walks away, saying he'll join the others, but I don't take a break, preferring to feed the kittens and keep busy clearing up after the ops rather than sit in the staff room where the atmosphere will be one of gloom. Losing a patient affects everyone, and if I'm feeling this bad about it, poor Ross must be feeling so much worse, but that doesn't excuse the way he spoke to me. I resolve to say something but, when we catch up later, as I'm ready to leave at the end of my shift, he speaks first.

'I'm sorry about earlier.'

'We don't have to talk about this now,' I say, aware that people are arriving for evening surgery.

'I know we decided on no house rules, but I think it's better not to bring work home, and this won't take long.' He pauses briefly before going on, 'You were right about doing X-rays beforehand – it's best practice.'

'How many clients are prepared to pay more for that, though?' I say, trying to cheer him up when he's been gracious enough to admit he was wrong. 'You did your best under the circumstances.'

'That's very philosophical of you, but I feel like I've let Leo and Stevie – and Bear down.'

'Leo will understand. These things shouldn't happen to a vet, but they do.'

'Thank you.' He gazes at me, his expression contrite. 'I'm sorry for the way I spoke to you too. I shouldn't have told you to shut up.'

'You're right. I know you're stressed out, but there's no reason to take it out on me – we're supposed to be on the same side.'

There are dark shadows under his eyes and the muscle in his cheek tightens and relaxes. It's been a terrible day and I can't bring myself to give him a tough time. All I want to do is give him a hug and tell him everything will be all right, but I can't risk betraying my feelings. I love him. There, I've admitted it to myself at last. I'm completely in love with Ross Curdridge.

'It's one of those days when you wonder why you do this job,' he says. 'It certainly isn't for the money and it isn't much fun.'

'You'd miss it if you gave it up. Imagine working in a bank, stuck at a desk all day, staring at figures, or—'

'Racing motorbikes or flying planes,' he cuts in with a rueful smile. 'Let's go out for a drink and something to eat tonight. We could both do with cheering up.'

'Okay, why not?' It makes sense when he's the only person who understands what I'm going through and vice versa.

'That's great. I should be back by seven,' he nods towards the consulting room door, 'patients permitting.'

'I'll see you then.' I relieve Celine of the kittens and, when I get home, I sit feeding them at the breakfast bar with the doors open onto the garden. Bindweed, covered with grandmother-pop-out-of-bed flowers, winds through the roses and brambles in the hedge at the end of the lawn; in the field beyond, several black and white calves are grazing with their mothers. I pour myself a glass of wine. I know it's early, but this is one of the rare occasions when really I could do with a drink. I take a sip and check my phone. There's a text message from Taylor.

Are you still up for meeting at leisure centre at eight? X

I text back. *Not tonight. I've had a bad day.*

What's up? she messages back.

It's work xx
Okay, as long as you're all right. X
I text back to reassure her. I don't mention that I'm going out with Ross because I don't want to hurt her feelings. I take my wine upstairs and soak in the bath before changing into a black and silver maxi dress and flat sandals. I blow-dry my long chestnut hair straight and put it up, then apply black mascara, eyeliner and silver eyeshadow to emphasise my blue-green eyes. I head downstairs, where I find Ross in the hall. He takes off his helmet and leaves it on the floor, but I don't comment. He stops and looks up at me, pursing his lips and uttering a low whistle as I walk down the steps. My skin grows warm as he speaks.

'You look amazing.'

'I don't know about that.'

'It's absolutely true. You are amazing!' he grins. 'You're also very argumentative.'

'I'm not.'

'Yes, you are.'

'All right, point taken. I give in.'

'I'll have a quick shower, then we'll go and have that drink.'

'Actually, I've already started,' I confess. 'Would you like one?'

'I'll wait, thanks. I thought we could walk to the Talymill Inn for a pint or two. It isn't that far if you go via the footpath.'

'Another couple of glasses of wine and I'll be on the floor.'

'I'll pick you up.'

'There's an offer I might not be able to refuse,' I say archly, but if he thinks I'm joking he's wrong. If he came on to me, I wouldn't turn him down this time.

'Shannon?' he begins.

'Yes?' I wait, wondering if he's about to say something deep and meaningful, what I've been waiting and hoping for, that this could be more than two people who've had a bad day drowning their sorrows, but he hesitates before shrugging and going on, 'Nothing. It's nothing. Give me ten minutes and I'll be with you.'

In my presence, but not really with me, not in the way I desperately want him to be, I think. I fancy him and I'm pretty sure he's attracted to me, so why not do something about it? I feed the kittens one last time before we go out, pushing my remaining doubts and obstacles aside. If he won't ask me, then I'll just have to ask him.

Chapter Sixteen

Through the Kissing Gate

Fifteen minutes later, we're walking through the fields towards the river. I glance at my housemate as we trample through the long grass beneath the leafy oak and horse-chestnut trees. He's wearing a grey T-shirt with a motorbike motif, jeans, and boots which seem too much for a warm August evening. His hair is damp from the shower, and his head is bowed, as if he's deep in thought.

'Are you okay? It wasn't your fault, remember.'

'Oh, the dog?' He turns to look at me. 'I feel sad about him, but it isn't that. I had some bad news this morning.'

'Why didn't you say?' I feel a little hurt that he hasn't confided in me. I thought he might have shared.

'Heidi rang to let me know her mum's been diagnosed with liver failure.'

Heidi again? I suppress a pang of disappointment that she and Ross are apparently still close enough for her to think it necessary to update her ex on the health of her relatives. I'm being harsh. I don't suppose you can wipe seven years of history just like that.

'She's devastated, of course.'

'I'm sorry.' I wonder what she's expecting, that he will dash to her side to console her.

'In spite of her faults, Barbara has always been kind to me. I spent a lot of time at her house – the wine was always flowing. The good life appears to have caught up with her, though.

'I'll drop into Petals and arrange to have some flowers sent to show I'm thinking of her,' he goes on.

I don't ask if he means flowers for Heidi or for her mother. It doesn't matter. He isn't with Heidi any more. He isn't in love with her, and if it wasn't for Bart, they wouldn't be in contact. He's told me that and I believe him.

'Life's a bitch,' he goes on, his eyes darkening as we reach a crossroads where two footpaths intersect. 'Which way now?'

'Keep straight on down the hill. We're almost there.'

The Talymill Inn is busy with tourists and locals. The car park is full.

'Only in Devon could you find a tractor and a pony and trap parked at the pub,' Ross observes with a small smile. 'Where would you like to sit? Inside or out?'

We settle for a table inside because all the seats in the beer garden are taken, and order food – a veggie lasagne for me and chicken curry for Ross – at the bar.

'Aren't you drinking?' I ask, when I see that he's on lemonade and lime.

He shakes his head. 'I'm not in the mood. Maybe later.' He rests his arm across the back of the seat behind me. 'How about a toast anyway? To friendship.' He raises his glass and I lift mine in return, chinking it against his. 'To being housemates.' His hand settles on my shoulder. 'Are you feeling better now?' he adds softly as the food arrives.

I nod. I think so, but I can only pick at my pasta. The loss of our patient, the news that Heidi is unloading her problems onto her ex and the wine, along with Ross's physical presence, has taken the edge off my appetite.

'Can I get you another drink?' I offer.

'Thanks.' He hands me his glass and our fingers touch. I pull away sharply, wondering if he's aware of the effect his touch has on me. Does he feel it too?

'I'll be back soon,' I say, standing up and moving away. As I'm ordering the drinks, I spot Stewart Pitt – one of the local dairy farmers and the guy who's left his tractor parked outside – propping up the bar.

'Hello, Shannon,' he smiles, exhaling hot, beery breath. He's dressed in a tatty vest which shows off his heavily muscled arms and pot belly.

'Hi.' I dig about in my purse for cash to pay the barman. I'm not keen on Mr Pitt. He's about the same age as Alex Fox-Gifford and has quite a reputation. In fact, there was a time when Maz operated on his dog and removed some women's underwear which turned out not to belong to his wife.

'I hear the new vet made a bit of a cock-up,' he goes on. 'Didn't he bust a dog's jaw?'

'It wasn't deliberate.'

'It's all round town. Lynsey found out from Stevie when she took the kids to Nettlebed Farm to see the animals today.' Lynsey is Stewart's long-suffering wife. 'I don't know why she does that when they can see our cows on our farm anytime.'

I can't help thinking that she probably wants to get away from her opinionated husband. I pick up the drinks from the bar and turn to move away, but Stewart doesn't want to let the subject of Bear go just yet.

'I bet Maz is pretty mad about it.'

'She's upset. We all are.' My face grows hot with irritation as I try to keep my cool, recalling that he's lost a dog before so he should have some understanding.

'This Ross chap sounds completely clueless, if you ask me,' he goes on in a booming voice, as if he's calling his cows in from the field.

'I'm not asking you,' I say sharply, aware that the conversation in the pub has stopped for everyone to listen in to his criticism.

'It isn't good for business, though, employing someone who doesn't know his own strength. I wouldn't trust him with my kids' pets.'

'You're making a judgement without knowing all the facts,' I say, sensing the pressure of a hand against my buttock through the material of my dress. 'I've seen how he looks after his patients and he's a great vet. I'd trust him with my dog anytime.' I give Stewart what I hope is a withering stare. 'I'm surprised you're such a gossip when you've so often been the subject of it yourself.'

He falls silent, his ruddy cheeks reddening further.

'You can destroy a reputation – or a marriage – in seconds,' I go on in a low voice, before I raise it so everyone can hear. 'Now shut up and get your hand off my bum.' I turn and walk away with the drinks, returning to the table, where Ross is gazing at me with admiration.

'Thank you for standing up for me. You were magnificent. I wouldn't want to be on the wrong side of you,' he says, letting me back into my seat. 'Who is that bloke?'

'One of the local farmers. I hope that little outburst doesn't get back to Maz and Emma. His wife is a good client of ours – they have a rescue dog called Raffles.'

Ross sits back down. 'Changing the subject, Maz and Emma have asked me to take on the new branch surgery.'

'Really? You didn't say.'

'They swore me to secrecy until their offer was accepted – it was agreed today. I know it will be a while until they exchange contracts and finalise the deal, but it looks like it will be a formality.' He grins. 'I hate secrets and this one's been killing me. What do you think? Emma's agreed to let me run it my way so it will be almost as good as having my own practice.' He half closes his eyes. 'I can't wait until I'm working for myself, pretty much anyway.'

'I suppose I should congratulate you.'

'I'm going to let my parents know that I definitely won't be going back now.'

'I thought you'd already decided that.' I wonder if he's trying to prove himself, even though he says that they don't matter to him and have no part in his life.

'I had, but I want my father to know I've done very well without him. He never thought I'd leave the family practice in the first place.'

'I'll be sorry to see you go,' I say, putting on a brave face.

'I'm not going far. It's the place in Talymouth, one of the houses that was on Godfrey's books.'

271

'But I like working with you. I've just got used to your ways and you're pushing off.'

'You've got the wrong end of the stick. I said I'd only do it if you came with me. What do you think?' He moves his glass in small circles on the table, making the bubbles rise to the surface.

'Really?'

'Why not? You're my favourite nurse. I know I can rely on you. And you're a lot of fun to be with,' he adds.

'I don't believe it. Thanks, Ross. That's amazing.' My blood feels like it's fizzing with joy. 'I assumed that Izzy would be given that role because she has more experience of running a practice.'

'Oh no, I couldn't possibly work with her full time. She's like a drug – all right in small doses. Maz is cool with it. She says that she'll advertise for either a trainee or a qualified VN for Otter House.'

'When do we start?' I can hardly contain my excitement.

'It's going to take a few weeks for the solicitors to do their bit and the sale to go through and then it will take a while to complete the building works.' He tips his head to one side, grinning. 'Especially with DJ doing it. But we're aiming for early in the New Year. The previous owners have already obtained planning permission for a change of use, so it should be pretty straightforward. I've said no lilac and insisted on making room for an operating theatre because there's no way I'm going along with Emma's idea of transporting surgical patients to the main surgery.' He hesitates. 'It will have to be just the two of us for a while, until enough clients have signed up for us to be able to afford a

272

receptionist. Do you think you'll be able to put up with me?'

'Now, let me see,' I say, touching my finger to my lip. 'I've managed to live with you for three whole weeks and we haven't fallen out so far.'

'I'm not sure what will happen about our living arrangements when the branch practice opens.'

'Oh? You mean, you'll give up the house in Talyford and move in?'

'Maz wants someone to live on the premises, but the flat will only have one bedroom . . .'

'We'd have to share,' I say brightly.

Ross is still grinning. 'I reckon someone has had more than enough to drink, but it's an interesting idea. You won't feel the same in the morning, though. Come on. We'd better make a move. It's quite a trek unless we call for a taxi.'

'I'd prefer to walk, if you don't mind.' I hold out my hand and he helps me to my feet. 'I hope you're not going to let the idea of running your own practice go to your head . . .'

'I think the drink's gone to yours.' He follows me out of the pub and down through the gardens to the river, where we wander back along the path where bats dart and swoop through the twilight. Something splashes in the water. An owl and its mate call back and forth from the trees.

'We were supposed to be out for a few drinks. It isn't my fault that you're stone-cold sober,' I say, to excuse myself for having drunk at least one too many.

'I don't mind. I couldn't face it tonight, not after the news about Heidi's mum.'

'Was it down to alcohol then?'

'She's been an addict for years.'

I stumble on ahead, worried that I appear insensitive, even though I didn't put two and two together earlier on when he first mentioned Heidi's mother.

'I'm sorry.' He catches up with me again. 'I'm not saying that I disapprove. You know me. I like a few drinks as much as the next person. It's just that this evening, I'm not in the mood.'

'You're upset for Heidi. You still miss her.' I reach the kissing gate that stands across the path on the way into the next meadow. We're almost home and I'm nowhere nearer telling him how I feel. I turn to face him, with my hand on the lever on the latch.

'I don't miss her as such. I miss being in a relationship. I miss the little things like holding hands, saying I love you and buying gifts – silly ones, like solar-powered dancing flowers, the things you didn't know you needed that you find at the garage when you're filling up with fuel – and—'

'Kissing?' I add hopefully. Steadying myself, I lean towards him and kiss him hard on the mouth before withdrawing slightly, closing my eyes and waiting for him to return the contact, my heart pounding with desire and anticipation. How long have we been waiting for this? How long have we been holding back? And for what?

'What's wrong?' I murmur, opening my eyes once more as he takes a half-step back. His face is pale in the moonlight, his expression taut. 'I don't understand. I thought you liked me. Oh-mi-god.' I turn away, confused and embarrassed at having misread the situation.

He catches my arm and moves around to face me. 'I've told you before – you're beautiful.'

'That isn't the same as finding someone attractive . . .'

'I find you attractive all right. You don't realise how hard it's been, living and working with you, and having to pretend I don't feel anything for you.' A light flashes across the river – a torch, or the head-lights on a car, I'm not sure. 'It might surprise you, but I think I know how you feel. I knew as soon as we moved in that I'd made a mistake in assuming we could be "just friends".'

I take hold of his shirt and pull him towards me. He grasps my wrists and holds me back.

'But,' he adds, 'I'm not going to take advantage of you while you're drunk.'

'It's all right. I know what I'm doing.'

'I don't want to wreck everything for one night of drunken lust.'

'Ross, you're so boring. Where's your sense of adventure?' I can feel his leg against mine as I try to pull him closer with my arms around his neck. 'I thought we were out to have some fun.'

He humours me, resting his hands on my waist.

'You are so pissed,' he groans.

'You're swaying,' I say, tripping against him.

'It's you, not me! Come on. Let's get some coffee inside you.'

'I'd rather have something else,' I mutter. 'Inside me . . .'

'That's outrageous.' He's laughing now as he takes my hand and leads me through the gate and up the hill to where the path joins the lane to Talyford. We walk along the verge to the ford where he picks me up and carries me across.

'What are you doing? There's no water,' I giggle,

clasping my arms around his neck and looking down. 'I can get home under my own self-esteem.'

'I doubt it when you can hardly speak, let alone put one foot in front of the other.'

'Will you carry me up to bed too?' I press my mouth to his cheek.

'I'll carry you as far as the front door,' he says, sounding slightly breathless. 'There's nothing more I want than to take you to bed and make love to you all night long, but you're in no fit state to make that decision.'

I start to protest, but he frowns at me, and adds hoarsely, 'You'll thank me for this tomorrow.'

'I can't see why . . .' He lowers me to the ground and lets us both into the house. The hallway is spinning, but it isn't just down to the alcohol. It's how Ross makes me feel, giddy with desire.

'Coffee, in this case, means just that: coffee,' he says firmly, and he makes us both a hot drink at the same time as preparing the kittens' milk. Sipping my coffee, I watch him feeding them as we sit side by side on the sofa. Although a strong dose of caffeine sobers me up a touch, it does nothing to restore my inhibitions. When he's put the kittens to bed in their temporary pen in the kitchen, he returns and sits back down, caressing my hand as he relieves me of my empty mug and places it on the floor.

'Time for bed,' he says, his voice trailing off as I turn and look him straight in the eye.

'That's a brilliant idea,' I murmur. I reach out and rest my hand on his thigh, feeling the tremor in the hot hard muscle beneath, and hearing the catch of his breath. My head is clear and my heart pounding when I lean closer and pause, my senses alert, my skin on fire for his touch.

'Shannon, are you sure?' he growls softly.

'I'm sure. I do know what I'm doing.' I nod and wait for him to decide. The tension is painful. I know he wants me as much as I want him, but will his conscience win? Very slowly, he tilts his face towards mine, until our lips are just touching. He groans and presses his mouth to mine, and it's better, more intense, more exciting than I ever imagined a kiss could be. Eventually, he pulls away and takes my hand.

'Let's go upstairs,' he says, his voice tremulous.

'I thought you'd never ask,' I whisper.

The next morning, I wake with a thumping headache. I shift in my bed, listening to the birds singing outside as the morning light sears the backs of my eyes. As I pull on the duvet, I hear a low moan. What the . . . ? There's a damp warmth at the back of my neck and a naked arm covered with dark hair lying across me. I turn my head very slowly to find Ross's face close to mine. He opens one eye and smiles.

'Hi gorgeous,' he murmurs.

'What happened? Did we . . . ?' I roll onto my back and press my hand to my forehead, as if the contact will activate my brain. The memories of last night come flooding back: drinks at the pub, the walk home and the kissing gate, me throwing myself at him . . .

Ross raises himself, leaning on his elbow, and looks at me with an appreciative expression.

'I think you know very well what happened. You seduced me.'

I remember it clearly now. He led me by the hand to the bedroom and kissed me some more before we made love. It was awkward at first, then passionate. He made me feel like I've never felt before.

He reaches across to kiss me on the cheek. 'I'm sorry, I tried to be a gentleman, but in the end, I couldn't resist,' he says with a wicked gleam in his eye. 'I've been fighting the urge to pick you up and carry you to bed for a while now.' He hesitates. 'You are lovely, Shannon, and if . . .' He falters. 'I'm not sure how to put this. There's nothing I'd like more than to change our housemate status to something more than friends. What do you think?'

'You mean lovers?' I say cautiously.

'I prefer boyfriend-girlfriend. It sounds more committed. I associate the concept of being lovers with infidelity – because of my father, I suppose. And I don't like the idea of being a couple of mates who go on dates. Again, it suggests that there could be a lack of exclusivity, and I'm just not into casual relationships.'

I want to say that I feel the same, but that would be a little hypocritical of me, considering how Mitch and I did casual for a while after we broke up. This isn't the time or the place. I gaze at Ross as the rays of the sun stream through the window and caress his face. In spite of the hangover, I'm smiling. Isn't this what I've been yearning for?

'I'd love to go out with you,' I say, as his hand moves across my belly and strokes the curve of my waist.

He grins and kisses me again before pulling away abruptly.

'That's great. We'll talk later. I reckon we're going to be late for work.'

I struggle to get out of bed and grab my dress from

where it's strewn across the floor, trying to cover myself up before I find some clean clothes from the wardrobe. Ross stands behind me with the duvet wrapped around his shoulders. He picks up my mobile from the bedside table.

'It's eight o'clock,' he says.

'What am I going to do?' I bite my lip. 'I should be looking after the inpatients. Izzy will kill me.'

'What you're going to do,' he says, taking my shoulder with one hand and holding the duvet at his neck with the other, 'is throw your scrubs on while I make you a coffee. You can take it with you.'

'What about you though? You're on ops.'

'I know – I'll catch you up. It's all right. I won't break any speed limits this time.'

'I'll have to give Tilly and Kit their breakfast at work.' I feel sick and a little apprehensive. What an idiot. I never have more than a couple of glasses of wine when I'm working the next day.

'Are you all right?' he asks gently. 'I mean about what happened last night. You aren't having second thoughts, because I'm not? I don't regret a minute of it.' He leans towards me and kisses my cheek. 'Go on, go and get dressed.'

Maz takes me to task when I arrive over half an hour late.

'What time do you call this?' she says, when I find her in Kennels feeding Tripod. 'Where's Ross?'

'He's on his way.' I cringe – I've never seen my boss so angry. 'I'm really sorry,' I grovel.

'I bet you are.' Suddenly, she grins. 'I'm pulling your leg. You look like death warmed up – maybe not a good analogy after what happened to poor Bear yesterday. A good night, was it?'

Honesty is the best policy, because she'll find out one way or another. 'I had a couple of drinks at the pub.'

'And some, I should imagine. I realise you and Ross had a bad day, so I'm not going to say any more. I think, from the look of you, the hangover is punishment enough. Just don't let it happen again.'

'I won't. I'll never drink again.'

'That's what we all say . . .'

Ross arrives a few minutes later – at least, I hear the sound of his motorbike as he turns up at the practice. But I don't see him for another hour or so, when he appears at the door into theatre, which is useful because it means I have time to feed the kittens before we start.

'Where have you been?' I ask as I top up the vaporiser for the anaesthetic.

'Are you trying to poison me?' he asks, half joking.

'I'm sorry. I forgot to do it last night.'

'Breaking the rules again, I don't know,' he sighs.

He's right. I should have given time for any escaping fumes to disperse.

'I'll turn the fan up.'

'Maz has been reading me the riot act. Apparently, I shouldn't be leading you astray.' A small smile crosses his lips. 'I told her it was the other way round.'

'You what?' I exclaim.

'I didn't drop you in it. I wouldn't.' He hesitates. 'Have you seen what we have on this morning?'

I nod, and wish I'd kept my head still, as my brain is knocking around inside my skull like a loose walnut. There are six patients on the list – a lot to get through at the best of times. We make a start on the ops, not stopping for coffee, deciding that it would be best to make up the lost hour at the beginning of the day, but we do take ten minutes outside in the fresh air. I sit opposite Ross at the table on the patio where Tripod is chasing butterflies.

'What are you thinking?' he asks quietly.

I blush, recalling the pressure of my lips on his and the heat in my blood, and how I felt lying in his arms. I pick at my nails and pop my finger joints. 'I was wondering if I should move out.'

'Why on earth would you do that?' He moves towards me. His scent, the warm musk of his body, is almost irresistible. 'Have you changed your mind?'

'I am fond of you,' I stammer.

'Fond? That's a pretty non-committal word.' He tips his head to one side. 'I'm confused. You don't want to go out with me?' His eyes are filled with pain, like a chastised puppy unsure what he's being told off for.

'No, I do,' I exclaim.

'But you don't want to live with me any more?'

'It isn't that. It's just that . . . what if it goes wrong?'

'Oh, Shannon,' he sighs. He reaches his hand across the table and touches his fingertips to mine. A molten ball of longing forms in my stomach. 'I understand where you're coming from and why you feel insecure, but I'm not a bad man. I have no intention of letting you down. I promise I'll always be honest with you.'

'It feels like we've done things the wrong way round – moving in together before dating.'

'How about we go on some dates? I'd like to take you out, spoil you and do all the things we'd do if we were just getting to know each other. I've wanted you for a long time, but I didn't want to make a move on you while we were living together. I didn't want you to think I was sleazy and I'd engineered it so I could get closer to you. I vowed to wait to see how we felt when the lease on the house came to an end.'

He grasps my hand tight. 'I've spent weeks in a state of pent-up frustration. Watching you wander about in your pyjamas – that vest and tiny shorts – and sharing the sofa with you in the evenings, pretending that my feelings are entirely friendly, has been hard. *Very* hard,' he reiterates with a chuckle.

'You cheeky . . .' I can't help laughing.

'I don't know how many times I've had to pick up one of the cushions and place it strategically across my lap.'

'I had noticed. I had to cuddle a cushion to keep my hands off you . . .'

'Why didn't you say anything?'

'I couldn't because of the rules, my self-imposed rules. It was about self-preservation. I was scared of being hurt. I was afraid you'd let me down, especially when I thought you might still be involved with your ex, but I know now that I was wrong.'

'You do trust me?'

I nod. 'Of course I do.'

'So where do we go from here?' He hesitates. 'How about I take you for dinner tonight?'

'I'm sorry, I'm supposed to be going swimming with Taylor and I bombed her out yesterday so I don't feel like I can do it again. I'm free tomorrow,' I add hastily.

'There's no hurry – we've waited this long. Another day won't kill us. I'll book us a table.'

We sit staring at each other.

'Is that it?' I say.

Ross grins. 'I think you've just agreed to go out on a date.'

I smile back. I might be hungover and tired, but there are fireworks going off in my head as we head back to the prep room, where we set our personal lives aside and get on with the rest of the list.

We anaesthetise a cat which has a collar injury, having become hooked up on a branch while climbing a tree in the churchyard. Ross scrubs up and puts on a sterile gown.

'Would you mind doing me up?' he asks.

'I'd love to.' I fasten the gown at the back, making the most of being able to touch him.

He tips his head back and leans into my hands. 'That feels good,' he breathes.

'Concentrate,' I say teasingly.

'Are you ready?'

'I think so. How is the patient?'

'She's good to go.' I check and recheck the cat's breathing and reflexes as she lies on the operating table and Ross starts to operate.

In spite of my lingering headache, I can't stop smiling. A date with Ross. I've never felt better, but apparently I still look a little out of sorts when I meet Taylor at the leisure centre after work.

'You look rough,' she observes as we walk along the corridor on the way into the changing rooms at the pool. 'What happened to you?'

'I've had a long day – and too much to drink last night.'

'You went out? You mean, you put a man before your mate?'

'I told you – we had a bad day at work. We lost a patient.'

'I'm sorry. I don't know how you cope. I couldn't.'

'Anyway, we went out to try to forget about it, and now we're going out on a date.' I lock myself into a cubicle and fling my towel over the door.

'Whose idea was that?'

'It was a mutual decision. It turns out that he's been holding back too.'

'I told you that two people of the opposite sex can't live together in a purely platonic relationship. I knew he had an ulterior motive for suggesting you moved in with him,' Taylor says from the cubicle next door, 'but I don't understand why it's taken him so long.'

I can hear water running in the showers opposite as she continues, 'Have you, you know . . . yet?'

'Do let us know. We're all ears,' a voice cuts in.

'Indeed we are, aren't we, Dot? I can't remember when I last, you know . . .'

Taylor giggles. 'I'd forgotten there were other people about.'

I know who they are – the ladies from the over-sixties swimming club. Mitch swears they deliberately get themselves into trouble in the deep end so he has to rescue them.

We continue our conversation on our way to the pool.

'So you haven't . . . ?' she whispers. I nod. 'Oh-mi-god, you have . . . Shannon, you're mad.'

'But it could work. We know each other well already. He's seen me looking wrecked and he still wants to go out with me. In fact, he's really sweet and thoughtful.' I think back to our conversation in the bedroom this morning when he made it clear he intended to commit to me. 'He won't let me down.'

'We'll see.' Taylor raises one eyebrow, but I won't let her reservations dent my optimism.

I move to the edge of the pool and dive in with the slightest splash. I re-emerge from the water with Taylor bobbing up alongside me. She dips her goggles and stretches the elastic over her head while I unwrap mine from my wrist.

'Do you want to borrow one of my dresses for your date tomorrow?' she asks. 'The flapper one would suit you – and it should fit. It's a bit long on me.'

'Do you mean the pale green one with the beads?' I tread water. 'That would be great, if you don't mind.'

'Come round and try it on after.'

When I get home with Taylor's dress in a bag, I find Ross has left a note and a present – a box wrapped in pink and black paper with a ribbon round it – for me on the kitchen worktop.

I've fed the kittens and gone to bed – I know, I'm a light-weight. Hope you had a good chat with Taylor. See you in the morning xx Ross

I unwrap and open the box – it's a selection of luxury chocolates from Lupins, the gift shop. I eat three before closing it again. They're sweet and a mixture of soft and hard centres, just like him.

Chapter Seventeen

Once Bitten, Twice Shy

Can you date when you are living and working together? This evening, I think, as I make a round of the inpatients before I go home, feeding the cat with the collar injury who is staying with us for an extra couple of nights, I'm going to find out.

Izzy turns up in Kennels.

'A little bird told me you're going out with someone special tonight.' She glances down at the chicken under arm. 'Not this one. This is Molly.' She is a fancy hen with a delicate grey and white lace pattern in her feathers which turn to fluff on her legs. 'She's egg-bound, poor little thing. Maz admitted her.'

'I didn't think she saw chickens any more.'

'You know what she's like. Besides, the client said they wanted to see a proper vet, not one of the farm boys. She might have called them cowboys, actually.' Izzy smiles and makes to hand over the chicken to me. 'I don't suppose . . .'

I check my watch. 'I'm sorry.'

'What am I thinking? You need to get away and get your glad rags on. Go on, off you go.'

I hesitate. 'It is all right, isn't it?'

'That you're fraternising with a colleague?'

'I'm hoping that it'll be a bit more than fraternising.'

'It doesn't make any difference what I think because you're going to go ahead anyway. It isn't exactly a surprise to anyone. It's fine with me, as long as it doesn't affect your work.'

Celine appears at the door. 'Maz needs a hand with a gerbil – she's struggling to catch it. I offered, but there's a queue at reception.'

'You go, Izzy.' I take the chicken. Ross will understand if I'm late.

She thanks me and disappears off with Celine, leaving me to find the patient a suitable cage where she can wait in peace and quiet for help to lay her egg.

'It's four-star accommodation for you,' I say, shutting her in one of the cages in isolation, with some newspaper and a nest of hay from the bag we keep for the rabbits and small furries, and making a mental note to remind Izzy to bring some more from the farm. As I leave her to it, I hear a cluck. I turn back to find her in the nest, her tail pumping up and down. She looks so distressed that I can't possibly abandon her and go home.

I check into the consulting room with Maz and Izzy, who are examining a gerbil – or at least the parts that are accessible between Izzy's gloved fingers.

'Can I go ahead and give the hen a warm bath?' I ask.

'If you wouldn't mind.' Maz looks up briefly. 'That

would be a great help. I'm going to have to admit this little chap for a touch of anaesthetic so I can get a proper look at this lump on his tummy.'

Izzy gives me a rueful smile.

I return to isolation, where I immerse the lower half of the hen's body in warm water for a while. She is too depressed to protest with more than a peck and a flap of her wings. I take her out, dry her gently and return her to her quarters.

'You look more chirpy now,' I tell her. 'Did I mention that I'm supposed to be going out tonight, so if you don't mind, an egg would be nice?' I leave her alone for ten minutes; when I get back, she's sitting with her head to one side and her eyes closed. I take a sneaky peek into the nest of hay, and there it is, the offending egg. 'Brilliant,' I murmur. 'Well done, you.'

I give Izzy the good news before I drive home with Tilly and Kit mewing in the back of the car, through the country lanes where the summer sun burnishes the wheat in the cornfields. The hedgerows are overgrown with brambles, the ford is a mere streak of damp mud and the brook alongside the houses in Talyford is nothing but a trickle. The heat is oppressive, and there are clouds bubbling up on the horizon, but I don't care because I'm going on a date with Ross – the first of many, I hope. I'm feeling sick with anticipation as I turn in to park outside the house, but there's a problem: a big black monster four-by-four in my spot, alongside his bike.

My fingers tighten on the wheel. Heidi and Bart? Not tonight? I reverse out of the courtyard, tyres slipping in the gravel, and park on the road outside. I check my mobile to see if there's a message. Nothing.

He's been off all day because he swapped a shift with Emma last week as one of the twins was off nursery with a bout of tonsillitis, so I don't see why he couldn't have given me some advance warning. It isn't much to ask.

I pick up the kittens, slam the car door and let myself into the house, pausing in the hallway to take off my shoes.

'I'm home,' I call, at which there's a gruff bark and Bart comes trotting in from the direction of the kitchen, diving straight at the kittens' carrier. I snatch it away and put them in the living room with the door closed. Bart turns back to his master who's following him. Ross is holding two bottles of beer. He hands one to me.

'What's going on?' I say quietly.

'I'm sorry.' He makes to kiss me. I turn my cheek. 'I'm afraid we'll have to postpone the date tonight.' He rests one hand on my shoulder. 'I haven't changed my mind – I feel terrible having to let you down, but I don't have a choice.'

'It's Heidi.' My heart is cold, like a slab of frozen fish. 'Where is she?'

'In the garden.'

'There'd better be a good explanation for this. Why tonight of all nights?'

'It's her mum. She's been admitted to hospital for a few days. Heidi needs me to have Bart so she can be with her as much as possible. I would have put her off, but it sounds pretty bad.'

'So she's going home this evening?'

'She wants to, but she's in too much of a state. I can't let her drive.'

'Oh, Ross,' I sigh.

'It isn't my fault.'

'I know.' I try not to sound bitter, but I hate the way he's dropped everything for her.

'I'm not doing it for her. I'm doing it for the dog. If I make it difficult, she'll find someone else to look after him and I'll lose touch. I can't let him go to kennels.'

How much longer are you going to let Heidi use the dog as a tool for emotional blackmail, I want to ask, but I bite my tongue. She must be feeling terrible.

'I can ring around and find her a room for the night,' Ross suggests.

'It's all right. She can stay here.'

'Thank you.'

For a moment, I wonder about offering to share my bed with him, but I couldn't, not with his ex-girlfriend in the house.

'How long do you think Bart will be staying?' I ask, realising the implications of having a dog to stay who can't be left for more than a couple of hours without tearing the house apart, who can't be kept in a kennel because he gets depressed, and who's somewhat temperamental at the best of times. 'Oh, it doesn't matter.' If Ross and I are going to have a future together, I'm going to have to embrace his troublesome dog. 'I'll keep the kittens in my room while he's here – he's welcome.'

Ross smiles wryly. 'Love me, love my dog.'

'You've washed the floor,' I say, stepping past him into the kitchen.

'Yes, does it meet your high standards?' he says with his hands on his hips and looking rather ridiculously proud of himself.

'You've done nothing around the house for weeks and you expect me to say how amazing you are for cleaning the kitchen?'

'I've done the rest of the house too,' he says, sounding hurt, and it's my turn to apologise. I put the bottle of beer on the breakfast bar and step onto the patio, where Heidi is sitting, staring red-eyed towards the hills, with a half-empty bottle of wine on the table in front of her.

'Hello,' I say. 'I'm sorry to hear about your mother.'

She turns to me with a small smile. 'Thank you – and I'm very grateful to you for letting me stay and for looking after Bart. It's such a relief to know that he's with people he can trust while I focus on helping Mummy get better.'

'I hope she gets home soon.'

'She isn't in hospital yet. She's going in on Monday.'

I glance towards Ross. He said she was in hospital already. Definitely. I didn't mishear. And, now I think of it, unless Heidi overheard us talking in the hall, he must have said she could stay before asking me if I was cool with it. He looks down at his feet. His big toe is poking out of a hole in his sock.

I wish Heidi all the best.

On my way through the kitchen, Ross catches up with me.

'Aren't you going to stay and have that beer?'

'I don't think so. It's been a long day and I don't want to sit here while you manage a case of dis-traught-ex syndrome.'

'Is that what it is?' He chuckles before quickly sobering up. 'I thought you'd got past the issues you had with me and Heidi. I'd help anyone out in an emergency, and Bart is partly my responsibility. I can't just duck out when it's inconvenient.'

I take a deep breath, fighting the strangling hands of disappointment at my throat. 'I'm fine about her turning up with the dog – her mother is ill and she can't look after Bart at the same time, that's understandable. And yes, we can go out on a date any time – we've waited so long, another day won't hurt, but what has upset me is that you've lied to me.'

'About what exactly?'

'Heidi's mother isn't in hospital yet, and you'd already said she could stay here.' I glare at him. I'm not letting him off the hook.

'Okay, I'll admit I was economical with the truth. I was trying to protect you . . . from yourself.'

'Me?'

'Yes, I didn't want you jumping to the wrong conclusion.' He pauses. 'Oh god, I've said the wrong thing again, haven't I? I can see it in your face. Shannon, please . . . anyone would think you were jealous—'

'As I have every reason to be,' I interrupt.

'I'm sorry. What else can I say? We've been living together for how long? Long enough for you to see that I'm not interested in Heidi, or anyone else, apart from you. Why can't you see that?' He holds out his hands and takes mine very gently in his fingers, turning them over and examining the lines in my palm. 'I was hoping that you'd let me prove myself. I can see that moving in together was a mistake, but that's with hindsight. It would be easier doing the dating stuff if we were living apart, but we're here now and I want us to be more than mates.'

I squeeze his hands in acknowledgement.

'Is everything all right?' Stepping away from him I turn to find Heidi has joined us. 'I thought I'd grab some water,' she adds. 'It's okay. I know where you keep the glasses.'

'Everything is fine,' I say.

'Are you going to eat with us? Only I picked up some fresh pasta on the way – as a way of saying thank you for looking after Bart.'

Us? I think. She's still under the illusion that she has a chance with Ross. A thought strikes me. He hasn't told her about us, has he? She doesn't know. I realise that she's sad and worried about her mother, and Ross is probably trying to protect her from further pain, but it isn't fair on anyone to hide the truth.

'It's very kind of you, but I'll leave you two to catch up. I'm going to take the kittens upstairs, feed them and go for a swim.' I reach towards Ross, putting my arms around his neck. He frowns and his eyes darken, but I am undeterred by his sensitivity to Heidi's feelings. Smiling, I lean up and kiss him on the lips. 'I'll see you later, darling. I won't be late.'

Heidi utters a sharp cry. 'Are you two—?'

'It had to be done. Look after her,' I say quietly to Ross and, to my relief, because I was afraid of how he'd take it, he touches my back and says, 'Will do, but are you sure you don't want to stay?'

I gaze at him. Why did I ever imagine he was still interested in Heidi? He's living with me. He's asked me out on a date. If we are to have any kind of future together, I have to trust him.

'Quite sure,' I say, and I take the milk I made up in advance from the fridge in the morning, a bowl of hot water to warm the bottles, and some kitten food, and head off to feed them, closing the door on Heidi's sobbing and Ross's voice, low with consolation and entreaties. When the kittens are curled up in their bed in my room, dozing off to sleep, I grab my swimming kit and drive down to the leisure centre.

When I return, Bart barks from the living room. I push the door open, a little anxious about what my reception will be like – both from the dog, because I'm still wary of him, and from Ross's ex. I'm relieved to find Ross lying on the sofa with a blanket and the dog on top of him.

'Hi,' I say. 'Where's Heidi?'

'I let her have my bed for the night.'

'How did it go?'

'Okay, I guess. I made it clear that I'm with you now and that she can't meddle in our relationship. I think she got it, although it was all rather traumatic. I'm shattered – I'd forgotten how wearing she can be. Poor thing, I do feel sorry for her though, even though she's obviously been deluding herself for ages. How was your evening?'

'It was good, thanks, although I was rather pre-occupied thinking of you . . .' I'd like to kiss and cuddle up with him, and run my fingers through his hair, but Bart's presence puts me off. 'I'm off to bed then. I'll see you in the morning. Goodnight.'

'Sleep well, Shannon,' he says. 'I know I will.'

The next morning when I wake up, Heidi's car has gone.

'She left at six to miss the worst of the weekend traffic,' Ross says when I join him downstairs in the kitchen, where he's tinkering with his motorbike. 'She's really upset about her mother and completely cut up about us.'

'I didn't want to hurt her feelings, but I'm not going to apologise.'

'You don't have to.'

'I had to do it,' I go on. 'I don't know why you didn't tell her, but it wasn't fair to keep stringing her along.'

'I know that now. You were right – she admitted she'd been hoping that one day I'd realise that I'd made a terrible mistake in breaking off our relationship—'

'It was more than that though, wasn't it?' I cut in. 'You were engaged.'

'I suppose that made it easier for her to jump to the wrong conclusion, that I was just having cold feet about the wedding, even though I explained, over and over again, that it went deeper than that. I feel bad about what's happened. I should have worked out that Heidi's offers to stay and look after Bart at the show and to cook dinner were her way of keeping me close. She's always been manipulative and I should have known that's what she was up to. As it is, I assumed she was being very grown up about the split.'

'And you like to do the right thing, even if you don't always go the right way about it.'

'I was proud of the fact that we could share the dog and stay friends.'

'What will happen now? With Bart, I mean?'

'I don't know. He's here for now and we'll have to find a way of keeping him separate from the kittens until they go to new homes in a month or so. We'll manage,' he adds optimistically. 'I just hope that Heidi doesn't start to make life difficult in future.'

So do I, I think, turning my attention to the motorbike.

'What's that doing in here anyway? I don't like you having the bike indoors. It makes such a mess.'

'I'm fettling with the engine. I want it to go faster.'

'Perhaps you'd better buy a bigger one.'

'I just might do that.' He drops an oily rag onto the breakfast bar and picks up a mug of tea.

'Do you have to?' I groan.

'I made this for you.' He moves across to me, kisses me lightly on the mouth and hands me the mug, complete with the black imprints of his fingers. 'I was wondering if we could start again, on the basis that we didn't really get started in the first place? I thought we could go and grab Seven on the way through town and take him and Bart for a walk by the river before going to the pub for lunch. What do you think?'

'Can you tear yourself away from the bike?'

'Oh, I think so . . .' He grins. 'Let me wash my hands and change my shirt.'

I feed the kittens while I'm waiting for him and, within half an hour, we're walking down by the river where the meadows are filled with summer flowers. Maybe it's the pressure of being on a date at last that makes me unable to think of anything to say. Ross seems similarly tongue-tied.

'It feels like there's rain on the way,' I say as we stroll along the bank, and then I feel like a bit of an idiot because it's the sort of remark my mum or Godfrey would make.

'I don't care. It always feels like summer when I'm with you.' Ross stops, leans towards me and touches his lips to my cheek. 'The forecast is for thunder-storms – we'll have to make sure we're back before they arrive because Bart hates loud noises.' He grimaces. 'I'm sorry. Now it sounds like I'm putting the dog before you.'

'It doesn't matter.' I smile as he takes my hand and squeezes it tight. 'We can drop into the practice and pick up some sedation for him, and there's food at home.'

We carry on walking quietly, hand in hand, until Bart takes exception to Nobby Warwick, Talyton's church organist, heavy drinker and opportunist, of whom some have said he would sell his own mother. The dog trots up with his hackles raised and a growl in his throat to where Nobby is fishing from under an umbrella.

'Hey, stop that. I apologise.' Ross pulls the dog away by the collar. 'The weather's unsettled him.'

Only a dog owner could say that, I think. That excuse for canine misbehaviour is a new one on me.

There's a squawk and a duck splashes through the water. Both Bart and Seven deem that it's necessary to run down the bank and plunge in to chase it off. Seven bobs up a little way upstream and swims against the current, getting nowhere close to it, while Bart utters a yelp and comes running straight out of the water, holding up one front paw. He comes limping over to us with blood dripping from his foot, staining the ground dark red.

'That looks nasty,' I say, as Ross takes a look.

'He's cut his pad. There must be some glass or something in there.'

I dig around in my pockets, trying to find something to stem the bleeding while we transport him back to the practice, but all I can find are a couple of poo bags.

'Shall I run back and bring the ambulance?' I suggest as a bolt of lightning streaks across the sky.

'I think it'll be quicker to walk him back.' Ross takes his shoe off and removes his sock, the one with the hole in it that he was wearing the day before. So much for maintaining asepsis to prevent infection, I smile to myself, as he wraps Bart's paw with the sock and the bags. 'That should do as a temporary measure.' He looks down and pats the dog's shoulder. 'I'm afraid you're going to have to walk.'

I call Seven back. He comes flying out of the river and gives himself a good shake and, in spite of everything, Ross laughs. 'I suppose it isn't going to make much difference. You were right about the rain – it's coming in with a vengeance.'

We walk back slowly into town, with Seven mooching along and making the most of savouring every sniff, while poor Bart hops along on three legs as the rain falls in fat, heavy drops.

'I wish I had the bike – I could have gone and fetched the ambulance,' Ross observes. 'Perhaps I should get a bike with a sidecar. I rather like the idea of Bart sitting beside me in goggles and a helmet.'

'As long as you don't expect me to ride in it.'

'Oh no, I want you on the back. That would be much more fun.' He turns as a heavy vehicle rumbles up alongside us, sending water splashing up from the gutter as it pulls in. A man with curly red hair opens the door of a shiny blue tractor and leans out. It's Murray from Greenwood Farm – I only recognise him because of Sherbet, the sausage dog, sitting in the cab with him. Bart barks when he spots him.

'It looks like you have a problem there. Can I give you a lift? You can hop in the trailer. It's a bit grubby, but . . .'

It's a bit of an understatement – although empty

now, the trailer is clearly used for transporting manure.

'It's good clean muck,' he goes on. 'It won't hurt you.'

'We're all right, thanks,' Ross says.

'If you're sure.'

'Quite sure. We haven't far to go.'

Murray slams the cab door shut and drives on.

Arriving at Otter House, drenched right through, Ross shuts Bart into a kennel. I put Seven in the one next door so I'm free to find a suturing kit and bandages while Ross fetches the drugs he needs from the DD cabinet, the cupboard where the controlled drugs are kept locked away. It takes two seconds but, by the time we're ready, Bart's dressing has slipped and there's blood seeping through the sock.

Ross's forehead is lined with worry.

'He'll be fine,' I say, trying to reassure him. 'He hasn't lost that much. It always looks worse than it is.'

'Heidi's going to kill me – she probably won't let me look after him again.'

'Don't be ridiculous.' I give him short shrift.

'I'm going to give him some sedation IV. That way, it'll be nice and quick.'

'I'll get him,' I offer, as he throws a gown on.

'I'll do it. He can be a bit touchy about being in a kennel.' He brings him into the prep area on a lead. 'I'm sorry about this, but every cloud has a silver lining. Once I'm happy with him, we can leave him here to sleep it off and pick him up on the way back from the pub.'

I take the lead and Bart sits quietly at my feet, his body trembling.

Ross draws up some of the sedative into a syringe.

There's a rumble of thunder and the rain starts to hammer down against the windows at the back of the practice. Tripod comes in leaving paw-prints across the floor, his coat spiked up like a punk's hair.

I find a kidney dish and some surgical scrub. 'Do you want me to warm up a drip?'

'No, we'll make it quick. I'll knock him out on the floor to save lifting him onto the bench. I'll check for glass then a couple of sutures should do it, and a bandage – one of yours, not mine, because yours are far neater.'

'And they stay on.' I kneel at Bart's shoulder with my plastic apron rustling over my T-shirt and jeans. He nudges me roughly with the end of his nose, as if to say, leave me alone. I wrap my left arm up around his neck and reach over to lift his right leg, flexing it at the elbow and placing my thumb across the vein at the front.

'All right?' Ross squirts a little surgical spirit onto the vein. The dog sneezes violently. I readjust my hold on him and let him settle down once more. I raise the vein by pressing my thumb across it so it fills with blood, and Ross takes hold of Bart's leg so he can slip the needle under his skin.

I don't know what it is, the shock of his injury or the surprise at discovering that what he thought was a friendly cuddle has turned into something more sinister and scary, but Bart stiffens. I can feel his muscles tense and the low growl that vibrates in his throat.

'Hey, that's enough of that,' I say sternly. 'Do you want to pop a muzzle on him?'

'He's fine. He wouldn't hurt a fly. His bark's always been worse than his bite.'

'I hope you're right.' I look straight into Ross's eyes as I take a firmer grip.

'Two seconds and you'll be out of it,' he goes on.

'Is that me or the dog?' I say lightly as Bart shifts his weight, straining against me.

'Hang on there, Shannon.'

'What do you think I'm doing?' I mutter. 'Get on with it.' I glance down. The needle is in at last, through the skin with blood coming back into the syringe. I release the pressure on the vein and Ross starts to inject the drug, at which Bart struggles and wrenches himself from my grasp. He turns on me, pushing me back so my head hits the corner of the prep bench.

'Get off!' Ross yells as he tries to haul the dog off, but Bart's on top of me, his weight squeezing the air from my chest and his mouth on my face. I can feel an agonising, crushing sensation as his teeth sink through my skin, and hear a terrible tearing sound, as if he's ripping the muscle from my cheek. I don't scream. I don't make a sound. If I play dead, maybe he'll stop playing with me.

Get him off me. Please. Help me.

The more Ross tries to drag the dog away, the more he hangs on, finding purchase on the flesh at the side of my mouth, and dropping all his weight onto my chest so I struggle to breathe. Through the pain, I can feel wetness across my face, tears of despair mingled with blood, and just when I think I'm about to die from lack of oxygen, I make one last-ditch effort to get rid of my attacker. I bend my knees and kick out as hard as I can, hitting the dog's belly with a sickening thud. Momentarily winded, he loses his grip with his jaws. Ross pulls him off and I hear the scrabbling

301

of claws on the floor and the slam of the steel gate on the catch and a shoal of black circles swim across my vision and coalesce, and that's the last thing I remember . . . Until I wake with a throbbing headache, lying on my side with a rolled-up vet bed under my head, and my hip digging against the floor. Ross is at my side, his hand on my shoulder.

'What the . . . ? What happened?'

'Hush,' he says, wrapping a blanket around my shoulders and helping me to my feet. 'You've bashed your head.' He holds up his hand. 'How many fingers?'

'That depends on whether or not you count thumbs as fingers,' I mumble.

'This isn't the time to be funny. How many?'

'Four,' I say, focusing on his hand. 'Three now. That's enough. I'm fine.'

'You lost consciousness.'

'I fainted. I wasn't out for long.'

'I'm worried you have concussion.' He pauses. 'Let me see your face.'

'It's nothing.' I can't stop shaking. I'm frozen to the bone, yet it's a warm day, or it was when we were out walking by the river. My lungs burn and my face, the right side, feels numb. I reach out to touch my face, where my face should be. It's wet and warm and I can taste the metallic tang of blood.

Ross grasps my wrist. 'Leave it.'

'Where's Bart?' My lips feel as if they've been disconnected from my brain.

'Don't worry about him,' he says curtly.

'But his foot . . . ?' It's coming back to me now.

'Yeah.' Ross looks completely stressed out and I want to comfort him because it isn't that bad.

'He knocked me into the prep bench. I bumped my head.'

'This is all my fault! I know him so well. I should have listened. I should have been more careful.'

'He's bleeding.'

'Forget the dog – I'll see to him later.'

There's something in the way he says 'see to' that makes my heart miss a beat.

'He was on top of you. He was out of control.'

'You aren't going to . . .' I start to cry.

'It's something I'll have to think about,' he says grimly. 'In the meantime though, what about you?'

I stumble and he catches me, holding me close against his body. 'Let's get you to the hospital.'

'I'm all right. Really.'

'Let me be the judge of that. Trust me, I'm a vet.' He tries to make light of it, but I can't miss the tension in his voice. 'Where are the keys to the ambulance?'

'On the hook behind the desk at reception – at least, that's where they should be, unless someone's forgotten to put them back.'

He grabs them on our way through to the car park, where he helps me into the passenger seat and sets off at considerable speed. The hospital is some miles away.

'Have you got your mobile with you?'

I shake my head then wish I hadn't. It hurts.

'You can use mine.' He thrusts it into my hand. 'Call your mum.'

I think for a moment, trying to remember her mobile number. I dial the landline for the shop instead.

'Mum, hi, it's me.'

'Hello, you,' she says. 'Is everything all right?'

'Everything's fine. Ross is driving me to hospital.'

Keeping one hand on the wheel, he grabs the phone from me. 'She's been bitten and taken a knock on the head. Yes, I think she'd appreciate that. Yes, in about fifteen minutes. Yes, I'll stay with her.' He cuts the call and drops the phone into the well between us.

'What did you have to go and do that for? The last thing I need is her fussing.'

'I'm doing the right thing,' he says, and I notice how the muscle in his cheek tightens and relaxes and tightens again. His eyes are dark with concern and his fingers blanch on the wheel as he travels along the dual carriageway, passing all the traffic.

'Can't you slow down a bit?' I say, clinging to the seat as my life flashes past my eyes, but he ignores me. I'm pumping an imaginary footbrake as we speed into the city.

'Didn't you see the signs? The ones that say thirty?'

He glances across to me. 'Of course I did.' And I'm just about to tell him to keep his eyes on the road, when he slows down to about forty-five.

'Aren't you worried about losing your licence?' I ask crossly.

'This is an emergency.' He relaxes into a brief smile. 'Do you really think the police will stop a veterinary ambulance?'

'Yes, if it's travelling at ninety miles an hour.'

Ross falls silent until we arrive at the hospital and park in the drop-off zone outside A&E.

'How do you feel now, Shannon?' he says, killing the engine.

'Relieved that we're here in one piece. Actually, I feel a bit sick.' I yawn, being careful not to open my mouth too wide because I'm scared it is going to hurt.

'I'm really tired.' My eyelids are heavy. I tip my head back.

'Don't go to sleep. Please don't.' Ross's voice sounds desperate but distant. I'm drifting again. 'Wake up.'

I'm vaguely aware of being bundled onto a trolley, taken straight through to a cubicle and being set upon by a team of medical staff. A nurse finds a vein in my arm and sticks a great big cannula into it, making me flinch. I lie back, exploring the inside of my mouth with my tongue, while a doctor checks my neck for any swelling that might interfere with my breathing and studies my face. No one will meet my gaze, apart from my mum; in spite of having argued against Ross making a fuss, I don't think I've ever been so pleased to see her.

'He told me what happened,' she says. 'Someone is going to pay for this.'

'It was an accident.' I try to make a joke of my situation, but it hurts to speak. 'I thought you might have brought me flowers.'

'Funnily enough, that wasn't the first thing that came to mind when I got the phone call.' She leans down and kisses my forehead.

No one will talk to me, not properly. They walk into the cubicle, and tell me I'm being brave, but how can I be brave when I don't know what's wrong with me? I raise my hand to remove the bandage from across my face, but my fingers are wrapped together in another sheet of material.

'Don't touch,' Mum warns. 'Now, darling, the doctor wants to talk to you.'

It's the A&E doctor, a young guy who is about my age, maybe younger, who explains that I'm going to have a scan of my head to check for bleeding because I've lost consciousness a couple of times, not that I remember, and then I'm going to be assessed by a plastic surgeon to decide what surgery I will need to repair my face.

I start to cry. I don't understand.

'How bad is it? Please tell me.' I'm shivering now with shock and a growing sense of fear.

Ross steps towards me. Mum frowns at him.

'I'm grateful for the way you rushed her here, but Shannon wouldn't be in this situation if it wasn't for your dog. This is your fault. My daughter's going to be scarred for life thanks to you.'

I try to interject, but it's too painful. I can't shut my mouth properly. My lips are dry and crusty.

'We don't know that yet.' His face is pale and drawn. 'I'm truly sorry.'

'Sorry isn't going to cut it.'

'I'd give anything for it not to have happened, and we can't know what the outcome will be until she's seen the plastic surgeon.'

'Oh, for goodness' sake. You're supposed to be a vet. Look at her – that dog of yours has taken off half her face,' Mum goes on insensitively.

'No!' I exclaim. 'Not that.' Even though I'm high as a kite on morphine, I am here.

Her hand flies to her mouth, as if she's just remembered my presence. 'I'm sorry, I shouldn't have said. I didn't mean it, darling. I overreacted. It's the stress.'

Ross takes a second look at me, not looking at my eyes but towards my mouth, his expression etched with regret.

'How bad is it?' I say in desperation. 'I need to know.'

'It's hard to say before it's cleaned up,' he says. 'You might need a skin graft which could leave you with a little mark.'

'A scar,' I correct him. 'It's called a scar.' Tears spring to my eyes, singeing a track down my cheeks.

'I'll make damn sure you do the right thing with the dog,' Mum says icily.

Keeping his eyes on my mother, who looks as if she might punch him, Ross sits down on the chair beside my trolley. He's a brave man!

What I want to say is, Mum, please don't interfere. Just leave it. This isn't the time or the place, but all I can manage is, 'I'm sorry, Ross—'

'Don't apologise,' Mum cuts in.

I glare at her before turning back to him.

'I think you should go now,' I slur softly, my mouth not moving as it should. 'Please can you walk Seven home?'

'Godfrey will be there – just ring the bell,' Mum adds.

'Is there anything else I can do?' he asks. 'Can I fetch anything, a change of clothes, phone charger?'

'I think you've done enough already. I'll look after her now.'

'Bye, Shannon. Please don't worry. I'll be back,' he says, taking his leave. 'Just let me know if you need anything – anything at all.'

'Bye,' I murmur. I close my eyes.

'You can't go to sleep yet, darling. They're ready to take you for your scan.'

I can hear the fear in my mother's voice and I know she's thinking of my dad. When she arrived at the hospital to see him, it was too late. She must be petrified that history is about to repeat itself.

307

Chapter Eighteen

Out of Sight, out of Mind

Mum has to wait for another couple of hours to find out that the scan of my head is clear. I'm admitted for surgery late the same afternoon, followed by transfer to a ward in the middle of the night. I drift in and out of a sickly post-anaesthetic sleep, having nightmares of big red dogs and losing track of time.

'Hi, Shannon, it's me . . .' The sound of Ross's voice seeps into my consciousness and I'm not sure if he's real or part of a dream as he kisses my forehead, not my mouth, which seems a little weird when we're supposed to be a couple.

'What time is it?' I mutter.

'Half past eleven. I couldn't wait until visiting hours to see you – I managed to sweet-talk my way past the nursing station. I've brought you your hair-brush, mobile and charger, Kindle and chocolates.' I open my eyes at the rustling of a plastic bag. 'The grapes are supposed to be kind of ironic – all hospital patients have grapes,' he teases, before growing serious, pulling up a chair and sitting down beside me at the head of my bed. 'It isn't funny. I didn't know what to get you.'

I thank him, but I really don't feel like eating. The side of my face feels tight and sore. 'It's good to see you,' I say, meaning that I feel much better knowing he's here at my side. 'Are the kittens okay?'

'I haven't forgotten them. I'm looking after them today, and Izzy and Celine have offered to take over from tomorrow until you're better.'

'I'll be out of here soon.'

'There's no rush.'

'There is – I can't wait to get back to normal.'

Ross fails to smile at all and my own smile seems lopsided. I reach up and touch my face, but my fingers come into contact with a mass of bandage instead. I walk them across my cheek, discovering that whoever dressed my wounds has used an awful lot of dressing material. Emma would disapprove – she hates waste. 'Use what's necessary and no more,' is one of her mantras.

'What did they do to you?' Ross asks quietly.

'They've trimmed the damaged tissue away, flushed and closed the wounds.' I make light of it. 'How do I look?'

He clears his throat before answering, 'As beautiful as ever.'

'You're being ridiculous,' I sigh. 'I'm wearing a bandage.'

'It's in your eyes,' he murmurs. 'I mean it,' he adds, and his words melt my heart. 'Has the consultant given you any idea when you can come home? The house feels empty without you.'

'I'm not sure if anyone's actually said.'

'Well, let me know when you know and I'll come

and get you.' He pauses. 'Can you remember what happened?'

'Some of it, but my brain aches when I think about it.' I gaze at him and he looks down at his feet, his shoulders slump and his forehead becomes lined with pain and regret.

'I'm so sorry. I wish I hadn't let this happen to you.'

'It doesn't matter. It's not your fault.'

'But it does matter. That dog is a complete nutter – I should have listened to you and done something about him before he hurt anyone. You've paid the price for my stupidity.'

'Oh come on, that's rather dramatic.' I reach out for his hand, but we don't quite touch. The distance across the blanket is like a chasm. 'I should have insisted on muzzling him.'

'I couldn't let you do that. Bart was badly treated before we got him and I didn't want him to think we were like his previous owners. Wearing a muzzle would have felt like a punishment.' Ross looks up. To my horror, he's close to tears. 'I should have treated his aggressive tendencies with more care. I should never have let Heidi bring him to the party.'

'No,' I say urgently. I picture Bart jumping up to greet him, wagging his tail, and a lump forms in my throat. 'You haven't . . . ?'

He shakes his head, his mouth turned down at the corners. He scratches at the back of his hand, leaving red weals.

'Not yet,' he whispers.

'You mustn't rush into a decision like that. Please don't do it on my account, I beg you.' I can't begin to imagine the guilt I'd experience if Bart were to be put to sleep because he'd attacked me. I touch the dressing again. 'It's nothing, just a couple of stitches.' At least, I think so. Although Mum was horrified when she saw the wounds, I'm pretty sure she was overreacting, as any parent would. I haven't seen the damage yet – I haven't wanted to look.

'I have decided, though. It's going to kill me, but it has to be done. I feel guilty enough already. I'd feel ten times worse if he went on to hurt someone else.'

Tears prick my eyelids. I'm not sure who I feel the most sympathy for, Ross or the dog.

'Oh, God, Shannon. I'm sorry. Please, I don't want you to feel bad about it. It isn't your fault. There, I knew I shouldn't have said anything – I didn't want to upset you.' His voice catches as he continues, 'Heidi is coming to see him tomorrow to say goodbye.'

'Oh, Ross, I'm sorry.' I shift myself towards the edge of the bed to try to console him, but one of the nurses appears to check my temperature and blood pressure and chases him out because the trolley staff will soon be here with lunch.

'You're welcome to come back, but during visiting hours next time,' she says. 'We can't have all and sundry on the ward getting under our feet.'

'I'll be back,' Ross says, standing up and kissing me on the right cheek. 'I'll text or call you later.'

I wish him goodbye and watch him stride out through the archway into the corridor without looking back, and I'm aching to follow him and tell him everything is going to be all right, but of course, it isn't. He and Heidi are about to lose their much-loved dog and I'm stuck in this hospital bed not knowing what exactly is lurking beneath the dressing on my face, because although I've been blithely imagining a neatly closed wound at the side of my mouth, I'm becoming afraid that it's more than that. The tingling sensation under the bandage is growing more intense and painful, but I try to put my concerns to one side until the consultant visits me with one of the nurses the following morning.

The nurse removes the dressing and the consultant checks my face – according to him, the puncture wound on my cheek is looking good and his repair to the injury at the side of my mouth is satisfactory.

'What does that mean?' I ask, feeling a little out of the loop. It's my face, yet I'm the only one not to have seen it. The nurse fetches a mirror and hands it to the consultant who holds it up in front of me.

I gasp. There's a deep, almost vertical crevice, a livid red scar about five centimetres long at the side of my mouth. It's swollen and shocking, but the consultant seems to think it isn't too bad. In fact, he's proud of his handiwork. He tells me to be patient because it will take time for the scar to fill in and fade a little.

'How much is a little?' I ask in a small voice. I can't believe this. I don't look like me.

'The cosmetic result will be better than it is now, but you will always have a scar.' My heart is beating fast and hard as he continues, 'We can consider revision surgery in the future, although that may not be necessary, and you can access support through your GP.'

'You are going to put another dressing on it?' I say, turning away from the mirror. I can't bear to look at myself. I don't want anyone to see me like this, especially not Ross.

'A light one,' the consultant says, 'and you can go home. My secretary will be in touch to give you another appointment at Outpatients . . . All the best,' he adds, shaking my hand.

The consultant leaves and the nurse puts another dressing on. She chats, but I can't concentrate. I look like a freak. I'm never going to look the same again. A wave of panic surges through me because I'm trapped in a new reality. How will Ross – how will anyone – love me now?

Images of Bart flicker through my mind: the way he looked at me with those cold, calculating eyes the first time I met him at the Country Show and how he snarled and lunged at Dave at the party . . . Ross knew what he was like, yet he stood by and let it happen. When he came to see me, I was in denial, but now I've seen what the dog has done, a new emotion takes over. Anger.

I phone my mother to tell her I'm free to go home and ask her if she'll pick me up.

'Of course I can, darling,' she says. 'I'll shut up shop and come and get you straight away.'

'Thanks, Mum.' My right cheek grows warm and wet with tears.

'I won't be long. I'll meet you on the ward.'

'I'll be at the main entrance,' I say, and I throw my things into a bag, pick up a letter for my GP, thank the nurses at the nursing station and make my way there. Half an hour later, Mum pulls in and I jump into the van. She turns in the driver's seat and throws her arms around me.

'You don't know how wonderful it feels to be taking you home,' she says, as I rest the good side of my face against her shoulder. 'What did the consultant say?'

'I saw it when they took the dressing off.' I burst into tears again. 'Oh-mi-god, it's awful.'

313

'I'm so sorry. I'm sure it will get better as time goes by.' She presses her lips to my forehead before sitting back and holding my arms. 'I suppose Ross is at work,' she adds rather stiffly. 'Have you got a key?

It takes me a moment to realise what she's talking about.

'Oh no, I'm not expecting you to take me back to Talyford.' I gaze at her and my throat constricts with grief and fear. Yes, fear, because I'm terrified about what the future holds for me. 'I want to come home for a while, if that's all right with you, and you think Godfrey won't mind. I need to get my head straight.'

'Of course. You're always welcome, you know that.' Mum smiles a small smile as she puts the van in gear and pulls away from the hospital entrance. 'The bed's made up – I got it ready, just in case – and I can't wait to see Seven's reaction. He's going to be over the moon to see you.'

As we reach the outskirts of Talyton St George, Ross calls on the mobile.

'Hi,' he says warmly. 'How are you?'

'Not good.' I'm not in the mood for talking to him at the moment.

'What did the consultant say?'

'He said I could go home.'

'That's brilliant. I'll give you a lift. I can be with you in half an hour. Just let me clear it with Maz.'

'No, don't worry. Mum's taking me back to Petals – we're on our way there now. I'm going to stay with her and Godfrey.'

'Oh, I was all prepared to look after you.' He sounds disappointed. 'It's all right. I'll pop in with some of your things – you'll need clothes for a few days.'

I thank him and add that I'll see him later.

Back at the shop, a dog comes flying through to see me, leaping up and down and squeaking. As a memory of Bart turning on me with his teeth flashes through my brain, I have to remind myself that it's only Seven and he would never hurt me. Seven rushes back inside to grab a slipper, bringing it back to me as some kind of present. I hug him, being careful not to let him lick at my dressing. I take a deep breath of roses and eucalyptus oil and relax. It's good to be home.

When Godfrey returns after work, he's pleased to see me, for which I'm very grateful. He makes coffee and cooks stir-fry and noodles for dinner; although I'm not hungry, I eat what I can to show willing. I'm sore, traumatised and on tenterhooks waiting for Ross to make an appearance with my things, because I'm not sure how I'll feel when I see him. He turns up on the doorstep later, with a suitcase of clothes and bits and pieces from the house.

'Can I come in?' he asks.

I look at the dark circles around his eyes and the stubble on his chin and I'm torn between a desire to console him and an impulse to send him away because it's his fault that I'm in this mess.

'Please . . .' he says gruffly, and my heart softens slightly.

I hold the door open for him and show him into the shop.

'I won't stop for long – I expect you're tired. I just wanted to let you know that I put Bart to sleep today.'

'I'm sorry.' I am because I can imagine how he's feeling. I'd be devastated if it had been Seven. 'How is Heidi?'

'She's extremely cut up as you'd expect, but she'll survive. Shannon I'm sorry too.'

'I can't find the words to explain how guilty I feel for what I've put you through. I know I've said this before, but I gave Bart one chance too many.' He holds my gaze. 'You do, don't you, when you love someone. If I could turn the clock back, I would.'

'I know,' I say quietly. Can I forgive him? I can live with the fact that he has had Bart put down, because I couldn't live with a dog I couldn't trust, but I can't forget that he took a risk, the outcome of which is that I'm going to be scarred for life. It's too soon, too raw and I'm still too angry.

'I'll catch you later. Go and get some sleep,' I say, dismissing him. He ducks towards me as if to kiss me, but I step aside, putting the door between us. He frowns as he says, 'Goodnight.'

'Night.' I watch him turn and walk back to the ambulance, before closing the door behind him. I'd love a hug, but I can't let him near me while I'm working out how to cope with my altered appearance and rebuild my life.

I start by calling Taylor, who's away on another course. She is appalled when she hears what has happened.

'I was there when that dog had a go at Dave and I heard what you said to Ross. I can't understand why he didn't get rid of him straight away. I would have done.'

'I hope I'd have been strong enough to make the decision earlier if it had been Seven who was going around threatening people, but it's hard to know how you'd behave if you were in that position. Ross adored that dog – I feel so guilty and furious with him at the same time.'

316

'I'm not surprised. I don't think I'd be able to bring myself to speak to him for a while.' Taylor hesitates. 'Is it really that bad?'

'It's much worse than I expected – all swollen and lumpy.'

'I'm sure it will get better,' she says brightly before pausing. 'I take it from your silence that you think otherwise? Please don't get too down about it. I'm certain there are things that can be done to fix it – and if everything fails, there's always make-up. There are some amazing concealers available now.'

'It's going to take a trowel and cement at the moment,' I say more harshly than I intend.

'I'm sorry; I'm not trying to be flippant or make light of it. I want to help. In fact, I really wish I was at home so I could take you out for a few drinks, but that will have to wait because I'm tied up here learning about staff motivation and blue-sky thinking.'

'Don't you think you're going to end up over-qualified to be a garden centre manager?' I say, glad of a change of subject.

'Possibly.'

'How's Dave?'

'Oh, he's absolutely amazing. He's taking me away for a weekend in London. I can't wait.' She hesitates. 'How does this leave you and Ross? You are going to have that date?'

'You've reminded me: I must give you your dress back.'

'You can hold onto it for now. You aren't going to let this wreck everything, are you? I've seen the way you look at each other – you're both completely besotted.'

'I don't know. I'm confused.'

'How does he feel about it?'

'He's been kind, coming to see me—'

'That's lovely,' she cuts in.

'I can't help feeling it's out of guilt.'

'He might feel responsible, but Ross adores you,' Taylor counters.

'He won't fancy me any more when he sees my face.'

'Surely he saw it when he took you to the hospital?'

'He gave me the impression it wasn't too bad.' When I think back, I recall that he was actually non-committal.

'Because he didn't want to upset you, I expect. Give him a chance, Shannon. I like Ross and I really don't believe he's one of those men who is only interested in a woman for her looks.'

'He went out with Heidi for years and look how gorgeous she is.'

'She looks amazing, but she's also rude and devious. Her beauty is skin deep and Ross knows that so you can forget about her.' I open my mouth to argue that I can't see why he should settle for me with my wrecked face when he could have absolutely any woman he wanted, when she goes on, 'Concentrate on staying strong.'

I promise her that I'll try, but when I'm rinsing my mouth in the bathroom, having waited for Godfrey and the prostate to use it first, I stare at my reflection in the mirror, picturing the horror that lurks underneath the dressing, and my confidence in the force of Ross's feelings for me washes away like mouthwash down the plughole.

The following lunchtime, Maz and Emma drop in to see me, bringing chocolates and wine, and a card signed by all the staff, and gently suggesting that I consider initiating a claim against the practice insurance over the incident and taking some time off work. When I talk it through with Mum and Godfrey in the evening, they agree that my lovely bosses are right, although I'm not sure. I'd like to get back to work – I'm missing it – but I don't see that it's worth seeing a solicitor about a claim when I won't be off for long. What's more, I'd feel like I was being disloyal – the vets at Otter House have been good to me.

Ross texts and calls me during the following couple of days to let me know how some of our patients are and asking me if he can come and see me, but I can't face him. He invites me out for a drink too, but I decline the invitation, saying I wouldn't be good company. His response is to drop by on his way home from work on the Thursday, but he's late and I'm already in bed, so Mum makes my excuses for me, something I suspect she's quite happy to do because she's quite clear that she blames him, while I'm wavering.

The following day I have an appointment with Nicci, my GP at the surgery in Talyton St George. Normally, I don't mind seeing her, but today I'm frantic, because she removes the dressing and tells me that I don't need another one.

'Are you sure?' I ask her.

She shows me the wound in a mirror – it's hideous, slightly less angry than before but still a major blemish at the side of my mouth. I touch it, rub at it and start to cry, because it's obvious that nothing I do is going to make any difference.

'I would avoid contact with the wound for now to

encourage healing.' Nicci hands me a tissue to wipe my tears.

'Please will you cover it up again?' I say quickly, because I can't bear the thought of anyone seeing me like this – not my mum, because she'll be devastated and I hate seeing her upset, not my friends and colleagues, and least of all Ross. How will he deal with seeing me like this? I look terrible and I don't feel like the same person. In fact, I feel numb with grief.

'What about going back to work?' I say hoarsely.

'I'd like to sign you off for another week to ten days. There's still a tiny risk of infection and you need time to readjust. I assume that part of your role is dealing with large dogs . . .' Nicci leaves that statement hanging, letting me think it through to its conclusion. Will I be able to cope, given my fragile state of mind?

'Thank you,' I say.

'It's important that you get out and about.'

'What about swimming?'

'I shouldn't yet. We'll discuss it when you come back in a week. Having said that, it helps in these situations to stay busy and positive. The scar from the puncture wound will fade to almost nothing over the next weeks and months, and the one at the side of your mouth will start to look less obvious with time . . .'

'But it will always be there,' I finish for her, an ugly reminder of what happened with Bart, of how life as I knew it ended. I've never been the most confident person in the world and this has shattered my self-esteem. I don't want to leave the doctor's surgery looking like this. People will stare at me, ask questions. Ross won't look at me any more. What man will?

'Shannon?' I look up at the sound of Nicci's voice.

'I don't think you heard me. There's lots of things we can do to help you. The consultant's letter has suggested revision surgery if you're unhappy with the cosmetic result of the repair further down the line.'

'That won't get rid of the scar, will it?' I say flatly.

'The impact could be reduced – you could have a skin graft or flap; although, you're right, you will be left with a blemish, whatever we do.'

'Can I have laser treatment?' I ask, remembering that one of Emma's twins had laser therapy to remove a birthmark on her face.

'It might be possible in the future, but you mustn't set your expectations too high.'

'What are you saying? That I should learn to live with it?'

'All I'm suggesting is that it's very early days,' she says tactfully. Before I leave the surgery, she offers me counselling and recommends a couple of websites with information and support for people with facial disfigurement. That's me, I think, with a heavy heart. I am disfigured, and that's official.

Chapter Nineteen

Changing Faces

Mirror, mirror on the wall. Who is the fairest of them all? The words of the fairytale come back to me as I brush my hair in the bedroom mirror when I return from the doctor's, walking in through the back door to avoid my mother, who's working in the shop. It certainly isn't me, I think, as I try flicking my hair forwards to hide the scar. It makes me look rather ridiculous, as if I'm modelling one of those crazy styles that you see in the hair magazines, so I 'borrow' one of Mum's scarves made from pale pink gauze from her wardrobe. It isn't really me, but I can tuck it around my neck and face to at least partially obscure the scar before I go and find her.

She's talking to someone. I hang back in the shadows at the rear of the shop, but when I realise that it's Frances and the conversation is bound to drag on, I make my appearance.

'Hello, Shannon.' Frances holds a bunch of lilies to her chest. 'I hear you've been in the wars, poor thing.'

'Hi,' I say, moving into the light from the shop window.

Her expression flashes from curiosity to surprise and then sympathy. My mum lets out a stifled scream and her hand flies to her mouth.

'Oh dear,' Frances says. 'That looks nasty.'

Mum bursts into tears, which is just what I didn't want.

'It's fine. I'll be all right,' I say, trying not to cry with her. 'Nicci says there are things they can do.'

'I'll leave you to it. I have to get these flowers to the church,' Frances says. 'All the best, Shannon. I'll see myself out.'

When she's gone, Mum makes tea. We sit at the table in the back of the shop, among the catalogues and glossy bridal magazines covered with images of flawless models. I turn them all face down so I can't see the brides' mocking smiles.

Mum dunks a biscuit before glancing up at me with a guilty look in her eyes.

'I know I shouldn't, but I'm a bit stressed. The plastic surgeon did say the repair wouldn't look great at first, but it's still a bit of a blow when you get to see it. You know you still look as lovely as ever. It doesn't change anything.'

I don't comment. She's wrong. Everything has changed.

People look at me in a different way, even Ross when he drops by after work, leaving the bike outside the shop. It is in darkness, apart from a small lamp at the back that lights the way into the living accommodation at night. I let him in, but don't invite him any further, preferring to talk in private among the plants and flowers rather than within earshot of Mum

323

and Godfrey. They are cuddled up on the sofa in the living room.

'How are you?' He unzips the top of his leather jacket.

'How's work?' I say quickly. I keep my face averted and my hand covering the switch on the wall for the main light.

'Not too bad, although it's much more fun when you're there. Lucky came in for a checkup – he's still in remission – and Izzy gave Merrie another bath, just to keep her skin allergy under control . . . Anyway, how are you?' he repeats. 'You didn't give me an answer.'

'I saw the doctor today.' Taking a deep breath and summoning all my courage, I turn the light on and point to my face. His eyes widen as he focuses on the side of my mouth.

'No,' he exclaims in a throaty whisper. 'That can't be right. Oh, god, it's . . .'

'Aren't you supposed to say I've never looked better?' I pretend to flirt with him and he smiles, but the smile doesn't reach his eyes.

'I don't know what to say. I'm so sorry.'

'You can be honest with me. I look like a freak.'

'Don't say that.' He reaches out and traces the line of my scar with the tips of his fingers, before leaning in and giving it a lingering kiss that makes my heart miss a beat as I recall the other kisses we've shared in the past.

'Seeing you like this makes me feel doubly guilty,' he goes on.

'I was angry with you when the consultant first showed me.'

'You can be as angry as you like. I've said before – it's my fault.'

I haven't the energy to rant and rave at him. He feels responsible and his dog is dead. I think that's punishment enough.

I stare at him. His expression is filled with regret and tenderness.

'When are you coming home?' he asks softly.

'I'm going to stay at Petals for a while longer.'

'Oh?' His expression darkens. 'I suppose that's for the best – your mum's around most of the day to look after you.'

'Godfrey's going to help me fetch the rest of my things.' I watch the blood drain from Ross's skin when he chews at his lip. 'I need some space . . .'

'You mean you're moving out?'

I nod as he puts his hands in his pockets, when all I want is to melt into his embrace and have him hold me, but I can't bring myself to say so. I don't want him going out with me because he feels sorry for me, because no one else will have me. I still love him, but how can he love me now?

'You can't, not permanently.'

'I'll keep paying the rent until the lease is up.'

'Don't worry about that. I'll manage for now, and when you're ready, you can move back in.'

I shake my head. 'That isn't going to happen.'

'Why not? Please, tell me it isn't forever. What can I do to make you change your mind?' His voice is raw with emotion when he continues, 'Shannon, I don't want to live there on my own. I want you back. I love you. You're my best friend, my—'

'No, stop.' He's breaking my heart, but I can't go back when the house, our home, is filled with memories of happy times and broken dreams of the future. 'I don't want to hear it.'

'If you knew how I feel about you, you wouldn't do this.' He looks at me intently. 'How can you think that something so . . .' He hunts for the right word. '. . . trivial would change the way I feel about you?'

'Is that what you call it?' The blood rushes to my face, making my scar itch and burn. 'I'm signed off work, the doctor's recommended counselling and I have the option of more surgery. It's not trivial. It's life-changing.'

'I'm sorry. I didn't mean to hurt your feelings.' He wrings his hands. 'What I meant was that it really doesn't make any difference. I know you feel devastated now, but the scar will fade eventually, and you will get over it. I know you will and I can help you, if you let me, and when you're ready to come back home, I'll be waiting for you with open arms.'

I don't know what to say. I'm not sure which of us is the most distressed. He stands in front of me, his eyes glistening with tears.

'Tell me what I can do to make it right,' he begs. 'I'll do anything.'

'There's nothing you can do. What's done is done.'

'Maybe it's too soon,' he says eventually, 'but I'm not going to give up. I'll be in touch tomorrow, and the next day, and the one after that . . .' He zips his jacket back up and wishes me goodnight. I lock the door behind him and watch him put on his helmet and jump on his bike before driving off, roaring away with my dreams of the happily ever after.

As the weekend passes, the glossy magazines in the shop, the actress and reality stars on television all contribute to my deepening sense of inferiority. I didn't think I judged people on their looks, but now I'm afraid that is exactly what I used to do. When

Taylor and I went out on girls' nights out, drinking and dancing, we used to talk about other women, envying them or criticising their appearance behind their backs. How I regret that now.

I find all kinds of excuses to stay at home until Ross calls me on Sunday afternoon to ask if I'd like to go out with him on Monday, his day off after his weekend on call.

'I'm sorry I haven't been able to do anything before – I've been flat out at work. I thought we could go and see Penny up at the Old Forge tomorrow. She's been asking if you could make a start on those training sessions you offered her.'

'Why didn't she ask me herself?' I say.

'She didn't want to put you under any pressure.'

'Well, I'm not sure . . .'

'I'd like to show you around the branch surgery too – I thought you'd like to see it. The sale was completed in record time and DJ is supposed to be making a start on the conversion.'

'I don't want to let Penny down, but I have another appointment with the doctor so I won't be free until later.'

'That's okay. I'll pick you up. I'll borrow the ambulance.'

'No, don't worry. I'll drive up to Talyford and meet you there.'

'Great. I'll see you tomorrow,' he says, and he cuts the call, leaving me wondering exactly what I've let myself in for. Training Trevor will be a doddle compared with facing Ross after his emotional pleas the other night. I have no appetite to get into that situation again, but I want to know that he's all right. I miss him.

The next morning, I walk to the churchyard to spend a few minutes at my dad's grave. There's a chilly wind whistling around the railings and the ancient yews, and the gargoyles pull frozen faces at me, but I don't care. I bend down to place a posy of flowers on the grave and trace the lettering carved into the stone as I have done so many times over the years. I talk to him for a while before I leave, feeling calmer and reassured because I know he loves me no matter what.

Next, I head for the doctor's surgery to keep my appointment with Nicci.

When I see Mrs Dyer with Nero, I cross the road to avoid having to explain my appearance, because that's what happens. People smile and say hi, all perfectly normally, until they spot the scar, when they either clam up and find some excuse to hurry away, or stop and stare, oozing sympathy and relief that it didn't happen to them.

Nicci asks me how I am and I respond saying I'm fine.

'Have you thought any more about having counselling?' she says.

I shake my head.

'How about going back to work?'

My mouth goes dry at the thought of facing up to all the people, and the prospect of coming across another dog like Bart. My palms leak sweat and my heart races, my breath quickens and all I want to do is run away and hide.

'I'm not ready. Can you sign me off for a little longer?'

'That's no problem. How about swimming? You can start that now – the wound's healing well and you could cover it with a light waterproof dressing while you're in the pool.' Nicci pauses. 'Shannon, I'm worried about you. You seem very low. You're bound to feel sad and there's no shame in that, but it would be good for you to make some plans, even small ones, like going out for a drink with a friend.'

'Oh, I'm going out later today.'

'Well, that's good. One step at a time. Let me know how you're getting on in the next week or so. There is always medication to fall back on if you need it.'

'Antidepressants, you mean?'

'Yes, you don't have to suffer. A short course can be helpful.' She smiles as she gets up to show me out of her consulting room, which is covered with photos of her horses. 'I prefer to call them happy pills.'

'I'll be all right,' I say, thanking her as I leave.

There's nothing that can make me feel better, I think, as I pick up the car and drive to Talyford. I park in the courtyard outside the house I shared with Ross and gaze out of the window, remembering with sadness the fun we had together, the party, sitting on the sofa chatting, the evening when we went to the pub and the morning after when we woke up in the same bed. I can't bring myself to go and knock on the door, and it crosses my mind that I should never have agreed to come. I sit clinging to the steering wheel until my ex-housemate emerges from my former home in shorts and a polo shirt, and walks across to open the driver's door.

'Hi, it's great to see you. I'm glad you could make it. I've spent a couple of hours mowing the lawn and weeding – I've done enough gardening to last me a lifetime.' He smiles ruefully and my heart does that familiar somersault at the sight of him because, even

329

though my appearance has changed, my feelings haven't. I still fancy him like mad. I still want him. I still love him and always will. 'Are you going to stay there all day?' he adds.

In response, I slide out of the car, change into my trainers and pick up a long lead and treats from the back before crossing the road to the Old Forge with him.

'You don't have to help me with this.'

'I want to,' he says, knocking on the cottage door, at which there's a flurry of barking and scratching, followed by the sound of Penny's voice.

'Out of the way, Trevor. Move.'

'This could be interesting,' Ross says, looking at me. Eventually, the door opens and Trevor flies out past us, over the bridge across the stream and into the road and back again. Ross tackles him before he can repeat the exercise in front of the tractor that's rumbling along the lane.

'Come in.' Penny reverses her wheelchair along the hallway and into the living room, where Trevor throws himself down on the floor, panting. 'You can see why we need help,' Penny goes on, red-faced. 'Thanks for catching him, Ross.' She turns to me and reaches out for my hand, giving it a brief squeeze. 'And it's kind of you to come along, Shannon, when you've been having a hard time of it.' Somehow, I don't mind when Penny's eyes settle on my scar, because she's been through far worse than I have. It puts my situation in perspective, at least temporarily.

'I said I'd do it, so here I am,' I say, feeling more cheerful at the thought of doing something useful instead of moping about at Petals. 'My plan is to have a chat about what the problems are before I take Trevor out for a walk to practise some sit and stay, and simple recall. We'll work on his behaviour indoors at another session.'

'It's good to see you out and about,' Ross says when we're walking down by the river a little later, with Trevor running about on a long lead. 'I've been worried about you.' He moves closer until I can feel his fingers tangling with mine. I brush them away, putting some space between us. When I look up, he's biting his lip, as if he's deep in thought, and I feel like a complete bitch for rejecting his approaches, even though I know it's right not to encourage him. Sometimes you have to be cruel to be kind. In my current mental state, my argument seems entirely rational. One day, Ross will thank me for it.

When we reach the footpath leading to the stile at the end of the Green, I spot some figures hanging around on the bridge, and suggest that we turn back.

'We could go a little further,' Ross says. 'What is it? What's bothering you?'

'I don't want to run into anyone.'

'Because of Trevor?'

'Because of the way people stare and make stupid comments about how I look.'

'Oh, Shannon, they don't . . . Do they?'

I nod as I try to haul Trevor in from the bottom of the riverbank where he's found an apparently fascinating scent.

'People are bound to be curious.' Ross hesitates as the dog splashes about in the water, stirring up the red Devon mud. 'Anyway, they're coming this way. I don't see how we're going to avoid them now. They're only kids.'

'Come here, Trevor,' I call, tugging on the end of the lead, as the sickening sense of panic returns at the sight of three teenagers, a boy and two girls, carrying cans of lager or energy drink, I'm not sure which. They clamber over the stile and move towards us, getting ever closer.

'I think you've caught yourself a dogfish,' the boy says.

'What happened to your face?' the taller of the two girls asks with a hint of challenge in her voice. 'Did he give you a love-bite?' She points at Ross.

'Didn't he realise he was chewing half your face off?' the other girl jeers.

'What did you just say?' Ross steps in, as I put my hand in my pocket and rustle the packet of treats I've brought with me, bringing Trevor scrabbling up to the top of the bank. He shakes himself hard, spattering the teenagers with muddy water. Laughing and screaming, they run away.

'That's right. You run, you cowards,' Ross yells after them. He swears and turns to me, sliding his arm around my shoulders. 'Are you all right?'.

'I'm okay, thanks.'

'You're trembling.'

'I'm fine.' I pull away and give the dog a treat. 'Trevor gave them a bit of a shock.'

'I didn't realise when the boy started talking that they were going to turn like that. The girls were vicious, like feral cats,' he says. 'I should have gone after them and given them a piece of my mind. What do they think they're doing, abusing people who are going along minding their own business?'

'It's better to let them get on with it,' I say, and I glance down at the river flowing past. 'It's like water off a duck's back.' Except that it isn't. I feel quite shaken and I want to go home.

'We'll go back,' Ross says quietly, and I'm grateful for his understanding. We return Trevor to Penny, giving him a wash in the stream on the way, and go back to Ross's where we stand beside my car.

'I'd love to give you a tour of the branch surgery,' he says when I tell him I'm going straight back to Petals. 'Go on, it won't take long. Please . . . DJ's been asking after you. He wants to know if the snake charmer – that's you – is available in case he finds any exotic creatures lurking in the new place.'

'Have you seen it then?'

'Of course. Maz wants me to be involved in the decision-making since I'm going to be working there. I'd like you to be part of it too.'

I bite my lip, tasting blood. My scar starts to throb. I can't do it. The more time I spend with him, the more I want him, and it isn't fair on either of us. It's torture.

'No, I'm sorry—' I begin.

'You're tired, I should have thought,' he cuts in.

'It isn't that. I really can't do this.' I catch sight of my reflection in the paintwork of my car and, even though the scar appears blurred, I can still see it, like a massive purple worm embedded in my face. I unlock the car and jump in. 'Bye,' I mutter as I slam the door shut. I switch on the engine and reverse, turning to face the road as he looks on, his arms folded across his chest, his brow deeply furrowed.

By the time I'm back at Petals, I have two voice-mails and three texts from Ross on my mobile but, to my shame, I can't bring myself to answer any of them. I take Seven to my room and cuddle up with him on the bed. He doesn't judge me on my looks. To him, I'm the same old Shannon.

I do everything in my power to avoid Ross, and virtually everyone else apart from Mum and Godfrey, which actually involves doing very little. I manage to motivate myself to drive to Talyford at the end of the week for a second, more successful training session at home with Trevor, showing Penny some strategies for taming her well-meaning but nutty Labrador before he goes away to what she calls 'finishing school'. I demonstrate how to use a training lead in the house, so when someone comes to the door she can secure him and stop him dashing out into the road, and I instruct her on the correct way to use treats as a reward for good behaviour. I do one last session with them on the bank holiday Monday, by the end of which I think we've gone some way towards stopping him running into Penny's legs when he's having what she calls a manic moment. I fail on the washing front, though. We practise with a few rags and the washing basket, but he can't resist ripping them to shreds.

'I think we'll have to leave it to finishing school to iron out that bad habit,' Penny says as we sit in the garden in the sunshine, watching him trot away to find a ball to play with. 'Thanks, Shannon. You've done a good job. I didn't have a clue what to do with him, but you've given me the confidence to tackle some of Trevor's issues.'

'I hope I've done enough to convince you and Declan that he can stay.' I rearrange the scarf around my neck – I'm boiling, but I won't take it off.

'I hope so too.' Penny changes the subject. 'How

are you, anyway? Ross says you aren't back at work yet.'

'When did you see him?'

'A couple of days ago. Declan saw him arriving back on his bike. He went over for a chat and asked him in for a drink. He seemed rather gloomy.' She clears her throat. 'I know it isn't any of my business, but you really should talk to him. He's devastated about what happened.'

'I know – he had to put his dog to sleep.'

'This isn't about the dog. It's about you. He's very upset that you didn't want to move back in with him. He doesn't understand why you've turned against him and he's worried that you're cutting yourself off from your friends and colleagues at Otter House.'

'I appreciate your concern,' I say awkwardly, because Penny is only repeating the truth. I am isolating myself because it's stressful putting on a brave face for other people, and I don't want to risk running into individuals like the yobs down by the river. I can't handle it.

'You will speak to him?' she goes on. 'It's a pity he isn't at home – you could have popped in and seen him while you were here.'

'Where is he?' I start to worry that I've missed something by not listening to his voicemails or looking at his texts in the past couple of days.

'He's gone off on his bike. He told Declan he was going to spend the bank holiday weekend on the road.' Penny smiles ruefully. 'I envy him his freedom.'

I look around at the paintings on the walls, wondering where he is and how he's feeling.

'I have to get mine from art,' Penny goes on, following my gaze. 'It can take a long time to heal, and sometimes it feels as if it will never happen, but it will. You just have to be patient and let people in. I'm talking from experience, but that's enough from me for now. Would you like a glass of wine?'

I decline, although it's tempting.

'I've promised Mum I'll go for a walk up on the escarpment or in the woods with Seven this afternoon. I think it's part of her campaign to get me out of the house.'

'Go for it,' Penny says.

'Let me know if you need any more help with Trevor.' I leave shortly afterwards and pick up Mum and Seven, but when we're up high on the escarpment looking down at the sea, I spot a group of people walking towards us – a family of grandparents, parents and children with pushchairs, kites and dogs. My heart starts to race and my skin prickles with heat. I touch my throat as I look around for an alternative path through the bracken and gorse to avoid them.

'Are you all right?' Mum asks as Seven presses his nose against my thigh.

'I can't breathe properly.' My chest is tight and my head is spinning.

'Come over here and sit down,' she says, taking my hand and pulling me towards a wooden bench that overlooks the grassy slope down to the beach.

'No, I have to get back to the car.'

'Can you manage that?' She reaches up and touches my forehead with the back of her hand, like she used to when I was a kid. 'Do you want me to call for help?'

'Please, don't. I'll be all right when I get home, I promise.' I stumble back along the stony path towards the car park, my legs moving faster and faster until

I'm running and my lungs ache with the effort. Seven stays with me, but Mum catches us up a couple of minutes later. I'm already in the driver's seat with the engine revving.

'What on earth is the matter?' she says, staring at me. 'Are you having some kind of panic attack? Oh, darling . . .'

'I can't face all those people. It's too much.' I bite my lip to hold back tears of relief that I made it without having to show my face to any of them. Mum touches my arm.

'It will get better,' she says. 'Look at you – it's only been a couple of weeks since you came out of hospital and the scar's smaller already.'

I glance at my reflection in the rear-view mirror, but I'm unable to share Mum's confidence. To me, it looks as red, uneven and vile as it was when I first saw it, and I am just as unlovable, and that reminds me of Ross and how much I'm missing him. I drive home, go to my room and howl silently with grief.

The whole episode gives me a headache and I use this as a reason not to leave Petals at all. Mum worries that it's an after-effect of being knocked out during the incident with Bart, but I assure her that it has nothing to do with it. I do text Ross, though, to check that he's all right and that he arrived back from his motorcycle tour in one piece. He calls me back and asks me out for a drink, but I turn him down, using the headache as an excuse.

'I'll ask you again,' he says, apparently seeing right through my evasion. 'You can't have a headache forever. I have to go – duty calls. See you soon.'

I feel bereft when he cuts the call, another sign that it is going to take a very long time to get over him, if

I ever do. I call Seven and retire to the sofa for the next few days.

On the Friday morning, Godfrey comes dancing into the living room with a mug in one hand and a plate in the other. 'For you, daughter of the love of my life.'

I thank him, taking the tea and putting the toast to one side.

'A smile wouldn't go amiss.' He utters a mock sigh. 'I'm trying.'

'You certainly are.' I force a brief smile.

'You're welcome. You know, I wish you'd at least think about going back to work. I hate seeing you like this. We're all very worried about you.'

'I am fine. I just need more time.'

'Very well.' He gives a little bow and disappears again. Mum is already in the shop attending to a delivery, while I'm still in my pyjamas, my favourite set with slouchy bottoms and a long-sleeved top with frayed cuffs. Seven sits and drools over the plate. In the end, I break up the toast and feed it to him, bit by bit. I know I shouldn't, but it makes him happy, and I don't have to explain to anyone why I haven't touched my breakfast. I sink back into the sofa with Jeremy Kyle on catch-up, watching people who are going through much worse times than me.

Seven jumps up beside me. I reach out and run my fingers through his silky fur as Godfrey calls through from the shop.

'Shannon, there's someone to see you.'

'Not now,' I call back. 'I'm not dressed.'

'I know you're decent. I've seen you.' He puts his head around the door and Ross pushes past him. I grab a cushion and hold it to my chest, as if it will dampen the rapid knocking of my heart.

'What are you doing barging in like that? You heard – I'm not in the mood for visitors.'

'Visitor,' he says. 'It's just me.'

'I'm sorry, he was very insistent,' Godfrey says in a tone that suggests he isn't sorry at all. He backs away and disappears off with his briefcase and shiny shoes, while Ross stands gazing down at me in his leather jacket and blue jeans.

'Aren't you going to ask me to take a seat?'

'If you must,' I say coolly, as Seven jumps down, picks up one of his toys and wanders over to greet him. Ross moves the newspaper that Godfrey's left behind, so he can sit down in the armchair opposite, leaning forwards with his knees apart and his hands on his thighs.

I recall the last time we were together, out training Trevor by the river, and up at Talyford outside his house, and how I drove away. Blushing, I touch my face, adding up how many of his texts and voicemails I've ignored. The ache of regret and longing returns. If it hadn't been for the accident, who knows what might have happened? We could be lovers . . . I suppress the memory of Ross holding me close, of making love with him and waking up in his arms.

'There are no ops this morning. Maz is chasing DJ to find out why he hasn't made so much as an appearance at the branch surgery in the past week and Emma's consulting. There's a bit of a lull, so I thought I'd come and see you.'

'You mean, they sent you.'

'You haven't been answering my calls or my texts again.' His expression hardens. 'I had to see you.'

'Now that you have, you can go back to work.' My

feelings for him come tumbling back like the surf crashing onto the beach from the sea, swirling and sucking me back to a time when I couldn't sleep for thinking about him. I can't weaken now. Whatever we had is over. Too much water has passed under the bridge for us to return to our easy friendship. I look away at the television to hide the scars. I wonder what Jeremy Kyle would make of our situation. Would he say: there are two sides to every story? Would he get us together to talk?

'Will you turn the sound down, or switch it off? We need to talk and I can hardly hear myself speak.'

Why do people keep telling me what I need? I have everything I require right here. I pick up the remote and stab the mute button.

'Thank you. This won't take long. I'm here to ask you when you're coming back to work. It isn't the same without you and I can't take much more of Izzy. I miss you.'

'I'm not sure.'

'I suppose you have to wait for your consultant's say-so.' He doesn't take his eyes off me. I pick at a thread on my sleeve as my faithless hound sits at his feet.

'I've had the all-clear,' I confess.

'That's great. Brilliant.'

'Physically, at least,' I continue, 'but Nicci's signed me off for another week so I can get my head straight.'

'The longer you leave it, the more difficult it will be,' he says quietly, his voice so gentle that it shatters my heart.

'But I'm not ready. I'm not sure that I ever will be. I've lost my confidence.' What use is a vet nurse who can't handle a big dog for injections?

'You can always start with the little dogs like Merrie,' he says, as if he can read my mind.

'And then there's this.' I point to my scars.

'What do you mean?'

'Don't pretend you can't see them.' I swear out loud. 'When I go out, people don't look at me. They can't see past these.'

'You're generalising. Our clients are bound to be curious at first, but they'll get used to it.'

I bite back impending tears. '*I'll* never get used to it. You don't have to put up with what they say and how they look at me. Even some of the people who've known me for years can't bring themselves to look me in the eye – when I look at their faces all I can see is pity. And you saw how threatening those teenage yobs were. You were there.'

'I'm so sorry.' Ross moves across to me, squats down and reaches for my hand. I push him away.

'I don't want your sympathy. I want you to leave me alone.'

'Have you talked to anyone, seen a counsellor?'

'No I haven't. I'm sick of talking about it.'

'If you took up Maz's offer of suing the practice, you could pay to see someone really good privately.' His tone is sharp and unsettling, as if he's losing patience with me. 'You really should do something. I mean, you're sitting here on your arse all day when you should be out there.'

'I'm happy as I am,' I say stubbornly.

'If you ask me, you're wallowing in self-pity. You haven't even asked about the kittens – who are doing well, by the way.'

'I have thought of them often.'

'They have homes to go to in a couple of weeks'

time. Well, Tilly isn't going anywhere – she's staying on as trainee practice cat as long as she gets on with Tripod, who is also on good form in case you're interested.'

'What's happening to Kit?'

'Celine's fallen in love with him – she's definitely taking him on.' He stares at me. 'I don't think you care about anything any more. I thought you were better than this.'

'Thanks a lot for the diagnosis.'

'I don't see any point in beating around the bush when I've tried every which way I can to help you. You need to snap out of it.'

'If only it was that easy,' I retort, seriously annoyed. Everyone knows you can't just snap out of a low mood. 'How can you have any idea what it's like for me? Every time I go out, I have the choice of sticking a load of Polyfilla in my face, or going make-up free and showing off the scars.'

'I wouldn't be hanging around shut up here all day every day, wasting my life. I'd be getting on with it.'

I've had enough. I stand up. 'Luckily, we aren't all the same. I wouldn't want to be like you, living at full throttle and so thick-skinned –' I hesitate, knowing I'm being harsh on him, but I'm furious – 'that you wouldn't notice if you'd had half your face bitten off.'

Ross glares at me. 'That's completely unfair. I'm trying to help.'

A voice in my head whispers that I'm overreacting because Ross does regret his actions, and maybe I'm being like this because I need to keep my distance, so I can fall out of love with him and stop looking back at what might have been.

'I'd like you to leave now. You can take your particular brand of sympathy and use it to upset
somebody else,' I say, but I'm not sure he's listening
to me because he starts up again.

'I've tried so hard to make you see what you mean
to me. I've stood by you, supported you as much as
you've allowed me to. You've been quite nasty to me
in return, yet I've still come back.' His voice breaks.
'I think you are the most beautiful woman in the
world. I love you, Shannon, with or without your
scars, and if you still refuse to let me in . . . Well, I'm
telling you now that if you let me go this time, I'm
not going to try again.' He pauses. 'There, I've said
it. It's up to you. Your decision.'

Ross is crying, I'm crying, and I can see through
my tears that he has a smear of dried blood across his
cheek where he's been scratched. He looks exhausted,
as though he's barely slept for months, but there's
something within me that stops me reaching out to
him and saying, stay, it's going to be all right. My
heart is as tight as a ball and I'm still smarting at his
stating of the obvious, that I'm wallowing. He stares
at me, his eyes beseeching, but all I can do is stare
back.

'Okay, that's it. I'm going,' he says, standing up,
'and this time, I'm telling you I won't come back.'

I raise my hand to wave him on his way, and he
turns and walks out for what I'm pretty certain will
be the very last time. It's over. I bury my face in a
cushion and sob until my tears run dry.

Chapter Twenty

On the Ball

For a long time afterwards, I half hope that Ross will turn up again, but why should he when I spoke to him like I did? *I* wouldn't. There are occasions when I wish I hadn't been so stubborn and could have opened up about how I feel, but I know I've done the right thing. I've just gone the wrong way about it. He's free to find someone else now. He doesn't have to put up with me and my scar.

Late summer turns into autumn and I settle into a routine, helping Mum in the shop every afternoon. I catch sight of Ross now and again when he's walking along the road or riding his bike past the shop, and Celine sends me a few selfies of her and little Kit when she takes him home – she asks me round for coffee, but I don't go. At the end of September, almost a month after Ross's final visit, I return to the hospital to see the consultant. He talks in depth about revision surgery. There's no guarantee of a satisfactory improvement in the appearance of the scar, which does look better than it did, according to him. To me, it looks the same, like a crevasse, except that the redness has been replaced by a purple hue and the swelling has gone down.

'Would you say that it affects your life in any way? That's the question you have to answer before you can make a decision.' He sits back in his seat behind his desk, his hands pressed together and his forefingers forming a steeple. 'If you decide to take this further, call my secretary and she'll make you another appointment.'

'What did the consultant say?' Mum asks when I get home.

I explain about the option of further surgery.

'I've decided not to have any,' I say.

'I think that's an excellent decision,' she says, giving me a hug. 'It's time to move on and plan the rest of your life. If you aren't going back to Otter House for whatever reason, you need to decide whether you're going to look for a similar job elsewhere or commit to Petals.' She gives me a look, meaning, Don't decide now, because I'll be revisiting this topic of conversation in the near future. I understand. I've been taking advantage and it's time I earned my keep.

'Are you sure you won't come with us?' Mum asks as I'm whizzing up a smoothie in the kitchen later the same evening.

'Thanks for the offer, but no.' The prospect of a long evening with the flat to myself is more appealing than playing third wheel to a couple of relapsed teenagers who can't keep their hands off each other.

'It's Godfrey's treat.' She slips a sequinned shrug over her shoulders.

'That's very kind of him, but I'm going to stay and keep Seven company.'

She gazes at me gently. 'I've told you, you can't spend the rest of your life dog-sitting. You should be out there. You haven't been swimming for a while. Why don't you give Jess a call and find out how she and Will are getting on, or arrange to meet Taylor? Don't leave it too long or they'll forget who you are.'

'I saw Taylor last week.'

'Only because she came to see you.'

'Are you coming with us, Shannon?' Godfrey joins us, moving up behind my mother, who jumps and makes an O with her mouth.

'She isn't.' Mum turns and kisses him on the lips; I'm praying they don't go into full snog mode when Godfrey breaks it off, taking her hand, and saying they must hurry because the table's booked for seven thirty.

'Don't wait up – not that we'll be late. I intend to make sure my lady is back for her bedtime.' Godfrey has a wicked glint in his eye and I can't help wondering if he's on Viagra.

'Goodnight,' I say, and I wait to hear his car drive off before deciding how I'm going to spend the next three or four hours. I notice that Seven is playing with one of the tennis balls Godfrey gave him, having bought them on offer at the garden centre the other day. He rolls the ball around the kitchen, picking it up and dropping it. I leave him to it, taking my smoothie into the living room, where I turn on the TV and sit on the sofa, glad to have the remote control to myself. Seven has other ideas, though, trotting in and dropping a ball at my feet.

'I'm sorry, I'm not up for this right now.'

He stares at me, his head cocked to one side and his tongue hanging out.

'I really don't want to play,' I say firmly. 'Please don't make me feel guilty with that look of yours.' His expression is quizzical, as if to say, 'Why not, when you're clearly at a loose end?'

Eventually he gives up, and I watch ten minutes of *Big Bang Theory* before he's back, dropping a second ball onto my foot, nudging at my shin and bowing before he grabs it up again and trots around the room, huffing and puffing and playing with it between his teeth. Okay, even my dog thinks I'm a party pooper. I bend down and pick up the second ball and throw it for him. With a yelp of joy, he chases into the corner of the room to pick it up, trapping it between his paw and the bookshelf. Unfortunately, he forgets to drop the one he's already carrying, and in a split second, his demeanour changes from joy to fear.

He drops one ball and retches, honking like a goose as he tries to clear the other ball from his throat. When that doesn't work, he stands still, hanging his head, strings of saliva sliding from his open mouth.

'Oh dear,' I say as calmly as I can. 'Let's have a look at you.'

I open his mouth wider, cautiously keeping my fingers over his lips so as not to get bitten. He takes a snorting intake of breath, which seems to make things worse. He stands gulping and quivering, his eyes filling with panic. Realising that this particular emergency isn't in any of the vet nursing textbooks that I've ever read, I grab my mobile from the arm of the sofa and dial the surgery, praying someone will answer straight away, as I check the position of the ball. I can just see it caught between his back teeth – he's squashed it and started to swallow it, goodness knows how.

I'm hoping for Maz, but it's Ross who answers the phone.

'It's Shannon here. I need you to look at Seven. He's choking on a ball.'

'Stay where you are. I'll be with you in ten.'

'I'll meet you at the surgery,' I say, knowing that he'll need forceps and maybe the endoscope, and he can't bring any kit on his motorbike. 'There isn't time to argue – he's turning blue.' I drop the phone as I stick my fingers into Seven's mouth – all right, I know about the risks of pushing the ball further into his throat, but desperate times need desperate measures. His tongue has a horrible purple hue. It lolls from his mouth and his back legs collapse.

I can feel the ball through his skin over his throat. I push it forwards from the outside, but it won't budge. I grab Seven, hold him up so he's facing away from me, and do the Heimlich manoeuvre. His chest pumps and heaves. He swallows and the ball moves further down, but at least that means he can breathe. He takes several gasping breaths – I can see the relief on his face – his tongue grows pink and, although he rubs at his mouth when I let him down to the floor, he seems calmer.

I cross my fingers and paws that the ball will stay put while I get him to Otter House.

I drag him through the back to the van, which is parked in front of my car, lift him onto the passenger seat and drive him down the road to the practice. Ross's motorbike roars up a couple of minutes later. Leaving his helmet behind, he carries Seven into the practice while I unlock doors and switch lights on.

'Is it a tennis ball?'

348

I nod. Seven sits on the prep bench, deep in misery and showing the whites of his eyes.

'They're like fluorescent dog-magnets.' Ross pulls up some sedation and gives the dog a shot into the vein in his front leg, making him sleepy and relaxed. I hand him a variety of forceps, grabbed from the cupboard, and he uses them one by one, trying to get hold of the ball.

'It's well stuck,' I say, my voice harsh with desperation.

'What goes in must come out. Ah, I've got it.' As he draws the ball through Seven's throat, it slips back again and blocks his airway. I snatch a stethoscope from the hook on the wall, and listen to his heart, which is beating far too fast.

'Hurry up,' I say, biting back the tears that are threatening to spill onto my cheeks. 'He's stopped breathing. Ross, do something!'

'Pass me the clippers, scalpel blade and spirit. Grab an ET tube.'

I feel as if I'm in a scene from a horror movie as I watch Ross turn Seven onto his back, clip the hair from his neck and squirt some spirit over his skin. He fits a fresh blade onto a scalpel handle, glancing at me as the metallic edge glints, reflecting in his eyes that are dark with concentration and worry.

'Have you done this before?'

'Many times. I know what I'm doing.' He makes a hole through skin and cartilage, takes the ET tube from me and forces it into Seven's windpipe before connecting it to the oxygen supply and a bag in case we need to ventilate or breathe for him.

'That buys us some time,' he says gruffly, but something isn't right. The sound of Seven's heartbeat has been replaced by my own pulse thudding in my ears. I slide my hand across his chest to confirm what I already know. His heart has stopped too.

'We're losing him.'

'Starting CPR,' Ross says, but I've already grabbed the crash kit and checked the clock. We haven't got long, three or four minutes at most before lack of oxygen starts to kill the cells in his brain.

'Don't worry about me,' he continues. 'Roll him onto his side and get some adrenaline into him IV.'

I do two minutes of chest compressions, with my elbows locked and one hand over the other, while he continues to try to dislodge the ball with a gag and a different set of forceps. There's a little blood trickling from Seven's mouth.

Stay on it, I tell myself. Don't give up.

'Got it,' Ross says, but there's no triumph in his voice as he delivers the ball and drops it on the floor. 'You squeeze the bag. I'll take over from you. Don't argue,' he adds, detecting my hesitation. 'You're no use if you're tired.' He carries out another set of chest compressions. At two minutes, he checks the pulse.

'Anything?' I ask.

He shakes his head, and I'm about to take over the compressions again when he touches my arm.

'Hold on,' he says, frowning. 'I can feel something.'

I give Seven another breath of oxygen then wait, willing him to breathe for himself. There's a quiver and the tiniest lift of his chest. I glance at his gums, but they're still pale and grey and I prepare to give him another breath.

'Leave it.'

'But he's blue and he isn't breathing,' I say sharply.

He might be the vet, but my instincts are crying out that my dog needs more oxygen.

'Hands off that bag,' he growls, taking me by the shoulders and pulling me aside. I try to shrug him off but his fingers press firmly into my flesh. 'Look, there's another breath,' he goes on. 'Give him too much oxygen and his body assumes it doesn't need to breathe.' He picks up another stethoscope from the crash kit and listens to Seven's chest while I watch for signs that he's waking up . . . or not. I feel sick to the pit of my stomach because I know the score. His chances of survival are low and, even if he recovers from this episode without brain damage, it's possible that he'll go on to have a second cardiac arrest.

'I'm sorry, Shannon. I shouldn't have yelled at you.'

'It's all right. I deserved it. You were right.'

'You realise this isn't looking too good,' he continues in a low voice.

I nod. I can't speak.

'If he gets through this, he's still up against it. We've done what we can, but it's up to him now. He's got to put up a fight, one he may yet lose.'

I check the tone of Seven's jaw, and touch the corner of his uppermost eye. He blinks.

'He's coming round,' I whisper, hardly daring to hope.

Ross's hand is on my shoulder. He clears his throat.

'It's a good sign, but there's a long way to go.'

I stifle a sob and somehow his arm is around my back and his breath is warm and damp in my hair.

'Hey,' he soothes. 'You've done your best. Let's keep focused. We'll leave the tube in for now – I'll suture it in place. I don't want to take it out too early because there'll be some swelling in his throat now the ball is out and we need to give that time to settle. You can set up for suction next to keep the tube clear. It's all right,' he adds, detecting my reluctance to leave Seven's side, 'I'm right here.'

I set up the equipment and clear the mucus and blood from the tube. I lean down and kiss Seven's head, my vision blurring.

'Come on, boy, you can do this.' I look into his eye and catch a flicker of recognition. He's in there somewhere. He blinks, lifts his head then falls back again.

'He's had a shock. You'll have to be patient.' Ross pushes a stool across to me. 'Sit down. I'll go and put the kettle on.' He smiles a small smile when I open my mouth to argue that it would be better if he stayed while I went to make tea. 'Any change, no matter how small, give me a shout and I'll come straight back. Are you okay with that?'

I nod and listen to his footsteps fading along the corridor and the doors swinging softly shut behind him.

He returns with two mugs of tea. I take a sip and choke myself. 'How much sugar did you put in that?'

'Just drink it.' He pulls up a second stool and sits down opposite me on the other side of the bench, and I don't know if it's deliberate or not, but his leg comes to rest against mine and we stay like that, watching over the dog lying between us.

Half an hour and more passes before he makes an attempt to get up. Disorientated and distressed, he starts to thrash about. I jump to my feet, leaning over him with one arm across his neck and the other across his flank, struggling to restrain him.

'I'm not sure what's going on,' I say, panicking again. 'Is he having a fit?'

'I think he's confused, trying to wake up too quickly.' Ross prepares a sedative and injects it, at which Seven relaxes and utters a deep snore.

'Is he going to be brain-damaged? Only I don't want him to suffer. Would it be fairer to . . . ?'

'Put him to sleep?' Ross finishes for me.

'You don't have to protect me,' I say, my voice cracking.

'Don't worry. If this reaches a point where I think that it's wrong to continue, I'll be straight with you. Don't give up on him yet. Trust me.'

I look at him. I do trust him with my dog. I'm pretty sure I could have trusted him with my heart too. He's a good man, but it doesn't matter any more. I wish I could be one of those people who wear their blemishes with confidence and pride. I'd love to be able to say, I don't care about my outward appearance, I'm still beautiful. Friends and family and all the counsellors in the world could tell me that I'm still gorgeous, but I wouldn't believe them. I'm not sure I'm even the same person on the inside after what I've experienced, even though everyone tries to drill into me that I am.

My loss of confidence is only one of my concerns though. I'm worried about being able to do my job properly because of my fears of big dogs and meeting people. If I can't work, how am I going to earn a living? I can't motivate myself to go swimming, and I'm frustrated at being stuck at home with Godfrey, even though he's being very sweet.

I don't know what I'm going to do.

I place a blanket across my sleeping dog, and call my mum to let her know what's happening. She wants to come straight back to see him for herself, but I suggest that she stays at home – it's too upsetting and he isn't aware of what's going on. I promise that I'll contact her as soon as I have any further news.

Ross fetches more tea – eating and drinking in Kennels is against the rules, but I'm on sick leave . . . Sitting here though, watching the rise and fall of Seven's chest, inhaling the scents of dog and disinfectant, and listening to the sound of Ross's voice, I realise how much I miss not only him, but work as well.

'How's it going being at home?' he asks.

'Much as you'd expect. I'm very good at watching daytime TV when I'm not helping out in the shop.'

'Can you do all that floristry stuff?'

'Mum's the creative one. I follow her instructions.'

'That's a change, you following instructions.'

In spite of everything, I find myself smiling.

'That's better. You know, we need you back here. It hasn't been the same here without you. I miss you, and the clients are always asking after you. I've had to work with Izzy while Maz and Emma look after the locum nurses. We've had three so far. The latest one's just left – she was lovely, but she could only fill in for a couple of weeks.'

'Are you trying to make me feel guilty?'

'It would be good to have you back.' He turns to Seven. His ears are flicking, which means the sedation is wearing off. Eventually, he comes round enough for me to settle him in a kennel, where he sits propped up on his front legs with a towel over his shoulders. He recognises me, pricking his ears and following the sound of my voice when I speak his name, but his eyes are glazed.

'He looks like he's been out on the piss,' Ross says, amused.

'Do you think he's going to be okay?' I ask, seeking reassurance that he can't give me.

'I'll start to relax when we're safely through the next twenty-four hours. Why don't you go home?'

'No, he's my dog. Why don't you go and get some sleep? You have to work tomorrow.'

'I'll stay here on the sofa and you can give me a shout if you need me.' He runs his hands through his hair and yawns.

'Ross,' I say as he turns to walk away.

'Yes?' He looks back.

'Thank you.'

'It's nothing.'

I sit, cuddled up with Seven in his cage with a blanket wrapped around me. As I wait, I hear the click of a cat-flap followed by a cat meowing, and Tripod comes stalking into Kennels with Tilly trotting along behind him, stopping to attack his tail. Tripod ignores her the first time, but on the second occasion he turns, hisses and bats her across the face with his paw.

'That's right. You tell her,' I say softly, a lump forming in my throat at the sight of the two of them: the old man who's doing so well on his medication and diet, and my baby who isn't a kitten any more. It's remarkable, and I'm praying as the cats come over to investigate that a miracle will happen for Seven too. I give them each a stroke and they wander away again, prowling and chasing after imaginary mice. I lean back against the side of Seven's cage and close my eyes, and I remember very little until the aroma of spice and coffee wakes me.

'Hey, sleepy.' Someone gently shakes my shoulder. 'Mind yourself. Don't bump your head.'

'Ross?' My mouth is dry and my body aches. .

'You really should be in bed.'

'In your bed?' The stress and lack of sleep must have made me mishear him. I gaze at him, a little shocked at being abruptly woken up, and my bottom aching from the hard floor. I feel a rush of blood to my face and my scars start to itch.

'You need some rest.' He helps me to my feet, his eyes filled with concern as I yawn and stumble into him. 'I should have made an appearance earlier.'

Suddenly, it all comes flooding back; Seven and the tennis balls, his frightening collapse . . .

'He could have died while I was asleep and I wouldn't have noticed.'

'You would have – vet nurses have a sixth sense when it comes to an animal in trouble,' Ross says. 'Come and have some breakfast; there's an egg roll and cinnamon swirls.'

'Shouldn't I feed Seven first?' I ask anxiously.

'We'll decide when you've had something to eat. You're no good to him if you're dead on your feet.' He lays out a feast on some paper towel, and we're eating breakfast when Izzy and Maz turn up. Izzy's about to say something when Ross nods towards the cages. 'We've had a rough night.'

Maz gives me a brief hug before she walks across to open the cage door, at which Seven struggles to his feet. 'What's happened to one of my favourite dogs? You've done a tracheostomy?' She turns to Ross as Seven sniffs at her knees and wags his tail, and I breathe a sigh of relief because he looks as if he's going to make it after all.

'It's a temporary measure, I hope. He choked on a tennis ball and went into cardiac arrest. We got him back and we're crossing everything that he hasn't suffered any lasting damage to his brain.'

'What brain?' Maz says lightly.

'Hey, don't be rude,' I say. 'He's one of the cleverest dogs I know.'

'He is,' she agrees. 'It's odd though, isn't it, how quick he is to recognise when your mum's having a hypo, yet he can't play safely with a tennis ball.'

He looks a mess with his neck clipped of hair and his fur knotted with dried blood. He coughs, bringing up a clot from his throat.

'Don't panic.' Ross looks at me. 'Let's have some suction.'

'Poor Seven,' Maz says, as Izzy and I hold on to him while Ross makes sure the tube is clear. 'I heard the bike go out last night.'

'I made it from Talyford to Otter House in record time.'

'So what happens with him now?' Maz goes on.

'I thought I'd leave the tube for another twelve to twenty-four hours. He ought to be under constant observation too, but I'm not sure how we'll organise that.'

'I'll do it,' I say, and I stay with Seven all day, stroking him, talking to him, suctioning his tube, fiddling with his drip and keeping him comfortable. Every so often, somebody comes in to check we're okay, bringing me tea or the offer of a quick rest break.

I sit leaning against the adjacent cage door, listening to the sounds of the practice, the familiar hiss of the autoclave, the clatter of an instrument tray being washed up in the sink, the hot smell of steamed drapes, the aroma of cat food and the occasional questioning woof from the terrier two doors down who's waiting for X-rays, and I find myself yearning to get back into the consulting room and theatre. Could I do it when it came down to it though, I wonder? Am I ready to re-enter the fray? When Izzy comes through with a rangy German shepherd dog with big teeth for a chest X-ray, I realise that I'm not sure.

Two days later, when I return to the practice after a break to shower and catch up with some sleep, Ross meets me in the corridor and gives me the go-ahead to take Seven home.

'I've removed the tube – his throat's fine,' he says.

'That's great,' I respond.

'I have to say I was bricking it the other night. I've never done a tracheostomy in my life,' he goes on, holding the door into Kennels open for me.

'But you said . . .' My mouth is opening and closing like a goldfish as I walk on through, turning to stare at him as I do so. 'You said you'd done loads.'

'I didn't want to worry you.'

'You seemed so calm.'

'It was all an act. I'm good, aren't I?'

'You are. I don't know how to thank you.'

'I can always think of something.' He is smiling and his eyes are on my face; I feel myself blushing because he says it in a light-hearted, suggestive manner with a glint in his eye. 'I want you back at work.'

Seven whines from his cage when he sees me, and barks to go out.

'It's all right,' Ross says, 'I've taken him out and given him some of that liquid convalescent diet. He's a miracle dog.'

'You're wasted as a vet. You should be a nurse,' I say, smiling.

'Any problems, give me a call on the mobile.'

'Are you sure it isn't too soon?' I say doubtfully. 'I mean, less than forty-eight hours ago, he was on his way out. What if he has another arrest?'

'You sound like a paranoid, over-attached owner,' Ross teases. 'You know the score. Unless you have a crystal ball like Mrs Wall, you can't predict what might happen in the future, but I can tell you with the benefit of experience that I don't see any reason why he shouldn't be okay now – as long as he plays ball, so to speak, and doesn't pick up any more foreign bodies. He'll be happier at home and make a quicker recovery.' He pauses. 'Maz hasn't been in touch with you?'

I check my mobile for texts and missed calls. There's nothing from my boss.

'Okay, I'll see you tomorrow at ten o'clock for Seven's checkup. I'm off home now and Maz is on call, but I'll leave my phone on in case you want me. I'll answer as long as I'm not on the bike.'

Thanking him again, I wish him goodnight. I think of him going back to the house in Talyford, and my throat tightens with regret because, if things had worked out differently, I would have been going home with him.

I put Seven on a harness and lead, and take him back to Petals, where he's overjoyed to see Mum and Godfrey. Much as he loves everyone, though, he isn't keen to return to Otter House, and the next morning he walks into reception with his head down and his tail between his legs. I chat to Celine while we're waiting.

'Seven's a VIP, a Very Important Patient,' Ross says, calling me through to the consulting room. 'You could have brought him straight through the back. How is he doing? Has he eaten anything?'

'He's had some chicken and rice.'

Ross lifts him onto the table and examines him. Seven is not impressed when he sticks a thermometer under his tail.

'That's all good,' Ross says eventually, looking up at me through his curly overgrown fringe. 'His heart sounds fine and his temperature's normal.'

'Do you want to see him again?'

'Same time tomorrow. By the way, Maz wants a word. She's in the office – Izzy will have Seven for a few minutes.' He whisks the dog back down to the floor.

'Thank you for keeping an eye on him,' I say as I take him through to the corridor.

'I don't mind,' Ross says. 'It gives me an excuse to keep an eye on you as well. I hope that doesn't sound creepy,' he adds quickly. 'What I mean is that it's always great to see you. You're looking lovely as always.'

I'm not sure how to respond.

'That's a compliment by the way,' he explains.

I find myself thanking him for a second time even though, deep inside, I can't believe that he means it. He's just trying to be nice, I think, which is sweet of him. I close the door behind me and drop Seven into Kennels, where Izzy treats him with a biscuit and holds on to him while I go and find Maz.

'Hi, Shannon. Thanks for coming to see me.' She shows me into the office and closes the door behind us. 'Have a seat. Would you like a coffee?'

'I'm all right, thank you.' I sit down on the chair in front of the desk. She sits behind it and smiles.

'How is Seven?'

'He's doing well, but Ross wants to see him again tomorrow.'

'That's wonderful news.' Maz rests her elbows on the desk. 'I thought you'd like to know that Kit's doing well with Celine. Apparently, he's getting bolder by the day. You've done a brilliant job with both of the kittens.'

I wonder if she's soft-soaping me, trying to flatter me into returning to work.

'Although I'm not sure about Tilly's future as practice cat,' she goes on. 'She sank her claws into my leg the other day – I'd chased her out of reception because she was winding up our canine patients, lying in wait under the shelves to ambush them.'

'She'll be in for a shock if she tries that with Nero.'

'She's so bold I don't think she'd care.' Maz changes the subject. 'I wanted to speak to you the other morning, but I thought it better that we didn't have this conversation while you were sleep deprived. I know we've mentioned this before, but you have to get on and sue me and Emma so you can get the compensation that you're entitled to for your injuries and loss of earnings. It's only fair. This –' she glances from my eyes to my scars and back – 'accident happened in the practice. You can put the money in the bank and save it for a holiday or put it towards a deposit on a home of your own. You aren't being disloyal or greedy, or hurting the practice, or alienating me and Emma. It's your right. We pay our premiums every year – this is what insurance is for.' She pauses. 'Think about it and, as soon as you decide to go ahead, let me know and I'll set the ball rolling.' She stops short and smiles wryly. 'That isn't the best way of putting it, considering what Seven's just gone through.' She reaches out and touches my arm. 'Ross said you did all the right things.'

'It was him, not me.'

'It sounded like a team effort.'

'You know what he's like.'

'I do. He's thoughtful, kind and a little mad. I'd appreciate it if you were gentle with him. He still feels terribly guilty for what happened. It's taken Alex and Leo many beers and late nights to persuade him to stay at Otter House.'

'Really? I didn't know.'

'He was all for resigning . . .' Maz hesitates. 'You can tell me to mind my own business, but I felt there was more behind it than what happened with Bart. Perhaps living together wasn't a good move as it turned out.'

I don't make any attempt to deny it.

'It's over now, whatever it was.' I've learned my lesson.

'So are you in the right frame of mind to make a return to work, do you think – only we really miss you?'

I take a few moments to decide. Bringing Seven into the consulting room with Ross this morning has made me feel that I really should give it a go. If I don't confront my fears now, it's likely that I never will, and I'll have to think about finding another job because I'm running out of money. I've discovered some alternative careers on daytime TV: doctor, chat-show host, antique dealer, heir hunter and cook, none of which appeal.

'I am, if you're sure you want me,' I say slowly.

'If you prefer not to work with Ross when you come back, I'll understand. You can be with me or Emma.'

'No, it's all right.'

'Thank you, but you can always change your mind.'

'What if I can't do it, though?' I ask, unable to disguise the rising panic in my voice. 'I'm not sure how I'll react when a big dog comes in for an injection. I'm still having nightmares.'

'When I came back from maternity leave, I remember wondering if my confidence would return.' Maz strokes her chin. 'I know it isn't the same, but being away from work for a while does things to your head. You have to think about everything that used to be second nature.

'How about making a staged return, perhaps mornings only for a week or so, and no large dogs to begin with? We want you back, Shannon. We all do. You can start tomorrow if you like.'

I decide to go for it, knowing that, if I delay, there's more chance that I'll change my mind.

'Tomorrow it is then,' I say, and Maz jumps up with a cry and leans across the desk at full stretch to give me a hug.

'That's wonderful. Oh, I can't wait to tell everyone.'

I'm touched that she's so pleased at the prospect of my imminent return, and I leave the office with a spring in my step, running into Ross, who is hanging around in the corridor as if he's been waiting for me.

'How did it go?' he asks.

'I've agreed to come back – Maz called it a staged return.'

'Oh, that's fantastic.' He steps towards me as if to

embrace me, then appears to change his mind. 'I'm so pleased.' His smile makes my heart somersault. 'I can't find the words to explain how much I've missed you.'

'Stop it,' I say, half laughing. 'You're embarrassing me.'

'When do you start?'

'Tomorrow. This afternoon, I'm going to ask Godfrey if he can recommend a solicitor to help me make a claim against the practice insurance for my loss of earnings. I feel bad about that, but Maz has convinced me that it's the right thing to do.'

'And she's right,' he agrees. 'Well, I'll see you tomorrow, unless . . .' He hesitates. 'Don't worry, it doesn't matter.'

'Bye.' I wonder as I fetch Seven what he was going to say. Perhaps he was planning to ask me out for a drink and thought better of it. I'm glad he didn't because I would have had to let him down. I touch the scar, feeling the gristle under my fingertips. I'm not one hundred per cent sure that I'm ready to come back to the practice where I'm among friends, let alone go out socially to a pub where there are bound to be people, acquaintances and strangers, who'll stare and ask questions and make me freak out. As I scuttle along the street back to Petals with the dog, I feel hot and panicky.

Chapter Twenty-One

Second Chances

Seven sleeps on my duvet, panting hot air in my face, because I don't have the heart to make him lie in his bed on the floor, and the next day I leave him with Mum while I go to work. For him life is all about cheese, biscuits, cuddles and walks, I'm not sure in which order, and there are times like today when I wish I was a dog.

Getting changed into scrubs at Otter House, I feel like it's my very first day all over again and, when I report to Izzy, I am decidedly nervous. I haven't been away for very long in the scheme of things, but I worry about being out of practice, that I'll have to think about how to use the autoclave and which instruments go into which kit for the different ops. Maz is right. I've lost confidence – not just in my looks, but in every area of my life – and I can't see how I'll ever get it back.

'It's good to see you back in uniform,' Izzy says with a welcoming smile. 'We thought you could help me out in Kennels to start with, and when morning

365

surgery starts, you can join Maz in the consulting room.' She raises her hand as I start to thank her. 'Don't thank me. She's the one who's organised it.' She sighs. 'It isn't your fault, but being one nurse down has been a right pain in the—'

'Hellooo!' interrupts a child's voice as the doors from the corridor open behind us.

'Hi, George,' Izzy says, turning to face him. He's wearing a white polo shirt and grey shorts, and carrying a red book bag. 'What are you doing here? Mummy hasn't booked you to do the ops?'

He chuckles. 'It's an insect day – Mummy forgot.'

'Does that mean I'm babysitting?' I ask hopefully.

'No, it's fine.' Maz joins us, her cheeks scarlet with exertion and some embarrassment, I suspect, at forgetting that there's no school today. I'm pretty sure she's done the same thing in the past.

'I'm not a baby any more,' George says.

'We know – it's a figure of speech,' Maz explains. 'I'm such an idiot – I had the letter stuck on the board at home and I still missed the fact it's an inset day for teacher training. Sophia's going to come and pick George up for me as soon as she's back from her ride. Humpy says she'll take you to buy a new hat at Tack 'n' Hack, George,' she adds but, as is the way with children, he's already onto another topic of conversation.

'What happened to your face?' He points at my scar and my hand flies up automatically to cover it.

'What did we talk about on the way to school?' Maz says quickly. 'I'm sorry, Shannon.'

'I can't remember,' he says.

'It must run in the family,' Izzy observes.

'It's all right.' He isn't being rude, just curious, but

it confirms my fears that everyone will be looking at me. 'Ross's dog bit me and I had to go to hospital to have stitches.'

'Was it bleeding?' he asks. 'Why didn't Mummy stitch it up? Does it hurt?'

'That's enough of the questions.' Maz takes his hand. 'You know what happened, and Shannon has work to do.'

'I wanna help.'

'Not now.'

'I wanna help,' George repeats, making to stamp his foot.

'Well, you can't,' Maz says wearily. I think she's a lovely mum, but sometimes juggling her job and children, and probably her husband, seems all too much. 'Unless –' she looks at me as her son's foot continues to hover in mid-air – 'Shannon's willing to show you how to feed Tilly and Tripod before Humpy turns up.'

'Of course,' I say, glancing towards Izzy, who rolls her eyes because she had other plans for me.

George has a wonderful time, squishing the sticky jelly from the sachets of cat food onto his fingers while he feeds the kitten; she mews and winds around his legs as if she's been starved, while Tripod sits patiently waiting for his special diet.

Ross puts his head around the door.

'Having fun?' he asks.

George responds with a grin as he wipes his hands on his polo shirt.

Ross's eyes lock onto mine. 'It's great to see you back.' The warmth of his smile makes me feel more apprehensive than ever. 'Nothing much has changed. Celine is still here, making long-term plans to become a vet nurse like you, and Frances drops by at least once a week for coffee and a natter.'

However, things have changed, I think sadly, when I find myself panicking at the thought of handling a dog – any dog – and struggling with the way some of our clients look at me when they catch sight of my face. For the first couple of days, my colleagues treat me differently too, metaphorically wrapping me in cotton wool. Maz will only let me handle the cats, a rabbit, and a tortoise called Charlie who comes in with rattling breathing and a sore mouth.

It isn't until after the weekend that I return to full-time work, feeling more confident. On the Monday morning, I'm with Ross in the consulting room. We've already seen a couple of cats for vaccination when the next client turns up with a dog. Emily has one of her children, a girl of about five years old, tagging along behind her in a dress and red wellies, hugging a black and white toy cat to her chest. Celine is about to start booking them in, but Ross calls them straight into the consulting room where I'm disinfecting the rubber mat on the table.

He looks at me. 'Why don't you swap with Izzy? She's clearing up after the dental.'

'I'm fine here.'

'But . . .' He frowns. 'Are you sure?'

'It's Sherbet. I've met him before and he's only a little dog . . . And you don't have to keep protecting me. I'll have to do this eventually. I can't be a cat nurse for the rest of my life.' It's thoughtful of him and I'm grateful that he's looking out for me, especially after the way I've treated him but, really, as I've said before, I've been doing my job for longer than he's been qualified to do his.

'So what has happened to Sherbet?' he asks as Emily lowers him down awkwardly onto the table. He yelps and then sits there, his hind legs limp and his tail still.

'He hurt himself,' pipes up the little girl, who has big blue eyes and strawberry-blonde ringlets of hair that tumble down over her shoulders. I can't help wondering how many sets of straighteners she'll get through when she's older. 'He fell off the bed. What happened to that lady's face?' she says, looking at me.

'Poppy, don't stare. It's rude.'

'Did you fall off your bed?' she goes on, oblivious to her mum's embarrassment.

'That's enough. You promised you'd behave if I let you come with me and Sherbet to the vet's.'

'It's all right,' I say. 'Really.' Like George, Poppy is naturally curious.

'I'm afraid you might report us to the social services, or whatever the pet equivalent is. Poppy put him in her bed, and when he got up, he slipped off the edge. I don't know how many times I've told her he isn't a doll.'

He's quite cute though, I think. I remember them bringing him for a booster jab soon after they picked him up from the Sanctuary, having offered him a new home. He's middle-aged, and his breath's a bit smelly, but they seem to love him all the same. I glance towards Ross.

'He's in a lot of pain,' he says. 'Let's pop a muzzle on to be on the safe side.'

I fish around in the drawer, take out a muzzle to fit his nose and slip it on, fastening it behind his balding ears. He looks surprised, and Emily even more so.

'He'd never hurt anyone,' she says, slightly affronted.

'I don't doubt it, but I'd rather be safe than sorry. Shannon, hold on to him for me.'

I hesitate. It's all right. I managed to work with Trevor, although I didn't have to restrain him for an examination or injection. Sherbet's only a small dog, and he's wearing a muzzle. He can't do anything except fidget, but an irrational fear takes hold of me as I take hold of him. He senses my state of mind, growling as he wrenches his head away and wriggles out from under my arm.

'Are you all right?' Ross asks gently.

'Give me a minute.' My heart is racing and my palms sweating. I'm shaking and hardly able to breathe. I can do it. I will do it. I *have* to do it.

'I can ask Izzy,' he persists.

'No,' I say sharply and I try again, aware that Emily is frowning disapprovingly. 'Come on, Sherbet, there's a good boy.'

I keep him still while Ross is examining him from one end to the other. When he touches the dog's back, just behind where his ribs stop, he yelps and tries to turn round, snarling and snapping through the muzzle.

'Mummy!' Poppy yelps too. 'The vet's hurting Sherbet.'

'He has to find out what's wrong, darling.' Emily has tears in her eyes as she takes a firm grip on her daughter's hand to restrain her.

'He's cruel.' Poppy glares at Ross. If looks could kill . . . 'Let go of my dog. He's my pet.'

'The vet is going to make him better. It's like when you went to the hospital to mend your head: it hurts at first and then it gets better. He is going to get better, isn't he?'

'I can't give you an answer yet,' Ross says calmly. 'I need to admit him and take some X-rays, or we can refer him immediately to the nearest specialist. Is he insured?'

Emily shakes her head. 'I kind of thought we'd risk it. I mean, you can't pay out on everything . . . Oh dear, Poppy, what's Daddy going to say? Sherbet needs to go to hospital.' I wait while she and Ross talk about the potential costs of investigations and treatment with no guarantee of a happy ending.

'I don't know what to do. I'll have to speak to Murray.'

'He's my pet,' Poppy repeats earnestly. 'I can pay with the pounds in my money-box.'

'I think Daddy's already borrowed them for the last bag of dog food. It wouldn't be enough anyway. What do you think?' Emily turns to Ross. 'What would you do if he was yours?'

I notice how a shadow crosses his face at the memory of Bart.

'I would suggest that we keep him in and get the X-rays done, then you can let us know what you want to do next.'

'What happens if we don't do anything?'

I gaze down at the dog, unhappy that Emily's even contemplating that possibility. I thought she was one of our more sensible clients, as in, willing to do anything within reason for her dog, not simply cast him away when he presents a problem.

'We can do the minimum, put him on cage rest and give him tablets or injections and wait to see if time heals.'

371

'I haven't got time to look after him.' She sounds desperate. 'I've got the girls, three little ones under six, and the farm. I can't nurse the dog as well. Murray's going to go ballistic. He thought I was mad letting Poppy have a pet in the first place.'

'There's no guarantee that if you decide to go to referral he'll get better anyway.' I know what Ross is saying. He's trying to make her feel better, less guilty if they genuinely can't afford to have Sherbet referred.

'You mean he could be permanently paralysed?'

He nods and hands her the tissues, and I find myself, not for the first time, surprised by the miracle of love. Sherbet is a funny old thing, a middle-aged dachshund with balding ears and a whip of a tail, yet Emily, in spite of what she's said before, clearly adores him.

'He's a poor old sausage, isn't he?' Poppy says, looking worriedly at her mum.

'He is.'

'I'll admit him and give him some strong painkillers,' Ross says. 'You can let me know your decision – it needs to be ASAP if you want to go ahead with surgery.'

Emily is in tears and Poppy cries as well, until I suggest that she leaves her toy cat here too.

'They can go in the same kennel,' I say gently. 'I'll look after them both.'

She seems to think this is a good idea and, with much kissing of Sherbet – I leave the muzzle on for that, just in case – and the toy cat, she leaves, holding her mum's hand.

'I hate these cases,' Ross sighs as he carries Sherbet carefully into the prep room. I bring the painkillers and set up a comfortable bed, clipping the inpatient

372

record card to the front of the cage. 'Let's get on with the X-rays. We can't afford to hang around. It isn't fair to continue if he's broken his back, and if he's slipped a disc, the sooner we can treat it, the better chance he has of being able to walk again.'

It isn't long before Sherbet is under sedation and Ross is looking at the pictures of his spine.

'In a perfect world, I'd do more tests to make sure it is that disc that's gone, but it looks pretty conclusive to me. If they have no money, we could have a go at surgery here.'

'Have you done a slipped disc before, or is this like Seven's tracheostomy, a stab in the dark?' I ask.

'I knew how to do it in principle. No, I've done this kind of op twice, although I'm no expert. I'm going to call Emily to chase her up. If she wants him referred, he needs to go now.'

'Do you want me to let him come round?'

'Good question. Yes, if she chooses to have the op done here, I'll do it after the evening consults.'

I keep my attention on the dog while Ross makes the phone call.

'Have you any plans tonight?' he asks me on his return.

I smile. 'I have actually.'

I notice how his face falls.

'I have a hot date as theatre nurse, I believe.'

'Thanks. You're a star.'

'I know,' I say, and later I realise I haven't thought about my scar since Poppy raised the topic. I've been too busy.

During the surgery, I monitor the patient under the drapes while Ross works on Sherbet's spine, the surgical site illuminated by the theatre light.

'Is everything all right your end?' I ask partway through. 'Ross?'

He glances up briefly. 'I'm sorry?'

'Is he okay?'

'Yes. Yes, thank you.' He looks back at the surgery, completely focused on the task in front of him. Beads of sweat start to roll down his forehead into his mask. I take a piece of damp paper towel and offer to mop his brow.

'That's better,' he says, relaxing for a moment. 'You couldn't do the rest of me, could you?'

He's teasing. I can tell from the sound of his voice and the twinkle in his eye.

'Keep your mind on the job,' I say lightly.

'I've missed you bossing me about.'

I make a note of Sherbet's pulse rate on the anaesthetic chart. It's gone up a little, but nothing compared with mine. I've missed Ross more than I can say.

He swabs at the incision. 'Suction, please.'

I press the button on the machine and listen to the sound, like someone sucking on a straw in an empty glass. As the op drags on, I fantasise not so much about the hot vet, but more of cold squash or cola with ice. I recheck Sherbet's vital signs and record them on his sheet. He's perfectly stable. Good shot, I tell myself.

Eventually, Ross pronounces the surgery over: he's released the pressure on the nerves in Sherbet's spinal cord. The dog is slowly coming round and I stroke his smooth, shiny coat. Returning him to Kennels, where the air is cooler, I wrap him in a blanket.

'Do you think he'll walk again?'

Ross shrugs as he removes his gown, mask and gloves, snapping them off his fingers and tossing them in the general direction of the bin.

'Hey, just because you're Supervet doesn't mean you can leave the place untidy,' I say, and he picks them up and puts them in the rubbish.

'I thought I was Speedivet.'

'I've given you a promotion. What you've just done is pretty amazing,' I call back as I flush the catheter on the patient's drip. 'I assume that Sherbet's staying with us for a while.'

'I don't want the little girl – what's she called?'

'Poppy.'

'Yes, Poppy. She means well, but I don't want to risk leaving him to her ministrations. He'll be better off having a holiday with us – three weeks' cage rest as a minimum – than falling off any more beds.' He yawns and his shoulders slump. He looks dead on his feet.

'It's gone eleven and you've been here all day. Go home and get some sleep. I'll keep an eye on Sherbet and call you back if necessary.'

'Thank you.' He yawns again.

'I'm sorry for boring you,' I say lightly.

'You could never bore me.' He gazes at me, his eyes soft and yearning. 'Goodnight.' And then he's gone, the sound of his motorbike fading into the night. Although he's no longer in the practice, I can feel his presence everywhere. I can't stop thinking about him.

I snooze for a while on the sofa in the staff room, where Tilly finds me, jumping up and lying across my shoulder, kneading with her unsheathed claws and dribbling. When I open my eyes, she arches her back and creeps away, as if terrified. For part of the night I sit up beside Sherbet, listening to him snoring, and looking at my reflection in the silvered back of the cage. My face looks distorted and indistinct; the surface isn't perfectly smooth like a mirror. I can't see my scar, but I can feel the pins-and-needles sensation pricking out its physical boundaries. Its psychological effects run much wider and deeper; sometimes when I'm alone, like now, I find myself consumed by it.

My patients seem not to care how I look, though, and my colleagues appear to have grown accustomed to my changed appearance in the few days since I returned to work. Apart from Ross: sometimes I catch him looking at my face, his eyes dwelling on my mouth, his expression one of sadness, quickly veiled when he realises I'm aware of what he's doing. I don't need his sympathy, but I need him. Having been apart for those few weeks, I've found out how much I've missed him as a friend, colleague and housemate. We've had our differences and I'm not stupid – things will never be the same between us because of what happened with Bart – but I could see us growing close again, not as lovers, but as friends.

At six in the morning, I give up on trying to sleep and make a start on the chores in Kennels. Ross returns at seven thirty, bringing coffee and croissants.

'How's he doing?' he asks, joining me.

'He's comfortable.' That's about all I can say.

'And you?'

'I'm fine.' I bite my lip, suppress the urge to add, 'Better for seeing you,' because his presence makes me feel more cheerful and less alone. He cares for me, I know he does.

'You need to say something to Maz and Emma

about your pay with doing these extra hours. They take advantage.'

'I don't think it's deliberate,' I say in their defence.

'How much do you think they earn? And they both have wealthy husbands. You should say something or put in an invoice for last night.' He pauses. 'You won't, will you, because you're too nice.'

'It's awkward because, if I ask for more money, it puts Sherbet's recovery in jeopardy.'

'But you're entitled to it.' He opens the cage door and squeezes one of Sherbet's paws to check for a reaction, but the dog is so desperate to escape that he doesn't give any indication as to whether he can feel anything, or not. 'Let's get him out of there.'

'I'll let you do it,' I say, not wanting to cause any damage. Sherbet has a large shaved area across his back and a long wound, neatly stitched and covered by a temporary dressing. He cries as Ross carries him to the bench. I place a towel on it to give him a more secure footing.

'You're a wuss. You've had enough painkillers to knock out an elephant. I think you're crying because you're afraid it's going to hurt.' Ross checks him over. He can support some weight on his back legs, he can feel him touching his hind paws, and he can wag his tail, but he can't stand on his own. Ross frowns and shakes his head. He looks utterly miserable.

I reach out and stroke his arm.

'Don't be so hard on yourself,' I say quietly. 'You've done the best you could, considering the circumstances. Others might have been quicker to give up on him.'

'Maybe that's what I should have done,' he says gruffly. 'I'm not sure I've done the right thing.'

'You said yourself that recovery can take weeks.'

'He can't walk, Shannon.' He swears. 'I was expecting some sign of improvement immediately post-surgery.' He runs his fingers through his hair. 'This is a disaster.'

I wish I could do or say something to console him.

'You know that feeling you get sometimes, when you try so hard and nothing seems to work out?'

I nod. I don't think he's just referring to Sherbet.

'That's how I feel right now.' He sighs. 'I'll have a chat with Emily later.'

I wish he'd confide in me. It isn't just the dog. There's something else that's eating him, but what is it? Heidi again? His father?

I have to admire Sherbet's bravery and determination, because a week later he's still with us, having been confined to his cage. The three vets have a meeting in Kennels to assess the situation. I hold on to Sherbet's front end, stroking his bald ears, which feel like rubber – not that there's any real need to restrain him. He isn't going very far.

'I'm really depressed about this,' Ross says. 'He's shown very little improvement; all I've done is raised everyone's hopes and dashed them.'

'It isn't your fault,' Maz says.

'You don't know until you try with these cases,' Emma says.

'What now? How long do I give him?'

'You can't give up on him yet,' I join in. I can't help it. I've been the one who's been feeding him by hand when he's too sad to eat, carrying him out to the garden, changing his bed and bathing him when he soils himself.

'I know you're fond of him,' Emma says, 'but Emily

and Murray can't afford months of rehab. It's already been a week and we've given them quite a discount on his hospital fees.'

'I'll do it,' I cut in. 'I don't mind coming in early and staying late.'

'You do that anyway,' Ross says.

'Yes, and we're very grateful for that,' Maz says.

'Not grateful enough to turn it into paid overtime, though,' he adds.

'Please don't.' I glare at him. I know he means well, but I don't want to upset the partners. Insisting on paying me for extra hours isn't going to help Sherbet's cause.

'She's too nice to ask you for more pay, but it isn't fair to expect a member of staff to be here day and night and stuck on the same salary,' he goes on, ignoring me.

'We can look into that later,' Emma says. 'What are we going to do about Sherbet?'

'I'm happy to match Shannon's generosity,' Ross offers. 'I'll come in early and stay late to give him the veterinary treatment he requires.'

'That's very kind of you,' Maz says, apparently warming to the idea.

'We aren't a charity though,' Emma says coolly. I know she struggled to balance the books in the past. It was before I started work at Otter House, when she went off on holiday, leaving Maz to pick up the pieces. I've heard from Frances that the bailiffs were pretty well knocking at the door. I don't see what the problem is now, though. The practice is thriving, unless the partners have overstretched themselves by converting the flat and buying and doing up the property for the branch surgery. Maybe Emma's just being tight. 'We can't do it for every client. Is it fair to offer free treatment to just one? It will be all over town in five minutes that we're doing discounts.'

Maz gazes at her partner. 'We've made similar arrangements before. We can keep the hospitalisation fees to a minimum, just enough to cover our costs. Which is worse? To miss out on a small amount of income or put the dog to sleep?'

'All right. You're right.' Emma looks at Sherbet. 'He's a funny little chap. We'll do this on the understanding that if he isn't showing steady improvement, then we make the decision.' She smiles. 'Thanks, everyone.'

I thank Ross later.

'I'm not sure Emma would have gone for it if you hadn't supported me,' I say.

'Maz would have done. You didn't need me, but, having done the op, I want to see this through. I've spoken to Emily and she's over the moon. She's bringing a bag of Sherbet's food in for him.'

'Where do we go next?'

'He has two more weeks of cage rest to look forward to, then we'll have to think about some rehab in the form of physio and hydrotherapy.'

'What if it doesn't make any difference and he still can't walk and lead a normal life?'

'We'll cross that bridge if and when we come to it.' He smiles and my heart melts. 'I'm learning that sometimes when you want something badly enough and it's really worth having, you have to be incredibly patient . . .'

I find myself remembering his words every now and then. He wasn't referring to Sherbet alone. He was talking in general. Is it possible that he means he's waiting for me? I wonder if I should say something to make it clear that the moment has gone, but that would be opening myself up to further hurt, like a wound breaking down. It's true, I think, that some things are better unsaid.

I keep myself busy. I tolerate Godfrey and the prostate, do a shift now and again in the shop for Mum, walk Seven and spend a lot of time on Sherbet's rehab, doing basic physio exercises to keep his muscles from wasting. I get to take him to a practice on the other side of Exeter for several sessions in a pool for dogs, learning from the qualified canine hydrotherapist who looks after it, but although he can move his back legs when he's in the water, he can't support his weight on them. I've perfected the art of using a tea towel as a sling to hold him up so he can relieve himself and take a few steps around the lawn, and I turn him regularly when he's in his kennel so he doesn't end up with bed sores.

I love Sherbet and he loves me. He yaps and wags his tail every time I walk past him.

'He's getting stronger,' I say to Ross when we have him out in the garden one morning. The dog pricks his ears and wags his tail, all excited, until he realises he can't chase the birds or play with the kitten, and his ears go down and he sniffs at the ground. I'm determined he's going to put on a good show, though, because I don't want anyone saying that he should be put to sleep.

'Look.' I lift him into a standing position and he holds it for two or three minutes, trembling towards the end when he sits back down. I place a treat about a metre in front of him. He sniffs the air and looks at me as if to say: you don't expect me to go and get that, do you?

I'm aware of Ross's expression. He looks decidedly doubtful.

'I'm not expecting him to be doing tricks or handstands or anything like that, but this isn't looking great.'

'He's being lazy,' I say quickly. 'He's got used to me picking him up all the time.'

I let him sniff at the treat before I put it back in its place. This time, he thinks it's worth going for, and he drags himself along on his front legs and snaffles it down.

'Good boy,' I say, before turning back to the arbiter of the final judgement. 'I know it isn't much, but he is happy.'

'I'm sorry, but I think you're living in false hope. No one could have worked harder than you—'

'Before you give up on him,' I interrupt, 'I've been researching the options and I reckon he'd do very well with a set of wheels. He's the ideal candidate. Please, he's got this far . . .'

'Yeah,' he sighs. 'I've only ever had one patient on wheels – he was an older dog with all kinds of problems and it's my opinion that keeping him going just prolonged the agony for everyone.'

'Sherbet isn't in pain, though, and his health is good. I think he'd adapt very quickly.'

Ross looks down to where the dog is gazing up at us, as if he understands every word.

'Okay, but I think Emily will say I'm off my trolley if I suggest the dog has one.' He smiles. 'I'll talk to her about it.'

'Make sure you use all your charms to persuade her.'

'Of course,' he says with a cheeky grin, before growing serious. 'Can I charm you into going out for a drink after work tonight?' he goes on. His eyes are filled with warmth, taking me back to a time before the accident when he made love to me.

'No, thank you,' I say, unable to stop myself blushing.

'Are you otherwise engaged?' he asks, raising one eyebrow.

'I'm busy, I'm afraid,' I confirm, relieved when he doesn't question me further. I don't want to go out in public unless I absolutely have to, and I don't want to go backwards now that I've got this far in getting my head straight. I still dream that Ross is holding me in his arms and kissing me, and my heart still skips a beat when I hear his motorbike, but I can cope with it. I'm in remission, like Lucky appears to be. When Jennie brought him in last with a scratch on his eye, she said he seemed back to his old self, and Maz couldn't find any sign of cancer when she examined him.

Emily agrees to order a trolley for Sherbet. When it arrives, he takes one look at it and turns away in disgust. I set it up, adjusting the padding and strapping so he's comfortable; although he isn't impressed with it dragging along behind him, he's ecstatic outside, wandering along the path, sniffing and running at the kitten with a yelp of pure joy at regaining his freedom.

Job done, I think. He has every chance of leading a long and happy life.

Chapter Twenty-Two

The World's Best Vet Nurse

'There's someone to see you.' Celine looks around
the door into Kennels. I'm scooping cat food into a
bowl for Tilly, who's sitting on the prep bench,
mewing for her meal. I know, I should chase her off,
but Izzy isn't about. 'Come on in,' she calls down
the corridor, and I can hear a scuffle of claws, a faint
but repetitive squeak and a child's giggles. I'm
about to remind her of another of the practice
rules – no clients beyond the consulting room –
when Poppy appears, tripping over her dress in
her red wellies, with her mum and Sherbet, who
rushes up on his trolley to greet me with a sharp
'woof'.

'Hello.' I squat down to greet him as the kitten
hisses and arches her back. 'How's my favourite
patient?'

'He's doing wheelie well, as you can see,' Emily
jokes.

'He sounds as if he needs some WD40 to me,'
Celine says.

'What are you going to say to Shannon?' Emily gives Poppy a nudge.

She frowns, holds her finger to her mouth and rolls her eyes towards the ceiling, as if she's trying to recall a dim and distant memory. Emily bends down and whispers in her ear. She smiles but, overcome by shyness, she can only stand there with her finger in her mouth now, as her mum speaks for her.

'We've brought you a present to say thank you for all you've done for Sherbet.'

'Happy birthday,' Poppy says, suddenly finding her tongue.

'It's a thank you present, not a birthday one.' Emily smiles as she hands Poppy a small box wrapped in gold paper, which Poppy solemnly passes to me.

'Thank you very much.' Suddenly, I feel as if I want to cry. 'It's a lovely thought, but you shouldn't have . . .' I read the label – Love from Poppy and Shebert xx – written in pink felt-tip pen.

'Open it,' she says. 'It's a special—'

'Sh,' Emily cuts in. 'It's supposed to be a surprise.'

'It's a special surprise mug,' Poppy goes on, her excitement uncontained, as she helps me tear the paper and open the box to find a mug with a photo of Sherbet on his trolley and 'To the World's Best Vet Nurse' printed beneath it.

'Oh, that's amazing, the best present ever.' I bend down to give her a hug. 'Thank you very much.'

'We thought you might find it useful. When we brought him in that first time, I couldn't have dreamed we'd take him home one day. He's brilliant with the trolley, except he gets stuck in the mud at times. Murray's planning to make him a new one, a cross-country version with wider tyres, so he isn't so restricted.'

'No, Mummy.' Poppy frowns and tugs at her mother's jacket. 'That isn't right. The elves are going to make it. I asked Father Christmas.'

'So you did. I remember now. We saw Santa and his reindeer at the garden centre the other day. Are you doing anything special for Christmas, Shannon?'

'I'll be working.' I'm on call with Ross. 'I don't mind – I'll have the New Year off.' I don't let on that I prefer to be here at the practice than with Mum and Godfrey, who are planning their first Christmas together.

'We'll see you at the manor for the New Year's do.'

'Yes, maybe.' I'm not sure I'll go this year, even though I'm invited as part of the Otter House contingent. I can't feel any great enthusiasm about spending hours glamming up and putting on make-up – I'm talking about thick, scar-disguising potions – so I can face attending a large social gathering where I'll end up fending off endless questions and, worst of all, sympathy. I can still sense it – though not with Emily. She's one of the people who've been able to see past my disfigurement. No, a party at the manor is too much for me. I'd rather be on my own than trying to pretend everything is normal.

'Happy Christmas, if we don't see you before.'

'And to you.' I watch Emily take Poppy's hand and head for the door with Sherbet's trolley squeaking along behind them. 'Just a minute,' I call after them. I pick up the can of clipper oil from the prep bench and give both wheels a quick spray. 'How's that?'

Emily pats her thigh, encouraging him to take a couple of steps towards her.

'I can't hear anything,' she says.

'Neither can I.'

It's the perfect result, I think, once they've gone. Happy dog, happy clients, and one very happy vet nurse. I smile at Sherbet's photo. It's wonderful to be appreciated, which reminds me that I need to do my Christmas shopping.

I'm leaving it a bit late this year and, a couple of days after Sherbet's visit, I find myself wandering through Talyton St George – having bought most of my presents in Exeter – looking for those last-minute gifts. I buy a top that Mum saw in the window of Aurora's Cave. It's all glitter and lace, and more than likely too long, considering how it fitted the six-foot, size six mannequin, but she said she loved it when we were walking past with Seven the other day. I decide to buy a bottle of malt for Godfrey from Lacey's Fine Wines, where Mr Lacey invites me to try some samples.

As I'm getting quietly sozzled, he asks after Mum and the shop, and wishes me the compliments of the season, as he puts it. While I watch him wrap my chosen bottle in tissue paper and slip it into a gift bag, I can't help wondering if he's deliberately making his customers tipsy so they'll spend more.

I almost fall out of the shop, tripping on the step, straight into the path of Penny's speeding wheelchair, forcing her to slam on the brakes.

'I'm sorry,' I say, as the chocolate lab with his pink nose and yellow jacket jumps up at me.

'No, *I'm* sorry,' Penny says, 'I really should have a speed limiter on this thing.' She's wrapped in a purple cape with only her eyes visible. 'Are you okay?'

'I'm fine. Hello, Trevor.' I try not to encourage him, but he's impossible to ignore.

'Are you busy? Only I've got another half-hour to kill before Declan can pick me up. Do you fancy coffee and a cake at the Copper Kettle – that's if you have time and you're not dashing back to work or something? My treat.' It seems as if she's already decided for me because she rattles on, 'My lovely dog is allowed inside now he's qualified.'

'He passed then? Clever Trevor.' I notice he has a piece of red tinsel fastened around his collar.

'Just, thanks to you,' she smiles as we make our way along to the Copper Kettle. 'I don't think he'd have made the grade without the time you put in.' I hold the door open and Trevor hurries on ahead, hopeful that there'll be someone to play with. He isn't disappointed. The teashop is packed with families who have taken shelter from the winter drizzle to wait for Father Christmas to make his annual parade along the high street. There appears to be a crisis, though, because rumour has it that one of the reindeer that Fifi from the garden centre has hired for the occasion is sick and having treatment from one of the Talyton Manor vets – and someone is trying to source a pair of horses or a tractor to pull Santa's wheeled sleigh instead.

Trevor greets everyone as if they're his long-lost friends, even those he hasn't met before. Most of the children adore him, but Cheryl isn't so keen. I can sense her bristling from behind the counter and hear the shake of disapproval from the metal cats that dangle from her earlobes. I take hold of his collar and drag him to a table near the door. I sit down opposite Penny, who removes her cape, revealing the colourful beads and some tinsel in her hair.

We order scones, jam and clotted cream, with a pot of tea.

'That dog is safe?' Cheryl asks when she brings our cream tea across. She gazes at my face as she lays cups and saucers from the tray across the blue and yellow gingham tablecloth, but doesn't say anything. It's as if she's noticed a piece of spinach between my teeth and she doesn't want to embarrass either of us by mentioning it. Sometimes, I feel like I am the scar. 'I don't want any of my customers getting bitten.'

'He wouldn't hurt a fly,' Penny says, hurt on her dog's behalf. He rests his head on her lap and gazes up with a mournful expression in his eyes.

'It's my experience that dog owners are blind to their pets' faults,' Cheryl counters.

'I'm the first to admit that Trevor has his issues,' Penny says sternly, 'but I can assure you that eating people isn't one of them. Now, can we enjoy our tea, or would you like us to leave?'

'I apologise.' Cheryl backs away. 'I didn't mean to offend you. I'm a cat person, not a dog lover.'

'And a very catty one at that,' Penny whispers when she's out of earshot.

Smiling, I pick up the teapot. 'Would you like me to pour? Is it the tea or the milk first?'

'Declan says it's the tea. Apparently, if you put the milk in first, you get some chemical reaction that spoils the taste. Or it might be the other way round.' She chuckles. 'He's such a geek when it comes to trivia.'

I pour the tea first and stir in the milk.

'I know that you put the cream on the scone first followed by the jam,' Penny says. 'I made that mistake when I had my first Devonshire cream tea. It was at a B&B on the way to Talymouth – the owner was really quite affronted.'

'How's work?' I take a bite of my scone and the cream and jam oozes into my mouth. I really should go back to the pool to swim away a few calories.

'Not bad. I've sold a good number of Christmas cards so far this year, and taken a couple of commissions.' Penny leans towards me. 'I'm thinking of opening a gallery here in town – I'm just waiting for the right premises to come up. I was planning to create a countryside retreat for aspiring artists, but I can't see how I can make it work financially. Too many people think that art should be for free.'

'That sounds interesting. My mother's boyfriend . . . no, old-man-friend, is an estate agent. I'm sure he'd help you out. Let me know if you want me to introduce you.'

'That would be great. I'll catch up with you in the New Year.'

'I expect he'll be at the party at Talyton Manor.'

'I'm not sure we'll be there. Declan and I will probably have a romantic night in with a bottle of wine and a DVD – and Trevor, I imagine. He'll be curled up on the sofa with us, no doubt.'

I smile ruefully. I envy them.

'Anyway, that's enough about me. How are you?' she asks.

'Better than I was, thank you.' There's a pause while I wonder how much to open up to her, and then I plunge on. 'I've been debating having more surgery, but I'm worried that I'll just be covering one scar up with another. I don't know what to do. I don't know how far to go. I mean, it will never be perfect, but right now –' I touch my face – 'I feel hideous. I hate myself.'

'I wish you didn't feel like that. You are a beautiful young woman.'

'I feel ugly, and then I'm angry with myself because so many people are far worse off than I am.' I stop abruptly, realising that I class Penny as one of them. 'I'm sorry.'

'It doesn't matter. I can't tell you how you should feel, but I do have some understanding of where you're at. If this is making you feel uncomfortable and you don't want to talk about it, just say, but sometimes it helps.' I nod as she continues. 'I don't know how much you've heard of my story.'

'Only that you were in a car accident.'

'We were living in London. Mark, my husband, was driving us home through Clapham and we came off the road, smashed straight into some railings. He died in hospital that night. He was a designer, making a name for himself in fashion. In spite of all our silly rows, we were deeply in love and our lives were really going somewhere. It all ended.' She snaps her fingers. 'Just like that. With one glass of wine too many and a moment's lack of attention.

'Sometimes I wonder what we'd be doing now. Maybe I'd be a mum.' She gazes towards some of the children, who have their noses pressed to the window, making sticky prints on the glass.

I catch a strawberry pip between my teeth. Penny's talk of her accident reminds me of Ross telling me about his friend on the day we went to the beach. It reminds me, most of all, of my dad, and how one morning he was there and the next, he'd gone.

'In that split second, I lost everything: the love of

my life; my mobility, dignity, freedom, and any chance of having children.'

'That's terrible.' I'm not sure what to say. Penny must have been devastated. 'I'm very sorry.'

'I spent months fighting the physical challenges and depression, and gradually, with a lot of support, I started to find my way out. I made a fresh start, moved here and devoted myself to my art. When I look at my paintings from that time, they're very dark. I suppose it was my way of expressing my grief. I painted my way through it. I started to make a living, my sister persuaded me to take on a dog for company, and then I met the beautiful man who's become my soul mate for this part of life's journey.'

I nod approvingly, although I'm not sure I'd describe the rather drippy and gangly Declan as beautiful.

'For whatever reason, I was given a second chance at love and living, and I've grasped it with both hands. It's okay. It's normal to mourn what might have been, but eventually you have to pick yourself up and move on.'

'But it's so hard,' I say quietly, playing with the crumbs on my plate.

'I'm not saying it's easy.'

'I think you're amazing. You always seem so happy, except for when you were having problems with Trevor.'

'Ah, you don't see what I put Declan through. I'm a bitch.'

'I can't imagine that.'

'There are times when the pain gets to me. I suffer from nerve pain. I used to embrace the shooting pains down my spine and legs as a sign that I was getting better, that one day I'd regain sensation in my toes and some strength in my muscles, enough maybe to walk again, but they're just one of nature's cruel tricks. It makes me angry and hard to get along with. In fact, I can be vile. I don't mean to be. I know how much I hurt him, but I can't help taking it out on him.' She shrugs. 'He's kind and caring and I don't deserve him. I'm the luckiest person in the world.' She pauses, looking at me with a twinkle in her eye. 'You're lucky too. You have people who love you: your mum, friends at Otter House, Ross . . . Everyone knows you're fond of each other. I've told you before – you only have to see the way he looks at you.'

That was before, I think, back when my life was relatively normal. I love Ross more than ever, but I don't see how he can feel the same way about me. He's a loyal friend. I only have to look at how he's been there for me even when I haven't necessarily wanted him around. I've been pretty hard on him at times, yet he's always come back.

The Christmas lights switch on outside, and a light comes on in my brain. The way Ross looks at me . . . A small shiver runs down my spine as I recall the heat of his gaze, the lightness of his touch as he held my hand, and his constant reassurance that everything would be all right. Is it possible that he does find me attractive in spite of the scars?

Penny giggles. 'Your face is going the colour of Rudolph's nose. Seriously, don't push him away – if you feel the same way about him, that is.

'Without the accident, I wouldn't be who I am,' Penny goes on. 'I like myself so much better – as I say I can still be pretty difficult when the pain gets bad, but before I was selfish and overwrought, a real drama queen. If you hide your scars, emotional or physical, you're denying who you really are. I expect you've heard it all before. I can't believe how many people have given me "the talk". Tell me to shut up, if you like.'

'It's all right. It helps talking to someone who's been through a tough time, and you've been through much worse than me. It's only my face, after all.'

'And your self-esteem. It isn't a matter of degree. It's a life-changing event that came out of nowhere. Promise me you'll be kind to yourself.'

'I'll try,' I say, as a scramble for the window interrupts the conversation. I find myself being jostled by several small children – and a couple of grown-up ones – trying to find space to look out onto the street, where a pony with feathery feet and a set of flashing antlers is pulling a cart through a crowd of people dressed in coats, hats and scarves. There are squeals and cheers of, 'It's Father Christmas!' and clapping. In the melee, Trevor snatches a bite of sponge cake from one of the kids, who turns to see where it's gone. Too late, I think, as the dog swallows without chewing, the evidence of his crime on its way to his stomach within the blink of an eye.

'Cake,' exclaims the boy, who can't be more than two years old. 'Gone!' He searches the floor between everyone's feet, but to no avail, and bursts into tears. A woman – his mother, I presume – sweeps him into her arms, wipes his cheek and points at another woman dressed in a red hat, green tabard and jeans, who's doling out sweets from a bucket.

'Look, there's one of Santa's elves. Let's go and say hi.'

'That's no elf,' I say in an aside to Penny. 'That's

my friend, Taylor. I can't believe that this is part of her management course.'

'It's probably elf-and-safety training,' Penny giggles again. 'I'm sorry – that was a terrible joke.'

I wave as Taylor is swept up by the crowd and carried along the street behind a roly-poly Father Christmas and the pony and cart sponsored by the Greens' garden centre. The excitement is too much for Trevor, who starts barking uncontrollably at the window.

'I think it's time to go,' Penny says, nudging at my arm. 'I'll settle up.'

'I'll take him outside,' I say, aware that Cheryl is glaring in our direction. 'Come on, boy.' Still barking, he tows me to the door. He doesn't stop for a good five minutes, by which time the crowds have moved on past Otter House and Penny has rejoined us on the pavement, with Cheryl standing in the doorway behind her.

'I'll thank you not to bring that dog in here again. He's a troublemaker,' she says, closing the door on us.

'So much for the season of peace and goodwill,' Penny sighs as a car draws up. 'Here's Declan. Thank you for your company, Shannon. We should do this again, but at an alternative venue. The garden centre does very good cakes and they give Trevor his own cup of tea there. Happy Christmas.'

'And to you too.'

'I hope you aren't too busy.'

I find myself hoping that we are so I have a reason to spend Christmas with Ross. I'm not up to asking him outright how he feels about me now – I'm too scared of rejection – but I think it would be good to spend some time together so I can find out.

Chapter Twenty-Three

Christmas on Call

Otter House closes for routine appointments for two days over the festive period, and I have some time off on Christmas Eve before I go back on call from six in the evening. In the meantime, I help Mum with the last-minute customers buying bouquets, poinsettia and sprigs of holly. In the quiet spells, she makes a table-top decoration.

'Will you be home for Christmas dinner?' She places a silver candle into the hole that she's drilled into a small log. 'Godfrey's cooking. He's bought some vegetarian roast to put in the oven.'

'That's very kind of him, but I might be at work. Who knows?'

She smiles as she picks out some holly clustered with scarlet berries. 'You're welcome to invite Ross.'

'I thought you hated him after what happened.' I trace the outline of my scar.

'I misjudged him. I was devastated when I saw what his dog did to you, and I blamed him because, being a vet, he should have known better, but he did try to do the right thing by coming to see you. He's been very persistent, especially when none of us have exactly made him feel welcome.'

'I didn't want him hanging around feeling sorry for me. I couldn't entertain the idea that he might insist on standing by me out of guilt. He's a lovely man who could have any woman he wants. I don't think he should waste his time on me.'

'Going back to work really helped you get over the depression. I know you haven't come to terms with how you look, but you're getting out and about more and things are very different now,' Mum says. 'For me, Ross went from zero to hero when he saved Seven's life, and I'll never forget that, but I'm not going to interfere in whatever is or isn't going on between you two. I don't like the idea of anyone spending Christmas alone, that's all.'

'Thank you.' I hand her the scissors to cut the holly. 'I will ask him.'

'We're eating at midday so we can visit Godfrey's sister and family in the afternoon.' She snips at a stem and attaches it to the log with a piece of wire. 'It's been quite a year, hasn't it? I'm the luckiest woman in the world. I just wish you'd found someone special too.'

I leave her to spray the arrangement with silver glitter when the bell jangles from the front of the shop, announcing the arrival of another customer. It's Aurora, Saba's owner. She walks inside in her black mac, short skirt and long boots, shaking rain from her umbrella and holding a tiny dog dressed in a pink coat under her arm. Seven barks from the kitchen – I've left him shut in because he's been trying to get into everyone's shopping bags and trolleys, tempted by the smell of the turkeys, chipolatas and hams from the butcher's shop.

'Hi,' she says, her gaze settling briefly on my scar. 'I didn't know you were working here now.'

'I'm helping out. I'm still at Otter House, but I have the day off because I'm on duty tonight and tomorrow. I didn't realise you had a new dog.'

'My partner thought it would be a good idea to have another to keep Saba company in her old age. He went out and found this little cutie.' She holds the dog – a cream chihuahua with big brown eyes – up to her face and it licks her on the lips.

'What's her name?'

'Diva. She came from a breeder who was giving up dogs, and she isn't a puppy so I don't have to go through the difficult stage. It's great – I've had her six weeks now and she's been no trouble at all, apart from being a little restless for the past couple of days. I must bring her to see one of the vets in the New Year – she needs her jabs.'

'She is sweet,' I say as Aurora lets me stroke her. She has the softest fur and reeks of Chanel. 'Have you come in for anything in particular?'

'I'm looking for a present for my mother-in-law, preferably a plant that's either prickly or poisonous, or both – I'm hoping she'll appreciate the symbolism.' She smiles. 'What do you think?'

Mum joins us, her sweatshirt spangling with silver glitter.

'Let me show you the planted baskets we have in stock, or I can make you up a suitable bouquet.' She turns to me. 'Shannon, would you mind putting the kettle on? I'm gasping.'

'Happy Christmas, Aurora,' I say. 'See you soon.'

'Not too soon, I hope,' she says, tucking the dog inside her mac.

I spend the rest of the morning in Petals, take Seven for a long walk by the river under dark rolling clouds in the afternoon, and settle down for the evening to watch television with Mum and Godfrey. At ten, having heard nothing from Ross and deciding that no news is good news, I make up my mind to go to bed.

'Aren't you going to leave a carrot out for the reindeer?' Mum asks as I wish her and Godfrey goodnight.

'Are you hinting that you'd like a sherry and mince pie?' I tease. 'It was funny how Father Christmas finished those when I left them in the fireplace, but the reindeer never touched the carrot.'

'I'll get up.' Godfrey stands up stiffly from the sofa. 'Would you like anything, Shannon?'

'I'd better not, thanks.' I retire to my room with Seven, who jumps onto the bed and curls up on my feet. I must have fallen asleep because the sound of my mobile gives me a jolt when it rings. I note the time as I answer. It's after midnight.

'Hi, have I woken you?'

'Ross?' I murmur. 'What's up?'

'I am, obviously.' He chuckles, but it's far too early in the morning for me to find anything funny. 'Happy Christmas! We have our first emergency of the festive season, and it has nothing to do with Santa.'

'What is it?'

'A Caesar.'

I jump out of bed and grab some clothes from the wardrobe. 'I'll be right over.'

Ross lets me in to the practice and follows me

through the back to Kennels. A familiar face looks out from one of the cages.

'Is that Aurora's new dog?'

'That's right. She's been unsettled all day; there's one big pup in there and it's stuck. I've got a kit ready. We need to be quick.'

We anaesthetise her and, while I'm doing a quick clip and prep, Ross scrubs up and puts on a gown, mask and gloves.

'Her other dog had to have a Caesarean,' I point out as I fasten the ties on his gown. 'It's becoming a habit.'

'She must have been got at by the stud dog at the breeders she came from. It's a pity they didn't warn her of the possibility she might be pregnant.'

I carry Diva through to theatre. Ross arranges the drapes for surgery and, within minutes, he drops a single puppy onto a towel in my hands. I clear the membranes from its face, check its heartbeat and rub it with the towel to stimulate its breathing.

'How is it?' he asks, checking to make sure there are no more puppies before sewing up.

'It's looking good.' Even though it's a big puppy relative to Diva's size, it's actually the smallest I've ever had to deal with.

'Boy or girl?' He chuckles again. 'I'm asking because you need the practice.'

'Ha ha,' I say dryly. 'How can you be so cheerful in the middle of the night?'

'You'd complain even more if I was grumpy,' he says, looking a little hurt.

'It's a boy.' I check the remnant of the umbilical cord and pop him into the bottom of a white wire basket on a heated pad and soft bedding to keep him warm.

When Ross has completed the surgery, I let Diva come round, by which time the puppy is crying for his mum.

'I'll call Aurora while you see if you can get him to feed.' Ross washes and dries his hands.

When Diva's awake, I introduce the puppy to her, letting her sniff and lick him before showing him where the milk bar is. He snuffles about for a moment before he latches on and sucks.

Ross returns and starts on the washing up, tipping the instruments into the sink.

'Don't say a word. The sooner we both get to bed the better.'

I frown at his turn of phrase.

'I mean, the sooner we get to bed separately,' he adds, blushing. 'Aurora is coming to pick mum and baby up in ten minutes. She's delighted – just as much about having an excuse not to go to her mother-in-law's as she is about the puppy.' He tries to unfasten the ties on his gown. 'What have you done?'

'Hang on.' I apologise. 'The knot's too tight. I'm going to have to cut you out.' I grab a pair of scissors from the draining board and snip through the ties. He strips off the gown and glances down at his scrub top, which is wet with surgical scrub. He pulls it off over his head right in front of me, revealing the V of dark curly hair across his chest. I bite my lip as he turns back to the sink, wets some paper towel and wipes the seepage from his skin.

'That's better,' he says, looking back at me with a glint in his eye. I know what it means, that Penny was right, and he still wants me. I don't know what to say. I've lost all power of speech and my face is burning. The autoclave completes a cycle, releasing a cloud of steam. The buzzer sounds from reception.

'That'll be the proud grandmother,' Ross says brightly, and he disappears to fetch himself a clean top while I show Aurora through to Kennels. Ross gives her instructions on how to look after the unexpected arrival and sends her on her way before offering to walk me home.

'There's no need.'

'I want to. I mean, I'll be happier knowing you're back safe.'

It's my turn to laugh. 'This is Talyton St George you're talking about.'

'I'll come back for the bike.' He throws on his leather jacket and changes into jeans and boots before walking me along the road. The streetlamps and Christmas lights are off and veils of cloud obscure the moon; all you can hear is the rain pattering on the pavement and dripping from the gutters. I glance towards him as we walk side by side in mutual silence. I can just make out his features in the shadowy darkness, but I can't tell what he's thinking.

'Is everything all right?' I ask. 'Are you missing your family?'

'It's the first Christmas when I haven't made plans to be with them, but no, I'm not going to mope about that. I've sent cards and phoned my mother – we had a good chat.'

'And your father?'

'I've spoken to him too. I've promised to keep in touch, and I'm going to make sure I remember never to treat my son in the same way as my dad did me.' He clears his throat. 'I'm not going back. My life is here now.' He pauses and swears lightly. 'That's the phone.' He fishes about in one of the many zipped pockets in his jacket, pulls out his mobile and holds it up to his ear. 'Otter House vets, Ross speaking . . .'

I wait on the doorstep outside the shop for him to finish the call.

'Why aren't people in bed at this time of night?'

'They're up because their kids can't sleep because they're waiting for Father Christmas,' I suggest.

'There's a cat on its way – apparently it's chosen tonight to start on the tinsel diet.' I can hear the humour in his voice when he goes on, 'I'll walk you back to Otter House if you like.'

Five minutes after our return, the client – Mrs Milton, a well-dressed woman in her sixties – shows up with a Siamese cat on a harness and lead. The driver of the car that brings her remains outside.

'Thank you for seeing us so quickly. We're staying with family in Talymouth and they recommended your practice. This is Ronnie. He's registered with a vet where we live, but it's too far to drive home tonight.'

Ross shows her into the consulting room.

'He's two, but he behaves like a kitten,' she continues. 'He was playing with the tinsel on the tree and it's got caught around his teeth.'

Ronnie, a seal-point with a cream body and brown ear-tips, paws and tail, perches on the edge of the table, a piece of gold tinsel hanging out of his mouth and scratches across his face where he's tried to remove it.

'Let's have a look.' Ross gently prises his mouth open. He has one attempt to untangle the tinsel, but the cat becomes distressed and starts panting and trying to get away, digging his claws into his arm.

'We'll have to admit him to be sedated,' he decides. 'When did he last have anything to eat – apart from tinsel, that is?'

'He had his usual cat food at six,' Mrs Milton says.

Ross is happy with that, so we take him in and send her home to wait until he's ready to be collected.

'It's beginning to look a lot like Christmas,' Ross sings as we wait for the sedation to take effect. 'What do you think? Is he ready?'

· I check Ronnie's reflexes and jaw tone. 'Go for it, otherwise we'll be here till next Christmas.'

'Very funny.' He opens the cat's mouth and starts to disentangle the string of tinsel from around his teeth, using forceps and scissors to snip it into sections.

'Has he swallowed any of it?' I ask, knowing that if he has this could be the beginning rather than the end of it, so to speak.

'This bit is going down the back of his throat.' Ross shows me. 'I'm going to pull on it very gently to see if it will come out on its own. If there's any resistance, we'll do a quick X-ray and go in.' It's a relief when the end of the tinsel appears, but Ronnie can't go home. 'We'll keep him in for observation for a couple of days.'

I know what that means: that I'll be checking his litter tray for tinsel.

We stay up for a while, watching Ronnie and drinking tea. At about three thirty in the morning, Ross starts to yawn, so I offer to take the phone while he gets some sleep.

'What about you?'

'I'm all right at the moment.'

'I think I'll stay here. There doesn't seem much point in going back to Talyford.'

'You can have the sofa. I'll go home for a while.'

I have a strange sense of déjà vu when he walks me back to Petals for a second time. The temperature has plummeted and our breath forms clouds in the light of the moon as we step outside the practice. Ross locks the door before moving up beside me and stamping his feet.

'That's cold enough to freeze a polar bear's you-know-what,' he says, grimacing, 'and the kind of night when you'd have to jump-start a reindeer.' He offers me his arm. I take it and we make our way along the icy street.

'I'm not sure who is holding up whom,' Ross laughs as we slip and slide into each other, bumping hips. He makes a show of catching me by the shoulders, using it as an excuse, I think, to get closer, wrapping his arm around my back and giving me a squeeze. The contact makes me shiver. I can smell his scent of musk and surgical scrub, and sense the warmth of his body through his leather jacket, a mix of sensations that reminds me of the taste of his kisses and the passionate embraces that we shared. The memories burn like fire inside my head and my heart.

'Shannon? Are you okay?'

'Yes,' I say, wishing that it was much further to walk home so I could enjoy his touch for longer and find a way to broach the subject of where we are going – as long as I've got it right and we do have some kind of future together. I fumble for the key in my pocket when we reach Petals, and unlock the door. Seven comes running through to greet us, wagging his tail. Ross gives him a pat.

'I'll see you later,' he says, turning back to me. 'Sleep well,' he adds.

I won't sleep for thinking about him, I muse as I close the door behind him, and I head for the kitchen for a glass of water before going to my room. Mum has left a pillowcase filled with oranges, apples and nuts, and a present on the end of my bed, as she always does every Christmas. The chocolates are on the mantelpiece so Seven can't get at them. There's a gift from Godfrey too and, even though I'm twenty-six, not six, I can feel the thrill of anticipation and excitement as I try to guess what's inside the wrapping paper crackling beneath my fingers. Seven sits on the bed with me, nudging at the presents with his nose.

'It's been quite a year,' I tell him. 'We've been through some hard times, but we've both come out the other side in one piece and the people we love have stood by us.' I feel quite choked. I have almost everything I could wish for – there's only one thing that's missing, and even that seems tantalisingly close.

I can't sleep and I can only have had half an hour or so of dreaming of Ross before the phone rings again.

'Hi, who's there?' The voice sounds familiar.

'It's Shannon. How can I help?'

'I bet you thought it was Father Christmas.' A man laughs and the phone crackles.

'I'm sorry,' says a female voice. 'Declan's had a few drinks.'

'Hello, Penny,' I say. 'What's happened to Trevor this time?'

'I'm not sure. I'm sorry for disturbing you at this

time of night, but he's lying around and being sick, and I'm desperately worried about him.'

It transpires that he hasn't been himself for a couple of days, but only took a turn for the worse during the past few hours.

'Can you bring him to the surgery or shall I come and pick him up?' I ask, although I know what the answer will be. Declan isn't in any fit state to drive. I walk back to Otter House to fetch the ambulance and wake Ross, who is asleep on the sofa with a blanket around him, his tousled curls spread over a cushion. I struggle to resist the urge to stroke his hair and check his vital signs.

'Time to wake up,' I whisper, but he's pretty well comatose. I reach out and squeeze his shoulder.

'Where's the fire?' he says, sitting up, eyes wide open.

'There is no fire.' I can't help smiling. 'We've been called out to visit Trevor.'

He stretches his arms above his head. 'You needn't have bothered to go home. You could have stayed curled up with me. Another time, maybe.'

'In your dreams,' I say lightly, although my heart is banging lightly at the thought of lying in his arms.

'You are always in my dreams,' he says, getting up. 'Let's go.'

We bring Trevor back to Otter House for observation and a drip, by which time it isn't worth going back to bed.

'We'll X-ray him after we've seen the two non-urgent cases at ten,' Ross says, bringing coffee and croissants. 'There's Nero, whose ear's flared up, and a cat with a sore tail. If we need to operate on Trevor, we'll do that before we have Christmas dinner.'

'I forgot to say that Mum and Godfrey have invited you to ours for lunch, if we're not busy and if you'd like to come along.'

'I was hoping to treat you to dinner and crackers. Maz and Alex asked me to theirs as well, but I turned them down. I thought it would be fun if it was just the two of us, like old times.'

I recall the long hot afternoons we spent on the patio at the house in Talyford, chatting and laughing over a salad and a glass of wine. There weren't many of them as it turned out, but they were precious to me. I savoured the time we had together. The prospect of celebrating Christmas alone with him is very tempting, and I don't suppose Mum will mind when she and Godfrey are still all over each other like a rash.

'I'll let them know I'm staying here with you.'

As it turns out, we would have missed lunch anyway, because Trevor needs an operation. Once he's under anaesthetic, I monitor his blood pressure, applying the cuff to his leg, inflating it and deflating it to get the required readings. I repeat it several times because it's much lower than I'm expecting – so low, in fact, that he should be dead.

'Would you mind checking this for me?'

Ross fiddles around with the cuff and machine.

'The cuff's all right, but when it's inflated, I can still hear a pulse.' He frowns.

'You haven't got the probe on your finger, have you?'

'Oh yes, that's my pulse. I'm sorry.' He casts me a meaningful glance as he readjusts the set-up. 'I'm tired. I haven't been sleeping.'

'You've been busy,' I say, trying to divert the conversation.

'I don't mean that,' he says quietly. 'That isn't why I haven't been sleeping.'

I take up the stethoscope and stuff it into my ears so I can block out any further personal discussion. Trevor is our priority, although we do need to talk.

I watch Ross operating and it feels like his hand has dived into my belly, grabbed me by the guts and twisted them up. I used to find him unbearably impatient, but he's shown that he can be gentle and steady – he tried so hard to stand by me after the accident and he persisted in coming to see me and trying to get me out and about. How many times did I reject him before he finally gave up? And even then I don't think he could have completely given up on me. Look how kind and supportive and . . . I want to say 'loving' . . . he's been to me over the past weeks since my return to work when he really didn't have to. I'm surprised he could bring himself to speak to me after how I behaved.

'I've found something,' he says, unable to disguise the triumph in his voice. He cuts into a section of the dog's intestines and pulls out a wodge of material, which he drops into the kidney dish on the instrument tray. 'What is it?'

I pick the stinking, brownish-green item up and rinse it under the tap.

'It's a sports sock,' I say, grimacing. 'Just what I've always wanted. Lovely.'

'Declan will be pleased,' Ross teases.

It's mid-afternoon by the time we've finished operating on not-so-clever Trevor. Ross has spoken to Penny, who says that he must have accidentally swallowed it while practising putting the washing in the machine. I wonder if he's going to get the sack as her assistance dog.

'That's it for now,' Ross says, leaving him to recover in a kennel. 'Let's have Christmas dinner – I thought we'd eat in the staff room.'

'Are you sure? I expect Mum has some leftovers we can warm up.'

'It's all here in the fridge,' he says. 'Come on, I'll do the clearing up in theatre afterwards.'

'You?' I say in mocking tone. 'What do you know about cleaning?' I give him a flirtatious smile as we move along the corridor to the staff room. 'Actually, that's an offer I can't refuse – but I'd rather we did it together.'

Ross holds the door open for me.

'Take a seat,' he says.

'I'd prefer to be doing something.'

'Just do as you're told for once and sit down.' He grins as he steps past me and pulls a bag off one of the shelves and places it on the worktop near the sink. I perch on the middle of the sofa, with Tilly lying curled up at one end and Tripod at the other.

'First things first,' Ross says, and he hands me the ends of two crackers. 'Pull!'

The crackers snap, sending the kitten flying off the sofa and skedaddling across the carpet to hide in the corner.

'Oh, poor little thing,' I say, jumping up to grab her and give her a quick cuddle before helping Ross find the contents of the crackers, which have disappeared under the sofa. Tripod continues to snooze.

'Do you want a crown?' he asks.

'Why not?' I say, laughing, 'but only if you wear one too.'

He slips one onto his head, but it tears as he tries to force it over his curls. As for mine, it falls over my eyes.

'Let's forget those,' he says. 'Would you like a fortune-telling fish or a whoopee cushion?'

'Neither, thanks. I don't want to scare the cat again, and I'd rather rely on Mrs Wall for some inkling of the future.'

'I've always been of the opinion that you don't wait to see what the future brings. You have to build it for yourself.' Ross turns away. 'Are you ready for dinner? I'm starving.' He takes two plates from the fridge and puts one in the microwave. 'Two roast dinners, one turkey, one unidentifiable object – I think it's supposed to be a vegetarian cutlet.' He warms the second one.

'Where did you get these from?' I ask, as Tilly takes a flying leap from the back of the sofa, aiming for Ross's plate, but ending up on the floor, having left paw-prints in his gravy.

'She thinks I should have bought one for her.' He pushes Tilly away as she makes a second and last assault on his meal. 'I picked them up from the Talymill Inn yesterday. A special order. What do you think?'

'It's great. Perfect for the busy vet and nurse on call.' I can't believe how sweet and thoughtful he's being, making sure we have the perfect Christmas on call.

'There's pudding too, but I forgot the brandy.' Ross shrugs. 'It's probably a good thing – setting fire to it might have set off the fire alarm.' He changes the subject. 'Have you got any plans?'

My forehead tightens. 'For this afternoon?'

'And for later, tomorrow, next year . . .?'

'Well, we still need to do theatre and check on Trevor . . .'

'We could drop into the new surgery tomorrow, that's if you're at a loose end and we aren't too busy. Maz asked me if I could run some of the boxes in the office over there. There's stationery and a delivery of syringes and needles. I thought you might like to put things away exactly where you want them. The more we can get done before we open, the better. I can't wait to have a place of our own. It will feel like it's ours.'

'I can hardly wait. I'll be able to do things my way, not Izzy's.'

'That's good to hear. When the idea of me taking on the running of the branch surgery first came up, I was afraid Maz and Emma were going to suggest Izzy joined me. She's a great nurse, but we don't work well together.'

I'm touched when he continues, 'I'd much rather spend time with you.'

Blushing, I get up to take the plates and put them to soak in the sink.

'Would you like dessert?' he asks.

'No thanks, I've had enough.' When I turn back, he's pulling a flat rectangular box wrapped in tissue paper from his jacket, which he's left over the arm of the sofa.

'I have something for you, a present. Go on,' he adds, as I hesitate.

'I haven't bought you anything . . .' I wish I had now.

'I didn't expect you to.'

Reluctantly, I take it from his trembling fingers and

open it. Inside is a necklace, a silver hare on a chain.

'It's the closest I could get to a rabbit,' he says softly.

'It's beautiful, thank you, but . . .' My voice falters. 'I can't accept it.'

'Why not?'

'Because.' I look up at him, at the lock of dark curls that falls across his cheek. I want to push it back and run my hands through his hair. I want to throw my arms around his neck and cover him with kisses. I want him to make love to me all day and all night for the rest of my life. 'It's complicated.'

'It was, but not any more. It's time we were honest with each other.' I read the pain in his expression, and the thought that I'm hurting him by rejecting his gift cuts through me like a knife. 'Shannon, we need to talk. Sit down.'

We settle down side by side. I can feel my pulse racing as he begins.

'I need to make it clear where I stand,' he says. 'I've tried so hard to prove to you how much I love you. I've done my best to be there for you, even when you made it clear you didn't want me around, and I don't know what else I can humanly do or say to convince you of the depth of my feelings. I've known for a long time that you are the woman for me. When I fall asleep, when I wake, the first thing in my mind is you.'

'Oh Ross,' I exclaim.

'Sh, let me finish. Perhaps I will never be able to convince you because you don't feel the same way about me. If that's how it is, I'd prefer it if you put me out of my misery. Well, I wouldn't. I'll be gutted and miserable for months, years . . .' His voice cracks with emotion. 'I know I'll survive. I'll be all right eventually, but there'll always be a small part of my heart that belongs to you. I will always love you.'

'Stop! Please.' I can't bear to see him like this. 'I haven't said that I don't want you.'

'Haven't you?' he says, his eyes wide with wonder.

'I've been really stupid. I didn't want you to feel you had to be kind to me out of guilt.'

'I'll always feel guilty about what Bart did to you. I don't think you understand how difficult it's been to see you, knowing that I'd allowed it to happen, but I had to because I couldn't bear to let you go without a fight. Think about it. If I didn't have feelings for you, I could have walked away and found someone else, but I haven't.'

'I know, and I'm grateful. You're a great guy and I'm very . . . fond of you.'

'That sounds like you're fobbing me off,' he says.

I stare straight at him. 'I'm giving you one last chance to escape. You could have any woman in the world.'

'I think that's a bit of an exaggeration,' he cuts in with a small smile.

'Why would you want me and my scars when you could go out with someone like Heidi who's flawless,' I go on, stubbornly. 'I don't want you choosing me because you're afraid no one else will look at me now, and you want to make up for what happened.'

'That's ridiculous, and quite hurtful. I haven't seen Heidi since she came to say goodbye to Bart. You were right. It wasn't healthy, keeping in contact. It gave her false hope. I was never interested. I wasn't interested in anyone else after I met you.'

'I don't understand why not – she's bubbly, attractive and very bright.'

'But she has a side to her. She's manipulative and good at putting on a show. You're worth ten of her.' He hesitates. 'I can't go on like this. If you really don't want me around, if you can't bear the sight of me, then tell me and I'll make plans to move on.'

'You mean it?' I say, shocked.

He nods. 'I couldn't stay here. Even after a few short months, there are too many memories. When I'm in the house, I hear your voice and see you all the time.' He holds my gaze, his dark eyes filled with desire and gentle recrimination. 'You have no idea how much I love you. If you could love me just half as much, I'd be a very happy man.' He takes the box from my hands and removes the necklace. 'What's it to be, Shannon?

'I want you to stay,' I say, biting back tears. 'I'm sorry if I haven't shown it – I do love you very much.'

'That's all I wanted to hear,' he says softly. He holds the ends of the necklace between his fingers. 'When I look at you, I don't see the scar. I see you, this amazing and beautiful woman . . .'

I let him place the chain around my neck. He fumbles as he fastens it, his fingers brushing my skin. I touch the silver hare.

'Thank you,' I say. 'I'm sorry for wavering, for blowing hot and cold and for pushing you away. I wish I'd been stronger.'

'You are one of the strongest people I've ever met.' His hand cups my chin as he moves in and brushes his lips across my scar. 'I adore you, Shannon. I want us to be a couple, if you'll have me. Will you have me?'

'Yes,' I whisper. I can hear a heartbeat in my ears – mine or his, I'm not sure. I can smell his scent of fresh sweat and surgical scrub. His gaze locks onto mine and he leans closer, until I feel the heat of his breath on my mouth and we're kissing and my head is swimming and all I can do is give in, reaching awkwardly with one hand to grab at his top and pull him closer . . . and his mobile rings from his jacket pocket.

With a groan of frustration, he grabs it and answers. It's Jennie to say that Lucky has torn one of his claws, chasing rabbits. It's bleeding, so he advises her to bring him straight over. He cuts the call and runs his hand down my back, resting it on the curve of my waist.

'We'll carry on from where we left off later on,' he murmurs.

'From here?' I say, kissing him full on the lips. 'Or here?' I kiss him again, deepening the contact as he wraps his arms around me and pulls me close.

'Or here?' he says, and we don't stop until the sound of a car rolling up outside interrupts us. Having checked on Trevor and Ronnie, and picked up a few bits and pieces that we might need for Lucky, I catch up with Ross in the consulting room. I can't stop smiling.

Thank you, Father Christmas, I think to myself. I must have been a very good girl this year.

Later the same day, I pop back to Petals to collect some clothes and personal items. I'm in the shop saying a quick goodbye to Seven, having given him a biscuit from his Christmas stocking, when Mum and Godfrey return from visiting his relatives. I wish them a happy Christmas and give Mum a hug before picking up my bag.

'I'm sorry we missed lunch,' I say. 'We were busy.'

'Are you off somewhere now?' Mum asks.

416

'Yes, actually, I'm going to Talyford with Ross.'

'Oh? That's a bit of a surprise.'

'Hardly,' Godfrey says. 'I don't suppose you'll be back tonight?'

'Um, I'll probably stay over – we're on call.'

'That'll be it then,' he says with a touch of sarcasm. 'He's a good man, Shannon. He's stuck by you even when you didn't want him around.'

Mum grins as if she's just worked out what's going on.

'You can drop by with the rent for the past few months any time,' she says, and when I frown, she laughs. 'I'm joking. You've been very welcome and I haven't paid you for any of the work you've done in the shop while you've been back, so I reckon we're evens.'

'Thanks, both of you,' I say, as a horn sounds outside. 'That'll be Ross. I'd better go. I'll see you soon.'

'There's no hurry,' Godfrey chuckles. 'We know what you'll be doing, don't we, my love?' He pinches my mother's bottom, making her giggle. I turn and flee, joining Ross in the ambulance. He leans across and kisses me.

'Let's pray that that phone doesn't ring. I'm taking you home.' He grins under the light of the streetlamp that shines in through the windscreen. 'I don't know about you, but I'm ready for dessert.'

Chapter Twenty-Four

Paws through the Door

We don't waste any more time. We are almost inseparable. On the last day of December, on a cold and sunny afternoon, I help Ross start packing in readiness for him to move out of the house in Talyford. Although we originally had a year lease, the owner is returning earlier than expected from their foray abroad, so it was decided by mutual agreement that they could have the house back as soon as the flat above the branch surgery was ready. DJ and his band of builders completed the building work, fitting and decorating just before Christmas.

We move some boxes and bags into the hall before getting ready to go out. Ross is dropping me off at the leisure centre for my first swim since I ended up in hospital, and it's also my first ride on a motorbike, for which he's bought me a helmet, jacket and trousers.

'You look hot,' he says as I check my new outfit in the mirror in the hall.

'Can we go fast?' I ask lightly.

'I have no intention of scaring you first time out.' He hands me a pair of gloves. 'And besides, I wouldn't risk breaking the speed limit. I have my good name to think about.'

'Since when have you worried about your reputation?' I put the gloves on to stop myself popping the joints in my fingers. The truth is that I'm a little nervous about placing my life in his hands.

'I've learned during the past few months that Fifi might be right about one thing. A sense of community is very important, and with that comes responsibility, and as I'm going to be in sole charge of the branch surgery very soon, I need to demonstrate that I'm the right person for that position. I mean, who's going to choose a nutter who races around out of control on a noisy motorbike as their vet when they can drive to Otter House to see Maz or Emma? What's more, I need to spend time with our clients, not hassle them out of the consulting room because I'm in a hurry.' He pauses. 'I'm going to that party at the manor tonight to prove that I'm one of them. Are you coming?'

I wasn't planning to go, but with him at my side I feel as if I can face anyone and everyone, scar or no scar.

'You bet,' I say, as he takes my sports bag to stow away on the bike, and within a few minutes, I'm on the back, clinging on for grim death as the trees and hedges – and my life – flash by. I can see the speedometer – we aren't going that fast, but it's still scary and, I have to admit exhilarating. We reach the leisure centre, having made a quick detour past the new branch surgery, and I take my bag. I lean towards Ross, my knees trembling, to give him a

419

kiss, but our helmets are in the way. I blow him a kiss instead.

'See you in an hour,' he mouths, before turning and roaring away across the car park and onto the street, in front of the terrace of Regency houses that are painted various shades of white. The road runs along the base of the red sandstone cliffs from the east side of the bay, and I watch him until he disappears.

I jog into the leisure centre and change, putting my belongings away in one of the lockers, before heading for the pool. On the way, as always, I catch sight of my reflection in the glass. No make-up. I decided not to cover myself up any more. I stand straight. No more hiding. This is me and I'm proud of who I am.

I walk across the cool tiles into the poolside area, which smells of warm chlorine. There are a couple of families with small children splashing about in the shallow end, two of the over-sixties' group women pounding through the water side by side, making waves, and there's Mitch, sitting on the lifeguard's chair, chatting to Gemma.

I haven't seen him for a while and I feel a little embarrassed for not having kept in touch, especially when he looks up, catches my eye and waves. He leans down and slides his arm around Gemma's shoulder, whispers in her ear and makes a show of kissing her on the cheek. I don't mind this blatant PDA. In fact, I'm happy for them.

I skirt the edge of the pool to say hi.

'I thought you'd given up,' Mitch says.

'I thought you were working mornings.'

'I reverted to tie back in with Gemma.'

'Hi, Shannon,' she says shyly.

'I wasn't allowed to swim for a while. How are you? Did you have a good Christmas?'

'It was great,' Mitch says. 'How about you?'

'I was on call, but it was still good fun.'

'Are you and Ross . . . ?'

I nod. 'We are.'

'Nice one. Are you coming out tonight? Gemma's having a party – everyone's invited.'

I glance at her face, looking for her reaction, but she's cool. I don't know how much she knows about me and Mitch, but she doesn't seem concerned that he's asking me to her party.

'We're going to Talyton Manor,' I say.

'Oh? What are you doing, getting down with the olds?' Mitch says. 'My brother's band are playing, there'll be beer and shots, and lots of people you know.'

'It's all right, thanks. We'll catch up another time,' I say, realising that we probably won't, because our lives are going in different directions. 'We'll have a drink after swimming one night. Perhaps Taylor will join us.'

'How is she?'

'The last time I saw her she was dressed as one of Santa's elves. She's going out with the chef at the garden centre. Happy New Year,' I add, before testing the water with my toes and diving into the deep end. I swim a couple of lengths before looking up in Mitch's direction; the duty lifeguard is too busy flirting to notice if anyone was drowning. I kick off from the side of the pool, sliding through the water like an arrow from a bow before surfacing and doing a few strokes of butterfly. I remember how much I love swimming and an idea begins to form in my mind.

Afterwards, Ross drops me off at Petals.

'I'll come and pick you up in the car at about eight thirty,' I say.

'No, I've booked a taxi both ways.' He smiles. 'Maz says there's champagne. I thought we'd make the most of it although, as she says, you've sampled plenty of it before.'

'Stop it,' I giggle. 'That was a very long time ago. I'll see you later.'

He blows me another kiss and rides off on the motorbike into the late afternoon sunshine and shadows, and I go inside to greet Seven and get ready for the party. I put my hair up, and apply full camouflage make-up, with glittery eye shadow and false lashes to emphasise my eyes as opposed to my mouth. I wear a long navy, figure-hugging dress and, underneath it, my trusty Doc Marten's. I complete the look with Ross's present, the silver hare.

Mum and Godfrey make their own way to Talyton Manor a few minutes before Ross arrives and helps me into the taxi.

'You look gorgeous,' he whispers as he slides into the seat beside me.

'You don't look so bad yourself.'

He's dressed in a black jacket over a grey T-shirt and smells of shower gel and toothpaste. I reach out to touch his face – he turns and gently bites my fingers.

'I want to eat you up,' he grins.

The driver clears his throat to remind us of his presence.

'You're going to the manor,' he says, pulling away from the pavement. I recognise him as one of the mechanics from the local garage. 'It's the place to be tonight. I didn't think the Fox-Giffords would hold another party up there after the old guy died, but there's been one every year since. They don't give up easily.'

Someone has placed tea-lights along each side of the drive up to the big house, adding to the party spirit, and there are cars double parked and a tractor and trailer outside, presumably to take some of the guests home.

'I'm glad you felt you could come along,' Ross says quietly when the driver's dropped us off, and we're approaching the front door. He takes my hand. 'I was afraid you might duck out at the last minute.'

I shiver at the sudden cold. The stars are sparkling from the clear night sky, and there's the beginnings of a frost twinkling from the lawn and overgrown flowerbeds.

'Let's get inside,' I say, my pulse quickening at the thought of all those people.

Members of the Pony Club are taking coats and holding out trays of buck's fizz and champagne on the way in while Sophia, Maz's horsey mother-in-law dressed in a pale grey ball gown and a moth-eaten fox fur with glassy eyes, and Alex Fox-Gifford wearing dark trousers, a white shirt and scarlet bow tie, are in the centre of the grand hallway, meeting their guests and showing them through to the drawing room.

Alex shakes Ross's hand and kisses my cheek.

'You might want to hide,' he says. 'The twins are on the prowl with that book of fairytales, and George is looking for anyone who's willing to play crocodiles.' His warning comes too late because the kids who have been sitting at the bottom of the oak staircase, lying in wait, jump out and come running across to see us.

'Someone's popular,' Ross says, as I whisk Elena into my arms and spill my drink on George, who's intercepted us with a plastic sword in one hand and the giant green crocodile in the other. The Fox-Giffords are worryingly warlike, I think, glancing up at the array of real swords displayed on the wall in the corridor on the way to the drawing room. Lydia tugs at my dress as Ross rescues my glass.

'Read me a story,' she begs.

'What's the magic word?' I ask, taking her hand.

'Story,' she says. 'No, it's per-lease. Per-lease tell me a story, thank you.'

'As you've asked so nicely . . .' I glance at Ross. 'Just the one, mind you.'

'I think I've heard this one before, so I'll mingle,' he says. 'Catch you shortly. I'll bring you another glass of fizz.'

I thank him and settle down on a footstool behind one of the shabby sofas in the drawing room, where a huge fire sputters and spits pieces of burning wood onto the Axminster carpet. The Fox-Gifford's pack of dogs is lying in a heap enjoying the warmth. Every so often, there's a yelp and one of them gets up and moves away from the fireplace, and the sulphurous scent of singed fur mixes with the smell of smoke.

I can see Delphi from the stables, Mum and Godfrey, Peter the greengrocer, Mr Victor the ironmonger, Mr Lacey, and Mr and Mrs Dyer. Ross is chatting to Leo and Stevie – so we really are forgiven for what happened to Bear – and to Jennie and her husband, Guy, who comes across as bit of a grumpy old man, in my opinion. Taylor is here with Dave, chatting to Fifi, and

Frances is with Lenny, admiring the antique vase that stands beside a Quality Street tin on a marble-topped side table.

I turn my attention to the book, which falls open on the twins' favourite, Snow White. As I start to read, Lydia leans against me and, quite unconsciously, I think, starts stroking my face. I reach into my bag for a tissue and wipe the make-up from her fingers.

'Mirror, mirror, on the wall, who is the fairest of them all?'

'You are,' says Elena. 'You look like a princess.'

'Well, thank you.' I'm touched. In fact, I have to blink hard to focus on the page – not that I really need to see the words when I know them off by heart. I read the rest of the story, the tale interspersed with some interruptions from George who feels that there has to be a role for a dangerous crocodile. The twins and I allow the handsome prince to kill it with his sword before he wakes Snow White from her poisoned sleep.

'And they all lived happily ever after, except for the crocodile,' I say, closing the book at the end.

'Because he died,' George says.

'Again,' Elena and Lydia say in unison.

'I'm sorry . . .' I look up to find Ross peering over the back of the sofa. 'It's my turn to be the handsome prince and I've come to rescue my beautiful princess if that's all right with everybody.' He passes me a full glass of champagne.

'It's more than all right with me. Why don't you three go and find someone else to read you a story? You could try asking Lucie.' She is George's half-sister and I'm pretty sure I spotted her among the Pony Clubbers when we came in.

'Let's do that,' George says, taking charge of the twins.

'Thank you,' I say to Ross as I rejoin him, slipping my arm through his as he takes a prawn vol-au-vent from a tray of food that is being passed round the room. They were Alex's father's favourite and a tribute to his memory.

'There's Taylor.' I lead him over to where she and Dave are standing beside a pair of dusty, floor-length curtains, and start chatting.

'You're looking fantastic,' Taylor says, embracing me.

'I know. I'm pretty fit, aren't I?' Ross responds.

'I'm not talking to you,' she exclaims.

He chuckles as she continues, 'I hear you went for a swim today. Make sure you let me know next time.' She glances down at her figure, her curves exposed by the tightest bodycon dress I've ever seen. 'I'm piling on the pounds, thanks to Dave's cooking. He brings me treats from work whenever he comes to the house. I can't resist . . .' She looks at him fondly and his cheeks flush deep pink.

'Actually, I'm planning a sponsored swim,' I say. 'Everyone's welcome to join in. The more the merrier.'

'That's the first I've heard of it,' Ross says.

'I only thought of it when I was in the pool today.'

'What are you raising money for? Cute fluffy animals?' Taylor asks. She isn't an animal lover.

'It's for a charity for people with facial disfigurement. I found them very useful for advice. There are others who are far worse off than me and I'd like to give something back to help them.'

'That's a great idea,' Ross says, squeezing my arm. 'I'll do it.'

'Will you? You don't like swimming in a pool.'

'I don't care if it's for a good cause . . . and I get to spend more time with you. I'll give it a go.'

'Count me in,' Taylor says. 'How about you, Dave? You're always saying you need to do some exercise.'

'I'm not sure it's my thing. I could count lengths or something.'

'We'll need a few volunteers to help out,' I say, thanking him.

There's a loud thud and a clunk at the window. Ross lifts one corner of the curtain away to reveal a Shetland pony with a massive mane and beady eyes standing on the other side, nudging at the glass and pawing at the ground.

'He wants to come in and join the party. Sophia must have shut him out for the night.' He lets the curtain go again, and I can see Dave's eyes widen with disbelief as he goes on, 'When I was staying here, the pony could come in and out as he pleased.'

'Where I come from, people have dogs and cats as pets, or geckoes at a push,' Dave says.

'I wouldn't have a pony in the house,' Ross says. 'It's sad that this place is in such a state. There are some amazing objects here, but everything feels neglected. Look at the paintings and antiques. They must be worth a small fortune.'

'I think those are majolica ware.' I nod towards the mantel, where a pair of colourful vases are half hidden behind a swag of holly and ivy, and smile to myself as I notice Ross's and Taylor's expressions change. 'I reckon that watching all that daytime TV might have paid off. I learned a lot from *Bargain Hunt.*'

'It's been quite a year,' Taylor says.

I raise my champagne to my lips. It certainly has.

At midnight, we see the New Year in and join in singing 'For Auld Lang Syne', after which Ross takes me in his arms and kisses me under the mistletoe, oblivious to anyone else. In the taxi on the way back to the house in Talyford, I'm aware of his hand resting on my thigh, his fingertips stroking my skin through the fabric of my dress. He grins as I place my hand on top of his, caging his fingers.

'I can hardly wait,' he says, when he's leading me up to his room.

'To move into the branch surgery?' I say archly.

'To get you into bed –' he pauses on the landing and presses his mouth to the side of my neck – 'and make love to you. Happy New Year, my darling.'

The following weekend, I pick up a solicitor's letter that's been delivered to Petals, detailing the settlement of the insurance claim, and Ross and I finish the preparations for opening the branch surgery. We borrow the ambulance again and take his possessions from the house in Talyford to his new home in Talymouth.

'Here we are,' he says as I pull onto the drive in front of a 1960s detached brick and tile house. There's a sign reading 'Otter House Small Animal Veterinary Group', with the practice logo, phone number and Ross's name and letters below.

'I can't wait to get started.' I switch off the engine and survey the car park. There's room for at least four cars and a motorbike.

'It isn't the most beautiful surgery in the world, but it's ours.' He leans across and gives me a hug.

'Let's get my stuff indoors, then we'll go and pick up yours.'

'Mine?' I gaze at him. I've been practically living with him since Christmas, but I have been taking one day at a time, not thinking any further than the immediate future. 'I put my things in the back.'

'I mean go and get the rest of it from your mum's.' His lips curve into a smile. 'You didn't think I'd let you go back to Petals? I want us to live together.'

'But there's only one bedroom.'

'I know. I'm not talking about being housemates. Are you being deliberately obtuse? We've been sharing a bed for the past week, and I can't bear the thought of giving up that arrangement. There's plenty of room for both of us here. Please, Shannon.'

'Yes!' I can hear shrieking – I think that it's me – before he silences the sound with his lips pressed to mine.

Eventually, we carry his belongings up to the flat, which still smells of paint and new carpets. We turn up the heating and open the windows. Then we go to collect some of my bits and pieces from Petals, where Godfrey makes us cappuccinos with his machine and Mum helps me pack.

'So you're off again,' she says, as we return to the living room with my bags. 'I suppose I was expecting it. We've hardly seen you the past few days.' She smiles suddenly. 'I'm pleased for you both. You must come for Sunday lunch next weekend.'

'You must come to us,' I say. 'I want to show off the flat.'

'Is there a garden? I expect you'll have a dog one day.'

'There's a small garden laid to lawn with a border

429

of mature shrubs,' Godfrey cuts in. 'I wrote the particulars for the property.'

'It's the perfect place,' Ross says with enthusiasm.

'Do you like the partial sea views?' Godfrey asks.

'You mean the glimpse of blue from the bedroom window?'

'That's right. It's more than a glimpse in my opinion.' It's a veritable vista, a feast for the eyes.

We make a move before it grows dark, returning to Talymouth where we unpack for a second time, then head for Otter House to leave the ambulance. Picking up my car, we drive to Talyford for Ross to collect his bike. We meet back at our new home; I have to pinch myself to prove that this is really happening, that I'm moving in with the man of my dreams.

The next day, I'm up early to check the vaccines in the fridge, and make sure the computer at reception is on and the phones are working. Ross shaves some wood from the consulting room door, which won't quite shut.

'There are bound to be a few teething problems,' he says happily. 'Maz suggested an opening ceremony, but I said I'd prefer to get on with it. I hope we'll have some clients turn up today. It's been advertised in the *Chronicle* as an open surgery, no appointment required, just to get some feet – or preferably lots of paws – through the door.'

I wander around making sure nothing is out of place. We have everything we need: a consulting room, staff room with a small kitchen area and cloak-room, a kennel area, prep area, operating theatre and X-ray room.

At eight thirty, the phone rings, taking me by surprise, so all I can say is, 'Hi, who is it?'

'Hello, it's Celine. I'm just ringing to wish you all the best. I'm so excited for you, although I'm missing you both already. It seems very quiet here.' She changes the subject. 'Did I tell you that Maz is looking for a new receptionist?'

'Are you leaving?'

'They've agreed to let me train to be a registered vet nurse. How about that?'

'I'm really pleased. I hope you realise what you're letting yourself in for, although you can always borrow my notes from when I did my diploma.'

'I know it will be hard work, but I'm made up. I'm one step closer to achieving my dream. You are my inspiration, Shannon.'

'Come and visit us soon.'

'Will do. Oh, and just to let you know that Diva and her puppy are doing well – Aurora dropped in to let us know. Oops, I'd better go. Izzy's giving me one of her looks.'

The phone cuts out.

'Is that our first client?' Ross asks, joining me in reception. He's wearing a light blue tunic over dark trousers and I'm in a navy tunic and jeans. There isn't a hint of lilac in sight.

'It was Celine wishing us luck.'

'I hope it isn't going to be too quiet,' he says anxiously.

'Hey, don't worry. It's early in the day.'

'We need enough income to employ a receptionist to help you out.'

'I'm all right,' I reassure him, but he starts pacing up and down, his hands in his pockets, stopping now and again to look out of the window. 'Calm down.'

He hesitates and turns to me. He smiles and my

heart turns over. 'I can think of plenty of ways to occupy those empty hours when no one turns up.'

'We'll be able to go for walks on the beach,' I say, although I know exactly what he means.

'You know, I feel as if I should have carried you over the threshold.' He grins. 'You're blushing.'

'I'm not.' I touch my face as he moves up to me, the reception desk between us.

'I think you are,' he says in a low voice, and he leans across and kisses me very gently. 'I love you.'

'Good morning, my lovers. Don't mind me.'

Ross steps back and I turn to face the door. Mrs Wall is leaning on her stick with Merrie at her side.

'Well,' she chuckles, 'who is it that doesn't believe in fortune-tellers and the ancient arts? Look at you two lovebirds. You doubted me, yet I knew this was going to happen all along.'

Ross groans. 'You're going to be insufferable now, aren't you?'

'Probably,' she says. 'No, make that definitely. I'll never let you live this down.'

'What are you doing here anyway?' Ross asks.

'I want to register Merrie here. You're our vet.' She eyes me up through her tinted glasses. 'For richer, for poorer, for better, for worse.'

'Let me take some details, Mrs Wall,' I say, taking over.

'How did you get here when you don't drive?' Ross asks.

'Fifi gave me a lift. She's good like that.'

After I've completed Merrie's details, I glance at Ross, who's leaning against the door into the consulting room, drumming his fingers against the wood. He raises his eyebrows.

I smile back. 'The vet will see you now.' I move around the desk and follow her so I can pick Merrie up and place her on the table.

'Goodness gracious me, I hope he's paying you two sets of wages,' Mrs Wall exclaims.

'So do I.' I'm joking. I'm being paid more than I was at Otter House. Ross made sure that the partners were taking the extra responsibilities as both nurse and receptionist into account.

'Do I receive a free consultation for being your first client?'

Ross appears to consider for a moment.

'I can agree to that, as long as I can take a selfie with Merrie to put up on the noticeboard.'

'He means a photo,' I explain.

'It's all right. I do know what a selfie is. I'm not completely illegitimate when it comes to computers. Lots of people took selfies with me at the Country Show. In fact, I'm planning on charging for every single one next year, then I won't need to bother with the crystal ball.'

'That's agreed then,' Ross says, examining Merrie from nose to tail. 'She's looking fantastic, the best I've ever seen her.'

'She's had every single tablet,' Mrs Wall says proudly.

'I feel as if I should give you a treat as well as Merrie,' Ross says.

I find the dog treats in a box in the cupboard under the sink.

'I thought you disapproved of being nice to people and animals,' Mrs Wall says.

'I've been persuaded to take a more relaxed approach.' He takes a treat and hands it to Merrie, who sits holding up one paw in anticipation. 'Shannon, have you got your mobile handy?'

I fetch it from reception and take a photo of him with the dog cuddled up to his cheek.

'Ah, that's sweet. When should I bring her back?'

'Shannon will count out some more tablets, a dose to be given every other day, and we'll see Merrie again in six months, unless you're worried about her before.'

'Oh? As long as that?'

'You're welcome to drop in any time for tea and a chat,' he continues.

'What did you say that for?' I ask when Mrs Wall has gone. 'We aren't running a seaside tearoom.'

'It might be more lucrative than this,' he sighs as he perches on the consulting room table.

'What do you expect? It's half past nine on the first day. In a couple of months, you'll be complaining that we're too busy.' The phone rings again, calling me back to reception. This time, it's Declan asking if he can bring Trevor to us to have his stitches out, seeing that Ross did the surgery. Ross is flattered, but it's another non-paying appointment.

Declan turns up half an hour later, and Ross removes the last stitch as I hold Trevor down on the floor.

'He's bouncing off the walls at home,' Declan says. 'Can we walk him now?'

'You certainly can. Have you decided what to do about him helping with the laundry?'

'I'm afraid he's very much a part-timer.' Declan smiles. 'We're planning to take on another dog. I know it doesn't always work out, having a working and a non-working dog in the same household, but the people at the training centre say they've known it to be successful in some situations. If we can find the perfect assistance dog, then Trevor can take early retirement.'

'What if you end up with another one like him?' Ross asks.

'That's impossible,' I say, happy that – from what Declan's saying – they're no longer considering rehoming him. 'He's a one-off.'

Later, I head into the staff room to make two coffees. We have all the right equipment – kettle, mugs, fridge and sofa – but there's something missing. I return to reception to find Ross is in the consulting room.

'I've got your coffee,' I say, at the same time as I notice the middle-aged woman and brindle boxer in there with him, along with a noxious aroma.

'It's all right.' He grins and nods towards the Costa cup with a lid that's on the table. 'Debbie here has brought me one already . . . Not really,' he adds. 'It's for you. A sample for the full works: parasitology, culture and sensitivity, everything.'

'The Boss here has the squits something chronic.' Debbie is running to fat, much like her dog. 'I own one of the guesthouses on the front – Bay View, it's called – and although most of my visitors like dogs, they don't appreciate the smell and I've been having to pretend we're having trouble with the plumbing.'

'When did this start?' Ross asks her.

'Before Christmas, if I'm being honest with you,' she says, the pink hue on her cheeks suggesting that perhaps she isn't. 'We've been at full occupancy over the festive season and I haven't had time to deal with it, but I'm here now.'

Ross advises a change of diet, as it seems highly likely that the Boss has been living the high life, begging turkey and biscuits from the guests, and he sends Debbie on her way to await the results of the tests.

'That's our first paying customer,' he says, washing his hands before drinking his coffee.

'You see, it is going to work out,' I say, sitting on the table and swinging my legs.

'You're right.' He gives me a long searching look that makes my heart lurch. 'We make a good team.'

'I know, but I've been thinking – there's something missing.'

'I can guess what you're going to say.' The expression in his dark eyes is soft and gently teasing. 'Aren't I enough for you?'

'You're more than man enough,' I say, 'but—'

'You're keen to hear the patter of tiny paws . . .' he finishes for me. 'I think we should pay a visit to the Sanctuary to see if we can find a suitable practice manager.'

'Canine or feline?' I ask, unable to disguise my excitement.

'I'd prefer a dog that we can take on long walks together.'

'I'll go for that,' I say, picturing us strolling hand in hand along the river or across the escarpment while our canine companion runs free, playing with the other dogs that we meet on our way.

'What else will you go for, Shannon?' He walks over to me and puts his mug down next to mine. I hear the chink as they touch. I feel his hands on my waist and his hair brushing against my cheek as he stands in front of me.

'You, I suppose,' I say, confused.

'I suppose? What's that *supposed* to mean?'

I look into his eyes. 'I love you,' I murmur.

'And . . . ?'

'I can't imagine life without you . . .'

'How about kids? You're great with George and the twins.'

'I'd like to be a mum one day.'

'I want a family too, not straight away, but in a couple of years when this place is up and running and we've had some fun together.' He pauses and I reach up and stroke his curls because, suddenly, he looks like a rabbit caught in the headlights, as if he's scared himself.

'Go on,' I say.

'Are you sure?'

I nod. My chest is tight with emotion. I can hardly breathe, let alone speak.

'Okay, here goes.' He touches his forehead to mine. 'I've never felt like this about anyone before. Since the very first time we met, when you mistook me for the courier, I've been falling in love with you a little more each day, apart from when you gave me hassle with Maz for being rude to Mrs Wall, and had a go at me for fixing the bike indoors, and on many other occasions I could mention.' I can tell from the tone of his voice that he's more relaxed now, almost smiling. 'I adore you and want to give you lots of babies, but I want to do it right. Shannon, darling, will you marry me?' He blunders on, not giving me a chance to respond. 'I'll prove that I can be patient. I can wait for as long as it takes for your answer.'

'I'm not going to keep you waiting,' I say, throwing my arms around his neck. 'The answer is yes.'

437

'Really?' He wipes a tear from my cheek. 'Are you absolutely sure?'

'Yes, yes, yes!' I slide from the table into his embrace, and we're both laughing and crying at the same time.

'You are so beautiful,' Ross says. 'I love you more than anyone in the world.'

'I love you too.' My heart is bursting with happiness as I press my cheek to his. I love him for his patience and loyalty. I love him for not giving up on me when I kept knocking him back. 'I will *always* love you.'

'I bet Mrs Wall didn't see this in her crystal ball,' he adds softly, but I reckon he's mistaken.

'She predicted it when she read my palm at the Country Show,' I say, recalling what she said this morning about 'for richer, for poorer, for better, for worse'. 'She made a bet with you, remember?' I smile. 'I think you owe her a tenner.'